The Calling

Defenders of the Faith in Apocalyptic Times, A Novel

By
Timothy A. Van Sickel

To Linda

Prepper Camp 2021

Tim Van Sickel

Places and characters in this novel are fictional and the creation of the author's imagination. Any resemblance to real places or people is strictly coincidental. The towns are real, use google maps to see the areas referenced.

Other novels by Timothy A. Van Sickel:

Righteous Gathering, Righteous Survival EMP Saga, Book 1

Righteous Bloodshed, Righteous Survival EMP Saga, Book 2

Righteous Sacrifice, Righteous Survival EMP Saga, Book 3

Righteous Soldiers, Righteous Survival EMP Saga, Book 4

Righteous Survival, Righteous Survival EMP Saga, Book 5

Righteous Revival, Righteous Survival EMP Saga, Book 6

All books available on Amazon in both print and eBook

If you have any questions, comments or suggestions/corrections, you can contact me at vansickelauthor@gmail.com

Table of contents

Contents

Biblical Inspiration

Mark 13:7-13, NIV
When you hear of wars and rumors of wars, do not be alarmed. Such things must happen, but the end is still to come. Nation will rise against nation, and kingdom against kingdom. There will be earthquakes in various places, and famines. These are the beginnings of birth pains.
You must be on your guard. You will be handed over to the local councils and flogged in the synagogues. On account of me you will stand before governors and kings as witness to them. And the gospel must first be preached to all nations. Whenever you are arrested and brought to trial, do not worry beforehand about what to say. Just say whatever is given to you at that time, for it is not you speaking, but the Holy Spirit.
Brother will betray brother to death and a father his child. Children will rebel against their parents and have them put to death. Everyone will hate you because of me, but the one who stands firm will be saved in the end.

Revelation 7: 4
Then I heard the number of those who were sealed: 144,000 from the twelve tribes of Israel.

Author's Forward

The Biblical quote from the Book of Mark are Jesus's words about His return. I feel they should have more relevance than any of the other Biblical prophesies. This novel portrays Jesus's prophesies being fulfilled, from major shifts in the earth's crust to wars and raging fires, to Christ's word being proclaimed to the nations.

The Book of Revelation speaks of the 144,000. They are selected, they are "sealed". It is my understanding that they bear a mark on their forehead indicating they are the chosen ones of God, and in John's vision they surround the throne praising the lord; 12,000 descendants from each of the twelve tribes of Israel.

Many theories and debates surround the 144,000. Who are they and what is their mission? Is it an actual number or a symbolic number? Some theorize that the 144,000 will be Messianic Jews that are called by God to proclaim Jesus as the true Son of God and the true Savior. If this is true, do they come before the rapture, increasing God's Kingdom before Christ calls us home? Or do they come after the rapture to save those who did not believe?

I don't proclaim to know the answers to any of these questions. I'm not a Biblical scholar. I am more of an evangelist. I am saved by the grace of God. I want everyone to know true peace, a peace that can only be found by knowing Christ as our Savior.

God has once again called me to write, this time using the 144,000 to place Christian characters in an action-packed apocalyptic novel. If you are hoping for a book that will answer all your questions of Biblical end times prophecy, you will probably be disappointed.

Personally, I don't think any work of man can portray what God has coming for His children and His creation. The Glory of Christ's return cannot be depicted by mortal words. Nor can the destruction and transformation of the earth be described better than how John describes it in the book of Revelation or by the prophets of the old testament. That said, I hope you find this end times story both thrilling and thought provoking.

Using literary license, I'm setting this story to follow a few of the 144,000 'chosen' in a pre-tribulation period. As the world begins to fall apart around them, these called individuals will have to deal with the idea that they have been given a directive from God to proclaim Christ to the nations as humankind's Savior. The Book of Revelation calls the 144,000 to be pure, virgins. Again, I'm using literary license. The characters in this book are not pure. Like all of us, they are fallen, they have sinned. But after they are called, they try to lead a 'pure' life. All Christians are called to proclaim Christ as Lord and to be pure. We all fall short of that high goal. The called in this book are portrayed to strive to reach that high bar that all Christians aspire to. Hopefully it will inspire you to be all you can be as a disciple of Christ.

Strap in for a high-powered thrilling saga of redemption and survival!

Prologue

It was over five thousand years ago that the stars and the planets aligned in such a way that God knew would cause a traumatic upheaval to the earth. He warned Noah, the only righteous soul on earth at that time, to be prepared. The same alignment of the stars and planets is about to happen again. God breathed the stars and planets, the entire universe, into life. He knew that another great upheaval was coming.

Five thousand years ago, before the great flood, the earth was as God created it. It was Pangea, a single continent surrounded by the seas. The great upheaval and ensuing flood caused the massive migration of the continents creating the world as we know it today. In the great flood, the earth was utterly destroyed and reborn. Virtually all ancient societies recognize this event.

Now, this alignment of the stars and the planets is about to happen again. It will happen just as God knew it would. He wishes that His people, the people that He created in His own image, would return to Him, be His true children. But His children are fallen, sinful. He gave them the freedom of choice. But once they bit from the tree of knowledge, they became sinful.

Over two thousand years ago, He came to earth Himself, in His trilogy, as His son, to become the final sacrifice for the sins of man. Yet man has continually turned away from Him. They profess to love Him, yet they kill His children in the womb. They profess to know Him, but covet power and wealth. Their quest for knowledge has increased to a point where they desire that their science will prove that He does not even exist.

Now, the planets and the stars will align once again. As foretold in the scriptures, the earth will be remade once again. God promised it would not be by flood. But a cleansing must occur before His triumphant return.

8

Five thousand years ago, only Noah was told of the oncoming wrath. This time, 144,000 are told, and they are to proclaim His forgiveness to all mankind. How many of those who are called will listen to God? Will anyone listen to them?

List of Main Characters:

Mustafa: Former ISIS fighter

Shawn: Street runner and geology major

Xi: Chinese farmer and Christian convert/pastor

Clarissa: Young Baptist woman and college student

Abaddon Rajani: Billionaire instigator

General Jerry Shapiro: General in charge of Special Forces

Frank Burns: G3, General in charge of Special Forces operations

Henry: G2, General in charge of Special Forces intelligence

Georgeanne Haquani: Social media super star

Michael: Head pastor: Shiloh Baptist Church, Los Angeles CA

Assistant/youth pastor: Dan

Chapter 1, The Fighter Is Called

Mustafa has no idea how his life is soon going to change. He looks with malice at the pleading girl beneath him and snarls. He punches her in the face as he rolls away from her defiled body. Snatching his worn but trusty AK-47 he heads towards the gunfire. The infidels are attacking their ragtag complex once again and his brief moment of pleasure with the Yazidi slave whore has come to an abrupt end.

He dodges left and right as he heads towards the firefight while keeping an eye on the sky. Will the Americans be sending air support? The evil empire has dealt their movement to start a new Caliphate serious setbacks. The Americans support the corrupt Muslims they are fighting; Muslims that tolerate a new Jewish nation. The Jews and their Christian allies are filth that must be exterminated from this world. He personally has killed dozens of Jews, Christians, and corrupt Muslims, both in heated battles and in bloody executions.

As Mustafa makes his way towards the fighting, he rallies several of his ISIS fighters, always keeping an eye on the sky and scouting for bunkers to shelter in. The bunkers have been established throughout the compound for cover from the incoming American missiles. He spies an ISIS mortar crew springing into action and hears the loud boom as their mortars are launched at the attacking forces.

Explosions erupt in the distance as Mustafa and his small squad of fellow fighters race towards the front lines. The mortars his people have fired are landing in the middle of the attacking forces. Mustafa rushes through the enemy fire one more time to reach the walls of the ancient village. In the perilous safety of the ancient stone walls, he meets with the captain of the guard to assess the situation and determine how to properly respond to the attack. He discovers that once again the Peshmerga are trying to breach their stronghold.

"The Kurds!" Mustafa exclaims. "They need to be exterminated once and for all! They cannot be trusted. We've had peace with them for three weeks. Why are they attacking us now?"

"Look over there," the captain states, handing Mustafa his binoculars. "They've brought in three tanks and a new artillery battery."

Explosions erupt behind them as artillery rounds land haphazardly throughout the compound. The two men dive for cover as shrapnel sprays across the area. Several of the frontline fighters receive shrapnel wounds as well as many of the citizens still trapped in the bombed-out town.

The two men cower behind the stone walls that were originally built several thousand years ago. Three old Russian T62 tanks come into range of the city walls and begin to fire at the ISIS stronghold positions.

"Mustafa, we have been weakened over the past few months. The Mullah is sending us more recruits. Until then, we need to hold this town," the captain says. "You need to rally an RPG squad to take out those tanks. We'll cover you."

"What! You want me and my men to move over a thousand yards through open territory to hit those tanks? We've got to get within three hundred yards to be effective. That's a suicide mission. Where's our artillery? We were firing mortar rounds at them as I was coming up here."

As Mustafa says this, he hears the thunk of mortar rounds being fired. He and the captain peer through a notch in the wall as the mortar rounds land all around the incoming tanks. Many dismounted troops supporting the tanks are killed or wounded by the exploding shrapnel, but the tanks keep moving forward, blasting precise rounds that take a toll on the ancient walls that surround their stronghold. As they watch the tanks move forward, they see one tank get stuck, its tread damaged by the mortar barrage.

Encouraged by their success, the captain orders another round of mortars to be launched at the two remaining tanks.

"Mustafa," the captain implores, "God is with us. Rally a crew to stop the infidels. You have seen our success. We have to stop those two remaining tanks. We'll support you with covering fire."

A fierce determination comes across Mustafa's face. He has seen one of the tanks taken down. God is with them. He decides to lead his people on a mission to take out the two remaining tanks. They quickly come up with a plan, as they have done many times in the past.

Before heading across no man's land, Mustafa gathers his small squad and explains the mission. They are used to dangerous missions and have seen many of their fellow fighters die. They are fighting for Allah, and this is the mission assigned to them. If they die fighting for Allah, they will go to heaven, they all know it, the Quran tells them so.

Using a detailed terrain map and their own knowledge of the land, they plot their attack. Minutes later Mustafa and his men are scurrying across the landscape, using every draw and wadi to get close to the approaching tanks. The captain of the guard sees Mustafa making his move. As promised, he has his men open up on the encroaching tanks and the supporting infantry units.

The tanks roll on as the infantry gets pinned down or killed by the sustained fire from the ISIS stronghold. For more than fifteen minutes the two sides exchange fire as Mustafa's men slowly get into position. From less than three hundred yards away, one of Mustafa's men pops up and fires an RPG that hits one of the tanks in the rear drive wheel. The ancient tank stops dead in its tracks. But it is not out of the fight. It turns its gun towards the attacking squad and fires. But not before another RPG is fired at the other tank, hitting it right at the seam between the turret and the main body of the tank, a deadly hit.

13

The projectile penetrates the aging tank. The munitions inside begin to catch fire and explode. The top of the tank blows off, killing all the fighters inside.

The two remaining disabled tanks continue to fire on the ISIS complex, even though they are unable to move. The Kurds rally infantry fighters to protect the disabled tanks. At the ISIS compound, the captain of the guard sees how the situation is unfolding and orders his people to fire on the Kurds who are trying to support the disabled tanks. He knows Mustafa and his team are working to take the tanks out of the battle.

Mustafa lies on the ground only three hundred yards away from one of the disabled tanks. A deafening boom lets him know that the tank is still firing at his compound. He rolls over to look at the five remaining members of his squad. He wipes the blood from his face, the blood splattered on him from his comrade that fired the last RPG. The blood smears across his face and streaks into his wild hair and unkempt beard. His face is already coated with sweat, grime, and dirt; it gives him a savage look. "You two circle around and take out the tank to the left. Yousef and I will take out this tank. Johan and Amoud, you provide covering fire. Allah is with us. We will prevail. Now go."

With those words, the final assault on the tanks begins. Mustafa and Yousef run and dodge as they make their way to the immobile tank still firing at their compound. As they get closer to the tank, more Peshmerga show up and the two men have to fight their way to their target. The fighting is bloody and at times the two engage in hand-to-hand combat. But Allah is with them. They reach the disabled tank that is still firing on their compound.

All they need to do is drop a hand grenade down the hatch and the threat will be over. Yousef rises and kills a Kurd still fighting to defend the tank but is shot in the process. He died fighting for Allah. He will see paradise.

Mustafa shoots the Kurd that killed Yousef. He climbs onto the turret of the tank. He's bloody. He's dirty. Sweat and grime streak his

14

face and body as he climbs to the top of the turret. The hatch is locked, he needs to let his grenade drop down the snorkel that lets air into the cab of the tank.

He pulls the pin to the grenade as he looks over the battlefield. They have won again. He lets out a wild scream. "Allahu Akbar!"

And then he stops, the grenade still in his hand, the firing spoon not yet released.

He stops because he hears a voice, the most pleasant and calm voice he has ever heard. Just the sound of the voice fills him with a calmness and peace that he has never known. For a moment, he thinks he has been shot and is going to heaven. He looks around and sees the battle still raging around him. More Peshmerga soldiers are fighting towards his comrades assailing the other disabled tank. So why does he feel like he's floating on air? Why does he feel such a great inner peace?

He hears the voice again. *"Mustafa, why are you trying to kill your brother? I love your brother just as I love you."*

Mustafa turns left and right, looking for who is speaking to him. He sees no one.

"I am here, Mustafa. I am in your heart. You will only see me by looking into your heart."

Mustafa feels an even warmer sensation. A feeling of peace. He also feels something he has never felt before. He feels love. He thought he loved his parents and his siblings. He thought he loved his fellow fighters. But now he's feeling a love that is so complete he cannot comprehend it.

The voice speaks to him once again. *"You have been chosen, Mustafa. Your sins are forgiven. From this day forward you will be pure. You will be my voice to the fallen."* A vision flashes before his eyes. It is a vision of heaven, and he is there, singing praises to the true Lord.

Mustafa is stunned. He looks in horror at the live grenade in his hand and tosses it as far away as he can. He begins to bang on the hatch to the turret. He shouts at the steal door. "Come out my friends. This is all wrong. You are my brothers, and we have to make peace." He looks around again and sees the devastation that has been caused to the land. He begins to weep. His eyes have been opened; he sees the true way. So many things have to change.

Chapter 2, The Farmer Is Called

It is a cold and rainy day in the northern state of Manchuria. Too cold for mid spring. Too rainy to allow the crops to begin to grow. Xi's strawberries were just beginning to flower when the cold and rainy spell hit. The cold and damp conditions could lead to root rot which would ruin this year's strawberry harvest. His asparagus crop is doing well but he has spent all day clearing drainage ditches to ensure that crop doesn't get flooded.

He and his two children, muddy and tired, make their way back to their modest home. He's proud of the home he has made for his family. After being forced to move because of the massive Three Gorges Dam project, Xi has been able to build a modest three-room concrete block home for his family. The concrete foundation that the government provided for him has cracked and they have issues with water seepage, but he knows there is no remedy. He must do his best with what he has.

He and his family have worked his new ten acres of land and have slowly turned his concrete block house into a home, despite all its faults. The main room in the house is actually quite large. It is twenty feet by twenty feet. It is what Americans would call a great room that is used as a kitchen, dining room, and living room. His two children share a small bedroom as does he and his wife. They feel privileged to have fully functional indoor plumbing, despite the leaks and occasional backups. At their old home they used an outhouse and got water from the town's well.

Xi thinks back as he washes up. Things could be worse. He misses the forty acres of land that he and his parents farmed, but his parents are housed nearby, and he has been given decent land by the government to farm. It is a much smaller parcel and he had to learn what crops to raise. But they are doing well.

He wishes he could take a bath, but he knows the government monitors how much water he uses. He washes up more thoroughly than normal because they will be having a meeting tonight in their home. Xi is a Christian, and tonight he'll be hosting a Bible study. He brims with pride that he and his family all know Christ and are actively working to spread the Gospel to their friends and neighbors. A passing doubt runs through his mind. What if the authorities find out he's starting a church at his home? They all would be sent away, separated for ever. He would never see any member of his family again, let alone any of his fellow Christians.

Xi smiles, knowing he has brought people to know Christ, despite the risks to him and his family. How much more could he do if he was not shackled by the Communist Chinese government? The communists want the state to be the people's religion. The government's goal is to create a utopia on earth through communist principles of shared wealth. Xi knows that will never happen. Only Christ can bring utopia. Only through Christ can one truly know peace. That is the message he brings to the people that gather at his growing church.

At that thought Xi pauses. Is he growing a church? Is he so blessed that he's actually starting a church?

"You are blessed my humble servant," a voice from nowhere states.

Xi stops scrubbing the dirt from his hands and looks around. Where did that voice come from? Does the government have a speaker in his bathroom? He has always suspected that there were cameras throughout his house.

He goes back to scrubbing his hands clean, ignoring the voice.

The voice returns. *"Only I can make you clean. You can never wash away your sins."*

Xi stops what he's doing. He looks around, no one else is there. He looks up, trembling.

"Is that you Lord? Are you talking to me?"

"You are a faithful servant. You are called. You have been sealed. Profess my name to the nations."

Trembling, Xi is dumbfounded, yet he feels an inner strength. He has known that his mission is to proclaim the word. But now, he sees his future laid out before him quite plainly. In a flash, he sees himself in heaven, praising his Lord. A warmth and inner strength grow inside him.

His eyes open wide. 'I have been chosen?' What does that mean? He's a Christian in a land that is hostile to Christians. Does it mean that not even the communist government will be able to stop him? An even greater peace sets on his soul. He wonders what he's going to say to his wife and family, because he knows all of their lives have just changed too.

Chapter 3, Foot Washing

The grenade Mustafa threw into the nearby wadi explodes harmlessly and he breathes a sigh of relief. The battle still rages around him. Amoud and Johan have established a fighting position only a few hundred yards away and are trying to pin down a Peshmerga unit converging on him. To his left he sees his other two squad members beginning their final approach to the other disabled tank. So many people are going to die. He has to stop it.

But how? All he knows is fighting and killing, it has been his life for years. How does he stop the killing? He rises from his crouched position alongside the turret of the tank and summons a new inner courage. He yells at the top of his lungs as he waves his hands over his head. "Tawaquf. Tawaquf, Tawaquf!! (Stop, Stop, Stop).

The firing slows as his people hear him yell for them to stop. They look at him a bit bewildered. What is going on? The firing from the ISIS stronghold continues as the Peshmerga begin to converge on Mustafa and his men.

Completely exposed, Mustafa stands tall and beckons for his men to rally to him. "You all must come to me, now. Pax, Pax, Pax! Come to me now," Mustafa commands.

Mustafa's men have known him for years. He's a good leader and fierce fighter. What he's now saying to do is out of the ordinary. But they trust him. He must have some plan that will allow them to win the day. Or maybe he's injured, and he needs their help. The remaining men of his small squad begin making their way to his position, dodging and running to avoid the fire from the encroaching Peshmerga.

Mustafa, seeing that his men are still being fired on by the Peshmerga, turns toward the approaching enemy and takes off his black turban, waving it in the air. This odd gesture catches everyone by surprise. The long black flowing cloth is seen by both the ISIS guard in the stronghold and the Peshmerga fighters and their commander. It is so completely out of the ordinary that both sides stop firing. The Peshmerga commander wonders how the big man atop his tank has not yet been shot.

Mustafa continues to wave his black turban as the fighting around him dies down. He has heard that waving a white flag was a sign of surrender in western cultures. He had no idea what waving his black turban would do, but it has caused the fighting to stop; at least for now. In the lull, he beckons his men to come to his position by the disabled tank, which has also stopped firing; the men inside not knowing what to do.

Mustafa's men arrive at his position just as a squad of Peshmerga arrive. They are all armed to the hilt; bloody, sweaty, and filthy from the day's battle. Both sides have lost brothers-in-arms in the last few hours. Now the armed combatants stand only a few yards apart, ready to renew their fight. Except Mustafa is standing between them all, himself bloody and grimy from the day's battle. Mustafa has an aura about him. Both sides see it. He's a man to be listened to, to be respected.

Amoud smiles, he knows that Mustafa is in charge. He knows that they will win the day. Somehow, Mustafa will bring them all a great victory for Allah. He looks at the Peshmerga fighters with scorn. From the walls of the ancient city, the captain of the guard watches intently.

Mustafa sees the scorn on Amoud's face. Mustafa can see the hate that he never saw before. It makes him sad. How can he show these people around him that God loves them? How can he show them that they are all brothers? Only moments ago the vision appeared to him. There is an answer, he knows it. Then he sees that all the soldiers carry canteens.

"Why are we fighting each other?" he asks the men surrounding him. "Would the world not be a better place if we loved each other rather than fought each other? Amoud, give me your canteen so that I might wash your feet. Let's all be so humble to wash each other's feet." The men around him look on in dismay. His own men are waiting for an opportunity to take control of the situation. The Peshmerga are equally on edge, expecting some type of trap.

But Mustafa's presence is great. He's in command of the situation, and his own men know it. Hesitantly, Amoud allows Mustafa to take off his boots. Amoud's feet are filthy, covered with sores and blisters. Mustafa pauses briefly, then proceeds to wash Amoud's feet. Amoud is astounded by the gentle care that Mustafa shows him, and by how good his worn and tattered feet feel from the soothing bath.

Mustafa beckons the Peshmerga leader to his side. "As you can see, I have laid my weapons aside. Let's start a movement towards peace. Let me show you that I respect you and love you as my brother."

The Peshmerga leader is chided by his men. "The great warrior wants to wash your feet! Let him! It is the act of a servant. He's surrendering! Do it." The Peshmerga leader submits, and Mustafa washes his feet. Seeing this, they soon all have their boots off and have their feet washed by their foes. Some willingly, some with hesitation. The act of service and submission changes them all. Minutes ago, they were willing to kill each other. Now they feel a fellowship they have never felt before.

***

The captain of the guard watches from the ISIS stronghold. He's stunned by what he sees. The local Imam is now with him. He tells the Imam what he's seeing. The Imam snatches the binoculars from the captain and watches the foot washing scene unfold. He swears under his breath. "An act of Christ as Savior!" The Imam turns to the captain. "Kill them all! Open fire on them."

"What? Those are our fighters out there!" the captain protests. "They went out on a vital mission to save our citadel. We can't fire on them. It could all be a ploy. In just minutes they may take the battlefield. We have to let this play out."

22

"When was the last time anyone, let alone an enemy, washed your feet?" The Imam asks.

The captain is befuddled. "I, uh, well, um. Mustafa is clever that way," he responds.

The Imam turns on the captain with wild eyes. "What is happening out there is not good for Islam. What is happening out there is evil and must be stopped. Have your men open fire. All of them must be killed. No one must know what just happened. Your prized fighter is an apostate."

But the Imam is too late. The act of love has already taken place. Too many people have seen it. Too many people were part of it.

***

Mustafa knows he's in trouble. He knows what he has done is antithetical to Islam's teachings. He knows he cannot return to the ISIS stronghold. As one of the Peshmerga soldiers finishes washing his feet, Mustafa rises and gives orders. "We need to get out of this place. The Imam will have heard of what we've done here. Consider us your captives and let's flee this place."

Amoud raises his rifle, ready to shoot Mustafa, thinking him a traitor to the cause. As he fires his weapon, one of the Peshmerga dives and knocks the weapon away. The shot gives a glancing blow to Mustafa's forehead at the hairline. It will leave a permanent scar and bleed a lot, but it is not a life-threatening wound.

Stunned by what has occurred, they all turn and flee, scurrying into the ravines and washes that head north, towards the Kurd's front lines. Gun fire erupts all around them as the ISIS stronghold opens fire. Mustafa, his men, and the Kurds meld into the wasteland as they make their escape. Amoud lays dying next to the abandoned tank, having been hit by the wild volley of fire from the ISIS stronghold defenders.

Secure in the depths of his vast estate, an old and decrepit man watches his highly secure news feeds and sees the foot washing ceremony. It alarms and angers him. The man's name is Abaddon Rajani. His entire life has been dedicated to sowing discord and undermining the Christian ethic of the western world. Some of his sources are regular news channels. Some of his sources come from highly placed officials from around the globe. He checks in with his closest allies. He pours over his own intelligence reports. Most importantly, he consults the stone idol that he believes has special powers.

He first came across the stone idol when he was in his early twenties. He was in Syria working as a geologist for a state-run oil exploration company. He had served two years in the Soviet army before getting his geology degree from a well-known university. With his combined degree and military service, the state decided he was a good candidate to send to an area known for troubles.

While in the Syrian/Iraqi border lands, he became amorous with a beautiful young local girl. The young lady was the daughter of a powerful chieftain and was already engaged to another man, the son of another chieftain. Abaddon found himself in a very hostile climate. He feared for his life. He requested to be reassigned, but his superiors laughed at him. He would either grow from the experience or be replaced.

After narrowly escaping a late-night assassination attempt, Abaddon found himself trembling in front of an ancient place of worship, not a church, not a synagogue, not a mosque. Just as a group of people searching for him were about to turn the corner, trapping him, an old man opened a door and beckoned him inside the ancient temple.

The place smelled of rotten wood and decay. Dust covered everything in sight and cobwebs were strung from every surface. The old man turned to Abaddon. "Welcome my friend. We have been

24

expecting you." That night, Abaddon was introduced to Baal. He escaped certain death and walked away with a small idol. Over the past fifty years he always kept the small idol with him. He is convinced that Baal saved his life that night and is the source of all his wealth and power.

As he gazes on the small idol, he speaks instructions to his loyal compatriots. These orders will be disseminated to the many people on the ground. Some of the orders will be carried out by people in power: politicians, media anchors, and other people of influence. Some of the orders will eventually get to the ground forces, the activists ... and the assassins.

Abaddon senses a disturbance. All the plans he has implemented are at peril. All the turmoil and decadence that he has sowed around the world is being undermined. He issues his orders before he finishes his glass of wine and heads to bed.

Chapter 4, The Street Runner

"I bet you twenty bucks you can't do it," Mike states.

Shawn looks at where the two cement block walls meet at the end of the alley. The top of the wall is almost fifteen feet high. "You're on," Shawn quickly replies.

Without even a moment's hesitation he runs straight at the corner of the concrete block wall. He leaps in the air as he approaches the immovable structure. His agile right foot hits the righthand wall about four feet up its surface. He uses his strong leg muscles to propel his body upward and to the left. As his body careens toward the other corner of the wall, he reaches up and grabs the top of the fifteen-foot barrier. He nimbly pulls himself to the top of the wall.

"Dude, why do you doubt me?" Shawn crows from the top of the wall.

"Why do you doubt me?" a voice responds to Shawn.

"What? Mike, did you hear that? Did you hear someone talking to me?"

Mike is standing in awe at what his extreme running friend just did; scale a fifteen-foot wall. "What, dude? That was awesome. How did you not crash and burn into the left wall?"

"Forget that dude," Shawn responds, shaken. "There's someone else here, someone just talked to me."

"What are you talking about Shawn? Are you paranoid? Did you start smoking weed again?" Mike queries his best friend.

Calming down a bit, Shawn looks around and then jumps down from his high perch, breaking his fall by bending his knees as he hits the ground and then tumbling forward before springing to his feet. He looks around, still spooked by the strange voice he heard. "Let's get out of here Mike. This place weirds me out."

"No way, dude. I get a shot at that wall too. You know the rules. If I scale it, the bet's off," Mike responds.

"Do not be afraid, I am with you," the voice states very clearly.

Shawn startles and looks around. His friend seems unperturbed as he tries to figure out how to scale the wall. "Did you hear that? Aren't you freaked out?" Shawn asks.

Mike turns and looks at his friend. "What up, brother? You look freaked out. I didn't hear nothin'. What are you talkin' about?"

"That voice, you didn't hear that voice? It told me not to be afraid. But it's weirding me out. Let's get out of here." Shawn has panic in his eyes.

"Bro, you have started smoking weed again. I didn't hear nothin'. But you're starting to weird me out too. Let's get out of here. Let's go get something to eat," Mike replies.

"I ain't been smokin' no weed. You know I quit that. It makes me lazy. I need to be in shape so I can get on that crazy obstacle show. I'm gonna win that contest and use the money to finish my degree." Shawn looks around once again, wondering where the voice came from. Calming down, he looks at Mike. "Yeah, let's go get a burger and a shake, high protein."

"I will always be with you," the voice says.

Shawn looks around but says nothing. His friend already thinks he's crazy. But now he feels like he's missing something. The voice was not menacing, it was calming, loving. Why did it scare him? He turns away and heads out of the alley with his friend. 'I will always be with you' echoes through his head.

"Why do you walk away from me?" the voice asks.

"I'm not walking away. I'm going to go get something to eat," Shawn says out loud.

"What? Dude, who are you talking to?" Mike asks, looking around.

"Did I say that out loud?" Shawn asks. "Mike, I swear, I'm hearing voices."

"Dude, you ain't going to make it to the big show if you keep smokin' weed."

"I ain't smokin' no weed," Shawn protests. "But someone is talking to me, clear as a bell."

"Well, maybe you should listen," Mike responds. "Unless the voices are telling you to do something stupid. You always hear about these freaks that say they heard voices."

"No, Mike. It's not like that. It's a good voice. But it scares the crap out of me."

They walk along in silence for a while, making their way towards a local diner to get their usual lunch. They turn a corner putting them on a busy commercial road. They walk past a homeless woman panhandling for money. It is not an unusual sight on the sprawling streets of Los Angeles; they pass by the destitute every day with barely a notice.

As they pass by the woman, Shawn hears the voice again. "*As you do for the least of these, you do for me.*" He stops and looks back at the woman. She's dirty and dressed in ragged ill-fitting clothes. As he looks at her, she smiles a toothless but genuine smile. Shawn stops. He walks back to her and smiles. "My friend and I are going to go get a burger and a shake. Would you like to come with us? I'd be glad to buy you lunch."

The woman smiles even more. "Oh, bless your heart my young friend. They won't let me in the restaurant. They don't like my type in there. But you could bring me a take-out. Would you do that?"

"They won't let you in? That's not right," Shawn responds.

"It's okay son. Too many people like me have caused problems. They don't want their patrons being disturbed. I understand that. If you would bring me something to eat, that would be just fine."

Shawn and Mike walk on and turn into the local burger joint. A waitress seats them and gives them menus. Mike immediately puts down the menu and looks Shawn straight in the eye. "What the heck was that? You want some stinky homeless woman sitting in the booth with us? God bless us that she turned you down. I don't think I could have eaten a burger with her stench wafting all around me. Are you nuts? What were you thinking?"

"I don't know, Mike. I've never done anything like that before. I don't know why I did it. It just felt like the right thing to do," Shawn responds, not mentioning the voice he heard.

"Well, next time you invite a stinky homeless person to have lunch with us, count me out, okay. I can still smell the urine stink that surrounded her."

Shawn does not respond in anger. Actually, he feels a peace surrounding him. "I just thought we should reach out to those in need. We always talk about helping those in need. I think it's time we start to act."

When the waitress returns, they order three meals.

Shawn hears the voice once again. "*Well done my friend, well done.*" He smiles but says nothing. He's no longer afraid of the voice. But he doesn't think he'll ever tell anyone about it again.

Chapter 5, The Meeting Place

They come in small groups and individually. It takes over an hour for the two dozen believers to assemble. Despite their stealth, they all still worry that they will hear a knock at the door. The dreaded knock of a Communist Party official.

As they wait for all of their parishioners to gather, they mingle together, sipping a homemade strawberry tea and talking about their lives, their kids. Some pray together for a particular ailment or family problem. Some laugh and joke about the inept local officials. More people arrive at their appointed times, staggered to avoid unwanted notice. When all the invitees have arrived, Xi calls the group together. As normal, he asks for prayer requests and updates from the twenty people who are crowded into his small home.

He takes notes as several people bring up both praises and prayer requests. In his mind a debate rages, should he say anything about his calling? He and his wife had prayed about his 'revelation' earlier, but he's not sure if it's something he should share.

"Proclaim the word to the nations," echoes through his head as he begins to organize his thoughts for the opening prayer. The Chinese are an obedient people. Xi will be obedient.

Xi prays over his growing flock for five minutes, then he prays for obedience and faith in following what God has called them to do.

In the time he had to prepare for the evening's gathering, Xi looked up as many verses from the Bible that say that the Word will be proclaimed to the nations. From the time of Abraham on, God states that the Word will be proclaimed to the nations. All people will kneel before the true Lord. His children will be more numerous than the stars in the sky and the sands on the shore.

Xi knows that he must tell his fellow Christians what has been laid on him. He knows that by doing so he's putting their lives at risk. He's putting his own life at risk too.

After his short lesson, Xi opens up. "God spoke to me today. He told me I was blessed, that I'm to proclaim His name to the nations. What happened to me today was not voices in my head. It was God talking to me." Xi tells his friends the entire story, then pauses and looks around at his friends and neighbors. He's hoping for some response. It is a discussion group, not a sermon. No one says anything for several minutes. Xi remains calmly quiet, he has peace in his heart.

Finally, a young woman speaks up. "If God called you to proclaim his Word, then we must help you. You have brought the Word to us. We know peace because of what you have taught us. I have joy and hope because of Jesus." She looks around for affirmation. Some heads nod at her words. "We will help you pastor," she states affirmatively.

An older man speaks up. "Is this 'calling' from the book of Revelation? Are you saying you are 'sealed'? If so, you are protected. But we're not. Are we to help you only to be killed for our efforts?"

"I don't know if it's from the book of Revelation," Xi replies. "I don't know if I've been sealed. All I know is that I've been called to proclaim the Word to the nations. I love our small group, but I don't think this is what the voice wants me to do. I think I'm to do something bigger."

"How are you going to do something bigger without us all getting thrown in jail?" the older man asks. "We all snuck in here out of fear of being discovered. How are you going to proclaim the Word by sneaking around? And if we don't sneak around, we'll all get thrown into a reeducation camp!"

"Then we don't sneak around anymore," the young woman's husband states. "So many of my friends and neighbors need to know that there is a God and that he loves them. They live in misery, working only to please the state and feed their children. Some of them have already asked me why I have become so happy and willing to help them with their problems. I'm too scared to tell them the truth. Who knows how they may respond? The government will pay them to turn in Christians."

"I feel the same way," a middle-aged woman interjects. "I have been watching some of the neighborhood children to free their mothers to do chores. They don't understand why I'm being so nice."

More stories are told around the room as people talk about opportunities to share their faith but are reluctant to do so for fear of the Communist Party coming after them.

"What if we just all came out as a group and told all our neighbors and friends?" Xi asks with enthusiasm. "Let's just come out in the open and tell everyone that they can be saved!"

The older man speaks up again. "Xi, what you are talking about is prophesized. It's in the scriptures. I'm retired and have had time to study the Bible. Your zeal is to be appreciated, but we should proceed cautiously and with discretion. Let's not make any decision now, let's pray about this and study the scriptures."

The rest of the evening is spent discussing the idea of boldly professing the Word without being arrested. Ideas on what scriptures to study are discussed. The meeting breaks up with a prayer said by the older man who fervently prays for their group to delve into the Word and seek God's guidance.

***

The young woman and her husband approach their home just before ten that night. They turn the corner onto the lane leading to their small home. They are startled to see many lights on at their home and several people milling around on the road in front of their house. They run towards their home fearing the worst. Is one of their children sick? Has there been some kind of accident?

As they near their home one of their neighbors runs towards them. He's pointing at them and yelling at two police officers further up the lane. "Here they are! Here they are! Arrest them, officers. They are the ones who live in that house." The young couple stops and looks around in shock. Why would their neighbor be telling the constables that they needed to be arrested? They move slowly towards their home as two constables approach them.

"Do you live there?" one of the officers asks very directly, with menace.

"Yes," the husband responds. "Is there a problem, sir? Our two children are in there with our babysitter. Are they okay?"

"The children are fine. The State will take good care of them," the officer replies harshly.

The young mother's heart both races and breaks at these ominous words. "You're taking our children? What have we done? You can't take our children. We're hardworking citizens. My husband works on the farms, and I help with the preschool program. We've done nothing wrong!" the young mother sobs as she pleads with the state official.

With disdain the officer looks down at the distraught mother.

"Apparently, you like to read to your children at night," the official states snarkily. The blood drains from both parent's faces. They have been reading the Bible to their children every night. "Your oldest son brought this out for your babysitter to read." The officer holds their Bible in front of them, sneering. "She has been taught to report these offenses to the state. You must come with us. You are under arrest for crimes against the state."

The couple is in shock. They meekly allow themselves to be handcuffed and led back down the lane towards the village police department. Their neighbors watch. No one says a thing as the couple is led away. To protest would expose them to arrest themselves as co-conspirators. To cheer would expose themselves as the snitches. The snitches want to remain anonymous. The snitches will be paid for their faithfulness to the state.

Chapter 6, The Fighter Sings

After being led away from the battlefield outside the walls of the ISIS stronghold, Mustafa and his four remaining comrades are at the mercy of the Kurds. They are led to a Peshmerga detention facility, where they are stripped naked and searched before being given what amounts to a loin cloth. They are separated and sent into small dark cells, with no furniture, just a threadbare blanket and a night pot. The heavy steel doors clang shut on each of them, locking them into a small confined darkness. Mustafa feels his way to the corner of his small and dank cell.

He lowers his large body to the floor and stretches out his legs. He's a hardened man, used to the rigors of combat and long days with little rest. This is not the first time he has been held as a prisoner. He spent four months as a captive of Sunni Muslims in Iraq before being freed in a short-lived peace accord. His current situation does not scare him one bit. It's just another day in a war-torn region where misery, hardship and death are part of everyday life.

Mustafa laughs heartily as he thinks about the day's events. "Forgive me Lord, for not standing up and dancing," he says out loud. "Your servant is tired and needs rest. I promise you, Lord, tomorrow I will sing and dance. I will sing your praises to everyone. The whole jail will hear me sing your praise. I will sing so loud that I will wake up the entire compound!"

He replays the day's events in his head. From his horrific actions to start the day, up through the attack on the complex by the Kurds and the bloody battle that followed. He thinks about what happened as he was trying to take out the old Russian tank. Tears come to his eyes as he recalls the revelation that was laid before him. He recalls clearly seeing himself in heaven, singing to the Lord in total bliss. That total bliss overcomes him again as he stretches out on the cold concrete floor of his cell. He falls asleep, exhausted, with visions of Christ swirling through his mind.

***

Back at the ISIS stronghold, the captain of the guard tells the four Imams who were quickly called together what he saw that day. It is late and he's getting tired. It is the fourth time he has explained the battle that culminated in the Peshmerga capturing Mustafa and his soldiers and then the weird foot washing ceremony. The Imams are particularly interested in the foot washing ceremony. He tells what he saw as best as he can remember, every detail.

They also question who else may have seen the foot washing ceremony. Who else had field glasses at the compound as the fight took place? He has no idea why this would be important. He tells them that the mortar squad's spotter would have had field glasses and may have seen what happened as well as two spotters for their heavy machine guns. Good field glasses are a prized item. Not too many people have them, he explains.

Finally, the Imams retreat to the inner sanctums of the local mosque. The captain of the guard eats a bowl of cold stew before heading off to bed. His head spins as he rethinks the day and the intense questioning from the Imams. He falls into a fitful, uneasy sleep. He never wakes up. He and everyone who may have witnessed the foot washing ceremony are murdered that night. Men faithful to the Imams take away the bodies, never to be seen or heard from again. A new captain of the guard is installed. No one asks a question about what happened to their old commander. Purges of those deemed unfaithful happen all the time. To even raise questions might have one marked as unfaithful.

As day breaks on the ISIS complex, the dusty signature of an incoming convoy can be seen approaching from the east. It is not a small convoy. It is a convoy of fighters led by one of the caliphate's best generals, a ruthless fighter and true believer. He has an imperative mission. The Peshmerga compound where Mustafa was taken must be destroyed. As in the days of the old testament, everyone in the Kurdish compound is to be killed, men, women, children, and most importantly, Mustafa.

***

Mustafa awakes abruptly. He looks around his small cell and smiles as he recalls the previous day's events. He drinks from the jar of water his captors left for him, silently thanking the Peshmerga for this small act of hospitality. Then he relieves himself in the night pot. With daylight now seeping into his cell, he takes in his surroundings. As he does so, he stretches, knowing his large muscles will cramp if he does not take care of his body.

His immediate bodily functions attended to; he resolves to make true his promise to the Lord. He begins by chanting. "God is good, God is good, God is great, God is great." As his chant grows louder, he thinks through the songs he knows. Singing is not encouraged in strict Muslim faiths. Neither is dancing. But he clearly saw himself singing and dancing before the Lord. He promised the Lord he would sing and dance, joyfully.

So, he begins to make it up. He begins to sing whatever comes to his heart. He begins to pound on the steel door to give his song rhythm. He begins to stomp his feet and twirl in circles. It is not pretty. But it is beautiful in a primitive way. And it wakes up everyone else held captive in the dank prison. Some of them yell at him to shut up, some join in with him. He pauses for a moment and hollers to the men who were captured with him.

"Join with me and sing," he hollers in his powerful battlefield voice. "Trust me my brothers, we're going to a better place. Let's sing and dance until our captors set us free!"

As the sun rises over the eastern plains, there is such a ruckus coming from the prison that the entire village is awakened. The night guards, along with the farmers and workers who are already awake, hear the unconventional singing and banging. The prisoners' commotion makes sure the entire frontier compound is awakened.

37

They all wonder what is going on that such a racket would be coming from the few prisoners in their jail.

The Kurds are a tolerant society and live peacefully with both Jewish and Christian families. An Orthodox Christian minister hears the singing, and his mouth drops open. The prisoners' chaotic singing is in many tongues, one of which is Aramaic, an ancient Jewish language, and they are singing praises to the Lord and to Christ. This is unheard of, but prophesized. Can it be? He hurries to the prison and tries to explain to the dumbfounded sergeant in charge that something of great historical significance is happening.

"These men, they seem to be talking in tongues!" the minister tries to explain.

"They are just trying to make a ruckus," the sergeant states. "They do this all the time, trying to disrupt us."

"No, no," the Orthodox minister interjects. "They are all singing the same song, but in different languages. Someone is even singing in an ancient language. Something is happening here. I need to find the one singing in Aramaic. He's a messenger, maybe even a prophet."

"Yeah, right," the young guard responds. "Look old man, stuff like this happens all the time. These guys get riled up and try to find a way to rattle us. Go get some breakfast and enjoy a cup of tea on your porch. We'll settle these rebel rousers down. It's nothing to be worried about."

The Orthodox priest is rattled but does not know what to do. The singing from the jail is clear. The message is clear. "Prepare ye the way for the Lord," the refrain that keeps coming around again and again.

The wizened priest looks to the south and sees a small but growing cloud of dust on the horizon. It makes him think his thoughts

38

are true. "Look to the south, young man. There is an attack force heading this way. Sound the alarm. I beg of you to sound the alarm."

***

In an expansive home on the shores of the Black Sea, Abaddon Rajani is approached by one of his trusted aides. "Sir, we have received some reports that you will want to see."

The curmudgeon of a man shoos away his nurse and waiter. He looks at his trusted aide with a grimace. "Don't be bringing me more reports of fake news. Damn it man, you know our people are the ones planting all the seeds of division. I want news of things we don't control."

The aide is used to being doubted and mocked, but he knows he has news his master will want to hear. His master is intrigued by anything that has religious connections. "There was a mass battlefield conversion in Northern Syria. An ISIS leader held a foot washing ceremony in the middle of a battle. We have coordinated a response. The ISIS fighter needs to be eliminated."

The wealthy man ponders what his aide has just told him. Abaddon Rajani has tentacles that reach far and wide. His vast wealth can influence even the most powerful countries in the world. His sources of information come from well-placed people in many governments. His ability to influence world events is only rivaled by the most powerful people in the world. And he has people working for him who can influence those powerful people.

"That is interesting. You were right to make sure this prophet is killed. Make sure our true allies stay in line. Keep me informed," he replies.

Chapter 7, The Runner, and the Lawyer

Shawn awakens as dawn begins to illuminate the southern California landscape. He looks at his phone. It is only 6:30 in the morning. His first class isn't until 10:00. He has studying to do, but it's not that important. He rolls over to go back to sleep.

"Wake up my son. Wake up and do what is right." Shawn clearly hears this voice, and it startles him. Then he thinks of the day before, and the voice that kept talking to him.

"Oh, not again. I want to sleep in. Leave me alone, whoever you are. Quit talking to me. You're freaking me out," Shawn says out loud.

"My child, you are one of the chosen. You have gifts. Use your gifts to honor me. You helped the widow yesterday. What about the orphans? Can you not help the orphans?" The voice asks calmly.

What the heck is this? Shawn thinks. Yeah, out of the goodness of his heart he bought the homeless lady a meal. It was a good deed and he felt good about it. What the heck is this question about the orphans and what does it have to do with him? "Go away! I bought the woman a meal. I'm not a bad person, leave me alone," Shawn says out loud. He buries his head in his pillow and tries to fall back to sleep. Fifteen minutes later his alarm starts sounding.

Shawn gets up and walks across the room to turn off the alarm. He swears he set it for nine o'clock, not seven o'clock. He looks around. Is there someone in the room with him? He groggily remembers talking with someone. Are his roommates pranking him?

As he presses the snooze button on the cheap alarm clock, his eye catches a glance at a piece of junk mail from a local charity. Big Brothers need your help ...

Shawn picks up the mailer. "*Can you not help the orphans?*" sounds loudly in his mind. "What the heck?" he asks himself as he looks to the sky. I don't even believe in you. What are you doing?"

The mailer states that there is a meeting for volunteers at eight that morning. Shawn tosses the mailer towards his overflowing waste basket. It hits the side of the waste basket and falls to the floor, laying face up.

"Shawn, are you up?" a female voice is heard from the hallway. "I made coffee and there are a couple of blueberry muffins if you're interested."

Shawn looks up with resignation. "So now you have Clarissa in on this gag. I give in. I'll go see if I can be a Big Brother." He opens the door to see Clarissa just down the hallway in the shared kitchen. She's in her tight clinging pajamas and Shawn takes a deep breath. He has always had a slight crush on Clarissa. She's not Hollywood glamorous. She's hometown beautiful; sweet smile, good heart, beautiful face and great curves. But most importantly, in the short time he has known her, she's genuine.

"I'll be out in a minute;" Shawn states as he searches for a clean set of clothing. He makes sure to find a fresh shirt that kind of goes with his semi clean shorts.

His heart races a bit as he brushes his teeth before heading down the hallway to the kitchen. He enters the common area to find it empty. There is a fresh pot of coffee and two blueberry muffins, but Clarissa is nowhere to be seen. Shawn pours himself a cup of coffee and wanders back to his room to get the Big Brothers flyer. When he returns to the common room, Clarissa is there, looking at her phone and eating one of the muffins. She no longer wears the clinging pajamas. She's dressed for the day, and her smile is brilliant.

"What gets our late-night Spiderman up so early?" she asks.

"Spiderman?" Shawn asks. "What do you mean by that?"

41

"Come on, Shawn," Clarissa replies. "We all know you're one of those wall runners. I saw you run up a wall, do a back flip and land on your feet. I think it's awesome. I hear you want to get on one of those reality shows. You have the talent, maybe not the drive, but you have the talent."

Stunned, Shawn replies defensively. "What do you mean I don't have the drive? I can do stuff that no one else can. I work at that. I boosted a fifteen-foot wall last night without even thinking about it."

"Proves my point," Clarissa says. "You did something you knew you could do. When you start doing things that push your limits, that's when you'll start to know your full potential." Shawn is left dumbfounded by this profound yet sensical statement.

"This is the first time I've seen you up this early. What's going on?" Clarissa asks.

Shawn is brought back to the here and now. He's smitten by this woman in ways he did not expect. He stutters a bit as he brings out the brochure for Big Brothers. He doesn't dare mention the voices he has heard as he explains that he thought he could be a good mentor.

"So, you've heard voices telling you that you need to do more with your life, with your talents?" Clarissa asks nonchalantly. Shawn's face goes pale. Does she know? Has she heard the same voices? No way, he thinks. It was just a coincidence of words.

Shawn smirks smugly. "Nothing like that, girl. It's like you said, I got talent. I should share that talent, right?"

Clarissa finishes her muffin and gathers up her books for her university classes. As she's getting ready to leave, she turns to Shawn with a smile. "Remember, Shawn, someone gave you those talents for a reason. Use them well." She winks at him, then pauses. "I hope all goes well at the Big Brother thing. I think you're a good person. If you need a reference, give them my name and number." She slips him a piece of paper and smiles as she pulls the door closed behind her.

Shawn is sweating from the encounter. It seemed as if Clarissa already knew everything about him. He felt like he was an open book while she was a complete mystery. He looks at the clock. He has fifteen minutes to get to the community center. He packs up the books and binders he'll need for the day's classes and heads out the door. As he thinks about the past twenty-four hours, he smiles. He looks to the sky. Is he going to hear more voices? He decides to think about Clarissa instead.

***

Clarissa arrives at the bus stop and breathes deeply. A half dozen people are waiting there for a ride to their job or to school. Although she sees a few people she knows, she stands back and does not engage them in the normal small talk. Instead, she silently talks to God. 'I know you called me, God. Please guide me and lead me.' She continues to talk with God about what she's to do and about her conversation with Shawn. She questions God about Shawn and is firmly reassured that God has called Shawn too. 'But he doesn't seem to know?' Clarissa protests. *"All who are called are different my daughter. Be patient. Trust me."*

Clarissa smiles. She feels the warmth welling inside her that she has felt many times since she accepted Christ as her Savior at a church retreat when she was a young teenager. The comfort is overwhelming and yet disturbing. She knows she has been called to do things that will stretch her faith, stretch her abilities, and open her to derision. To follow the path she's been called to follow will veer her far away from the comfortable life that a law degree would give her. The path that she's to follow will be a much harder life. But the joy wells up in her again. She's going to follow a path of adventure that will lead to salvation for those who truly need to be saved.

"I'm all in, God. I gave you my life ten years ago, and I'm not turning back now," she says out loud. She gasps as she realizes she just proclaimed her faith in public to people she barely knows, and to complete strangers. She blushes as she looks around at her fellow commuters. A few people smile at her. A few scowl, including one with a rainbow shirt espousing LGBTQ.

A middle-aged woman, a health care worker from the way she's dressed, walks over to her. "I heard what you just said. I wish I had that kind of faith. How can you be so strong when so much is going wrong?"

For a second, Clarissa panics. What is she supposed to say? Then the words come to her. "God loves each and every one of us. He loves you just as much as he loves me. He created the earth and all that occupies it. That includes you and me. He's my father. He's your father too. I'm not sure how to explain it better."

The woman's face turns down, "My father was jailed when I was a toddler. I've barely seen him over the past thirty years."

A moment of uneasiness overcomes Clarissa, but she reaches out and hugs the woman. "The father I know will never leave you," she whispers in the woman's ear. "He's your father in heaven."

"I know that," the woman says as tears stream down her face.

The bus comes to their stop and their moment of intimacy stops too, as a dozen people board the bus. Clarissa manages to sit next to the woman. She puts her arm around the woman and gives her a warm hug. Clarissa thinks of her calling to profess her faith. Now is the time. She leans close to the woman and whispers in her ear. "Accept Jesus as your Savior and know God as your father. Confess your sins and you will find peace, even in this chaotic world."

The woman buries her head in her hands and begins to sob. "I know that's what I need to do. I have heard it many times. But I'm not strong enough. I've done so much wrong. How can I be forgiven?" Clarissa and the woman talk quietly as the bus makes its way along its route. Several miles down the road, the bus comes to a stop. Across the street is a Planned Parenthood clinic. The nurse gets up suddenly. She straightens her uniform and wipes a tear from her eye. "I have to get off here. Please pray for me." Before Clarissa can say anything, the woman gets off the bus along with two young women, both showing signs of life in their wombs.

Dumbfounded, Clarissa leans back in her seat. She thought she was on the cusp of actually having someone proclaim Jesus as their Savior. And then it didn't happen. Should she have chased the nurse off the bus and not let her into the abortion clinic? That would have been a dramatic confrontation. Is that what she was supposed to do? She's bewildered, upset. She had explained God's love so well, only to see her efforts fall to pieces. How is she to proclaim the Word to the nations if she can't convince a fellow bus rider who is open to hearing the truth?

"Faith can move mountains. A small seed grows into a mighty tree."

Clarissa looks around, still not accustomed to hearing this reassuring voice. The rest of the riders on the bus are unphased. It's like nothing has happened. Some gaze out at the passing surroundings. Others are transfixed on their phones and iPads. Did she just witness to a nurse who works at an abortion clinic? Or was it all a dream? She doubts her own faith as she replays in her mind what just happened. 'God, I thought you were with me. Where did I go wrong?'

"Faith can move mountains. A small seed grows into a mighty tree," is repeated in her mind. She shakes her head, not knowing what to think as she waits for the bus to stop at the university.

Chapter 8, The Cleaner's Mission

The alarm claxons begin to ring. The young Peshmerga sergeant realizes that the approaching dust cloud could very well be an attacking force heading their way. Other outposts have also reported the approaching threat. The watch captain comes to the southern gate of their compound and quickly assesses the situation. He ignores the pleas of the Orthodox priest and immediately radios the compound commander.

"Colonel, there is a fast-moving force heading from the south. It's big, larger than anything we've seen since the Turks attacked us last fall. You need to get up here."

"Is it the Syrians?" the colonel asks, perturbed.

"I don't think so, sir. It's coming from the south, not the east. Bring the Americans too. This looks serious. I think you should alert the northern response group," the captain responds.

Moments later, as Kurdish troops begin to man fortified positions and mortar crews get their tubes ready for battle, the colonel, and his entourage, including two American Special Forces soldiers, arrive on the scene. By this time, the approaching column has begun to spread out. The dust cloud grows wider as the attacking forces move to encircle the southernmost Peshmerga outpost.

The American captain does not hesitate to get on the radio. He does not even consult the Kurd's commander. With a few curt sentences, several armed drones in the area are put on high alert. The drone operators are already tracking the column and immediately have their feed showing live footage on the Special Forces captain's iPad.

It is not easy to discern the scope of the attacking force through the dust clouds, but when switched to infrared, the scene comes into focus. The captain, though young, has been in several serious battles. His first sergeant, with over twenty years of

46

experience, is looking over his shoulder. The first sergeant swears under his breath. "That looks like the gates of hell have been opened, captain. That small fight yesterday really ticked them off."

"I need to show this to the colonel," the young captain responds. "Get on the radio with Command. Incirlik and Aviano need to scramble at least two squadrons. They need to alert the Jordanians and Israelis too." The first sergeant is already activating his secure SAT phone as he nods grimly.

The Peshmerga colonel quickly comes to the captain's side, knowing that the American will have live feeds from their drones and satellites. "It's serious, Emek. It looks as if they have sent everything they have our way."

Emek looks at the screen. "That is everything they have! That has to be at least nine tanks and dozens of troop carriers."

The captain widens the screen, showing more small red dots converging on their position. "They're also bringing in technicals and support trucks. They plan on taking out this position."

"Why?" the colonel asks. "Our attack yesterday should not have provoked such a large response. They are throwing everything they have at us." As he says this, they see more red dots, indicating the heat signature from an engine, start to encroach from the east. "Look at that, those have to be Syrian forces." The colonel stops for a moment and wipes the sweat from his brow. The captain is shocked too. The Syrians have been fighting against ISIS. Why would they be supporting them now.

The captain grabs the elbow of his first sergeant. "Top, look at this, make sure command knows this." Top looks at the screen and scowls. Without saying a word, he signals that he's on it. The captain knows that if he's seeing it on his iPad, then command sees it halfway around the world too.

The loud thunks of mortars being fired is heard. The enemy's scout vehicles are now within range. Soon they see explosions in the distance as their rounds begin to come down on the leading edge of the attacking force. The battle has begun. The ISIS forces return fire, but they are too far away to be of any significance. Meanwhile, the Kurds, along with their American allies, continue to ramp up their defenses. Busses, trucks, and cars stream out of the compound heading north, carrying the few remaining women and children that still live in the war torn village.

***

"Do you hear that, Mustafa?" Mahmoud exclaims. "Our friends are attacking. Soon we will be free."

Mustafa smiles at his longtime comrade, "I'm already free, my brother. Jesus has freed me. That battle that you hear outside, those fighters, they come to kill me, not to save you."

"You are a hero, Mustafa. Our friends will not let us stay captive here. But why do you say Jesus has freed you. We all know he was a mighty prophet, but only death in Allah's service will assure our place in paradise," Mahmoud replies, a bit conflicted.

"Let me explain, my friend. We're told that Islam is the religion of love, right?" Mustafa asks.

"Yes, my friend, Islam is the religion of love. We all know that," Mahmoud replies.

"If Islam is a religion of love, then how is the path to heaven through a battlefield? How is killing another man who does not believe as you do, showing love? Mahmoud, I saw something yesterday. I saw true love. God loves us. Each and every one of us. He loved us so much that he came to earth in his trilogy, as a man, and died for us. That man was Jesus. There is no greater sacrifice than to give one's life so others may live. That is what God did through Jesus. And I saw myself in heaven, praising Jesus. It was very clear. My friend, Jesus is the way to heaven. Jesus is love. Killing people is not love. It is very clear to me."

"But what about the prophet, Muhammad?"

"Muhammad proclaimed violence on those who were not of his faith, it is in the Quran. Why didn't Muhammad proclaim love for those who did not believe? If Muhammad truly believed in love, then why did he proclaim violence to promote Islam? If Islam is the religion of love, then we should be reaching out to our enemies, embracing them, helping them. Jesus truly proclaimed love. His love is for all people."

"But the impure must be eliminated, erased. Only then can we be pure."

"How does killing those who do not believe as you do make you pure? There is the fault in what Muhammad proclaimed. Islam does not give anyone a choice. Believe or be killed. Jesus gives us a choice, there is no earthly consequence for not believing in Jesus. Jesus's promise is eternal."

Mahmoud looks confused. He has never doubted his faith in Islam. Now, a man he respects greatly, has shaken his faith to the core. If Islam is love, then why do they kill those who do not believe? His senses are shaken.

***

Halfway around the world, in the Special Forces Command Center on the Gulf Coast of central Florida, people are moving. Far flung units are being spun up, alerts are being sounded, and calls are being made.

They can see the troop movements that are converging on the remote Peshmerga village. They see that even the Syrians are converging on the outpost, which happens to be the American base for one of their Special Forces units.

"Henry, what the hell is going on here? Why such an intense movement on this ragtag remote village?" General Jerry Shapiro, the commanding general asks his G2 who is in charge of intelligence.

"We're researching that right now, sir. There was a small battle at the ISIS compound south of there yesterday. The Peshmerga rounded up three old Soviet T-62 tanks and attacked the ISIS outpost. That violated a local cease fire agreement worked out a few weeks ago. The ISIS fighters apparently were able to defeat this attack. My best guess is that ISIS is retaliating for that attack. Maybe they are trying to send a message for breaking the cease-fire agreement."

"This is more than that," General Shapiro states as he watches the battle begin on the high-tech screens in front of him. Drones, satellites and even ground force cameras are displaying the developing battle on the high-definition screens around them.

"Have your people research yesterday's fight, Henry. Something happened that pissed them off. Search all drone footage and any satellite feeds we have. Get any ground assets activated to find out what happened." General Shapiro looks at the screens as the ISIS and the Syrian forces converge on the stout Kurdish outpost. They see the explosions as the Kurd's mortar rounds begin to land around the approaching enemy forces.

The G3, Frank Burns, a three-star general in charge of operations, has been standing next to his boss, General Shapiro, as this discussion has taken place. General Shapiro turns to his trustworthy aide. "What's our tactical situation, Frank?" he asks.

"That has been an aggressive but stable base for two years, Jerry. They have withstood several attacks and two long-term sieges by both ISIS and the Syrians. But they have never seen an onslaught like this. The Kurds have about two hundred reliable fighters with several heavy machine gun emplacements and a very good heavy mortar squad. We have eighteen elite operators in the village, Marine Recon and Special Forces."

"Any tanks or heavy artillery in the area?" the general asks.

"The Kurds are moving six Russian T-92 tanks and a battery of American 105 howitzers to support them, but they are an hour away. They will be late to the battle."

"What assets do we have to support them?" the general asks. "We have planes in Turkey. Get them in the air. We can't have another Benghazi situation that leaves our people dead due to lack of support."

"That's a peculiar situation. The Turks have locked us down. They have not explained why. We have two squadrons in the air from Aviano. They are three hours out."

The command staff of the Special Forces watches a battle halfway around the world play out. They do everything they can to bring American power onto the battlefield. But the situation spun up out of nowhere. The reluctance of the American allies in the area to help them leaves the General with few options, and many questions.

***

The G3 finds a moment to send a clandestine message. It only takes a moment for the zip drive to send the data cache detailing the battle that just occurred around the world, pinging from server to server, hiding itself deeper and deeper into the web. Its origin and its destination are totally obscured before the data cache reaches its final destination.

Frank wipes the sweat from his brow. It is not from concern about his fighters on the ground in Syria. It is from the act of treason that he just committed. But he is tired of the endless wars. He sees this as a way to stop the useless loss of American blood.

Chapter 9, Xi Coming Out

The knock at the door is faint. The sun will not rise for two more hours. The hard-working farmer is still in deep slumber. The woman knocks at the door a bit louder, waking one of Xi's dogs. The barking dog wakes Xi up. He looks around groggily for a moment, as anyone wakened from a deep sleep would. The dog barks again. In a flash, Xi senses danger. Adrenaline pours into his bloodstream, and he becomes fully awake and alert. His senses tell him something is wrong as he hears the knock at the door. A knock at the door at four in the morning is not good. He quickly dresses and heads through the large main room to the front door.

He peers through the curtains to see who might be outside. It could be Communist Party officials coming to arrest him. As he looks timidly through the curtains, Xi hears a voice, *"Do not be afraid."* He jumps back, startled. The voice speaks again. *"I am with you."* The voice is calming, soothing. Xi feels a comfort he has rarely felt. He knows it is the Holy Spirit entering him, giving him strength.

He saw through the curtains that it was an old woman at the door. His mind races. Why is there an old woman at his door in the middle of the night? His scared mind tells him it's a trap. The communists have developed some evil scheme to ensnare him. But the good side of him tells him to fight his fears. He just heard the Holy Spirit tell him that He's with him. Xi moves to the door and opens it wide. "Come in, come in," he beckons to the old woman. "Let me put a pot of tea on and then you can tell me why you're making this late-night visit."

The woman looks around with fear in her eyes. She looks behind her before she enters Xi's home and securely shuts the door. "No need for tea, no time for tea, your friends have been taken. They were waiting for them when they came home tonight."

Xi almost drops the tea kettle in the sink as his mind races. But he finds calmness settling over him as he remembers the voices he has heard, the peace he has felt. The sensation is almost unsettling. He wants to panic. Instead, he settles his mind and focuses on the situation. He finishes filling the tea kettle and puts it on the stove. Then he turns to the old woman and offers her a seat at their kitchen table. In the better light of the kitchen, Xi recognizes the woman as a neighbor of the young couple who comes to their meetings. The woman has come to a few of their meetings as the young couple's guest.

With a warm smile Xi extends his hand to her. "You are Nan. I have met you before. Li and Hui have brought you here a few times."

Nan blushes as she looks around nervously. Then she leans forward, obviously shaken. "Li and Hui were taken into custody tonight. Their babysitter found a Bible in their home. She reported them to the Party officials." Nan looks around again, fear in her eyes. "I didn't care at first. It's none of my business. But then I saw them take the children away. I have children. The state should not take children away from their parents. I wrestled sleeplessly half the night, and then decided to come tell you. I felt that you would know what to do. You're a man of God."

Xi feels a burden laid on his shoulders that he never expected to feel. Two of his fellow believers have been taken into custody. He knows from scripture that those who believe will be persecuted. His small group of believers met in secret so the communist officials would not know who they were. Yet, Xi always knew this day would come. For years, his small group of believers grew, and he was content knowing he was helping people find the love of Christ and eternal life.

What does he do now? Two people he has brought to know the Lord are in danger. They will be sent to 'reeducation camps'; their children destined to be sent to communist families, brought up praising the state, worshipping the state. '*You are sealed. Proclaim my name to the nations.*' Xi is startled as he hears the voice once again. He jumps up from the rickety stool he's sitting on. One of the stool's legs breaks and he falls forward, hitting his head on the kitchen counter. A gash is cut on his forehead and begins to bleed profusely. The older woman jumps from her seat to provide assistance and begins to wrap his head in a few threadbare dish towels.

Wu, Xi's wife, comes into the room, awakened by the commotion. She's startled. "What is going on here?" she exclaims. She tries to keep her voice calm, to not wake the boys or disturb the neighbors. Her first thoughts are of infidelity or some kind of home invasion. As she looks at the pleading eyes of the older woman wrapping her husband's head in bandages, she knows the devil planted those thoughts.

She rushes to her husband's side and begins to assist the stranger in cleaning and dressing the wound. As they clean his face with cold water Xi begins to regain his composure. Wu rushes to their bathroom to get a few medical supplies. As farmers they deal with unexpected injuries often. The state has allowed them a few medical supplies like gauze and tape. They also have a few of their own home remedies that have been handed down over the centuries.

The cut is neither deep nor long. Head wounds usually bleed a lot, even with small cuts. The brain requires a constant and steady flow of blood, making head wounds bleed far worse than a scuffed knee or cut finger. After applying pressure for several minutes, the wound begins to clot. Wu applies some salves and a small bandage. "That's going to leave a scar", she says with concern.

Xi looks up at her and smiles. "It's okay my love. It's okay." He struggles to his feet with the two women's help. "Let's go into the living room where we can talk." Wu guides them to their cheap couch and matching love seat, the cushions are already showing wear, the backs and sides are made of pressed wood and also show heavy signs of wear. The two teenage boys rough housing has accelerated the breakdown of the furniture.

Xi's head begins to clear as he sips on the tea he brewed almost an hour ago. The green tea has medicinal value, and the vapors help to clear his head. Wu sits beside him, but stays distant, wondering what is going on. Why is a strange woman in their house just before dawn, and why is her husband's head bearing a wound that will leave a scar? The older woman is quiet, embarrassed at the odd situation. Xi is smiling as his brain begins to function again.

Wu sees Xi's eyes begin to focus. "What is going on Xi? What is happening? Who is this woman, and why is she here?" Wu crosses her arms and looks at her husband with accusing eyes.

Xi is still trying to understand everything that has happened and how to explain it. He hears the voice again. *'The truth will set you free'*. His mind tries to think through all that has happened, and he realizes that only the truth can explain what has happened. He cannot dodge the truth.

"We can no longer build our church in the shadows." Xi states to his wife. "It is not what God wants us to do. We're to proclaim the Word to the nations. It is in the scriptures."

"And you will be sent to jail just like my neighbors," the visiting woman states with grief. "I watched them being taken away. We will never see them again. Their children will never see them again. How does that help you?"

Wu looks at Xi in confusion. She doesn't understand what is going on. Xi explains as his mind clears. "The young couple from our group returned home to find some Communist Party officials at their home. Their daughter had brought a Bible to their babysitter for her to read to them. The babysitter reported it to the party officials. The parents are in custody and the children are going to be raised by the state. Our friend came here to tell us this. Her name is Nan. She has been here several times as a guest."

Wu grasps Xi's hands and begins to cry as the story is completely told. "What have we done? They are in jail for what we taught them. We gave them that Bible. We encouraged them to read it to their children. Now they are in jail and their children; who knows what will happen to them?"

Wu begins to get angry. "I told you this would happen! You have brought anguish on another family! Your ideals have not caused us harm; even worse, it has caused another family harm. Xi. We have to stop. This is a path to destruction. No good can come from this."

Xi claps his hands loudly, which completely interrupts his wife's thoughts. He looks around the house fiercely. "Devil, you are not welcome here. Your voice of doubt will not be tolerated. Leave now."

As Xi commands the evil spirit to leave, Wu collapses on the flimsy couch. Xi steps over and covers his wife with hugs, kisses, and calming words. His wife looks up at him with peace in her eyes. "I'm sorry to have brought doubt to this home." She hugs her husband tightly. "There are so many threats, so many pitfalls. You are right, we must move forward in strength. The sun will be rising soon. We must have a plan if the communists begin to round us up to take us away."

Wu gets up off the couch and walks towards the kitchen area. She pours a cup of tea and stares out the window. She says nothing else. Xi knows it would be best to let her absorb what she has just heard. Let her just process what has happened. But Xi knows she does not yet know the full truth, and the truth will set them free.

Nan sits in the corner of the living room on the couch as she watches the couple work through this situation. She's somewhere between stunned and amazed. In the midst of a family dispute, she witnessed the devil being told to leave. And from what she's seeing, the devil left. Do Christians have the power to tell the devil to go away? Who are these people? What powers do they have?

"Wu, I have more to tell you," Xi states calmly.

"I don't know if I'm ready for more," Wu replies, still sobbing from having the devil's words cast away from her.

"I don't know how to tell you this, but I have been chosen. I have been sealed. I'm to proclaim God's Word."

Wu looks back at her husband. "So, tell me something new. You have been preaching the Word here for three years. How does this change anything?"

"You don't understand. Like I talked about at last night's meeting, God has spoken to me. I have been sealed. I saw myself in heaven praising Him. The fall I took tonight that left the gash on my forehead. It is the seal. What we've done so far is good. What is about to happen is going to be great!"

Wu ignores what her husband just said and begins to ready breakfast. The boys will be up soon, they will be hungry.

Nan looks around the worn room. Is this the room of a prophet? She feels a warming sense throughout her body. Is she in the presence of God? Without asking she's offered a plate of scrambled eggs with fried strips of mutton and a piece of cornbread. The breakfast is more food than she normally eats all day. Are all Christians so well taken care of, she wonders? But the state persecutes them. How does this family live so abundantly? She eats slowly, wanting her body to absorb every nutrient on the plate.

Wu sets a plate in front of Xi and then sits next to him with her own plate. Nan pauses as the couple prays. They give thanks to the Lord for the meal before them and ask that He guides them through the day. The prayer is a simple yet meaningful acknowledgement to their God.

Other than the prayer, the couple has been silent. Both Xi and Wu need to contemplate what is coming. Xi is the first to speak. "You are right, Wu. We must be ready for what is going to happen today. God is going to work miracles. We will make our plans expecting miracles to happen."

Chapter 10, Shawn steps Up

Clarissa thinks over what has happened to her as the professor drones on about tort law. The dream she had was so vivid. She was in heaven praising the Lord. And she saw Shawn there. What is that all about? She was raised as an evangelical Baptist and is proud of her faith. She lets people know her faith. She does volunteer work for Birthright and has helped several women come to know Christ through that ministry. But what is she supposed to do with the revelation laid on her in her dream? She shakes it off, it was just a dream. She has always had an overactive imagination. But what about Shawn being in her dream? Her overactive imagination starts to take her places she knows she shouldn't go. She focuses on the lecture, expunging from her brain her thoughts of Shawn.

Thirty minutes later the lecture is over. She heads to the library. Her next class is not for two more hours. She's to meet one of her classmates to study, then she'll get lunch before her one o'clock class starts.

As she's walking through the well-manicured plaza, her phone rings. She pulls the phone from her pocket and looks at the number as she always does. It is not a number she recognizes. She's about to hit delete. A synapse in her brain tells her to answer the phone, and she hits 'accept', rather than 'delete'.

"Clarissa, Clarissa. We need to meet. We need to talk." The urgency in the voice startles her. She's ready to hit delete but doesn't.

"Who is this? Why are you calling me? You're freaking me out," Clarissa says into her phone, frustrated and ready to end the call.

"It's Shawn. You gave me your number this morning. I signed up for Big Brothers this morning and I want to talk with you about it."

Clarissa smiles, relaxes. "Oh, cool. Sorry for freaking a bit. I didn't recognize the number. I'm on campus. Do you want to meet for lunch?"

"That would be great. I'll be there in about half an hour. I have two classes this afternoon. Can you meet me at the Trojan Cafeteria near the bus stop?" Shawn says with warmth in his voice.

"I know where you mean. I'll meet you by the MLK statue, Okay?" Clarissa responds.

"Yeah, I know where you're talking about. Wow, I didn't even expect you to answer your phone, now I get to buy you lunch."

"Slow down a minute mister, this ain't no date," Clarissa interjects, her Baptist upbringing kicking in.

"Oh, no problem man. I just wanted to thank you for making me breakfast this morning," Shawn replies. "And I want to talk with you. I mean I need to talk to someone. I think you're the person I need to talk to."

Clarissa smiles at Shawn's awkward words. "Okay, see you in thirty minutes."

Thirty minutes later, Clarissa waits patiently by the fountain and statue. She's smiling as she watches the self-preoccupied people walk by. Most have their heads stuck in their phones, barely noticing what is going on around them. One young man literally walks into the chain surrounding the fountain. Rather than being embarrassed at his ineptitude, the young man curses at the statue for being in his way! Clarissa cannot help but laugh.

The young man hears her laughing and looks her way. "Are you laughing at me? Do you think that's funny?" He starts heading her way with malice in his demeanor.

Clarissa meant no harm in her casual observation, but obviously the young man took offense. She tries to make the situation good. "I'm sorry for laughing, but you nearly walked right into the fountain. Rather than looking at your phone, why don't you try looking at the great big world around you. It's rather beautiful, including the fountain that you nearly walked into."

"You bitch, now you mock me," the young wiry man states angrily. "I could have won that game I was playing if not for you. Now I have to go back to level forty-six."

The gamer fiend is only a few steps away from Clarissa at this point and she begins to worry for her safety. The gamer is clearly unhinged, there is anger in his eyes.

Shawn, a bit delayed by a short detour the bus had to take, sees the confrontation unfolding from afar. He rushes forward, nearly knocking a few people down as he races towards the fountain. He sees the young punk reach Clarissa as he's still thirty yards away. The young gamer brings his hand up to slap Clarissa for the offense of laughing at him. Shawn, the able street runner, reaches back and snatches his backpack off his shoulder and hurls it through the air, using the shoulder strap to increase its velocity.

The twenty-pound projectile hurtles through the air, smacking the gamer punk square in the shoulder, knocking him over, sending him into the shallows of the fountain that he almost walked into only a few moments ago. Several people in the area had seen the whole situation develop. Many of them cheer as Shawn rushes onto the scene. But rather than checking on Clarissa, who is obviously shaken, Shawn reaches in and grabs the punk gamer out of the fountain.

The punk gamer is dripping wet and grasping his shoulder as Shawn pulls him onto the sidewalk. The young gamer, who was about to strike Clarissa, suddenly becomes the victim. "Did you see that?" he asks the crowd that has gathered around. "This guy just nailed me with his book bag. I guess he got jealous that I was hittin' on his lady friend, so he smashed me with his book bag. I want witnesses. Who just saw this racist white guy smack me down for hitting on his black ho? You all saw it. The white man crushing the black man once again.

Why don't you come over here and just step on my neck and kill me you racist bastard?"

The crowd begins to separate. The white folks walking away, not wanting to be drawn into anything that could rile racial tensions. A few minorities begin to gather around the punk gamer, starting to support his version of the story, seeing a black man once again being the victim of racist violence.

Clarissa is dumbfounded as a mob quickly forms, denouncing Shawn as a racist. "You all have to be kidding me," she hollers at the encroaching crowd. "Shawn is my friend. This pig was about to assault me. You have this all wrong."

The gamer punk jumps up on the wall to give him an advantage over the gathering crowd. "Don't listen to this whore. She sold herself out to the white man. That man smacked me down. He's full of white privilege. He thinks he can be the big defender of our black women. Who is he to say how we should treat our women? Take that bastard out. Get that privileged bastard. He's white scum."

Racial tensions have been running high across the nation, around the world. Even the slightest offense can start a mob reaction. The punk has managed to start a mob reaction to a non-event. He has taken classes on how to stir up situations like this. He never thought he would do it, but the lessons of oppression and white entitlement have been hammered into his brain for years. Even though he knows he provoked the incident, he relishes seeing the mob close around the white man and the black whore.

"He smacked me down!" he hollers as he holds his shoulder, feigning injury. "He's just another white man holding us back."

The crowd begins to grow vocal as they gather around Shawn and Clarissa. More than half the crowd is made up of millennial whites who have been told that they need to make amends for being born the way God made them. The whites are more aggressive and angrier

61

than the few blacks in the crowd. A chant is started, "racist, racist, racist."

Clarissa prays silently for strength and wisdom. None of this was part of her dream. She's close to panic as she fears for Shawn's safety. She's a black woman, they dare not molest her, unless the gamer punk has his way. But Shawn is in serious jeopardy of being violently beaten as the crowd gets larger and angrier, egged on by the punk gamer and a few other agitators who have come on the scene. Clarissa closes her eyes again, praying for wisdom. *"Faith can move mountains. The power of the resurrection is in you."*

Clarissa looks up. 'Do I have that power?' she wonders as she stares at the clear blue skies above her. She feels a strength welling up inside her. She steps up on top of the wall surrounding the fountain, giving her a perch above the crowd.

"In the name of God almighty, I command you all to stop now!" she yells overtop the crowd. Her voice is loud and firm. It is a voice to be obeyed, full of conviction. The crowd stops. They grow silent and look up at the black woman defending the white man.

Clarissa is stunned at how quickly her words were heeded. She knows why. It gives her confidence. "That man is speaking for the devil," she states loudly as she points to the gamer punk. He tries to respond, but Clarissa will not have it. "Be silent," she commands the punk before he can open his mouth.

She looks back over the crowd as they mill about. The crowd is not sure what to do, transfixed by this powerful woman who is speaking to them. She points at the gamer punk. "That man was about to assault me when Shawn threw his bookbag and knocked him into the fountain." She turns her finger towards Shawn. "The man you want to pummel as some kind of white supremacist, saved me from being beaten by a black man."

The crowd starts to look back and forth between Shawn, Clarissa, and the punk. Why would the black woman lie to them? Why

62

would the young black man stir them up? Have they been duped? Why would the young black man call the black woman a whore? It starts to sink in that they were about to attack a man for no reason. Clarissa sees the confusion and doubt. Her mind clears, her will is strengthened.

"Why do we hate?" she asks the crowd. "You wanted to hate Shawn. You want to be angry. Why? That young man nearly walked into a fountain because he was too involved in a game he was playing. It made me laugh. Because of that, this campus almost became the site of a riot. Why? What happened to acceptance? What happened to love thy neighbor? Why are we all looking to be a victim rather than looking to succeed on our own merits?"

Clarissa has their attention, so she pleads her case. "You are not victims. You are not oppressed. We're all unique individuals created by God and loved by God. Celebrate it. Love your neighbor. There is no room for hate in heaven. Stop the hate. Embrace love."

With that final statement, Shawn helps her down off the fountain wall. The crowd starts to talk about what she said. Some grumble that she's just another Jesus freak. Others ask themselves 'why not love?' 'Why is there so much hate?' 'Why not start the love right now and turn their backs on the hate?'

The crowd begins to dissipate, some grumbling that there was not a fight, some praising the Lord that it all ended peacefully. More importantly, some walk away wondering why there is so much hate. There should be more love. Where does that love come from? Where does that love start. It has to start with them.

By nightfall the incident is talked about around the large campus. Several versions of the story are told. One version is that a racial riot almost broke out on their campus, but a smooth-talking black coed calmed things down. Version two is that a black Aunt Jemimah saved a white supremacist from getting his ass kicked. Version three, A black woman preached love over hate to diffuse a tense situation.

No one knows the truth, because even those who were there all tell a different story. The gamer punk still proclaims that he was beaten down by the white man. The jumbled phone videos do not provide any conclusive storyline. It is just another day in a divided country.

***

After talking with many people and answering a lot of questions Shawn, and Clarissa are some of the last to leave the area. Finally, they get a couple of sandwiches from the nearby Trojan Café. They sit quietly at a table with a large umbrella to give them some shade.

"I know this is not a date, but what a first date it would be!" Shawn exclaims. "Could you imagine telling our grandkids this story?" Shawn assumes and old and wizened voice. "Oh yes, there was your grandmother about to be attacked by this punk. I hurled my book bag at him and saved her. Then a riot nearly broke out and your grandmother saved my life from a bunch of self-loathing snobs." They both laugh, needing the moment of levity.

They talk about the near riot with both grave sincerity but also with the ability to laugh at the stupidity of the entire situation. The gamer punk almost convinced the crowd that he was the victim. They talk about what would have happened if he had been able to convince the crowd that he had been attacked for no reason. The country is in turmoil over black men being confronted and killed by law enforcement officers. Both agree that the situation could have gotten very ugly.

"I have one thing to say about all these protests against the police," Clarissa states. "In almost every one of those situations, if the black men had just listened to the officers, they would not have been shot. I know some of those situations look pretty bad. But you know what, Shawn? If they had just allowed the officers to do their job, not resisted arrest, most of those people would be alive today. We all have to pay for our sins sooner or later. Those are my brothers. But they broke the law. They were in denial of their sins. That don't work in my book. If you break the law, you got to stand up for the consequences of your actions. That's what God asks us to do.

"Sure, there are some bad cops, and things need to change. But we need to take responsibility for our actions, for our families. We have to quit being victims and embrace the great opportunities that are before us. A black man was elected president of this country. That means any of us can rise to the most powerful position in the world. I was raised by a single mom in Watts, yet here I am attending law school at USC. I don't understand the oppressed mentality. Are things perfect? No! But should we be rioting, burning down our neighborhoods, burning down the country? Heck no!" Clarissa is worked up. She saw a situation nearly go out of control on lies and propaganda. She yearns for all people to succeed.

Clarissa continues her short sermon. "The thing that needs to change the most is my people need to embrace the sanctity of life. We don't care about life anymore. Not for our babies, not for our children, not for our men. It's so sad."

Shawn is taken aback by this outpouring of emotion. He reaches over and warmly grasps Clarissa's hand. "There are a lot of problems with our country, our society. I don't think we can solve them all right here and now."

Clarissa looks up. "I know, I know. But I feel that's what I'm supposed to do. And you're supposed to help me."

Shawn once again is startled. Is he supposed to help her? How? Why? What the heck is going on? Sure, she's a good looking and smart girl, but what is he getting himself into.

"I don't understand what you're saying." Shawn states.

Clarissa looks around. The café is mainly vacant, they have some privacy. She knows she needs to tell Shawn what she knows, what she saw.

"Shawn, I saw you in a dream. Not just any dream. I was in heaven. I was with a holy host. I was called to proclaim the Word to the nations. You were there too. I saw you singing praises at the throne of the Lord almighty. It was awesome, it was beautiful. I never felt so fulfilled in my entire life. And then we were commissioned by the Savior himself to proclaim His Word."

She looks up at Shawn, looking straight into his eyes. "Were you there? Did you have the same dream?" She unintentionally clasps Shawn's hand a bit tighter. She needs confirmation. She wants to know she's not crazy.

Shawn does not break with her gaze as he absorbs what this beautiful and sincere woman has just told him. 'Why does he get the crazy ones?' races through the back of his mind. The front of his mind is captivated by what she has just said. He was in heaven with her, that is totally cool. He was raised with Christian values, but not in a Christian home. He remembers sometimes going to church on Christmas and now and then on Easter. His knowledge of the Bible is virtually nil. But he's intrigued and begins to think.

"Some weird things have happened recently," Shawn replies. "I didn't see myself in heaven, but I have heard voices. Voices asking me to do things I normally wouldn't do."

Clarissa brightens as she hears this. She remembers hearing a voice say that all are not called in the same way, to be patient. "Tell me more," she says earnestly.

Shawn, having sworn not to talk about the voices, opens up and tells his story.

Chapter 11, The Village

Dawn breaks over the sprawling plains of northeastern Manchuria. The golden light of the sun starts to warm the millions of acres of farmlands that have fed generations of families for centuries. Xi lets the sun shining through the window warm his body before turning to hug his wife as he heads out the door. He gets his boys started on the morning chores and gives them instructions for the day.

"Papa, you talk like you won't be here today. Is something going on?" his oldest son asks.

"Friends of ours are in trouble. I have to go help them," Xi responds truthfully.

"In trouble with the state?" the boy asks.

Xi stops what he's doing to ponder the question. "They are in trouble for believing in God."

The young man looks at his father. "Why can someone be in trouble for believing in God? I've thought about this a lot. There has to be a God. Even if you believe in the big bang theory that they teach us in school, there had to be something to cause the big bang. At some time there was a Creator. Something brought our universe into being. None of my studies can explain how the universe came to be, therefore there has to be a God, a Creator. It's pretty clear cut as far as I can see."

"You are wise way beyond your years," Xi responds. "That is what I have to explain to the government officials today."

"You can do it pop, I have faith in you," the teenager responds enthusiastically.

Xi smiles at his son's optimism. "Well, young man, I appreciate your confidence. I have staked my faith in God. That is where you need to place your faith too. That is where we get our strength to make it through the day."

"I know what you mean papa. God is our true father. I have that figured out. Be safe papa." The teenager gives his father a rare hug. Xi embraces him with both arms.

"Make sure you and your brother get all your chores done before I get home tonight. And don't forget about your studies." Xi smiles at his son as he turns to walk to the village.

His mind races as he leaves his property and starts the two-mile walk to the village where the young couple is being held as enemies of the state. What is he going to say? What is he going to do? His only plan is to expect miracles. Is that a good plan? *'If I am with you, who can stand against you.'* Xi looks around upon hearing this. Was it a voice out loud, or did he hear it in his head? He swears he heard it come from heaven.

He sees a farmer ahead of him, moving two dozen pigs to the village. This hardworking farmer and millions like him keep the cities supplied with food. He quickly catches up with his neighbor. "More pigs for the slaughter, I see," Xi remarks. "No offense, my friend, but they seem a little lean."

"They are all lean, Xi. There has not been enough feed to get them properly fattened. But the council has to meet its quota. They ordered me to bring in the best I have. I'm going to be a thousand pounds underweight. But what can I do?"

Ahead of them they see another farmer herding sheep to be put on the train to the slaughterhouses. Xi looks behind him to see more farmers pushing their livestock into town. Even from a distance he can see that all the animals are not fully nourished. They are all going to slaughter much leaner than they should be. The council will not be able to meet its quota. The council will be under great duress because of this. If they cannot meet the state's quota, they could not

68

only lose their prestigious positions, they may also be sent away to the concentration camps for being disobedient.

Xi realizes he's walking into a cauldron. The council will be concerned about meeting its quota. They will have little concern for a small local produce farmer when they fully grasp the shortfall in production that they face. Still, he does not lose faith. Two hummingbirds come flittering by and pause to gather nectar at a few spring flowers. Xi marvels at their beauty and grace. He continues to walk forward with purpose. He fully expects God to be with him. The God he knows works miracles.

Xi enters the outskirts of the village. The muddy roads are full of livestock from all over the precinct. He should have known that today is the day the train comes up the small spur to collect the state's allotment of livestock to be shipped to the slaughterhouses. The animals are already lined up to be brought onto the scales. After being weighed, they will be sent to pens until they are loaded onto the train.

Xi watches as the animals are brought onto the large scale, counted, and then weighed. He has seen this spectacle before, but he usually avoids the village on this day. It is too busy and too hectic for him. Two dozen goats are brought onto the scale. "Chen, twenty-four mature male goats, two thousand one hundred and eighty kilos." Xi looks over at the owner of the goats and sees a tear roll down his face. The weight should have been well over twenty-seven hundred kilograms. The farmer will be punished, his rations restricted. He watches two more weigh ins. Both fall short of their allotment.

Xi has lingered long enough. He's not here to watch how poorly the farmers have fared. It has been a tough spring. He knows this, but the state doesn't care. His mission is to free his two followers. He turns and heads towards the small precinct police building. It's a concrete block building with few windows, a rather grim and imposing building. He thinks over the situation as he walks up and opens the door.

A woman is sitting behind a stout counter with a strong Plexiglas screen in front of her. It is like something you would see at a bank that has been robbed too many times. The woman looks up from her paperwork.

"Are you here to see someone? Do you have and appointment?" she asks quickly, annoyed at being unexpectedly interrupted.

"You arrested two friends of mine last night. I want to know why, and I want to see them," Xi states calmly.

"Do you have an appointment? If not, then you must set up an appointment. State your name, I'll check the appointment list."

"My name is Xi Whu. I don't have an appointment so don't bother checking. May I speak with the watch officer please. I would like to speak with the couple that was arrested last night. They are friends of mine."

"Xi Whu, you can't meet with anyone without an appointment. The commander is very busy today. I could schedule an appointment for next Thursday at one o'clock," the woman states as she shuffles some papers around.

"I will meet with him today. Tell the commander to come here now or I will go to see him." Xi feels confident as he says these words. He's not sure why, but he knows he'll be seeing the commander very soon.

The stout woman behind the desk looks at Xi oddly as she presses a hidden distress button. Two officers come through a side door. Before Xi can react, one of them hits him with a taser while the other takes him to the ground and handcuffs him. The taser causes Xi to fall limp to the floor. The officers take him into custody. As Xi is led away, the woman behind the desk remarks snidely, "I guess now you'll get to see your friends that were arrested last night."

The two officers take Xi into the small jail and throw him in the only empty cell. Next to his cell is the cell holding the young couple. They watch as the barely conscious Xi is tossed into the cell next to them. "Pastor, pastor!" they both holler. "What are you doing here?" They begin to sob. "We didn't say anything. How did they know? Are they going after all of our brethren?"

Xi begins to stir as the effects of the taser begin to wear off. He starts by trying to move his fingers and toes. Soon he starts to regain all bodily functions. He shakes his head to help him regain his senses. After flexing his knees and elbows, he stands up. His mind is still blurry as he looks around. His eyes begin to focus. He sees the young couple in the cell next to him. He starts to remember why he's there. His thoughts start to become clear. He looks at the young couple and smiles, "Okay, this is a start. I told them I wanted to meet with you. The next step is to meet with the commander of this little operation."

The couple looks at their mentor with mouths agape. They have no idea what is going on.

Xi starts to stretch out his muscles, trying to fully regain his senses. "We're going to be leaving here soon," Xi states. "These are cramped quarters; you should stretch out and get limbered up."

The young couple looks at Xi through the steel bars that separate them. "What are you talking about?" the husband asks.

"God is with us, He is going to work miracles today," Xi responds confidently. "I need you to pray for God to be with this village today. Pray for his presence to be here."

Xi grabs the steel pot that is there for his bodily functions. He picks it up and begins clanging it against the steel bars, making as much noise as he can. It only takes a few minutes for the two guards to come into the jail. He is ordered to stop his ruckus.

He stops the clanging. "Tell the village leaders that I need to meet with them. They will be short for their quota. I can help them meet their quota."

The guards look at him and laugh. "Shut up fool. You're already in enough trouble." They turn and walk away. Before the door closes behind them Xi starts clanging on the bars with the night pot. The larger of the two guards turns and fires a taser at Xi, hitting him square in the chest. He keeps the trigger pulled for a few seconds. Xi drops to the ground, convulsing as the electrical charge courses through his body.

"Maybe that will shut you up for a while. Cause trouble again and we'll take you out back for a real beating," the behemoth of a man snarls.

Xi's body aches from being hit twice by a taser in less than an hour. As he starts to regain his senses, he begins to move and stretch as he did before. The couple in the cell next to him are terrified. They watch Xi regain his strength and stand up. Xi looks at them. "Please pray for us and the village," he asks earnestly. With that request, he picks up the steel pot and begins making a ruckus once again.

The two guards wait a few moments before entering the jail cell area, hoping the crazy farmer will stop on his own accord, but the clanging continues. Once again, the larger guard draws the taser and aims it at the prisoner. Xi raises his hand as the guard takes aim with his taser. "Stop now or the wrath of God will come upon you!"

The guard laughs as he fires the taser once more. The electrical projectile glances off the steel bars, ricochets off the block wall and smacks dead on into the head of his partner, who falls to the ground as the electrical charge races through the wires, sending the smaller guard into convulsions. The larger guard quickly releases the trigger and starts to tend to his comrade. The smaller guard needs a few moments to recover from the taser. His speech is slurred, and his movements are slow as he begins to regain his composure; a taser to the head can have lasting impacts.

Seeing that his long-time work mate is injured and may have long lasting mental injuries, the lead guard begins to draw his sidearm.

"In the name of the Lord, I command you to stop!" Xi states forcefully. He looks directly into the eyes of the guard. "There will be no blood shed in this jail. Bring me to the council, I can save them."

The guard snarls. Who is this country farmer that challenges his authority? He pulls his side arm and aims it at Xi. He pulls the trigger, but nothing happens. The weapon is poorly built and poorly maintained. The firing pin has seized up. He pulls the trigger several more times to no effect.

Xi looks sternly at the guard. "No blood will be spilt. Listen to me! Bring me to your council. I can save them," he states.

The guard looks around. He looks at his useless handgun. He thinks about what the farmer has said. His mind is in total confusion. The man in front of him should be dead.

Xi can see that the guard is thinking things through. "Your weapons will not work against me. I'm not here to harm you, I'm here to save you. In the name of the Lord, you are commanded to bring me to the village leaders."

The young couple has been praying as all this has been unfolding. They pray even harder and more fervently, seeing the guard is on the verge of capitulation. Their eyes are wide open at seeing the faith of their leader standing so strong against what should have been certain death.

The guard's right hand slowly reaches down to his belt where there is a large ring of keys. "What do I say to the village council?" the guard asks, his voice trembling. "What do I say to the village constable?"

"Tell them that I have a way for them to be saved. Tell them that the quota can be met. Let me out of here, and I will tell them myself," Xi responds.

The guard fumbles through his keys and unlocks Xi's cell. "I'll bring you to my commander. He can figure it out from there."

Xi grasps the jailer's hand gently but firmly and looks straight into his eyes, a clear indication to the jailer that Xi is in charge. "My friends will be released too." It is not a request, and the jailer knows it. Trembling, he unlocks the young couple's cell.

Xi looks at the large man and smiles, a warm and genuine smile. "You are afraid. Don't be afraid. In the Bible it says 'do not fear' three hundred and sixty-five times. You are afraid because you do not know Christ. He loves you. With him there is no fear."

"What do you mean, 'there is no fear'?" the guard asks as they start heading towards the door.

"My Savior, my God; he made the heavens and the earth. My God knew me before I was born. Everything you see he created including you and me. Because I love him, he loves me and protects me. He loves you too. If you love him, believe in him, he'll protect you too. Through him you will have eternal life."

Many thoughts run through the guard's head. Only moments ago, he had hit this man with a taser and tried to kill him. Why is he telling him of this loving God? But the farmer is speaking truth. The farmer should be dead. Is his God protecting him? Now he's taking the farmer to the council who will surely determine he should be executed, and his family sent away. He thinks of the power he felt in the jail cell when the farmer spoke to him. He still feels that power coming from the farmer. He could easily overpower the farmer, handcuff him and deliver him to the council as his prisoner. But he knows he would fail. He decides this man, this meager farmer, must be a holy man.

74

"Tell me more about your God," the jailer states earnestly, as they head towards the railroad station.

"You already know him my large friend. You just have not acknowledged that he exists. He is the Creator. He is your true Father, and He loves you."

"You've said all that before," the jailer replies. "How do I become like you, fearless?"

"You can only become fearless through love," Xi states calmly. "Love God, who created you, and love your neighbors as God loves you. Knowing God will make you fearless."

The guard looks around at the growing crowd as they get closer to the rail station. Herds of animals are everywhere. He sees the eyes of despair and fear all around him. He knows that look of fear. It is fear of what the state may do to them if they step out of line or do not meet their quotas. Fear surrounds him, he can feel it. But the farmer still has no fear as they march to meet with the village officials.

What the farmer said starts to sink in. He has always known there must be a God, a Creator. The idea that hate only brings about violence and more fear rings true. His heart begins to turn. He feels it in his soul as he acknowledges that there has to be a God. His mind races as he thinks about a God as his Father. Not a father that would beat him, but a father that would love him. He starts to walk a little straighter and a little taller. His fear of what is about to come starts to disappear.

Chapter 12, Mustafa Discovered

In the bowels of an intelligence facility on the west coast of Florida, a young sergeant reads a report from a Peshmerga soldier who was present when they took the four ISIS soldiers captive. The Peshmerga soldier made a statement about a foot washing ceremony, right in the middle of the battlefield.

The young sergeant's grandparents are anabaptist and he had attended several foot washing ceremonies while growing up. He knows the significance of this ritual right away.

He flags the report and forwards it for further review. As he hits the send button he knows he needs to take additional action. The report could sit in the 'cloud' for days. He knows that something has stirred up a hornet's nest. He's not sure what or why. But he does know what he just read needs immediate attention. What he just read is biblical, maybe even apocalyptic.

He should go to his Lieutenant with this information. But the Lieutenant is young and dumb. His platoon sergeant would know what to do but he's not on duty. The information he has needs to be forwarded up the chain of command as fast as possible. He's a mere E5, a lowly sergeant. Who is he to decide that? He trembles as he tries to decide what to do.

His buddy at the workstation next to him looks at him. "Luke, what's up? You don't look so good."

"I got some serious intel here, Josh. I think the LT will blow it off as nothing."

"Then go to the captain, dude," Josh responds. "Even the captain knows the LT ain't worth a crap. If you got serious intel, go to the captain."

"I'm a newbie here. I can't just go to the captain," Luke states timidly.

76

"Show me what you got. If it's important, then the captain will want to see it." Josh reads the intel report and Luke's written assessment.

"Seems weird," Josh responds. "So, this group of people stop and wash each other's feet in the middle of a battle?"

"Not just a group of people, enemies!" Luke exclaims. "One minute they're trying to kill each other, the next minute they're washing each other's feet. Would you want to wash my feet?"

Josh looks down at Luke's boots, sturdy but well worn. "Hell no, dude. Who knows what stinky disease you got going on down there," Josh says as he wrinkles his nose.

"That's my point," Luke implores. "This does not happen. This is a Christian act of service and love. An ISIS fighter does not start washing his enemy's feet in the middle of a battle. They want to know what happened in this battle that was different. This is it. This does not ever happen except for in some devout Christian churches."

"Dude, that's pure gold. There was some kind of battlefield conversion. And both sides are Muslims," Josh states as he reads through the report once more. "All of a sudden a dozen Islamic guys wanting to kill each other perform this distinctly Christian act? I'll go to the Captain with you. He'll want to see this."

***

Two hours later, drone footage is found showing the twelve fighters sitting in a circle, apparently washing each other's feet. The resolution is poor, but the actions reflect the report from the Peshmerga soldier.

"What is the status of the battle at the Peshmerga village?" General Shapiro asks pointedly.

"It was over run about thirty minutes ago," Henry, his general in charge of intelligence responds. "About a hundred fighters are fighting a retreating battle to the northwest where a strong line of defense has been set up by the main Peshmerga forces. As you know, we had eighteen operators in that village. We have four confirmed American casualties. The ISIS prisoners are with our remaining forces."

Frank, the G3, speaks up before General Shapiro asks any questions. He knows the general will want to know how the operation is progressing. "We have two squadrons of F35s out of Aviano supporting the fleeing fighters. The Peshmerga have enough tanks and artillery on their defensive line to stop what's left of the raiding ISIS group and the Syrian forces that are supporting them."

"What else do I need to know?" General Shapiro asks. "I'll have to brief the president again. I don't want any surprises. What about our allies in the area?"

"The Jordanians and the Saudis both launched aircraft as a precaution. Neither left their own airspace. The Iraqis are still in too much turmoil to react at all. The Israelis are on high alert, expecting some kind of action from the Palestinians or al Qaeda."

"So, we don't have a full-blown international incident?" the general asks.

The General's high-powered staff looks around, not wanting to comment. The G2, a long-time friend of the powerful general speaks up. "We're warriors sir, not politicians. Today's actions need to be looked at in a geopolitical aspect. That is above our pay grade. We protected our soldiers on the ground using the assets available. Turkey denied the use of our aircraft out of Incirlik. That is troubling. The Syrians supporting an ISIS attack is troubling too. The foot washing ceremony needs to be brought up as well. It is the oddity of the whole situation."

The general looks around at his staff. He sees doubts and concerns. But they are paid to have doubts and concerns. How is he supposed to tell the president and his cabinet that a foot washing ceremony may have caused the whole event? He thanks his staff as his report begins to formulate in his head. A foot washing ceremony caused a major battle where the front lines have been relatively peaceful. What the heck is a foot washing ceremony and what is its significance? The general tells Henry, his general in charge of intelligence, to meet him in his office. He needs more information.

***

"What the heck is a foot washing ceremony and why did it cause such a dust up?" General Shapiro asks Henry, his G2. A young sergeant is in the room, along with a naval chaplain.

"Jerry, I was raised as a Presbyterian. I know that Jesus washed the feet of his disciples at the Last Supper," Henry replies. "But I haven't been to church in ten years." The G2 looks at the Chaplain, a bit embarrassed as he says this. "Finding time for church is hard while trying to raise three kids and keeping the world from blowing up at the same time."

"Confess your sins to God, not me," the chaplain replies, trying to infuse a bit of humility into the situation. Chaplain Kaufmann is a captain, a high-ranking officer in the navy, with twenty-six years of service. The naval captain turns to the army general. "A foot washing ceremony is a Christian tradition. Very few Christians actually practice this tradition. Washing another man's feet is an act of submission, an act of service. As your G2 said, Jesus washed the apostles feet at the Last Supper." The chaplain pauses for a moment. "General, I don't know your faith. Are you familiar with the last supper? Do you know Christ personally? I don't ask from an evangelical standpoint. I ask because I need to know from an intelligence standpoint." tinkle

General Shapiro's face blushes at this question. He regains his composure and responds in a diplomatic fashion. "I was raised a Lutheran, we went to church on Christmas and Easter. When we had kids in the house we went to church on Christmas and Easter too. Assume I don't know what you are talking about."

The chaplain pauses for a bit. How does he explain the love of Christ to a three-star general in a few short sentences? "I assume that you know Christians believe Christ is the son of God. By washing the feet of his apostles, Christ showed that he was there to love, not rule. He set the example that acts of service, acts of love are the acts of people who truly know God and his love."

"Okay," the general states. "The foot washing thing is an act of service. I get that. And I get that it takes a lot of love, call it submission, to wash someone's feet. Hell, I'm not washing anyone's feet. Maybe my wife's, but that's a different story."

The naval chaplain leans forward. "That's my point, General. You would wash your wife's feet because you love her. That is the same love that Jesus was expressing to the apostles."

The general does not respond for several moments as he ponders this. "So, what's this got to do with our dust up?" the General asks.

"The ISIS fighter had a battlefield conversion," Captain Kaufmann replies.

"Okay, that happens all the time," the general replies. "We know all about fox hole conversions, people find faith when bullets are flying."

"A prayer said in a foxhole is not the same as washing your enemy's feet," the Captain replies. "These are Muslims. Christ's actions at the last supper would not be something brought up in their madrassas. You wanted to know if something significant happened at that battle. This is it."

"I still don't get it," the general responds. "Why would this make the ISIS commanders act so violently and so quickly. They convinced the Syrians and the Turks to join them in just a matter of a few hours."

"Which is why it was such a significant event," the captain responds. "Sergeant, let the general know your thoughts."

The young sergeant stands. He never dreamed he would be briefing a three-star general when he signed up just four years ago. He takes a deep gulp of air as he tries to organize his thoughts.

"I'm a Christian, sir. I look at this from my upbringing as a Christian." Luke pauses to put his thoughts together. "What I have been taught is that twelve thousand people from the twelve tribes of Israel will be called to proclaim Jesus prior to His return. No one knows when this will happen, or how. This report plus other things I have seen in the news makes me think that the 144,000 have been called. ISIS knows this too. So do the disciples of the antichrist. They have to stop anyone who has been called, especially an ISIS fighter, one of their own."

"That is crazy talk. What the hell do you mean?" the general asks.

"End times prophesy," the captain responds.

"Whoa! Wait a minute," the general replies, aghast. "I've heard dozens of end times theories over the past thirty years. I'm not going to waste any more time on them now. This foot washing thing is no different than a stray asteroid that may hit the earth. C'mon, man. Are you really wasting my time with this? I have to brief the president in less than an hour."

The general stands, pissed. At that moment the room rocks slightly. Books fall from the shelves lining one of the office's walls. Water glasses tremble, the general has to grab his desk to keep from falling over. Everyone in the room is stunned, not knowing what to do. They are in central Florida; they don't have earthquakes in Central Florida.

In less than a minute, the trembling stops. "What the hell was that?" the general hollers over the alarms going off all over the place. Car alarms and fire alarms are sounding across the military complex.

The G2 looks around, visibly shaken. He grew up in Southern California and has experienced moments like this before. "That was an earthquake, General." He stands and looks out the window, his naturally curious mind wants to see if there are any serious effects from the tremor. He sees downed utility poles and people streaming out of the local buildings. Car alarms are screeching everywhere. "General, we should initiate Def Con Three protocols."

"Def Con Three?" the General asks. Def Con Three puts the military base on high alert. Def Con Four means war is imminent, Def Con Five means the country is at war.

"We don't get earthquakes here,'" Henry responds. "If we felt an earthquake here, what happened around the country? You need to ramp up this base for the worst-case scenario. Better to be prepared than caught flat footed."

The Three-star General realizes the common sense of Henry's suggestion. With the push of a hidden button on his desk, the Central Command complex goes on high alert. The sound of the military claxons joins in with the cacophony of alarms already filling the air. The claxons let the people on the base know what to do. The disciplined men and women of the compound begin to report to their duty stations. The most important function of this military base is to monitor and react to threats to their widespread military forces. The soldiers of the base will not neglect this duty under any circumstances.

***

Abaddon Rajani is on his smaller yacht, a 35-foot boat set up for fishing, when he receives a call. He has his crew return him to his home base immediately. Fishing is fun but controlling the world's politics is his business.

Once on shore he is escorted to his secure communications room. He watches a short video clip and digests the information. The Americans have gone on high alert. They have even brought in Christian experts on the situation. He asks the few men in the room to leave so he can digest this information. As he is left alone to think, he turns to a blank wall and presses a button. The wall opens to reveal an ancient idol, a statue of Baal. It is an exact replica of an ancient statue found in the middle east. The original bas relief statue was carved over three thousand years ago. The statue is both comical and terrifying, featuring a man with the head of a goat with horns protruding from its head. The body of the statue is comical with its straight lines and too pure imagery of a man. The eyes of the statue are what are terrifying. They seem to be glaring right at you, piercing your soul, following you.

Abaddon kneels before the statue. "I have followed you, my god. I have promoted the sacrifice of children in the womb. I have sown division among the races. I have made the right be wrong and the wrong be right. You have blessed me for my faithfulness. I am rich and powerful. But as you told me, a new power is coming. You told me to be prepared for this. You told me to tell you when this happened. It is happening now. I covet the power you have given me. Tell me what I need to do to continue to dwell in your favor."

The old man waits for an answer. No answers come from the ancient and evil statue. But his mind churns evil thoughts.

Abaddon dwells on his past as he looks upon the statue. He was brought up in poverty in East Germany. When the Berlin wall fell, he was shining shoes at a local barber shop. He soon found that by listening carefully to his clients he could use their words to his advantage. He used his eaves dropping to take gambles. It did not take him long to gain wealth and power. He found that knowing the secrets of wealthy people was extremely valuable. He expanded his network, starting with shoeshine boys and maid servants who heard valuable information. It did not take long for him to have informants in all levels of government. His tentacles started to spread worldwide.

83

Sixty years later, he is now one of the richest men in the world with the ability to shape world events. He sees himself as a savior of the world, a man able to save humanity from its own stupidity.

Chapter 13, Commitment

It is late evening in Los Angeles. Shawn and Clarissa are eating tacos from a food truck. They are sitting together at a picnic table set up to accommodate the many food trucks that serve the campus. "Shawn, I know you'll think this is crazy, but as I said before, I saw you in my vision. You were with me in heaven, and we were singing praises to the Lord,"

Shawn hears her once again tell him she saw him in heaven. He thought he was crazy. But here is someone just as crazy. "So, not only am I hearing voices, you're telling me you're seeing visions?" Shawn asks. "I thought I was crazy. I bought a homeless woman a meal last night. I never do that. I volunteered to work with troubled kids this morning. Again, that is not what I normally would do. I'd rather sleep in until nine and then go to the gym until my classes start."

Clarissa looks at Shawn with loving eyes. She knows Shawn has been chosen too. He just hasn't fully realized it yet. She moves to a chair next to Shawn and puts her arm around him, not in a sexual way, in a comforting way. As she touches Shawn, Clarissa has a moment of clarity. Thousands of scenes flash through her mind. The scene she cannot shake is of her city, Los Angeles, crumbling and broken. Startled, she looks around.

Her gaze returns to Shawn, she has fear in her eyes. She sees fear in Shawn's eyes too. "Shawn, you look like you just saw a ghost," Clarissa states, alarmed.

"I just saw Los Angeles being burnt to the ground," Shawn replies. "It was weird. Right when you touched me, I saw this apocalyptic scene. Buildings falling, roads upheaved, bridges crashing to the ground." Shawn looks at Clarissa and backs away. This woman's touch had him see horrific scenes. Is she the devil? Is she a demon?

Shawn doesn't know what to do. He likes the dark-skinned beautiful woman sitting next to him, but her touch made him see horrific things. Should he get up and walk away?

'*Stay. She is your helper, your mentor,*' Shawn hears.

Shawn looks around. "Did you hear that?" Shawn asks Clarissa.

"I did," Clarissa responds. "God wants me to be your helper."

Shawn's mouth drops open. Eyes wide he looks directly at Clarissa. "You heard it! That's nuts! What does that mean?"

Clarissa puts her hand on Shawn's hand. "It means I'm here to help you."

This time, Clarissa's touch brings warmth and peace, a peace Shawn has never known. He hears the voice again. '*You are mine. Follow me.*'

Shawn starts to cry. He looks up to the sky. He has only one option. "Yes, Lord, I will follow you."

The ground beneath his feet begins to tremble as he proclaims his faith in Christ. He looks over at Clarissa as she tries to keep their food on the table. It is only a minor quake and the tremblings soon end.

"Does the earth always quake when someone chooses to believe in God?" Shawn asks seriously.

"No, you silly man. But angels are singing in heaven at your decision," Clarissa replies with a smile. "Welcome home my friend. Our journey has just begun."

***

The tremors that hit southern California and central Florida are felt in many places around the world. From the southeastern United States to the northern reaches of Siberia. Some local news casts report the minor abnormal tremors, but they do not make any national news broadcasts.

The scientific community takes a much more alarmed look at the seismic activity that their far-flung sensors report. At the United States Geologic Survey (USGS), scientists look at the data and are bewildered. The largest quake is in central Siberia, measuring six point zero on the Richter scale, not a big quake but definitely significant. What is more significant is that quakes happened all around the globe. The USGS records earth tremors around the world. They happen every day all across the globe. Most are minor, no one even knows they happened. But this time more than one hundred quakes occurred measuring over five on the Richter scale. That's more than a hundred quakes that people felt; the entire earth truly shook. The on-site scientists don't know why. The bigwigs are called and the brainiacs are notified. Something unusual definitely happened. It does not take long for the scientists to wonder if the White House should be notified. A memo is dutifully written and forwarded to the correct undersecretary of geologic sciences.

Some of the lead scientists go to bed that night knowing they did what they were supposed to do. A few scientists go to bed fearful. The data they saw did not match anything they have ever seen or predicted.

***

On the fourth floor of a non-descript building in Shanghai, a half dozen highly educated scientists look at their data. They squabble and bicker about its significance. How much damage could this series of earthquakes cause?

In America, structures are built to withstand earthquakes, the question is always why did the earthquakes happen? In China, the question is how much of the infrastructure survived. What major projects may have been damaged? In China, inspectors are paid off and regulators are bought and paid for. Corruption in the construction of government projects is notorious. The biggest question is the stability of the Three Gorges Dam and the many other newer hydroelectric dams across central China, where once wild rivers have been dammed up for flood control and hydro-electricity needs.

The highly trained scientists pour over the reports and request on-site inspections. Preliminary reports indicate that there are a few bridges that have failed, and some remote villages will be affected, but there is no significant damage to any major infrastructure project. Reports are dutifully filled out and submitted, only to be buried in a quagmire of inefficiency.

In governmental agencies around the world, the same thing happens. Reports are made and submitted. No major destruction occurred, so the news media never even hears of the story. The largest movement of the earth's crust in seven thousand years goes unreported. The scientists know it happened, but their reports are buried in a quagmire of apathy and bureaucratic red tape.

***

Shawn, having just accepted Jesus as his Savior, looks up, tears still making his eyes glisten. "Clarissa, this is so overwhelming. I can't tell you of the joy I feel." He turns to Clarissa and his face becomes serious. "That was a real earthquake. We need to get home. There may have been major damage somewhere."

"You're right," Clarissa responds. "Let's get home. We'll talk more once we get a better handle on what has happened."

Chapter 14, Better Pastures

"Take me to the scales," Xi tells his guard as they enter the village's commerce district. "The village council will be at the scales." The jail guard leads the way to the scales, shooing away the farmers and their herds of livestock as they trudge down the muddy street.

They come to the railway depot where the scales to weigh the livestock are set up. The mood is grim. The village has not met its required quota. The village leaders could face dire consequences for failing in their duties.

"Bring me to the front of the village council," Xi requests.

"My new friend, they are squabbling, even enraged. You are a mere farmer accused of sedition. How am I supposed to present you to them?" the guard asks.

"Present me to them as I am," Xi responds. "Do it now, do not hesitate. Be loud and make a ruckus that I'm a religious zealot. Tell them how I overpowered you and forced you to bring me here."

The guard looks at Xi and grins. This man has set him on a path to freedom, he feels it in his heart. He'll do what this man of God asks.

"Clear the way! Clear the way!" the guard bellows at the crowd surrounding the village elders. "A man of God wishes to speak to the elders! Clear the way, clear the way."

A half dozen Chinese soldiers protect the village elders. One of the soldiers grabs Xi's jail guard. "You are a seditious bastard. There is no God. There is only the state. You are a disgrace," the soldier states as he tries to take down Xi's guardian.

All attention turns to the commotion that has been stirred up. Xi knows now is the time to act. Xi leaps to the stage that has been set up to monitor the scales. He says a silent prayer for words. He knows what he's doing is the work of God. He believes in miracles.

"Stop now!" Xi yells in a shrill voice. The commotion continues as the communist soldiers try to subdue the jail guard while the village elders flee from the main stage.

"Stop now," Xi says again, forcefully but calmly. "I'm here to save you." He turns and looks directly at the village council who are trying to flee from the mayhem. He repeats his message. "I'm here to save you."

This time, people do stop. They turn to listen.

Xi begins to speak. He does not know where his words come from, but he speaks confidently.

"The train will not come today. It will be delayed. Send our herds to graze in the fields of clover east of the town. When the train comes tomorrow your livestock will meet your quota. This is a promise from God."

A commotion breaks out, some people want to take Xi back to jail. As violence is about to erupt, a woman in charge of monitoring the trains slips a note to one of the councilors. 'Train delayed 24 hours due to landslides.'

The village elder shows the note to his comrades; they are stunned. How did this simple farmer know this would happen? They order their Captain of the Guard to restore calm to the crowd. The lead elder walks to the center of the elevated weigh station. "It appears our so-called man of God is right. There have been landslides on the rail line. The livestock train will not be here until tomorrow. There were minor earth tremors that caused some small landslides."

The crowd hushes at this announcement. Xi moves to the center of the stage as people look at him with astonishment. No one tries to stop him as he begins to speak. They feel a power emanating from him that they do not understand; he has prophetically predicted that the train would be delayed.

"Friends and neighbors, God loves you and wants you to prosper," Xi states loudly. "You were not created to serve the state. You were created by God to serve Him, to love Him. My God, the great Creator, wants you to thrive, not just survive. The Lord has told me that if we let our flocks graze on the clover to the east of the village, they will grow fat. Send all the flocks to the east. Any that graze to the north, west or south will perish. Send your flocks to the east, as far as they may wish to graze. When the train arrives tomorrow our flocks will overwhelm the scales."

Xi turns to walk away from the podium. The village elders surround him with several armed soldiers. Xi can be arrested for talking openly about God. The large jailer moves in with several of his compatriots and stands tall next to him as the communist guards threaten to arrest him.

Just before the situation has a chance to become violent, an elder statesman from the village speaks up. "Why are you harassing this man?" he asks. "He said we would have an extra day. Moments later we found out we do have an extra day. Now he's giving us advice on how to fatten our herds. Should the man be imprisoned for giving us advice?"

"He's blasphemous against the state," a senior guard snarls. "No one is allowed to talk about God in public. Christians are not allowed to practice their sorcery in the open."

"We can't let our herds graze to the east," a local farmer states. "That is government land. It is off limits to our herds."

"It's also the lushest land in the valley, full of clover," another farmer replies wistfully. "You may call Xi crazy, but he's right. We need to let our herds graze on the state's land east of the village."

The village elder turns to the senior communist sergeant. "Is there a reason our flocks and herds cannot graze on the public lands to our east?"

91

"Those lands belong to the state. They are reserved for the state," the guard responds.

"So, our flocks and herds should be allowed to graze there," Xi states confidently. "Our flocks and herds are being sent to the state, they belong to the state. It only makes sense that they graze on state land."

The senior elder smiles. "That makes sense to me." He looks at the senior guard. "Do you object to the state's herds grazing on the state's land?"

The senior guard is befuddled. He has never had to argue. He has always been listened to as the final authority. How can he say that the state's herd cannot graze on state land?

"But he's blasphemous!" the guard bellows, pointing at Xi. "He must be arrested."

"Let's see what the scales say tomorrow," a junior guard says, smirking. "They were three thousand kilos short. If they don't make the weight, we can put the entire village into detention camps. This God-fearing guy can proclaim the Lord all he wants as he slaves away in the mines along with all his friends."

As all of this is being discussed, the farmers and herders are sending their animals to the east of the village, into a state-owned preserve, lands that have never been molested by herds of grazing animals.

The local people discuss what has been happening. Meanwhile two young children are reunited with their parents. "Momma, Poppa, I didn't mean to get you in trouble. I like the Bible lessons," a young girl proclaims tearfully as she hugs her parents.

The parents look down at the innocent child lovingly. "It's okay, honey, you were following your heart and your love for God. It's all going to be okay," the father states assuredly.

Chapter 15, Earthquakes

Clarissa's phone rings at five thirty in the morning. She awakes, startled. Phone calls this early are never good.

"They've happened all around the world," Shawn states stoically.

"What? Is this Shawn? What are you talking about? Why are you calling me in the middle of the night?" Clarissa replies, a bit aggravated.

"What? What do you mean? You started this," Shawn replies. "I've been reading and studying all night. I'm all in on the Christ as Savior part. I have that figured out and I'm saved. It's the chosen part I've been digging into. I'm Jewish on my grandfather's side. He immigrated here before WWII. But that is not even the half of it. The earth quakes. They happened all over the world, not just in southern California."

"I believe, Clarissa, I believe!" Shawn states emphatically. "So, what do we do now? This is the real deal. We need to let people know."

"Slow down. What are you talking about?" Clarissa asks, confused, as she tries to shake herself awake. "Let me make some coffee and wake up a bit. It's too early."

"Make a big pot, we have a lot to discuss." She nods her consent to have coffee with him.

***

Half an hour later, the two sit on the small balcony of their shared apartment overlooking the sprawling and crowded Southern California metropolis. The skies begin to lighten, showing the smog filled air of the densely populated area, multitudes of cars already filling the streets. Clarissa pulls a wide pick comb through her long wet curls as Shawn hands her a cup of fresh brewed coffee.

"Tell me about the twelve thousand from each of the twelve tribes of Israel," Shawn asks as he sits down in the chair next to Clarissa.

Clarissa looks at Shawn. He's glowing, almost feverish. "Shawn, you're distressed. We should pray. We need the Holy Spirit with us to guide us, to lead us. Will you pray with me?"

"Yes! Let's pray. I need calm. I'm freaking out, things are happening that I don't understand," Shawn replies.

"None of us can fully understand God's plans, but we can talk to him. He'll guide us." Clarissa takes Shawn's hand in hers and bows her head. "Dear God, hear our prayers. We're lowly servants in your kingdom. But You have asked the least of us to proclaim Your Word to the nations. I saw You in a vision. Very clearly, the chosen ones from the twelve tribes of Israel were bowing down before You, singing praises to You. In the glory of Your presence, You commissioned us to proclaim your salvation to the world. Dear Lord, I saw Shawn there too, and he has come to know You, to accept You as Lord, and Your Son, Jesus as his Savior.

"We accept Your commission to extol Your greatness, and proclaim that our salvation comes through Your Son Jesus. Dear Lord, we humbly ask that You grant us wisdom, patience, and fortitude to fulfill the mission that You have laid upon us. We ask that Your Holy Spirit be with us, that You fill us with the desire to proclaim You, that we become fearless. Let us fully understand Your forgiveness, Your love, and the promise of eternal life in heaven. Lead us, guide us, empower us with Your Holy Spirit. In Christ's most Holy name we do pray, Amen."

As Clarissa prayed to God, she felt Shawn's hand release its tight grasp and become more like a loving touch. She opens her eyes and looks to her roommate, her new companion in their new mission.

He's weeping. He looks up and uses the napkin from his coffee cup to wipe his eyes.

Shawn looks at Clarissa through his teary eyes. He clenches her hand again, firmly, not in fear, but in assurance. "Wow, Is this what it's like to know God?" He stands up and looks out over the smog filled city. He looks back at Clarissa with a smile. "We have to go and tell them. They need to know God. His wrath is coming, It has already started."

Clarissa's smile turns to a frown. She was at the peak of joy in knowing she brought someone to know Christ. Now that person is telling her that the wrath of God is already coming, but she knows this. It is part of God's Word. She and Shawn are to proclaim His kingdom to the nations. She's filled with joy and dread at the same time. How are they going to proclaim God's Word into this cesspool of sin? So many before have tried. What will make them succeed? Theologians and learned titans of the Word have tried and failed. How are two nobodies going to change the souls of millions.

As this thought runs through her head, she feels the floor briefly begin to shake. It stops very quickly but leaves her a bit rattled. The tremor was not enough to make anyone panic, but enough to rattle the glass. It is enough to rattle Shawn. "The quakes, I almost completely forgot about the quakes. Clarissa, this has never happened before. It won't make the news, but quakes were recorded around the world. Most of them were minor, but some caused damage. The thing that no one will report is that the quakes happened all around the world. Usually, they are isolated. Yesterday they happened all across the globe, all at the same time."

"How do you know this?" Clarissa asks.

"My major is in geology," Shawn responds. "One of my professors showed us how to gain access to a program that shows the seismic readings from around the world. It's run by the UCGS and is public, but most people don't know about it. I'll grab my laptop and show you."

A few minutes later they sit together at the kitchen table looking at Shawn's laptop. "Take a look at the seismic activity last night." Shawn pops up a screen that shows a portion of the globe with green, yellow, and orange dots all over the globe. Clarissa is startled by what she sees. The screen is covered in dots. "The green dots are minor quakes, 3.0 or less, they happen all the time," Shawn explains. "No one even notices they happen. The yellow dots are more significant, quakes of 3.0 to 4.5. These quakes can be felt but usually don't cause any damage, like the one we just felt. The orange dots are quakes from 4.5 to 6.0. They can cause damage, but not on a large scale. From 6.0 to 7.5 would show up in red and anything over that would have been purple, those are major quakes that cause serious damage."

"Okay", Clarissa responds. "It's a lot of quakes I guess, but I don't see any reds or purples. What are you trying to show me?"

Shawn clicks a few buttons, and the same screen appears but with far fewer dots. "This is from two days ago, this is normal." He hits a few more keys on the keypad and the same screen appears with a minimal number of colored dots. "Another normal day. Now let me show you last night again." He jabs a few keys, and a blank screen appears. "What? Let me do that again," he states. His fingers dance across the keyboard for a few seconds. "Site unavailable," appears on the screen. "No! They've already started to scrub the data! I told you they won't want this released. Something ain't right. But I got screen shots. I know what I saw."

Clarissa's mind is racing. She's putting her dreams and visions together with what she just saw. Is this the start of the end times? Is this real? She thinks of her parents and siblings. She does not know their hearts, but she was raised in the church. As the gravity of what is happening consumes her, she prays they truly know Christ as their Savior.

While she's having these thoughts, Shawn is furiously hammering at the keyboard. "Now I'm locked out!" he exclaims as his

96

computer freezes. "Look, I'm locked up. They might have frozen me because of the data I was trying to look up. He quickly pulls his thumb drive from his computer. "Those sneaky bastards will try to erase my backup," he states, holding up the thumb drive with concern.

Clarissa is pale. Is this really happening? What do they do? She takes a deep breath and tries to calm down. She says a silent prayer asking for guidance and wisdom. "God, what do we do now?" she asks not knowing what the answer will be. Her mind races. "I've got a laptop. Show me what you saved on that thumb drive," Clarissa states.

"Great!" Shawn responds. "I'll make sure you're not connected to the net. I'm going to unplug your modem. Then we'll look at it again."

Five minutes later they both are bewildered at what they are seeing. The data is clear. A massive number of minor quakes occurred around the globe. It is significantly above any normal seismic activity. "Does this have something to do with the visions you saw?" Shawn asks?

Clarissa is looking to the sky through the doors that lead to the balcony. Her thoughts delve into her memory of the Bible lessons she has learned and studied. God will never again destroy the earth through flood, that is a promise. But God did say he would destroy the earth through fire. If all the volcanic power stored up under the earth's crust were to be unleashed... The earth would be destroyed by fire!

***

Halfway around the globe, the animals from Xi's village gorge on the clover and hay on the state lands. Xi returns home to have dinner with his wife and two sons.

"How did the village weigh in work out?" Xi's wife asks.

97

"It was delayed. An earth tremor caused a landslide. The harvest train won't get here until tomorrow. The village has an extra day to fatten up the livestock."

"And how did things go at the jail, where our two friends were being held?"

"Our friends were released." Xi responds stoically. "I convinced the guards that they should let their innocent prisoners free."

"You know I know," Xi's wife responds. "The rumor mill travels fast. The guards tried to kill you. Don't do that again. I can't run this farm and raise these boys without you." She slops a large spoonful of rice and goatmeat on his plate. "Do you hear me! You could have been killed!" She stops and falls to her knees. "Xi, don't get yourself killed." She starts sobbing. "I need you, the boys need you. The church we've started needs you."

"The church we've started is going to grow to the point where no building can hold it, nothing will be able to stop it," Xi responds. "I'm going back to town tomorrow. God has already started to work miracles. I have to be there to proclaim His Word. I'll be safe, I promise you. You should come with me."

"Who will tend to the farm? Who will look after the chores?" his wife responds.

"Be calm, my dear. Don't be afraid. God will look after us," Xi replies. "If God will ensure that the sparrow is fed, surely he'll look after our needs."

Wu joins her husband at the dinner table. Since it is late, the two boys have already been sent to bed. "Did they really try to kill you?" she asks

Xi blushes. "We should pray for blessings my dear. Let's not dwell on what has passed. Let's look forward to the bounty that is to come".

***

Abaddon looks at the reports of the earthquakes. He had a dream that the earthquakes would be coming. People will begin to panic when they see the widespread devastation. In times of panic, people can be manipulated. He makes a few calls, sends a few emails. Things are put in motion that have been planned long in advance. For too long, freedom has reigned. The common man needs to be controlled. In times of crises man will look to a higher power for strength. He intends to be the force behind that higher power. A unifying world power.

Chapter 16, Allies

The Orthodox priest makes his way to the narthex of his church. The hallways are crowded as he tries to make his way through. Finally, he reaches the source of the commotion. A man in beggars' clothes is anointing people at the entrance to their elaborate cathedral.

"You there, you filthy man, stop what you are doing! How dare you defile this place. This place is meant for the holy, the devout. How dare you baptize people here!" the bishop proclaims as his robes of satin and silk flare behind him.

Mustafa looks up and sees the pious man approaching. He smiles. He knew he would come. He's the great proclaimer of this church. "Come and be saved," Mustafa says. "I knew you would come. Refresh your soul and let us make plans together."

"Refresh my soul! What are you talking about?" the bishop shouts, astounded.

"You know all the rules and rituals, but do you know Christ? Come and be baptized in Christ," Mustafa responds calmly. The crowd pushes the bishop forward to the baptismal pool. His robes and garments are stripped from him as he gets pushed closer to the place of baptism.

He's humiliated that his prestigious garments are being stripped from him. But Mustafa walks up to him and grasps him firmly while looking directly in his eyes. "Your wardrobe does not make you a man of Christ. God knows your soul. He does not care about your clothes. Join me. Be baptized again. Renew your spirit."

The Orthodox priest stands almost naked in front of the makeshift baptismal pool. He looks into the eyes of Mustafa. In an instant his genealogy flashes in front of his eyes. He's a Levite. In that same vision he sees his genealogy all the way back through Isaac, Abraham, Noah and even Adam and Eve. Tears come to his eyes.

100

"Are you the one?" the priest asks.

"No," Mustafa says. "I'm one of the twelve tribes who is to proclaim Him. So are you." Mustafa plunges the older man into the baptismal pool. "May the mercy of Christ wash you clean of sin and renew your soul."

Mustafa raises the Orthodox priest from the cleansing pool. Water streams from the priest's long hair and full beard. The priest's eyes are wide, and his smile is broad. He wraps Mustafa in a bear hug. "I have been a Pharisee. I have been a man of rules and rituals. Now God has set me free. Brother, we're to work together. We must let the nations know that Christ is King."

Mustafa, the reformed ISIS fighter hugs the learned and respected Orthodox priest lovingly. "You are my brother. We will do great things together. God has ordained it. We will proclaim it."

***

The Special Forces captain watches as his first sergeant discreetly records the whole episode. They have been watching over and protecting the ISIS fighter since they entered the Kurdish free lands. The Kurds consider Mustafa an ally, since he not only abandoned the ISIS cause, but has also provided them with intelligence that has allowed the Peshmerga to win some local battles. Mustafa is a hero to the Kurds. They have always been tolerant of Christians. They pay no heed to his antics and his preachings. But the Americans have been told to watch him, and to protect him.

"Push that up to command," the captain tells his first sergeant. "That was significant."

The first sergeant scans the area before submitting the video with his report.

Just then, one of the team's operatives breaks in on their local voice coms. "Nine o'clock, at the base of the bell tower, three unknowns. They are armed."

The captain quickly moves his binoculars to the targets. "I see them," he states. "Murphy, intercept now."

"No can do," Murphy responds. "They are beyond my position."

"How did you let them slip by!" The captain responds, agitated.

"They looked like normal Peshmerga, we need to go arms live now," Murphy responds.

"Arms live," the Captain responds. As he relays this message, the three targets mingle into the throngs surrounding the Orthodox church and the market square.

"Lost them in the crowd!" Murphy states.

"Same here," their other sniper announces.

"Friggin great, we have three potential threats in this crowd," the first sergeant states. "We need to get control of this situation, people."

"Time to rein in our target," the Special Forces captain states. "Jones, take him off of the stage, let him know of the threat."

***

On the dais in front of the Orthodox church the preacher is speaking to the people gathered there. "Christ does not want us to fight against one another. Christ does not care if we follow the rituals and rules that we've established. Christ wants us to love our neighbors. Reach out to our neighbors in love, be they Jew, Muslim, or agnostic. Turn now and embrace your neighbor. Do it now, don't wait."

As he says this, gunfire erupts, aimed directly at the priest. What he's saying is blasphemous to Islam. His words have to be silenced. The three ISIS infiltrators have a mission to complete.

Just before the assassination attempt starts, Mustafa sees someone he knows in the crowd. Someone he recognizes from an ISIS training facility. Someone he taught infiltration and stealth tactics. Knowing what is coming, he rushes the priest and hurls him to the ground just as the gunfire erupts. The sudden movement of Mustafa disrupts the assassins' plans. Both Mustafa and the priest are unscathed by the assassins' bullets.

The Americans and their Peshmerga allies have no choice but to open fire on the three ISIS fighters. For two chaotic minutes bullets fly in the crowded church courtyard. The three ISIS fighters are taken down. Unfortunately, there are casualties. Some by friendly fire, but most of the casualties are caused by the ISIS militants firing indiscriminately into the crowd of new believers, knowing their mission failed. Three women, two men and four children are caught in the ensuing battle as the Americans and their Peshmerga allies engage the assassin squad.

***

The entire action is seen live and recorded halfway around the globe in central Florida. In just a few minutes the video of the firefight is in the hands of the G2. Having been rebuked by his commanding general once for talking about end time's philosophy, he's reluctant to wake his boss at this early hour. But ISIS sent an assassin squad into a Peshmerga stronghold. This is not an attack on a remote village. This was an attack in a major stronghold. And the ISIS convert was right at the center of the action. Henry tries to go back to sleep. It is all just a coincidence. He'll be sure to mention it in the morning briefing.

But something nags at him. He cannot sleep. He does something completely out of character for him, something he has not done since he was a child and he used to pray with his mother before going to bed. He gets down on his knees and prays. He asks for guidance, for wisdom, and to be forgiven. Henry says his prayer earnestly and expects some great revelation. But he feels nothing. Being awake and active, he gets dressed and heads to his office at the fort. As he travels the fifteen-minute drive he talks to God.

Out loud, Henry pleads, "Why don't you answer me? I'm asking for your help, but you are not helping. Things are happening that involve you. I'm on your side. I'm trying to do what is right. Please God, answer my prayers." At that moment, Henry thinks about what he is saying. Is he a Christian? Is he an evangelical Christian? He doesn't go to church, but he does believe in God. Why does he expect God to intervene? He just said he was on God's side, but does he truly believe? What does that even mean? These thoughts run through his head as he navigates his way onto the sprawling military base.

The G2 parks his car and passes through the security checkpoints before he walks into the massive room full of well-trained soldiers monitoring situations from around the world. He can watch real time negotiations happening in Afghanistan between a Captain and the local tribal elders. On another screen he can see a crew sweeping for roadside mines in Iraq. Another cubicle shows reconnaissance on a drug cartel's activity in Mexico. He starts to marvel at the amount of real time intelligence that is right at his fingertips. He has always taken it for granted. But to stop and see what the American worldwide intelligence apparatus monitors in real time is amazing, almost frightening.

"General, we didn't know you were coming in so early," the major working the night shift states. "The Colonel is in his office with all of the latest intelligence. There are things happening in China, some strange military moves, and there is the dust up at the Orthodox Church in the Kurdish free lands. I can round up some specialists if you want."

"No, Major, that's not necessary. Let me just absorb what's going on." The major salutes the general and backs off. She's the person who flagged and forwarded the video of the firefight at the Kurdish church. She steps back a few feet and lets her commanding officer walk the floor, looking at anything he finds interesting.

After a few minutes, the general stops. "Show me the live feed from the Kurdish church."

"Right this way, General." The major leads the general to the area where they are monitoring the Kurdish stronghold. There are seven live feeds. Five are from soldiers on the ground. One is from a drone overhead; one is from a satellite.

The Orthodox priest is speaking to a hushed crowd as Peshmerga EMT tend to the wounded and police try to assess the situation. "That's interesting," the general states. "The crowds are still there. I know the Kurds are resilient, but a firefight happened there less than an hour ago. The crowds are still there. They have not fled to their homes. Bring up the volume."

A technician turns up the volume from the soldier's mic who is closest to the dais. A translator's voice is heard.

"We're not a forsaken people. We're a blessed people. We do not have to be divided; we can be united. We all know there is only one true God. What will unite us is to know that he sent his son, Jesus, to save us from our sins. He was sent to save both the Jew and the Gentile, the final sacrifice to atone for our sins. The way forward is through unity, unity in faith, faith in God, and faith in Jesus, His son. The commandments we're given are to love our God and to love our neighbors. Join with me in prayer. Repeat my words and take them into your heart, make them your own.

We believe in one God, the Father almighty, maker of heaven and earth, of all things visible and invisible.

We believe in one Lord, Jesus Christ, the only Son of God, begotten from the Father before all ages.

God from God, light from light, true God from true God, begotten, not made. Of the same essence as the Father, through Him all things were made.

For us and our salvation, He came down from heaven and became incarnate by the Holy Spirit and the virgin Mary and was made human.

For our sake He was crucified under Pontius Pilate, he suffered death and was buried.

On the third day he rose again, in accordance with the scriptures.

He ascended to heaven and is seated at the right hand of the father.

He will come again with glory, to judge the living and the dead, and His kingdom will never end.

We believe in the Holy Spirit, The Lord, the giver of life who proceeds from the Father and the Son, who with the Father and Son, is worshipped and glorified, who has spoken through the prophets.

We believe in the holy apostolic church.

We affirm one baptism for the forgiveness of sins.

We look forward to the resurrection of the dead, and to life in the world to come, Amen."

Henry watches, mesmerized. "They just prayed a prayer acknowledging Christ as Savior, right?"

"The Nicene Creed, I do believe," the sergeant responds.

"Yes, I remember it from days gone by. A powerful statement of faith. Sergeant, what do you estimate the size of that crowd?"

The sergeant glances at a side note on the screen. "Our drone has one thousand three hundred and seventy-six people on site, sir."

"And the crowd is growing. More have been arriving," Henry states. "Can you tell me the crowd size before the firefight?"

The sergeant had recorded that number. "Yes sir. There were six hundred and forty-nine people in the area when the assassins opened fire."

"Rather than the crowd dispersing, it has doubled!" Henry states, astounded. "That never happens. Look, is that the ISIS fighter coming to the dais?"

"Yes sir," the sergeant replies.

Mustafa is seen approaching the dais. Dressed only in a torn and dirty loin cloth, the large man is an imposing figure. His hair is long and wild. His tangled and matted beard reaches to the middle of his chest. There is blood on his arms and chest from tending to the wounded. The sun glistens off the sweat that covers his hardened muscles.

"Is he Samson or is he John the Baptist?" the sergeant asks as he looks at the scene on the monitor in front of them.

The giant of a man begins to speak with passion. "Brothers and sisters! Join me, join us in knowing Christ and knowing freedom. Two days ago, I was fighting you on the battlefield. I was a savage beast ready to kill you, my enemy. I met Christ that day. I was told to love you. Come and be baptized in the name of Christ so you can know the love that I know." The wild-eyed man's short testimony is captivating and intriguing.

The general and the sergeant watch as the throng of people begin to line up to be baptized. Several more Orthodox priests strip down to a loin cloth, and after being baptized themselves, begin helping to baptize the newly converted faithful.

"Have you ever seen anything like this?" the General asks the sergeant.

"I've heard of such things. An evangelist, Billy Graham, did things like this from what I've heard," the sergeant replies. "But this is the Middle East. It is known that the Kurds are tolerant of Christians. But for over a thousand people to turn to Christianity at once. General, this is biblical."

The general watches for a few more moments, many thoughts twirl through his head, including the prayers he had beseeched to God. Is this his answer? Did he expect God to speak directly to him? Maybe God does that sometimes. Maybe God speaks in other ways. How is he to know? His mind races. Is he an evangelical Christian? He feels a warming in his heart, a peace settles around him. He makes a decision.

"I need copies of this footage sent to me. Get it to Chaplain Kaufmann of the navy and Army sergeant Luke Parsons. Let them both know I want them in my office at 0700 hours." The general has a little over an hour to digest all he has seen and come up with a plan.

Chapter 17, Blessings

"Father! Father! You must come and look at the strawberry crop," Xi's youngest son exclaims as he shakes his father awake. It is the youngest son's duty that day to make sure the animals are fed and to take care of the other early morning chores. Xi slowly wakes from his slumber and starts to focus on his son. He grabs his glasses off of the nightstand to help him see.

As his vision comes into focus, he sees that his son is beaming. "Good morning young man," he states, emphasizing their morning ritual of always starting the day on a positive tone. "You have good news? I hope you started the tea. I need my tea before we get on to serious business."

"Your tea is ready father and I have gathered the eggs," the teenaged boy states. "But you must come and see the strawberries. The rot is gone! They are plump and ready for harvest!"

Xi's eyes widen. "How can that be! Yesterday the crop was almost completely lost." Then Xi remembers the events of the previous day. He foretold that the village's crops and herds would be multiplied. He was not concerned for his own crops. Did the Lord perform miracles? After getting a cup of tea, he walks with his son to the edge of their strawberry field. As far as he can see there are bright red strawberries ripening in the morning sun. He falls to his knees and thanks the Lord. His mind races as he thinks of the village and the herds that need to be weighed in.

"Wake your momma and brother. I'll cook breakfast. We're all going to town today. Today is going to be a glorious day. Today there will be a great harvest."

The young man has no understanding of what his father is saying other than the fact that he gets to go to town. That alone sends him into high gear. His mother and brother are soon awake and getting ready for a rare family trip to town.

While the kids are busy rounding up goods that they can sell at the farmers market, including several bushels of plump strawberries, Xi's wife pulls him aside. "Yesterday you were arrested and almost killed. Don't you dare put our children in danger. I love you, and respect you, but do not put our children in harm's way."

"I understand what you are saying," Xi states, trying to comfort his wife. "God worked miracles last night. Our crops were ripened, and I know the village's herds were fattened too. We will see more miracles today. It is God's will."

Xi and his family begin to walk the few miles to town. They take turns pushing the two handcarts brimming with produce that they will sell at the local market. As they enter the outskirts of the village, they encounter more people crowding the road heading to town. Many of the farmers are also pushing well ladened carts of ripe produce.

"I have not seen such an abundance of crops in many years," Xi's wife states. "So much produce may force us to lower our prices and cut into our profits."

Xi smiles at his wife as he pushes the laden handcart through the muddy ruts in the road. "I will not complain if God has granted us an abundant crop. There is a more important crop to be harvested. These people need to know God. They need to know who has blessed them with the bounty that they have harvested."

Xi's wife looks around at the overflowing handcarts being pushed into the town. "You did say that God was going to work miracles. Did He really work miracles?"

"I think so." Xi responds with a broad smile. "We'll truly know when they weigh in the herds." They continue their trek in silence as more people gather around them, heading towards town.

When they get to town, Xi sends his sons off with baskets of produce to fulfill contracts with local businesses. He sets his wife up to sell more produce from their carts in a makeshift farmers market. Once everything is settled, he heads off to watch the scales.

He positions himself at the eastern gate of the city so he can see the herds as they are being brought in. The shepherds and cattle wranglers are smiling as they begin to bring in their flocks and herds. The animals are fat! Not fat from one day of eating clover. They are fat like animals that have grazed on a prime land for the entire year.

One of the wranglers sees Xi and recognizes him from the day before. "You were right! How did you know? That big guard said you were a man of God. Did your God do this?"

Xi responds. "My God works miracles."

"I want to know your God," the cattle wrangler states as he pushes his fat herd past Xi.

More plump flocks and herds pass by. Xi silently praises God for doing what He did. Xi's prayers were answered, his confidence in God grows. The train's whistle blows announcing its approach to the remote town. Xi moves to a spot close to the scales so he can watch the weigh in.

Once again, the animals are brought to the scales to be weighed before being sent to the loading corals. It takes several hours to weigh all the animals. Xi watches as the scales tip heavy. The village will meet its quota. He rejoices in knowing that his neighbors and friends will not be cursed and whipped for failing the state.

By noon, the weigh in is completed. The village exceeds its quota. A few of the local elders start to make speeches, praising the work and diligence of the farmers. One of the elders spots Xi in the crowd and asks him to say a few words.

The village elder makes an introduction. "You all know the train was supposed to come yesterday, and we did a weigh in. We came up short. A local farmer, one of your neighbors, predicted that the train would be delayed. Not only that, he told us how to fatten our herds. Xi, come up here and say a few words."

Xi looks to heaven and prays. Is this his opportunity? Is this his time? As he makes his way to the stage, he sees soldiers in the area. Some are soldiers that are always present in the village. Some are soldiers that came in with the harvest train. He sees the large guard from the jail that he met the day before and nods in recognition. The newly converted guard assesses the situation very quickly. He has told several of his friends and workmates of the previous day's events. He has told them that he tried to kill his captive to no avail, and how Xi embraced him in love. He does not know enough to tell of his conviction, his conversion. But he does know enough to convince his friends and fellow guards to ally with him.

Seeing Xi walk to the stage motivates the guard. He knows the soldiers from the harvest train will not take kindly to what Xi is going to say. He springs into action. His motivation is strong, like nothing he has ever felt before. He has no idea why he's acting in such great haste and with such clarity, but he senses in his soul that he's doing the right thing. Moments later he walks up onto the stage just as Xi does. Four other guards follow him. From the stage he looks around. His hasty plan is working. The large guard and his four allies walk onto the stage and stand behind his new friend as Xi begins to speak.

Xi takes the microphone from the village elder. He turns to look at the large jail guard standing behind him. The jail guard stands there, firm and stern. Xi gains strength from this show of faith by the guard and his allies. Jesus was able to spread God's Word because the Roman's rule created a time of relative peace through the strength of their armies.

"Thank you for allowing me to address such an esteemed assembly of our people," Xi begins politely. "I ask that we all praise God for the blessings that he has bestowed on us."

The crowd hushes at this statement. They do not know God. They have been taught from childhood that the state is the provider,

112

that the state makes all things happen. To praise God is a totally foreign concept to them. Xi knows this and begins to explain.

"I believe in an almighty God, who created all things and knows all things. He is a God who can work miracles. Yesterday our flocks and herds came in well short of the village's allotment. I told the elders that they would have an extra day. Due to the landslides, that happened. With that extra day I gave advice on how to make sure the flocks and herds met their allotted weight. They listened to me. With just one extra day, we've met our assigned allotment. I beseech you all to know that God worked a miracle right here in our village."

One of the village elders thinks that what Xi is saying is blasphemous. He moves to take the microphone away from Xi. The jailer moves to stand in his way.

Xi smiles at this gesture and continues. "How many of you woke up this morning to find your fields full and abundant? How many of you were able to buy anything you needed to feed your families at the market today? We just watched the scales. People, that all happened because God loves you. Look around you at the state's soldiers. They are mad and angry. Why? We made the quota. They should be happy. But they are angry. They are angry because I have told you about God. Look around. Miracles happened last night. Only God can perform miracles."

"Take the mic away from that man," a soldier from the train yells. He's quickly succumbed by a few of the jail guard's friends.

A strong and wiry man jumps on stage and abruptly takes the microphone from Xi. "I went to bed last night thinking my broccoli crop had gone bad because of the heavy rains. I woke up this morning to find an abundant crop. Yesterday our herds fell short, today they exceed the scales. I don't know this God, but I want to meet him. I want abundant crops. I want abundant produce. I don't want my children to wonder if there will be food on the table tomorrow. I want a God who loves me."

One of the elders walks onto the stage to take control of the situation. He knows that the state will hear about this blasphemously and retaliate against them. Xi takes the microphone before the man of the state can get there.

"People, I want you to know the love and peace that I know, I want you to know forgiveness. I want you to know the gift of eternal life. You can only know that gift by accepting Jesus Christ as your Savior." Xi is ready to bring it all home. He's ready to do an altar call. He knows that hundreds of new believers will come forward. They have all seen the miracles. God is supreme. Then shots ring out. Chaos ensues.

***

The officer in charge of the train knows he cannot allow the blasphemy to continue. He puts in a secure radio call to his captain and then gives him a live feed from his cell phone. His captain tells him to shut down the assembly at once. Lethal force is authorized if needed.

The young officer is stunned by what the elders of the village are allowing to be preached. The state abhors any religion. It is to be stifled. It is to be shut down at all costs. But here a "Man of God" is allowed to spew his lies to the people. It must be stopped, and his superiors have given him permission to act.

The young officer orders his men to remove the heretic from the stage. He follows behind his men as they move to take the stage, ready to give his own speech about fealty to the state. He has never met resistance. He is the state. His word is law. When several armed guards, the jailer's friends, stop him from taking the stage, he's infuriated. "I speak for the state. You must disarm and obey my commands. "

The local guards have been told of what happened at the jail. They have seen what has happened with the local farmers' crops. The "state" has not brought on any abundance. The "state" has not provided in any means whatsoever. The man of God has brought about miracles. The guards stop the young officer and his men. Food on their families tables is more important than faithfulness to the state.

That is when the gunfire erupts. The young officer orders his men to take the stage by force. The local guards react. Thirty seconds of mayhem ensue. The locals win the day. The dying words of the young lieutenant bring about foreboding thoughts to the villagers. "Your false God cannot defeat the state. The state will always win."

***

Abaddon watches from his remote location as the Chinese imperial forces are defeated. Reinforcements must be sent right away. The stronghold of totalitarianism is being threatened. Through diverse channels, strong messages are sent. Strong actions are promised.

Chapter 18, Parting The Waters

"How do we get the word out?" Clarissa asks. "How do we let people know? The state powers are already shutting us down, shutting us out."

"Let's calm down and think this through," Shawn replies. "We're to be God's messengers. You told me that. God would not give us a mandate and not give us a way to fulfill his mandate. There is a solution to the problem."

Clarissa calms down and begins to think things through. Shawn is right, there has to be an answer. They have to find that answer. Maybe the problem is they have the wrong question. They want to tell people about the imminent threat caused by the recent earthquakes. Maybe that is not what they are to proclaim. If their mission is to save souls, then it does not matter how the earth's destruction happens. Their mission is to save souls, not tell how the earth may burn up in a ball of volcanic fire.

"Oh my, Shawn," Clarissa exclaims. "It doesn't matter how the earth comes to an end. What matters is what we do before it comes to an end. It doesn't matter that we're being shut out of the data. What matters is what we do with the information we have. We know. We have to let everyone know."

"Clarissa, If I can't get the data, how do we prove what is about to come?" Shawn replies.

"We don't need to," Clarissa responds, "that's my point. We know what is going to happen. We don't have to convince people of what is going to happen. We need to convince people of what to do."

Shawn looks at Clarissa, not understanding what she's saying. "So, we convince people to run for the hills for no reason?"

"No, you silly man," she responds, laughing. "What good is running to the hills going to do? Would that have worked in the time

116

of Noah? Running for the hills is fruitless. We have to tell people to turn to God, just like you did."

Shawn takes a seat as he digests this information. He begins to think out loud. "God spoke to me. God changed me. Can that happen to other people too? Why not? It happened to me. But how can we reach millions of people? It would be easier to prove the earth's crust is moving than to prove that God exists." Shawn buries his head in his hands. "I have two choices, prove the impossible or prove the improbable."

Clarissa has been watching and listening as Shawn has debated what he knows, and his options. She sits silently for a few minutes, letting Shawn think things through. She offers her advice quietly. "Prove it with science or proclaim it with faith. You know you can't prove it with science, so that leaves only one choice."

"I have to proclaim it by faith," Shawn replies. He does not say it with enthusiasm. He says it in a resigned manner. Clarissa knows why. Stepping out in faith is a hard thing to do. There is no science. There is no math. There are no facts. There is only faith. Does God exist? Did He create me? Does He love me? If He loves us all, why is there suffering and wars?

Clarissa sees the confusion racing through Shawn's mind. She prays for him. She prays for clarity and confidence. Man is fallen, man's inhumanity to man is rife throughout history. Slavery, war, submission, violence, thievery. Since the fall of man, they have all been present. It is only through Christ's final sacrifice that our sins are forgiven. Through that forgiveness we find true love. Man's aspiration for true love is the one thing that has kept humanity righteous. Clarissa prays that Shawn sees true righteousness in God's will.

Shawn opens his eyes with clarity and sharpness. He looks at Clarissa. "We have to do this. Where do we start?"

"Right here and right now," Clarissa replies. "Let's call everyone we know. We're having a barbecue at the community pool this afternoon."

Shawn is a bit shocked. "A community barbeque? Why?"

"To preach God's love, you silly man. We have to start somewhere. How better to attract a crowd than offer free food at a pool?" Clarissa responds, smiling.

"Can we pull that off this quickly? We need to let the complex management people know what we're planning. We'll need permits, we'll need to order food."

Clarissa kisses Shawn on the cheek. "It will happen. Let's not talk about it, let's just do it. By the way, you're going to be the main speaker."

"What! What are you saying!" Shawn interjects. "I'm no good at that!"

Clarissa looks at him and smiles again as she picks up her phone. "That's what Moses said. Tell your story, that's all you need to do. God will take it from there." She calls her pastor first, then her youth minister, briefly explaining her plans, asking for their help. Soon many calls and texts are sent throughout her church community.

***

Three hours later the pool party begins. The youth pastor is flipping burgers on the grill and Clarissa is serving iced teas and lemonade. Shawn is talking with a few members of Clarissa's church. There are only about twenty other people there, which is not bad for a weekday afternoon on short notice. They posted several handmade signs around the neighborhood about the pool gathering, encouraging mothers and kids to attend at no charge. The extra hotdogs, chips,

118

and popsicles to feed the young mouths is not a significant expense for the church's budget.

By two o'clock, over fifty people have converged on the community pool and more people are arriving, lured by the crowd and the aroma of grilled burgers. Most are mothers with their children. A few are local tween-agers with nothing better to do. Some are gang bangers looking for a free lunch. Clarissa walks to the side of the pool and begins to speak.

"Hey, ya'll. Listen up," Clarissa shouts over the noise of the party. People quiet down. "We invited you here out of love. Our community needs to come together in love. We've all heard about the shootings that have been happening. We've all heard about the strife happening after the last election. That is not good for our community, it is not good for our nation. There is only one way forward, and that is through love. Stop where you are and turn to the person closest to you. It might be your brother or sister. It might be your mother or father. It might be a total stranger. I want you to hug that person and tell them you love them. No nodding and smiling. Say it out loud; I love you."

Clarissa stops as she watches the people in the pool and the surrounding area turn and hug each other. She smiles at the reaction and eggs them on. "I see a lot of hugging, but I don't hear the 'I love you' part. Say it with me now, come on now people, 'I love you'. Say it to your neighbor." She hears the phrase repeated and sees the hugs get deeper and stronger. This is a good start, she thinks.

It is a mixed-raced neighborhood, so it is a mixed raced crowd. Some of the gangbangers join in on the hugging. Some stay distant and watch the crowd. In Los Angeles, you are never out of sight of the gang bangers.

She has the people's attention. The crowd has grown to over a hundred people eating free food and cooling off from the heat. "One of my friends wants to talk to you, tell you a rather intriguing story." Clarissa pauses for a moment. The crowd hushes. Clarissa lowers her

119

voice to a whisper, just loud enough for the hushed crowd to hear. "Have you ever heard from a prophet, a man of God?" She raises her voice a bit. "We called you here to listen to words of wisdom, to hear the words of a prophet. Please give your attention to my friend Shawn, a man of God."

Shawn takes the mic from Clarissa, his normally white tanned skin showing beet red in embarrassment. Thinking quick on his feet, Shawn stands tall and raises his hands and face to the heavens. "Lord almighty, hear my voice. If it be your will, part these waters!" He dramatically brings his hands down and stares at the middle of the pool. Then he spreads his hands out as if trying to push the waters of the pool aside.

And a miracle happens. The waters begin to spread, a channel begins to form in the center of the pool. Shawn's eyes open wide. He prays to the Lord as he continues to mimic pushing the waters aside. Water begins splashing over the side of the pool, running across the concrete berm and into the grassy lawn. The people in attendance at first are amazed, then they begin to panic as the water from the pool begins to cause a small flood as it washes around them. Shawn brings his hands together and yells "Stop!" The flooding stops and the pool returns to normal, with a few waves splashing back and forth.

The crowd is stunned, as is Shawn. Clarissa and her church family are in shock as well.

"The power of God is in all of us," Shawn states strongly. Powerful words begin to flow from his lips. "God created the earth, parted the seas, and raised his Son Jesus from the dead. He is a God of love and redemption. He has authority over the heavens and the earth. He has authority over life and death. He has offered all of us the choice of life over death. If we believe in Him, then we choose life over death. If we believe that his Son, Jesus, rose from the dead, then we too can rise from the dead. If we repent our sins and follow His ways, then we can have eternal life." Shawn stops and looks around at the stunned crowd.

"Clarissa asked you to love your neighbor. I ask you to do something even more important. I ask you to believe in, and love God. With all your soul, with all your heart, and with all your strength, love God. I am a man of God. I'm not a prophet. I'm a Christian. If God is calling you, if you want to know God and everlasting life, the everlasting love that He offers you, please come forward to be baptized in Christ's name."

Shawn lowers his arms and looks over the crowd. Many people begin to come forward to be baptized, some smiling broadly, some weeping, some in stunned shock. Others are hurriedly gathering their children and possessions and fleeing. Some sit in shock and talk amongst themselves. 'What just happened?', 'Is he the devil?', 'Is he a prophet from God?', 'Was it some kind of parlor trick, like they see on TV?'

The youth pastor prays with his people over the miracle they just witnessed. He and a few of the stronger parishioners begin to mingle with the naysayers and doubters. "You have seen a miracle from God. You are blessed. Please, do not be afraid. Stay and listen, come and learn." Their urgings stop a few of the people who were ready to leave, panicked and bewildered.

"I've seen stuff like that on TV," a skeptical gang banger tells a young evangelical woman from the church. "Me and my boys think you're running a scam. When are you going to pass the collection plate?"

She stops and stares down the four intimidating young men. "You saw the seas parted on TV?" she queries. "How do you think they did that?" She puts her hands on her hips defiantly, looking at them as if she expects and answer. The young men remain silent, not ready to address the brash dark-skinned woman. The women they know do not talk back, do not ask questions.

"I know you, Jeffie," she says, pointing at one of the young men. "You tried to cup me under the bleachers in eighth grade." The young man she's pointing at blushes. "Tell me how that white boy pulled off a parlor trick? I tell you all, I believe, and that scared the crap out of me. He parted the waters! Tell me Jeffie, how did he do that?"

"Don't fall for her jive, Jeffie," the gang banger leader states. "We've seen this kind of stuff on TV. They use mirrors and splits screens, CGI and all those modern technologies."

"Bingo, give a star to the A student. He knows how the magicians do it," the young woman responds with sarcastic enthusiasm. "Now, mister A student in magic, show me the mirrors. Show me the split screens. Show me the CGI." She gestures with her hands at the open spaces around them. "Do you see any mirrors?"

She pauses and looks at the four thugs, expecting an answer. The four gang bangers squirm under her stern gaze.

"There ain't no mirrors, are there smart man? You just saw this with your own eyes. That wasn't magic. That was God right here in LA working miracles. You heard the man. Life over death. Love or hate. It's your choice. You saw God in action with your own eyes. Are you going to walk away from that?" She looks over the four men once more. "You all are into drugs, sex and thuggery. You think only of yourselves. You have no love except for your own ego. God graced you with the privilege of seeing one of his miracles. Get off your lazy selfish butts. God has plans for you. Or stay where you are and maybe get killed tomorrow in a drug deal gone bad. Life eternal with God in heaven, or death here in the hood. It's your choice."

She turns and starts to walk away. "Don't be like that," the gang banger leader says. "Why do you have to come down all righteous on us. We're just trying to get by."

The young woman turns and looks at the four young men. "God created this earth. He created you. Do you think He created you to just get by? He has plans for you, great plans. But you settle for just getting by. I'm not being righteous; I'm bringing you the truth. Your path is your choice." She turns and begins walking back to the shallow

122

end of the pool where the pastor and Shawn are baptizing new believers. She hears a few stifled words behind her, then the crunch of sneakers on gravel. A broad smile breaks out across her face, someone is following her. Angels are singing in heaven; a soul is being saved.

Chapter 19, Changed Hearts

The village elders are divided. Half the elders side with Xi, his converted jail guard, and his well-armed friends. The other half are appalled at what has happened and fear the state's reprisal.

"Look out there, he's in open defiance of the state," one elder whispers to another as they cower behind the scales after fleeing the violence. "More people are coming to hear him speak. The state's strong stance against this man has not scared people away. It has drawn more people in!"

On the stage, Xi has resumed preaching God's love. His wife and close friends have set up a baptismal station and are baptizing new believers. There is a long line of people waiting to feel the warmth of forgiveness and the hope of eternal life.

"The state has no answers to your questions," Xi proclaims to the growing crowd. "Why are you here? Who created you? What happens when you die? God answers all these questions. God created you, you did not evolve from an ape. You are here to serve God and your fellow man; you are not here to serve the state. And when you die, if you love God and His Son, Jesus Christ, you will go to heaven, eternal peace." Xi raises his right hand which firmly grasps a Bible.

"It's all right here. All the questions you might have, are answered right here in this book, a book the state has banned, a book the state does not want you to read. God loves you. He's the one who made your crops abundant. He's the one who wants you to thrive. Join the many who have come forward this day to accept Christ as your Savior. God will not let the state overpower us. God is stronger than the state. I beseech you all to embrace God's love. The state is a passing entity. God's love is eternal. He'll never forsake you, He'll never leave you."

The two elders watch as more people line up to be baptized.

"He's a powerful speaker," the younger man states.

124

"Very powerful," the older man replies as he breaks from the hidden alley and makes his way to take his place in the long line. He has toiled under the yoke of the state for decades with no hope, no light, no joy. He has been told all his life to toil for the state and then he'll die. For the first time in his life, he's hearing the word of hope, love, life. Even life after death. He decides that a glimmer of hope is worth the persecution the state will bring down on their village.

It is the first time in his many years that he has even felt hope. His life has been one of drudgery, compromise, bribes, and thievery. The higher in the ranks of the party he grew, the more corruption, thuggery, and thievery he saw. He never liked it, but he participated in it. It was how the system worked. He sees a way out of the system he hates. He embraces Christ and is baptized.

Xi's wife is the one who baptizes the elder. "You are washed clean of your sins. Love God, love your neighbors, and lead a righteous life. You are, and always will be, a child of God."

The elder raises his head from the shallow pool and feels cleansed. He looks around at his fellow villagers and sees smiles, not frowns. His eyes more clearly see the fertile valleys and meadows. But most importantly, he feels an inner warmth. "I have sinned against you Lord, creator of all the earth. Please forgive me," he says out loud. It is the first prayer he has ever said in sixty years. It brings him warmth and comfort. He smiles as he joins a group of other new believers. They hug each other and talk about what they have just experienced.

Even as they share their joy, they have questions. Hundreds have been converted, but there is not a Bible among them. The few people from Xi's congregation do what they can to teach, and answer questions. One of Xi's sons runs back to their farm where there are a dozen Bibles. He brings them back and they are quickly absorbed by the crowd. The splines are cut creating many small portions of the Bible so that more people can read at least a part of the holy book.

One woman ends up with the Book of Psalms in her hands. She begins reading out loud with a clear and sonorous voice, she quickly draws a large crowd. The village elder begins to read the Book of Genesis and draws his own crowd. As the day progresses towards dusk, a thousand people are dispersed across the village, listening to the Bible being read to them in rapt joy.

Xi takes a moment to eat some fresh mutton stew. He looks around and smiles broadly. He expected miracles. God works miracles, and God did work miracles. He thinks of tomorrow. Will it be a day of retribution from the state? No, God will not allow that to happen. But he must prepare these people, these new followers of Christ, for the persecution that is to come. There are so many scriptures that he can reference, from Daniel being spared from the lion's den to Peter and the other disciples being let loose from jail. But he settles on talking about Paul converting his jailers and writing to the faithful while being jailed by the Romans.

Xi rises from his brief respite. He sends word out that he wishes to address the newly faithful. As he makes his way back to the stage by the scales, a crowd gathers. The village square is filled to brimming. The crowd extends into the streets and lanes of the village. Xi looks around in amazement. The crowd is so large that people from nearby villages must have come to see what is happening. Xi silently prays that he speaks God's truth. Then he opens with a prayer.

***

From a distance, the stouthearted elder makes another report to his contact in the province's bureaucracy. "The Christian continues to preach to the people. Now people from other precincts are showing up. If you just send a squad or a platoon, they will be overwhelmed. This is a serious rebellion," the elder implores.

The mid-level bureaucrat makes notes in his daily log. He wants nothing to do with this. "You need to get control of the situation. If the state has to send troops, it will reflect poorly on your leadership," the bureaucrat states.

126

The elder tries to think of a way to get the oafish bureaucrat off his duff. "These rebels have already killed the lieutenant in charge of the train guard! Our own guards have turned against us. I have no way to regain control of the situation."

"Is that what you want me to enter into my logs?" the oaf responds. "I don't think you want me to do that. Look buddy, friend to friend, let things cool down and take back control of your village in the morning. If I record what you have told me, you will be the first one the state comes after. They will hold you responsible for everything."

The disgraced elder thinks about it. It is true, he'll be held accountable. His future is very bleak if he cannot deal with the situation at hand. If the state is brought in, he'll fall before they even begin looking for the preacher and his followers. He'll need to make up a story to cover for the dead train guards. With a few bribes he can bury that situation. But what to do about the preacher and his followers. Maybe his oafish bureaucrat friend is right. Let the night pass. Address the situation in the morning.

He walks through a few back alleys to his six-room apartment on the third floor of a bland concrete building. His apartment is no nicer than anyone else's, except it's larger. The wiring is faulty, the plumbing is poorly done and there are cracks in the walls because of the improperly poured foundation. He can't complain about any of it. He received kickbacks and bribes from all the contractors. But that is how business is done in a country with no moral authority.

He opens his door and smells fresh vegetables frying in sesame oil. The fragrance is wonderful. He has never smelled such fine cooking in his own house. It smells like the meals he has eaten with some of the provincial leaders that he has occasionally had the honor to dine with. He follows the aroma into the kitchen where his wife is happily making a fine dinner for him. He sees fresh goat meat ready to be sliced and sautéed to go with the fresh vegetables.

The fine smells of the delicious meal his wife is preparing momentarily allows him to forget all his troubles. The rebellion taking

127

place in the town square leaves his mind as he takes in the smells of the dinner his wife is preparing.

Their marriage is strained. He has not always been faithful. But his wife has been faithful to him, always seeing the best in him. She has always tried to be good to him. He assumes this is another attempt by his wife to gain his good favor. And it is working, he embraces his wife as he absorbs the aroma enveloping their kitchen.

"What is the occasion?" he asks his wife. "This looks like a sumptuous feast."

"Dear, surely you have heard about the bountiful crops that our farmers brought in?" his wife responds. "I've never seen our markets so full. I was able to buy all of this fresh food at today's market. They say our village has been blessed. I was told a man of God has come and blessed our crops. I'm not sure what that means, but my dearest, look at what we have!"

Upon hearing this, her husband explodes. "This is from the prophet?" he exclaims. He begins throwing the pots and pans around the room, splattering the well-cooked dinner on the walls and floor. "He's the devil. He's going to bring ruin on our house. I want nothing to do with any bounty from his proclamations." With his final statement he hurls a wok at his wife's head as rage overcomes him. She's nimble enough to duck the object and flees their home, sobbing. She has no idea of what she did wrong. But she determines that it will be the last time she'll let her husband abuse her. Once again, she goes to her sister's house to escape her husband's wrath.

Chapter 20, Mustafa's Warning

It is three in the morning. Darkness envelopes everything. Sunrise is still three hours away. The older man hesitates as he reaches out to shake his newly found brother awake. He has heard stories of how battled hardened men will kill people who suddenly wake them from a deep sleep. He says a prayer for his life. He reaches for the large man's shoulder, just to give him a gentle nudge. In a flash, the sleeping man's hand shoots up and grabs the priest's hand. The sleeping man pulls the priest down and rolls on top of him. In just a moment the priest has been put into a deaths grip. The priest shakes, thinking his worst fears are coming true. The large man plants a kiss on the old man's forehead as he begins to laugh.

"Father, I know you have much to teach me," Mustafa exclaims, as he releases the Orthodox priest from his bear hold grasp. "But I think I could teach you a few things too. There are escape maneuvers you should know. And you're not very good at being stealthy. I knew you were outside my door when I heard the boards creak in the hallway." Mustafa releases the priest who quickly regains his footing.

The older man steps back from Mustafa and shakes off the scare of being bear hugged, almost killed, by this giant of a man. "You must come with me my new friend," the Orthodox priest states. "Many people are interested in you. Your old friends want to kill you. Your new friends may not really be your friends. You are called. You are chosen. Many people fear your message."

Mustafa stands up and stretches. His hands reach to the ceiling of the room as he reaches up, stretching out his back and legs. He then bends down and stretches out his legs, leaning this way and that, pushing his legs into abnormal positions.

"Mustafa, I'm not sure if you heard me," the priest says, as he watches this stretching regimen. "People want you dead. Both

Muslims and Christians want you dead. We need to find a safe refuge. I believe you. We've been chosen. We need to proclaim Jesus."

As Mustafa does deep knee squats, he looks at the priest. "Okay. I believe you too. Now I want you to do these exercises with me. If I'm on the run, then so are you. I love you brother, but I don't want to have to carry you. Let's start by loosening up."

The priest is about to protest, but a light goes off in his head. The former ISIS fighter is right. Being agile and fit would be an asset. He starts by stretching out, as Mustafa directs him. His wiry muscles ache, but after just fifteen minutes of exercise, he feels ten years younger.

Mustafa gently settles on the floor, with his legs crossed under him. The priest tries to do the same but can't. His wiry old muscles won't allow him to tuck his feet under his butt. So he reclines as he rubs his aching and stiff muscles.

"So, tell me again why you came and woke me at three in the morning?" Mustafa asks.

"We're called, we're part of the Messianic Jews who are called to proclaim Christ as Savior."

Mustafa smiles, "Yes we are. It is such a great honor! We've done great things in His name already. I look forward with joy to see the things He'll do through us. Which causes me great confusion. Why do we need to run? I have never run. Now that Christ is with me, I see no reason to run at all. This is the birthplace of Christianity. I think we need to stand here, firmly."

The priest pauses to regain his thoughts. "Mustafa, there are plots developing to take your life. I have many contacts. A reliable source told me that ISIS wants you dead. Because of recent events, the Americans have taken a great interest in you as well. The Special Forces people that have helped to protect you now want to take you into custody. The Peshmerga believe you are a prophet and are

130

helping to hide you. But the Americans have eyes and ears everywhere. They want you."

"ISIS is dangerous and dedicated, but they are fools," Mustafa replies. "I do not fear them. I know their tactics. I know how they think. The Americans should be our friends. Why should we be afraid of them?" Mustafa asks, pondering the situation.

"The American people are our friends," the priest replies. "But the American Government, they are power hungry. We speak of a new freedom that they have been trying to sequester for years. For decades, the American government has been trying to undermine Christianity. Through their schools and through their governmental programs, they have been undermining the church. We've seen it from afar. We've called for reform, but we have had no voice. Maybe you are the voice we have been looking for."

"That doesn't answer my question," Mustafa replies. "We should embrace the Americans, but not the American government? Why, is there a difference?"

"It's hard to explain," the priest replies. "Let me put it this way, does ISIS represent the people's hearts?"

"No," Mustafa replies. "ISIS is the radical fringe of Islam."

"Exactly," the priest replies. "Most Americans are God loving people. But the people in control of the government, they are power hungry. They want nothing to do with God. They want power and wealth. God liberates people from the state. So, the state's ultimate desire is to eliminate God, making people dependent on the state."

Mustafa stretches once again as he takes in these new thoughts. He's currently a free man in the land controlled by the Peshmerga. But the Peshmerga are allied with the Americans. If the Americans want him, the Peshmerga will give him up. Is he really a free man?

"My new friend, we have to rely on our faith," the large man replies. "Maybe God anointed us to become captives of the enemy. Maybe from within the walls of our captors we will be allowed to proclaim His kingdom. I have read the Bible. I know Paul was a captive of the Romans. Even from his imprisonment he proclaimed God's kingdom. Maybe we will be allowed that same glorious fate."

"Those who pursue us know that," the Priest responds. "If they catch up with us, there will be no time in prison. There will be no time for writing prophetic letters. I have friends, we have to leave now."

Mustafa looks at his new friend. "You have friends who are neither American nor Peshmerga?"

"They are Christians," the priest responds. "They can smuggle us out of the area. They have done it many times."

"Smuggled out of the area?" Mustafa queries. "Why should I want to leave here? I'm a man of God!"

The priest understands the prophet's objections. Running seems to be admitting defeat. But they are not running, they are moving. "Christ came during the Roman empire, right?" the priest asks.

Mustafa ponders the question. "Yes, so what of it?"

"It was a time of stability, Pax Romana," the priest replies. "The Middle East is in crisis. The Word needs to be proclaimed from an area of stability, not from an area in crisis."

"But the church started here," Mustafa exclaims. "We cannot abandon the Holy Land."

"We will return. The promised land will not be forgotten."

Mustafa looks to heaven. "You said we would be exiled. You said we would return. I pray, dear Lord, that I may return."

The earth rumbles under their feet. It rumbles strong and long. They both dive for a doorway and stay crumpled up under the strong structure. Mustafa, the strong man, covers the seventy-year-old priest with his body as the building they are in rattles and shakes. Rubble and stone begin to fall all around them.

Chapter 21, Making Plans

"What Happened?" Clarissa exclaims. Clarissa and Shawn are at their shared apartment.

"I don't know," Shawn replies. "You mentioned Moses, I just acted it out."

Clarissa stands on the couch and screams excitedly. "But you made it happen! The friggin seas parted! Did you see that? The water parted. How did you do that?" She jumps off the couch with a smile brimming from ear to ear. She looks to Shawn, waiting for his answer.

"I didn't do it, God did," Shawn replies. "I just started speaking. You told me God would give me words. I spoke what God told me to speak."

"And you performed a miracle!" Clarissa exclaims. "A twenty first century miracle! Everyone says God is dead. Maybe people will start to see that God is not dead. Shawn, what you did, it could change things. We should watch the news. Surely someone recorded it on an iPhone. Surely some news media outlet will report it."

Shawn is still contemplating what happened. He's looking at his hands in bewilderment as Clarissa tunes in to a well-known national news outlet. The top story is about unexpected new fighting in the Middle East, and a rebellion starting in a northern province of China. Clarissa's phone starts to chime with incoming calls and texts. As Clarissa is about to start reading the texts, Shawn stands abruptly. "We should pray. Something is happening, something beyond our comprehension. We need to pray."

Clarissa puts her phone aside and mutes the TV. "You are right. God is moving, God is working around the globe. We need to seek his guidance." The two pray together for several minutes. They pray for wisdom, patience, guidance, love, and compassion. They both speak to God, seeking to follow his will, asking for the Holy Spirit to guide them. When they are done praying, they embrace, weeping tears of joy.

The door to their shared apartment is thrust open and one of their roommates, Mark, enters. "Hey, can you all help me with the groceries," the roommate asks as he walks into the shared living space. He looks up to see Shawn and Clarissa embracing. "Hey, none of that here," he chides. "No public displays of affection in the common areas. You know the rules. Off to one of your bedrooms with all that." He winks at Shawn as he continues. "I knew there was something between you two. I'm happy for you."

Clarissa and Shawn step apart, blushing. "No, it's not like that Mark. Clarissa and I had a moment of clarity. A God moment. I need to tell you about it," Shawn states.

"Dude," Mark responds looking at the television. "You're on the news." He grabs the remote and turns up the volume.

"This prank video is making the rounds on social media," the news anchor states. "A modern-day Moses pretends to part the waters at a public pool in Los Angeles, causing a near riot. David Blaine would be jealous of this trick as you can see the prankster parts the waters by spreading his hands and invoking the words of Moses. We have an exclusive interview with someone who was at the pool party. Marcia, to you."

"Marcia Hemmingway reporting from Los Angeles. I have with me an eyewitness to the pool prank where supposedly the waters were parted. This is Julia Franks who witnessed the prank. Julia, tell us what you saw."

Julia is visibly shaken as the reporter puts the mic in front of her. "You all keep calling it a prank. I don't know why. I saw it with my own eyes. That man, he called on God to part the waters, and the waters parted! I was with my two children, we had to run from the waters splashing out of the pool. It was crazy, but I saw it."

"There you go, life in these modern times," Marcia interjects. "Pranksters scaring people just trying to escape the heat. Back to you, Asa."

Mark hits mute as the news moves onto another story. "Shawn, you're moving on from street running to full blown magic tricks? And you made the news! Bro, you have a career! Sign and date my shirt dude, you're going to be famous."

"That was no trick," Shawn replies. "God parted the waters, not me. I asked Him to do it, and He did."

Mark looks at Shawn like he's crazy. "You asked God to part the waters at some local pool. And God parts the waters? Bro, I want a hot girlfriend. Can you ask God for that? Your talking crazy my friend."

"Mark, your friend is not crazy," Clarissa responds. "It's all over YouTube, over a hundred thousand views already. Watch the whole thing. There are no parlor tricks."

Mark takes Clarissa's phone and for several minutes watches the full video.

He looks up at his two roommates. "How did you do that?" he asks, his voice trembling. His two roommates remain silent. He looks back and forth between the two, expecting an answer. But he already knows the answer. "God did it?" he finally admits. Shawn and Clarissa nod, smiling. "I got to get this figured out," Mark states as he turns to head to his room.

Clarissa grabs him by the shoulder and hugs him. "There is nothing to figure out, Mark. God is real. He loves you. Come to him and he'll accept you as you are." Mark pushes by and goes into his room, closing the door tightly behind him.

All this time, both Shawn's and Clarissa's phones have been buzzing and twerping. Calls and texts have been flooding in. Clarissa picks up her phone. "I have over forty text messages already."

Shawn looks at his phone. "I have over thirty, and sixteen voice mails. How do we respond to this?"

"We're called to proclaim the Word to the nations. We can't do that by responding to each text or voice mail. God has given us a platform. We must use it."

"You mean go to the press?" Shawn responds. "They'll eat us alive. They are already spinning what has happened as a prank. We need help."

"Did someone come to help you part the waters?" Clarissa asks. "He'll help us. And we have allies. One of my texts is from my pastor. I'm calling him now."

She dials his number. He picks up after the first ring. "Pastor Michael, something is happening, and we need your help," Clarissa states warmly, confidently.

"I saw the news clips and Dan told me what he saw." Pastor Michael responds. "I'm getting in my car now. Where are you? I'll come to you."

"We're at our apartment. Things are a bit crazy, but I swear to you pastor, it is God working. Pastor Dan, the youth pastor was there. He saw it all. There were no tricks, no hidden mirrors. We need to talk. You know I know my scriptures pretty good. I want you to think about the twelve thousand from the twelve tribes of Israel. That may sound crazy, but we need to talk about it."

"That's from the Book of Revelation," Pastor Michael responds.

"Yes, pastor, pray about it, think about it. We'll expect you in about twenty minutes." Clarissa hangs up and sees that ten more texts have shown up on her phone. She decides to ignore them.

"Your pastor is coming over?" Shawn asks. He looks anxious and scared. "Is he a good guy? Can we trust him? What about these twelve tribes of Israel? Is that about the chosen ones? Will he be able to explain that? Oh my God. Clarissa, will he be able to understand it? Will he believe what is happening?"

"He won't believe what is happening if you keep freaking out," Clarissa replies sternly. She looks at her roommate and assesses the situation. He did not grow up knowing Christ. Now all of this has been thrust on him. He's smart and competent. How must he feel, having been 'called'? "Shawn, I have known Christ for many years. He'll be with you. You are probably scared and confused right now. That's okay. So am I. But I know God is not only behind us, he's beside us, and in front of us, leading the way. He has set a path before us. We need to be stout and follow that path." She chuckles. "Isn't it ironic that He chose a man who is a street runner, a man who can make a path where no one else can see a way forward, someone who sees obstacles as challenges. God is awesome!"

Shawn hears her words and smiles. He has always seen the world as a challenge. He has always fought to overcome the challenges. This is another challenge. He hears the voice again, '*I have been preparing you for this*.' Shawn looks up. "I'm ready, help me, guide me." With those few words, Shawn feels a comfort come over him, the Holy Spirit enters him again.

Silence fills the room for a few moments, until Mark bursts back into the room. "I've looked at the videos like five times. Dude, how did you do that?"

"It was an act of God, Mark," Shawn replies quietly. "There is a God, and He loves you. You can try and explain it anyway you want. But I'm telling you the truth. Believe me and believe in God."

138

Mark starts to shrink back against the wall. Fear comes into his eyes. "You, I mean we, uh, I, you," he mutters on as he crumbles to the floor. "Don't hurt me, don't judge me. I'm just trying to get by." He says as he lays weeping on the floor.

Clarissa runs to his side and embraces him. "Mark, oh Mark, you have it all wrong. We're not here to judge you, we're here to love you. Your judgement comes from God. And if you accept Jesus Christ as His Son and your Savior, then your sins are forgiven. We're here to spread that message of love and salvation."

Mark thinks of all the lies he has told, all the times he has been mean and spiteful. How many other times has he been sinful? He cowers on the floor, fearing demons are going to come and take him away, but the hope of salvation penetrates his fears. "I can be forgiven for my sins?" Mark asks meekly. He knows in his heart he's a sinner. If there is a God, Mark knows he'll not pass judgement.

"Profess Christ as your Savior and the Son of God," Clarissa replies quietly and calmly as she holds Mark in a loving hug. "Repent for your sins. Begin to lead a life loving God and loving your neighbor. If you do that, then your sins will be forgiven. Christ has a place in heaven for you."

Mark sits up and looks at Clarissa, then looks to Shawn. "I believe you, there is a God. I want a place in heaven. Lord, forgive me for all I have done. I do believe in You and Your Son, Jesus Christ."

With those few words, Mark feels an inner warmth. A comfort comes across him that he has never felt before. Worries wash off his shoulders and strength enters his heart.

He looks from Clarissa to Shawn in astonishment. He stands up and embraces Clarissa, then turns to Shawn and embraces him too. "Wow, God does love me. I have never felt like this. What do we do now?"

"We tell the world, Mark, we tell the world," Shawn replies with a smile.

Just then they hear wrapping at the door. "It's me, Clarissa. Pastor Michael."

Mark opens the door and wraps the pastor in a big bear hug. "I just accepted Christ, pastor. I'm saved! Do you know how awesome that is? Well, you being a pastor, I guess you know. But I want to tell everyone!"

Pastor Michael hugs the young man. "Welcome home my friend, welcome home." He stands back from Mark, holding his shoulders as he smiles. "We will need your enthusiasm. I always love to meet a new believer."

Shawn looks past the pastor and sees that a small crowd has gathered on the street. Some are praying, others holler obscenities at them. He quickly closes the door as the pastor enters into the common kitchen area. The pastor embraces Clarissa, and they exchange welcomes. Then the pastor turns to Shawn and embraces him warmly too. Shawn feels a power, a sense of love that allows him to calm down.

The pastor stands back from Shawn and looks him over from head to toe. He's sizing him up. He knows he cannot judge the man from what he sees. Only God can judge his heart. But the pastor is in uncharted waters. No one has performed miracles for centuries. Is the man before him a fraud? Or a man of God? "From what I've seen, you performed a miracle today. Tell me how it happened."

Shawn feels a warmth from the pastor and replies honestly. "I did not perform any miracles today, God did."

"I saw the videos," the pastor responds, challenging Shawn. "You raised your hands and parted the waters."

"You're missing the most important part," Shawn responds, recalling what happened. "I asked God to part the waters. I didn't do it. God did."

Pastor Michael takes a step back. It is the answer he wanted to hear, but not the answer he expected. The man before him is not claiming any part of the miracle.

"So how did it happen?" the pastor asks, genuinely curious.

Clarissa jumps in and explains how they decided to have a pool party and how Shawn was to be the main speaker. "Shawn said he wasn't good at talking to large crowds. I told him Moses said the same thing."

Shawn picks up the narrative. "I'm not a good public speaker. And I don't know a whole lot about the Bible. So, not knowing what to say, I said what Moses said at the Red Sea. And the waters parted. It scared the hell out of me."

"We need to go back," the pastor says. "Before the pool party, Clarissa, you saw yourself in heaven, praising the Lord. And you saw Shawn there too."

"Oh, most definitely," Clarissa responds. "That's why I asked you to think about the twelve thousand from the twelve tribes. I clearly saw my heritage back to the tribes of Israel. I'm a descendant from Isaac. It is implanted on my brain. I could write it out for you."

The pastor ponders this for a moment, then he looks to Shawn. "What is your heritage? Do you know it?"

Shawn thinks for a moment. "I'm from the clan of Reuben. I know my heritage as well. I could write it down for you too. As a matter of fact, I can trace it all the way back to Noah if that helps." Shawn ponders this for a minute. "Pastor, two days ago, I didn't know who my great grandparents were. How do I now know my lineage back four thousand years?"

"You both have recent scars on your foreheads. Did you know this?" the pastor asks.

"We've been in a few tussles in the past few days," Shawn responds. "Clarissa saved me from a crowd of rowdy coeds. But if you are wondering about us being chosen. Pastor, we're chosen. That is why you are here. We need your help. We're called to save thousands, if not millions. We can't do that from this isolated apartment. You know how to reach millions. God will give us the words. We need a platform to deliver the Word."

"We've had a platform to deliver the Word for years. How is your message going to be any different?" the pastor asks.

"For the same reason you are here," Shawn replies. "God is working miracles."

"God parted the waters, pastor," Clarissa states slowly, thinking as she speaks. "It has already made some news channels and the video is going viral on social media. An interview with Shawn would be a hot commodity. You should interview Shawn and we can post that to YouTube."

Pastor Michael is beginning to realize that there is a story here that needs to be told. He begins to talk out loud. "It should not be taped; it should be live. If what you are saying is true, then it needs to be done live. Shawn, are you okay with that?"

Shawn is beaming from knowing his best friend has been saved. The joy it brought him is resounding in his heart. The opportunity to tell his story to the world sends chills down his back. "I'm all in, pastor," Shawn responds.

"They're going to come after you. They are going to dig into your past, they're going to try and destroy your past and your family," Pastor Michael responds. He thinks back to how he was undermined every step of the way while building his church. He dreamt of a church with a few hundred members. Now he has a church with several thousand members. And every day new attacks occur.

"I already have our clerks checking you out. People have come to us many times, looking for a platform. If you are a fraud, or if what you are saying is not biblical, we won't air it. That said, I want you at our studio tomorrow morning at ten o'clock. I've seen the videos. Something is happening. I'll contact our local media."

Clarissa looks at her phone which shows over 60 texts and thirty voice mails. "What do I do about all these texts?" she asks.

"Pick out the important ones and answer them. Ignore the rest, they just want to pick a fight. Let's bring the fight to them on our own terms."

Chapter 22, New converts

The dust and debris from the minor earthquake is long gone from their robes. They are in the back of a nondescript Volvo van on their way to a little used airstrip. A small plane awaits them. It will fly them out of northern Iraq and into Turkey. From there, they are to be flown to eastern Europe. The priest and the ISIS fighter will be secure from unknown attacks and able to regroup in peace.

While on the plane, Mustafa ponders his calling and their current actions. He turns to the Orthodox priest and shakes him from a distressed slumber. "We need to preach the gospel to all the nations," Mustafa says as the priest is jolted wide awake. "It is repeated throughout the Bible. You may look at me as a hardened fighter with little education, priest. But I'm well-schooled in both the Bible and the Quran. As an elite ISIS fighter, we were taught to know our enemy, know how he thinks. So, I studied the Bible and the Quran. I have taken and passed online theology classes." Mustafa chuckles, "I'm only fourteen credits away from being an ordained priest!"

The priest's eyes widen a bit as he looks at his companion. "That explains a lot," he states. "Your sudden conversion raised my eyebrows. But your ability to preach the Word, your knowledge of the scriptures, that really got me thinking. I know the Holy Spirit will give us words, but you speak to the masses as a man who knows God's words."

"I know God's words," Mustafa replies. "When He came to me on that battlefield, it all became clear. I knew. Which is why I say we should not run. Jesus himself said that we're to proclaim his Word even to the rulers of the nations. We cannot proclaim His Word from the basement of a warehouse. It needs to be proclaimed from the steps of the palaces. But we're fleeing the battle."

The priest responds slowly, after considering Mustafa's words and thinking of the strength of his own faith. "How many words can you speak if you have a bullet through your head? Who will hear your teachings if no one is allowed to hear what you say? I know God is on our side, but we must be prudent, we must be wise. The forces of evil are widespread. Governments around the globe are pierced with corruption. Countries that were founded on religious freedom now shun religion. Even the American fighters that helped to save us would have turned us over to corrupt leaders. We would have been silenced, never to be heard from again."

"So, who is helping us? Where are we going?" Mustafa asks.

"These are Christian soldiers from many nations. God has blessed them with many skills. Some are pilots, some are doctors, some are soldiers, some are technicians. They are loose knit but capable. We're going to Albania, where I have trusted friends. We will be hidden and can make plans as we evaluate the situation."

Mustafa shakes his head. "The best plans are made on the battlefield, as the battle is being engaged. Plans made from afar never work out."

Mustafa's words strike the priest's heart. He has made many plans from the safety of his domain. But the action is in the field. Hearts are not won from a citadel. Hearts are won on the streets. This street fighter has a point. They cannot just make plans, they must engage in the battle, the battle for the human soul. That cannot be done from a safe space. There can be no more pontifications. There must be action.

"When we land, I want you to engage. I want you to tell your story. I want you to say whatever God lays on your heart. Let's start proclaiming as soon as we can."

Mustafa smiles. "As soon as we land, I'm to proclaim the Lord? But you said they are all already believers? What good is that? I will be 'preaching to the choir?' as I've heard it called."

145

"There are always non-believers in the choir. And it is good to get the rest of the choir enthusiastic about what they are doing," the priest responds. "It's a start. Hopefully a start of something big."

"Christ is coming! I think that is something big!" Mustafa exclaims. "Let's get started!"

Their plane begins its final approach to the private airport and moments later they have taxied to the small terminal. Following his security team, the priest exits the plane. He expects to be met by a few of his Orthodox friends and clergy. Instead, he's met by a cheering crowd of over a hundred people. He instantly thinks of what he told Mustafa on the plane. He looks up to the heavens. "God, may you speak truth through your chosen people." Two of his close clergy friends look at him, wondering about this strange greeting. Mustafa steps off the plane behind him. The priest turns and beckons him to speak.

The crowd hushes as the massive warrior walks down the few steps to the tarmac. He has an aura about him that demands respect and attention. He moves with confidence and despite his large size and many battle scars, a peace seems to surround him, exude from him. Some would call him confident and capable. But a better description is assured and called.

In a loud and clear voice, heard by all in their native tongue, Mustafa states confidently. "Praise be to God in the highest, the creator of all things! Praise be to Jesus, His Son who came to save us from our sins. Praise be to the Holy Spirit who is with us, to guide us. May the purity of the Holy Trinity be proclaimed to the nations. May all who wish to be cleansed of their sins come forth and be washed in the blood of Jesus through baptism."

The two friends of the priest are stunned. "He is speaking in tongues!" one exclaims. The other begins to weep. They have heard many alter calls, but none as straight forward and direct, and they have never heard anyone speak in tongues. They watch in astonishment as people begin to come forward to be baptized.

"Come my friends! Strong believers and new believers, come forward and have your faith refreshed", Mustafa implores. "The final battle is coming; we must be washed anew to face the coming trials. Come and renew your faith, renew your strength in your faith." The line grows longer as believers are encouraged to renew their faith. Mustafa's new Orthodox friend smiles as he watches, and then begins to sing as he joins Mustafa in helping to Baptize the faithful. The song is picked up and amplified. Soon the song of praise is echoing throughout the airport and across the nearby valleys and mountains. More people come to see what is going on. The baptismal line grows. By nightfall, over a thousand people have been baptized. Feasts are being prepared and songs of joy are being sung.

Night has fallen. The small village is in full blown celebration as they rejoice in their newfound faith. Mustafa finds his Orthodox priest friend near one of the roasting pits. He clasps his massive arm around the older man's shoulder. "Look at what God has done!" he proclaims with joy. "The Holy Spirit is alive and well here. You were right to bring us here. We will revive our faith before returning to the Holy Land."

The priest returns Mustafa's embrace. "New believers have come to know God, and the choir has been invigorated. You have done well my friend. You have done very well."

Mustafa steps back from the priest and looks at him with a large smile. He reaches out and brings the other two Orthodox priests into their embrace. The two 'friends' had been rather cold to the events of the day. But as Mustafa reaches out to include them in what has happened, an electricity flows among the four men. The Holy Spirit binds them. They are all on the same mission, their mission may not follow the same path, but their mission is the same, proclaim God as creator and his Son as Savior.

One of the younger priests turns to his compatriots. "We're united under Christ. We must remember that. There is much to do. We must build on what has happened today."

Chapter 23, Social Media

A small group of people have been working all morning to get the message right. "Social Media is very fickle. Get the message wrong and it could all blow up in your face," Georgeanne Haquani tells them. She's a young social media influencer with a large following. She's one of the few Christians with over a million twitter followers. A friend of Pastor Michael helped them to get a Zoom meeting with her. After seeing the video from the pool party, Georgeanne readily agreed to help them.

"But we must proclaim the truth," Shawn states adamantly. "It was a work of God. Everyone there knows it. I know it. I'm not a street magician."

"A lie makes it halfway around the world before the truth even leaves the starting gate," Pastor Michael states. "Any coverage of this has been proclaimed as a hoax, a street prank. And that is what people believe. How do we combat that?"

"You were smart not to respond in public right away," Georgeanne responds. "You could have easily gotten an interview with some local media, and they would have turned your words inside out and upside down. 'Right will be wrong and the righteous will be persecuted.' My version of what the Bible says, but you know what I mean."

"So, what do we do?" Clarissa asks.

"Tell your story. Tell the truth," Georgeanne responds. "I have never been on mainstream media, yet a million people tune in to see what I have to say. I speak the truth, even when people don't like what I have to say. My messages on abstinence have more views than any other subject, and more negative comments. They also have more positive comments because I didn't let anyone filter my views. I stayed committed to my convictions."

"How do we go about getting our message out?" Shawn asks. "How do we tell our story, the truth?"

"Part of that is very easy, speak the truth. But getting people to hear the truth, that is the hard part," Georgeanne responds. "Pastor, how quickly can you get a crowd at your church? Offer free food or something, we need a big crowd."

"I guess we could put it in the bulletin. We'd need to gather volunteers to have a festival with a large crowd. Give us two weeks and we can put together a pretty good gathering," Pastor Michael responds.

"Step up to the plate, pastor!" Georgeanne responds. "Shawn and Clarissa got a few hundred people in a matter of hours using their own resources. You can get a thousand people at your church tonight if you work at it. You have a speaker that parted the waters. I think people would be interested in what he has to say."

"Oh nnno, I'mmm not going to bbbee the main speaker again," Shawn stutters. "That's what ppput us in this ppppredicament. I'm nnnot good at that kkkind of thing."

Clarissa is starting to see the big picture that Georgeanne is painting. "Shawn, this is not a predicament, it's an opportunity. Pastor Michael will be there to do most of the talking."

"But if you all want me to pppart the waters again, I dddon't know if I can do that." Shawn replies nervously.

Pastor Michael looks at Shawn. "You know that God parted the waters, not you. God was with you; he'll be with you again. He'll speak through you."

"Sounds to me like you all are gaining some faith," Georgeanne states. "I can be at your church in an hour. I want to be part of this. God is moving. Pastor, get your service team moving to feed a thousand people at your church tonight. I know you have the resources to get that done. I'll be at your church within an hour. Don't make any public comments until I get there. Then we're going to blast this miracle around the world. We'll tell it on our terms, with truth and integrity, in a way that anyone who fights it will look foolish. God bless, see you all soon." Before anyone can say anything, the media socialite signs out.

"Wow, she's asking a lot," one of the church elders that Pastor Michael brought with him states. "Food for a thousand people in what, six hours? How are we going to pull that off? And for what, a shyster who we barely know?"

Shawn hears these words, and it troubles him. He wants to get angry, but there is no anger in him. He looks at the woman who has called him a shyster with sympathy. "Why do you doubt me? Why do you doubt God's Word?"

"I don't doubt God's Word, young man. I doubt you. Look at you, a street runner, disrespectful of people's property. You have no knowledge of God's Word. Yet you come to proclaim his Kingdom?" the woman states snidely. "I'm to believe you have been chosen to proclaim his Word? You haven't worked an honest day's work in your life."

"How many days of your life have been without sin?" Shawn asks quietly. The woman blushes at his comment. Turning angry she tries to reply. But Shawn speaks first. "I'm not here to proclaim my innocence. I'm here to proclaim the innocence we can find in the blood of Christ. It is a message that needs to be proclaimed to the nations. I'm not schooled in the Bible, but I'm pretty sure that's a mandate given throughout the scriptures. Please, be my friend, please join us in this mission."

The woman looks at Shawn with scorn. "God would send a clean man, a healthy man, not a filthy degenerate like you." She turns and looks at Pastor Michael, "Do you believe this man and his groupies? They are filthy with sin. I bet they are sleeping together. We need to walk away from this den of sin."

150

Pastor Michael looks at Shawn and Clarissa in a new light. The woman is a trusted member of the church, voted by the congregation as an elder, a leader. He cannot dismiss her concerns. Is he caught up in the hype of the moment?

"Jesus said that brother would turn against brother, sister against sister. What harms has Shawn caused you?" Dan, the youth pastor asks. "You have fulfilled the scriptures. Repent for your sins and join us in proclaiming his Word. I was there, I saw the miracle. Would you reject John the Baptist because of his lifestyle? When was the last time you mingled with the fishermen coming into the docks down at the piers? Are they also below your expectations for an apostle of Christ?"

The woman stops as she's heading out the door. She recalls the words of Christ from the Gospel of Mark. The man proclaiming to be a prophet did not reprimand her. The man asked her to join him. A false prophet would have condemned her. A true man of God would reach out to her in love, offering the forgiveness of Christ.

The woman feels the Holy Spirit descend upon her as she hesitates at the doorway. Why does she doubt? Why is she fleeing from action? Here is an opportunity to act. Yet she doubts. It may be crazy, it may be something beyond belief, but it is something she must do. She turns around and heads back into the small apartment.

She looks at her compatriots. "It will take a miracle to put together food for a thousand people in six hours. Do you even have a menu in mind?"

"God is in the business of working miracles, Miriam," Pastor Michael responds. "What do you think our team can put together? Roasted chicken, potato salad and coleslaw is pretty standard fare. And cake too. Gotta have cake."

"We'll need five hundred chickens!" Miriam exclaims. "Two hundred pounds of potatoes, a hundred sheet cakes, who knows how many cabbages! Pastor, we normally have a month to organize

151

something like this! I'll start making some calls, but this is not going to be easy."

"Miracles, Miriam, miracles. Make it happen. God is with you, with us," the pastor responds with a smile.

"I'm on-board Pastor. Now, we should get the word out to the congregation. That will also allow our prophet time to clean up, and maybe get a haircut."

"Music, we need music," Clarissa interjects. She's part of the church's praise band and has the right connections. "I'll start making those calls now. I'm assuming we'll start things off at six?"

"You got it," the pastor responds. "We'll also need our small group leaders here as well as our outreach people. I'll start making some calls."

***

Twenty minutes later, the group gathers in the office complex of the twenty-five-acre church campus with all its resources including a sports field and picnic grounds.

"Do a 'one call', pastor," Miriam suggests. "We need the congregation to know what is going on. We need their prayers. I've already talked to Julian Saylor. He's putting together a menu and is going to start ordering the food. He said he would send someone to get one of the church's vans to start picking things up. He says there is no way to get all that he needs delivered on this short of notice. He'll be at the church picnic grounds by two o'clock to start the fires in the roasting pits. He's concerned about getting enough volunteers here. So put that in your one call alert."

Pastor Michael gets busy on the phones too, calling board members, fellow pastors, and other key church members. After forty-five minutes, their church is awake and moving. He prayerfully composes his one call message. He writes it out before recording it to be sent to over a thousand of their congregants.

"Dear church members, your action is direly needed. We will be hosting a gathering tonight with a special speaker who has a powerful message. This is a spur of the moment event, we expect over a thousand people to attend. We expect most of these people will be newcomers, not members of our congregation. We urgently need people to get to the church to help prepare. Anyone who can help with cooking is desperately needed. Julian Saylor will start food preparation at two o'clock. We also need van drivers, welcomers, and mentors. Most importantly we need your prayers. Miriam Walker said it would take a miracle to pull this off. Well, our God works miracles. Please help in any way you can. One final request, please don't call the church. Our secretaries are going to be swamped. Just show up when you can, willing to help out."

John Philippi, an associate pastor, whistles as he listens to the pastor's one call. "That's a tall order, Mike. I'll start calling our small group leaders, then head out to see how I can help Julian with this herculean effort."

"Wait till you meet Shawn," the pastor replies. "He's an honest man. God laid this on him, and he wants to do his best. Have you seen the videos?"

John smiles. "Only what I saw on the local news. They really try to play it as a magic trick. But it looks real, and the people they interviewed, they didn't see it as a parlor trick. You obviously believe this is the work of God. I'll follow your lead. If I see something fishy, I'll let you know."

As John is leaving the pastor's office, Clarissa enters with a young woman in tow. She's a petite woman, dressed nicely in a long flowing skirt and loose-fitting blouse. She does not look like any of the fab girls that one thinks of when they think about a social media influencer. No tattoos, no purple hair, no body piercings. The young woman would most likely be called geeky, or maybe earthly. "Pastor,

153

this is Georgeanne Haquani." She turns to Georgeanne, "Georgeanne, Pastor Michael Roberts."

"Pleased to meet you Georgeanne, have a seat."

Georgeanne takes a seat on the edge of a large chair. "Pleased to meet you too, Pastor. Where is the gentleman who parted the waters? I want to talk with him."

"He's not here right now. Clarissa, can you give Shawn a call?"

"I'll have him here right away," Clarissa responds. She looks at Georgeanne. "He's had a rough couple of days. He was going to get cleaned up before coming here." Clarissa gets Shawn on the phone and he confirms that he'll be on his way in a few moments.

"You were there when it happened, right?" Georgeanne asks. "Tell me everything that happened. Don't leave out anything."

Once again, Clarissa explains the day's events, along with the belief that she and Shawn have been called as part of the chosen ones as described in the book of Revelation. Both Georgeanne and Pastor Michael sit in silence as she tells the entire story.

"I didn't know all this about the earthquakes and the fight at the campus," Pastor Michael states. "You are saying this is the end times. That Christ is coming soon."

"I don't know when Christ is coming," Clarissa states, she's visibly shaking as she thinks through everything she has just said. They both could think she's crazy. She puts her head in her hands. "It all sounds crazy now, but I saw Shawn in heaven. I was there too. We were praising Jesus." She looks up, strength returning to her eyes as she looks at the two of them. "It was beautiful. More beautiful than you can ever imagine. And lovely! The music! The songs! Oh, dear Lord, it was majestic!" She stands up and raises her hands to heaven. "It was real, and I will do God's will."

Just then, there's a knock at the door and Shawn enters without waiting to be let in. He looks at Clarissa and smiles. He is cleaned up and his face is beaming, almost glowing. "She's telling the truth. We're chosen. We're to proclaim the Word to the kingdoms. We're to glorify God. Help us in that mission. It is your mission too." His confidence and exuberance infiltrates the room.

Georgeanne looks at Shawn intently. "You have a wound on your forehead." She looks at Clarissa. "You have a mark on your temple."

Shawn begins to explain. "There are a hundred-forty-four-thousand of us around the world with similar marks. Twelve thousand from each of the twelve tribes. We're sealed. I'm from the tribe of Gad. Clarissa is from the tribe of Rueben. I can give you my lineage back to Isaac if you want, but it would take a while. It was revealed to me and is imprinted in my memory."

The pastor and the socialite stare between the two, wondering, thinking. Clarissa sees signs of doubt. Their story is too incredible to believe. She starts to recount her lineage out loud, just as if one were to read it from the Bible, starting with her father and stating all his sons. She only gets back four generations before she's told to stop.

Georgeanne is smiling. "This is good. No, this is great! You may not have noticed, but I set my phone here and set it to record. It is not as good as using my go-pro, but what we just got is pure. You can't make that up, you can't rehearse that." She turns to the pastor. Give me fifteen minutes and I'll have something to release. Trust me, it will go viral."

The pastor wipes a few tears from his eyes. "You believe them too? What they say is unbelievable, yet completely within the realm of scripture. Let us see what you come up with before you release it, okay? I want to talk with these two for a bit." Pastor Michael turns to the two messengers. "So, Shawn, you said that you did not know what God wanted you to say. And you, Clarissa, you said the Holy Spirit would give him the words to speak God's message. That is straight from the book of Mark. Jesus said it would happen. I have had seeds of doubt, but I don't anymore. It is our mission to proclaim His Word. I can look at it as doing what we're called to do. You both are just icing on the cake, or maybe a kick in the rear end to get to doing God's work. Nothing like a good old-fashioned miracle to help move things along."

"Be careful what you wish for Pastor," Shawn replies. "What is coming will be brutal. We will all be tested."

Shawn pauses for a minute. "I want to get some fresh air, stretch my legs. I'll be back." With that he heads out the door of the stuffy office. He needs fresh air and open spaces.

Chapter 24, Rumors

The Special Forces Central Command in central Florida is working at a war footing. A high-level staff meeting is underway. "Jerry, this is the situation. The Syrians and ISIS are both poised at the border with Turkey. The Israelis and the Saudis are backing up Turkey, but the Iranian's and the Iraqis are siding with ISIS. The Egyptians are staying out of it but will most likely side with the Saudis. Meanwhile Boka Haram and their allies have gone ballistic in east Africa. There are reports of serious incursions in Somalia, Nigeria, Chad and even Kenya."

"Wars, and rumors of wars," General Shapiro mutters, thinking back on his meeting the previous day with the chaplain and the young sergeant. "What can you tell me about China? I hear there is a rebellion going on there, in one of the northern provinces."

"We don't have much intel, sir but satellite images show something is happening. What we can gather from social media is some kind of prophet is defying the local military. The Chinese will quash that insurrection by the end of the day," Henry responds.

"What else is happening?" General Shapiro asks. "Tell me things that are out of the ordinary."

"Wildfires are raging not only in Australia and California but also in Brazil and Argentina. There was an extraordinarily high number of small earthquakes around the world, but they caused very little damage. There is a major uprising going on in Paris over high fuel taxes. Authorities fear the riots could spread across the country. I have more sir, should I go on?" Henry asks.

"Anymore weird stuff, like that ISIS fighter washing feet in the middle of a battle?"

Frank Burns, the general in charge of operations responds. "The ISIS convert seems to attract a crowd everywhere he goes. He held a large baptism event in southern Turkey. We had plans to nab him, but he found some friends in the Orthodox community and flew out, apparently to Albania, where another mass baptism took place. We're putting a team together to snatch him. We're not sure if he's a danger to us or to himself, but he could instigate more battles. We need to get him silenced."

"Why silence a man who preaches peace?" the general asks.

"The man is preaching peace in an area that is known for war. We're in the business of conducting wars," the G3 replies honestly. "If peace broke out in the Middle East, God forbid! We would go out of business, lose our funding. We have to snatch this guy."

"Let the ISIS guy go. That is an order. Keep an eye on him, but don't touch him." General Shapiro looks up and ponders. This world could use some peace. What has continual warfare brought them? Dead soldiers, collateral damage, wasted billions of dollars. There has to be a better way.

General Frank Burns ponders this same question. He has been convinced that all religion is bad. He is convinced that religion is the source of all wars. He is enlightened and knows that science is the true path to freedom. Any belief in any God is a distraction from science. He will pass on any information he can to make sure the ISIS convert is neutralized.

Looking down and shaking his head General Shapiro asks if there is anything else on the weird scale. "Actually," the G2 responds. "Your sergeant friend from yesterday flagged a video of some guy pretending to be Moses. Well, maybe succeeding in being Moses. You can decide." Henry plays a short video from a local news cast that downplays the event as a hoax. But the video speaks for itself.

The group of high-powered military men watch the video three times. "That's no hoax," General Shapiro states. "I want to talk with that young man. What do we know about him? How soon can you have him here?"

158

"The kid's name is Shawn Simmons, twenty-two years old, a student at USC, geology major. He's a fitness buff and does what's called street running, which is a kind of urban acrobatics," Henry replies, reading from a freshly printed report. "But it would be easier to grab the ISIS guy in Turkey or Albania, or wherever he is than to grab this kid. We have no jurisdiction."

"We can keep an eye on him, right?" Frank asks. "We can send someone to talk to him. That's not against the law." Frank knows this is another threat to the enlightened movement. He will be sure to send a report on this development.

"We already have assets moving into place, Frank," Henry responds. "Now we need to get down to business. We have assets in several hot spots...." The men discuss the technical aspects of American Special Forces that are deployed around the world. Frank wonders how he can control the assets that are assigned to monitor the situation in California.

Chapter 25, The Word Spreads

The sun rises over the fertile hills of the Manchurian province. It is a rare day that Xi sleeps in. He's snuggles closely with his wife. As he wakens, he hears the sounds of his teenage boys doing their chores. The cows are mooing, the ducks are clucking. He hears the pigs begin to eat as they are fed their morning slop. "Sleep some more, my dear. I'll get your tea and start our breakfast. You had a big day yesterday," Wu coos into his ear.

Xi throws the covers aside and springs out of bed. "Yesterday may have been a big day, but today will be even bigger. I have to get to town. I'll have tea and a rice cake with honey. Have the boys yoke up the donkey to our cart." Ten minutes later he's on his way to town. He knows the communists will not sit idly by and let the rebellion he started the day before stand.

How can he keep his rebellion peaceful? He has no answer to that question. He resolves to give himself up to the soldiers rather than see his village decimated. He started the rebellion. He'll stand up for its consequences. His resolve hardens as he nears the village.

And then things begin to change. Neighbors who just days ago would barely talk to him, come out with smiles and greet him warmly. 'Thank you for letting me know about God,' 'I feel redeemed,' 'I know that I'm not a slave,' are comments that he hears.

Xi starts to realize something. For almost a century these people have toiled for the state with no hope for the future. Christ offers them hope. Once this miserable existence is over, there is a heaven, there is a future. What does anyone have to live for if your existence stops when you die? But if there is life after death, in heaven? That changes everything.

As Xi gets closer to the village, he becomes caught up in a traffic jam. Not a traffic jam of commuters late for work. It is a traffic jam of carts burdened with produce, and livestock ready for market. Donkeys and oxen pull carts and wagons ladened with goods, along with a few trucks, all heading to the village. Xi wonders what the heck is going on. He questions one of the farmers driving a dozen goats along the road to the village. "What's going on? Why are there so many people on the road?" he asks the herder.

"You haven't heard? There is a wise man in the village. He can make your crops and herds multiply. He even talks about a God who offers eternal life."

Xi stops for a minute. Then he starts talking with the young farmer. "It's not the prophet that nourishes the crops and the flocks, it is God. The prophet is just proclaiming God as creator and Savior. It is God who is giving us abundance. Do you believe this miracle has come from God, young man?"

"I got a dozen fat goats that two days ago were thin and scrawny. I want to meet this prophet and thank him," the young farmer replies.

"Don't thank the prophet, thank the one true God who sent him." Xi moves along as quickly as he can through the crowded lane. He needs to get to the village square to tell the true message.

He comes into the village square and sees pandemonium. Farmers and merchants are everywhere, some squabbling, some waiting patiently. One of the village elders sees him and marches up to him with several of his guards. "Do you see what you have caused? These people expect their herds to be blessed. They think you have some kind of magical powers. How are you going to address this crowd? We need to calm things down before the state quashes us. There are troops on the train scheduled to arrive tomorrow morning. It will get ugly if we don't show a united front supporting the state."

"I started this, let me help to make things right," Xi responds. "Will you allow me to take to the stage? I promise you; I will speak the truth to the gathered people."

"The state considers us in rebellion. You need to bring these people into order. Say what you need to say." The elder makes way for Xi to speak from the village square.

The elder introduces Xi to the crowd from the ramshackle stage in the center of town. The large crowd dutifully quiets down. "I know you are all excited about the events of the past few days. We're all happy that we met the state's allotment and still have plenty of food for our families. It is my pleasure to introduce the man who helped this happen. Some say he's a prophet; some say he's a man of God. I call him my neighbor and friend." The elder turns the stage over to Xi. He hopes the man can make things right. His life is at stake if the soldiers arrive and determine the village to be rebellious. He knows what happens to village elders who cannot keep their people in line.

Xi prays silently before addressing the large crowd. He prays that God speaks through him and that he's faithful in proclaiming His Word.

Xi walks up to the microphone with confidence. "We're all God's people. He created us and he loves us," Xi states boldly. "The state enslaves you. God gives you freedom. With God, you have eternal life. With the state you only have death. It is God who blessed your crops and flocks. Join me in knowing God and having eternal life. Come and be baptized."

The crowd is in shock. They expected some dribble about the state being in charge. To hear a message of deliverance through God was not what they expected. The village elders are dumbfounded and shocked. Rather than recant, the prophet has doubled down. They begin to argue amongst themselves.

From the stage in the town square, Xi continues. "Yes, there is more to life than fulfilling the states quota. We trudge along all day in fear of the soldiers, in fear of the state. Our lives are spent trying to please the masters, trying to meet a quota. When we fear the state, our lives have no meaning."

"What if we spent our days praising God as our Creator and Father? What if we acknowledge that we didn't evolve from some creature that crawled out of a swamp, but were created by God, in His image? What if we spent our days loving our neighbors instead of resenting them? Look around you. Do you appreciate your life? If you acknowledge God, your answer will be yes. With God in your life, you begin to appreciate even the grass you walk on, you begin to understand that the whole world is a miracle. He created the mountains, the rivers and every living thing around you. And He created you too!"

"My friends, we've been trained to worship the state as our provider. But that is completely false. It is we who provide the state. And It is God who provides us with the means to keep the state satisfied. We need to worship God! He's the provider. The state is a leech that drains our blood. Jesus, God's son, shed His blood for us. He does not ask for our blood, He asks for our love. Come, join me in offering your love for Jesus. Be baptized in the Lord."

As Xi is speaking, many people move forward and join him on the town stage. The jail guard and several of his friends come forward and discreetly take positions to protect Xi as they have been trained to do. A dozen of Xi's church members come forward to stand with him including the couple he freed from the jail. A few farmers, who witnessed their cows getting fattened for the scales come up to the crowded stage. Even two of the village elders come forward to stand with the prophet. Some of Xi's church members bring a barrel on stage, full of water, and Xi begins to baptize new believers.

"Can you believe the audacity!" a woman exclaims.

Her husband responds. "Yes, I do believe." He makes his way towards the baptismal line.

A banker turns to a prominent store owner. "He's going to bring down the wrath of the state on us all. And some of our elders are joining him. We must make plans to show we have no part in this."

163

"You are part of the state, you have made me pay bribes for years to get the loans I needed," the businessman replies. "This man doesn't ask for any bribes. He asks for truth and justice. Through his God he gives a purpose to our lives and offers a life in heaven! I want to believe in something bigger than meeting our quota. I want to believe in something bigger than turning a profit at my store. You can stand here and abide by the state. I'm casting my lot with this prophet and his God."

"What? Are you kidding me?" the banker stammers. "You'll cast everything aside to follow this rube and his fairy tales?"

The store owner turns back to the banker. "I never believed that my forefathers crawled out of a swamp." A smile breaks out across his face. "This God that Xi speaks of, He created me, and He loves me. That is something that gives me hope. Come my friend and join me."

The banker snarls and turns away. He begins to take mental notes. He knows he'll need to defend himself against the soldiers who will be arriving the next day. He'll save himself by turning in his neighbors. Hundreds are lined up to be baptized. Sounds of singing and praise fill the air. The feasts and festivities he sees around him disgust and trouble him.

"Tomorrow will be completely different", he says to himself. "I won't be part of this rebellion." He turns and walks back to his home, a four-bedroom condo with a new kitchen, complete with leaky pipes and drafty windows.

He makes a full report and sends it to his superiors. It eventually is read by a man in a dark office on the shores of the Black sea.

Chapter 26, Set Up

"How can I help out?" Julian hears once more as he checks on the coals in the roasting pits.

"See Joan, she needs help in prepping the tables and tableware," he responds without even looking up. He turns to his right and hollers loudly. "Pit two is ready for cooking." Two men bring over a rack full of split chickens fully seasoned and marinated. They place it over the roasting pit. They quickly bring over another rack and place it over the other side of pit two.

Julian moves back to pit one. "Amy, Mike, be ready to rotate both racks. Rack one should be flipped in ten minutes, rack two should be flipped in thirteen minutes." His volunteers move into action. They are used to Julian's exacting demands, having helped cook many meals for various service projects. They do what is asked and set timers on their phones. They make harmless jokes as Julian rushes away to ensure the serving crew is getting set up.

"If I didn't love that man, I'd hate him," Mike quips.

"He's a demanding boss, but he knows what he's doing," Amy replies. "It's like the iron chef meets Joel Osteen. The people gathering here have no idea that their meal is being prepared by a five-star chef. Set your timer, let's not upset the man." In the distance they hear the sounds of their praise band setting up and tuning in.

***

"Jerry, can we get a sound check," Lisa shouts.

"Give it a go," Jerry hollers back.

"Do re mi fa so la ti do," Lisa sings into one of the mikes. The sound check goes on as the band sets up their equipment and begins to get ready for the night's program.

While this is going on, other volunteers are bringing out tables and chairs. In just a few hours, over a hundred volunteers have shown up to help get the grounds ready for the impromptu event. The pastor's one call has worked small miracles. Now they are getting ready to release the invitation to the public.

Georgeanne, the social media optimizer, along with Pastor Mike, a few church elders, and Clarissa, have been working to get the message right. The editing is done, the music has been blended, the message has been fine tuned. There are two videos to be released. One is forty-five seconds long. It is powerful, showing the parting of the waters and an invitation to tonight's event and ending with a great tease. The second is three minutes long with more facts and more intrigue, but with the same compelling video and the invitation to come to their event.

***

Shawn walks out and looks over the church's complex, he is stunned to see the activity. He smells the aroma of the roasting chickens. He hears the praise band warming up. He sees the volunteers setting up the tables, chairs and side tents. 'Is all this for me?' he thinks. 'What am I getting into? I'm not ready for this.'

"If I am with you, who can stand against you? You are to proclaim my Word," Shawn hears. *"Do not be afraid, I will be with you."* Shawn straightens and looks around. Where did that come from? His mind calms down. It came from God.

As he sees all that is going on, he smiles and begins to gain some confidence. He looks at the stage at the back of the large pavilion. He sees a challenge. He runs straight at one of the picnic tables set up outside the pavilion. He leaps onto it, then springs up toward the roof of the structure. He grasps the edge of the roof and pulls himself up. He rushes to the peak of the structure where he stands and looks over the church's campus.

166

He stands twenty-five feet above the ground on the peak of the pavilion's roof, smiling. His acrobatic antics have gathered a few spectators. One of them is Julian. "Hey you, this is not a playground. Get off that roof. Who do you think you are? This is not your personal jungle gym. We have serious business to be conducted here."

Shawn smiles at the man and winks. "I'll be right down my friend." With that he turns and runs down the roof, leaping as he reaches the eave. He crumbles into a ball as he hits the ground and rolls once before springing to his feet. He turns toward Julian with a smile. "No more gymnastics my friend, I promise."

Julian looks at Shawn, a frown crossing his face. "Young man, we have serious business to conduct here. You are distracting my people. Why are you here? Maybe we can help you."

"I'm here for the same reason you are. We've been blessed by God with talents, gifts. We're to share those talents." Shawn looks at Julian's apron. "I take it you have been blessed with culinary skills. Thank you for being here."

"Yes, I'm a good cook," Julian responds, smiling proudly. "I like to share. People would pay a lot of money to eat tonight's meal at one of my restaurants. Tonight, people will be treated to my skills as God's blessing. But who are you, roof runner?"

"I'm no different than you. I'm doing what God called me to do. God called you to cook good food. God called me to proclaim His Word."

Julian looks at the young man sternly. "You are the speaker? You are the man who parted the waters, as I have been told?" Julian steps in closer. He looks over Shawn skeptically. "You are a brat. But you take care of your body. You have clear eyes and good teeth. God uses us all in ways we don't understand. I like you. Come, have some bruschetta. Nourish your body."

A helper quickly appears with a plate of appetizers and they talk a bit while eating. Julian is brusque, but genuine. Shawn can see his heart through his demanding personality. As they finish their small plate, Julian leans in and hugs Shawn. "Speak the truth, young man. Speak the truth." As he steps away, Julian wipes a tear from his eye. Then he turns abruptly towards the roasting pits. "Did you turn the racks on number three? Rotate the racks on number one. Let's make sure these people get properly cooked chicken tonight. We have a reputation to defend. Our guests get only the best, our 'first fruits' just as the Bible tells us."

Shawn stands there for a moment. He wipes a tear from his own eye. He looks around at the bustling crowd. Some are incredibly talented people. Like the members of the band, doing sound checks and rehearsing. Others are blessed with the diligence to do the mundane; and do it with joy. The people butchering the chickens, the people setting the tables, the people getting ready to embrace a crowd of strangers. None of them will be recorded in history as making a great mark. But all of them will be recorded in God's book. All of them will be gaining a greater seat in heaven, even if their chore for today is to set up chairs for this evening's event. Not because of what they do, but because of why they do it.

Shawn turns and heads towards the church office that he saw from the peak of the pavilion's roof. He wonders what new developments he'll find there. He's glad he took the time to exercise, limber up. He feels better about the upcoming event.

Entering the administrative door to the church, one of the church's secretaries recognizes him and leads him to the pastor's office. He knocks softly before entering. "I understand there's a conspiracy going on here to free the people of the constraints of this world. I'd like to offer my services to this glorious agenda."

Clarissa looks up with an eyeroll. "Always the grand entrance," she says. The group laughs.

"This is what we've come up with to release on social media," Pastor Michael states. "We didn't want to release it until you had a chance to review it."

Georgeanne hits the play button and both segments are played. Shawn watches in silence with the rest of the crew. No one says a word. After the two segments play, Shawn speaks up. "I still can't believe that was me. I'm still dumbfounded. I don't know my Bible that well, but I do know we're encouraged to pray. Let's all pray." Shawn starts, asking for the Lord to give him words to use him to glorify His kingdom. The others join in, praying in different ways for the evening's event. Pastor Michael ends the prayer seeking God's blessing on all they do.

"So, let's release these videos and see if anyone responds," Georgeanne states.

"Go for it," Shawn responds. "Do you really think we can get a crowd here in only three hours' notice?"

"I have two million followers," Georgeanne responds as she hits the post button. "A lot of them live here in the LA area. God is moving this project. People will come to see the man who parted the waters. People respond to miracles."

"What about all the fires?" one of the church elders asks. "The winds are whipping up and two of the major freeways are threatened. There's also a new fire in the hills around Malibu. They are telling people to stay home so those that need to evacuate have safe travels."

Pastor Michael frowns as he recalls his scriptures. "Do we flee in the face of the fires? Or do we call more people to God's kingdom to fight the fires? We're doing God's work."

Chapter 27, The Return

"I must return to Syria, to Damascus," Mustafa states definitively. "It is the land where Christ's disciples first proclaimed His Word to the Gentiles. Then I will make my way to Jerusalem. You have friends, make this happen or I will walk to Damascus on foot. You cannot keep me here."

"We're making plans, my friend," the Orthodox priest replies. "It may take some time. We just can't fly into Syria unannounced. We have to clear the way."

"God will clear the way," Mustafa responds. "I know people. Here is who you call." Mustafa lays out a plan that includes many high-level contacts and their phone numbers. "Tell the people who you talk to that I have an extremely important message to deliver. These people know me, they will make things happen. I need to make a few calls myself to make arrangements for our security detail. I have people I can trust in Damascus."

***

The Orthodox priest meets with his friends in the church's dining hall. "He insists that he returns to Syria, Damascus to be precise."

"We can't let him go," an older priest responds. He has been told to keep Mustafa in their area of control. He is not sure why, but the directive was very firm, so he persists. "He brought almost a thousand people to the altar last night. Our church is filled with people today. This man speaks in a powerful way. If he goes to Syria, he'll be killed. We can't let him go."

"You tell him that. He has given me the plans on how to get to Syria. Am I to tell him it's too dangerous? I'm to tell a man, who has literally faced down tanks on the battlefield, that it is too dangerous to go to Syria? I would rather join him in his mission than stand against him!"

The priest has an epiphany, he would rather go to Syria with Mustafa than sit with these stodgy priests and proclaim the Word to their dwindling congregation. He makes a bold proclamation. "I will help him return to Syria. And I'm going with him. You can help us, or you can stand aside. The Word needs to be proclaimed. Jesus did not shun sinners, he embraced them. The Bible tells us not to shun our enemies; we're to embrace them. We still have churches and believers in Syria who are under attack. We can't let them wither and die. Here is a way for us to embrace our brethren with the possibility of growing the church in Syria. Can any of you deny this opportunity?"

"It is a fool's errand," the older priest proclaims. "I am the senior priest here and I say this mission should not take place.

This statement falls on deaf ears. "I will go with you too," the young priest states. He looks around at his sullen compatriots. "This is the spark that is needed to start the fire. I have family in Syria. They are starving to hear the Word. We have a brave man, a called man, let's follow his lead."

Mustafa joins the group with a large tray of food and a friend. "Hello, my friends," he says exuberantly. "Let me introduce you to Jon. I have known about Jon for many years. He has provided ISIS with a lot of valuable intelligence. It took me a bit to track him down, but with God's help, I tracked him down." Mustafa sits down and starts to dig into his meal. Between slurps and gulps he tells of how he knew about and found Jon. The priests are aghast, the on-call repair man for their church was an ISIS spy! "Jon and I have had a long talk. He's on our side now. We're going to liberate his sister and her family who are in northeastern Syria. In return he's going to help us. It is something he has always wanted to do, but he feared for his sister's life. He's going to feed false information to ISIS and the Syrians. A double agent as the Americans would say. Now, let's get down to planning this mission. Funny, mission has a whole new meaning to me now." He laughs and smiles at his new friends.

171

The group discusses the plan to get into Syria for almost an hour. There are two sides, and they are firm. The Church establishment will not condone sending them to Damascus; too many of their clergy have died or fled already. The two enlightened priests are dead set on going with Mustafa. They firmly believe it is God's calling.

Mustafa turns to the leader of the establishment group. His eyes are piercing and true. "You cannot stop us from going to Syria. I have resources and contacts to make it happen. God is with this mission. We do not ask for your permission or your blessing. All we ask for is your support. We ask for access to your logistics and communications. If you cannot grant us that, then I will dust the dirt from my sandals and move on."

The recalcitrant priests know this direct Biblical reference. Jesus said to move on if your message was not being received. They are being referred to as one's to be left behind. The reluctant priests look at each other and communicate silently. The older priest sighs. "We do not condone this mission, but we will support it. God sent you to us, and you have worked wonders. But God has other plans for you. We will not stand in God's way."

***

Mustafa works his contacts diligently all afternoon, making preparations for their flight into Syria. He's a wanted man for betraying ISIS. He makes arrangements to give himself up to the main Imam of the largest mosque in Syria. He's assured that he'll not be turned over to the murderous ISIS mercenaries, but will be subject to the Imam's decree. Both of his new priest friends are apprised of his plans and they begin to wonder. They are willfully walking into the belly of the beast. Are they strong enough to do this?

They walk with Mustafa to a small plane. They have no luggage; they have no supplies. "What are we to do when we get to Syria?" the young priest asks. "It seems we're walking right into the hands of the enemy."

172

Mustafa smiles and laughs. "All my life I have been walking into the fire. I think God has always been preparing me for this. Just as God was in the furnace with Shadrack, Meshack, and Abednego, God will be in the fire with us." Mustafa laughs a belly laugh as he recognizes an irony, a God thing. "It is three of us just as it was then. God is consistent in those kinds of things. Let's go my friends, into the fire, into the furnace!"

They board the small plane and begin their flight to a small airstrip in the Bekka Valley. During the flight, Mustafa regales them with stories of his time as an ISIS fighter. He tells them of being held captive by the CIA for two weeks. "Waterboarding! That was the best they had! We're trained for waterboarding. I laughed at them. No, it is ISIS to be afraid of, they have no conscious. They will cut you, beat you, burn you. They look at Christians and Jews as less than human. Therefore, they feel they can treat us as beasts, as an owner would treat a disobedient dog, yet worse." He tells of his six months in captivity by rival Muslims. He opens his tunic and shows the scars that riddle his body. "I told them everything they wanted to know, except the truth. A man will say anything when he's being tortured."

The young priest turns pale at the sight of the disfiguring scars. He cannot imagine the pain Mustafa had to endure. The older priest has seen these scars on people who have been captured by ISIS. Sometimes they are let go to tell their horrific stories. More often they are crucified, burned at the stake, or killed in some other horrific way. ISIS, Boka Haram and the Taliban are well known to treat infidels with utter disregard to their humanity.

Seeing the trepidation on his fellow travelers' faces, Mustafa has concerns. These are men of faith. It is their calling to proclaim the Lord. Then he thinks for a minute. Proclaiming the Lord to your parish, to your neighbors, is fulfilling the Lord's mission. But proclaiming the Lord to all the nations; that is not something that is ordinarily done. Proclaiming the Lord in the heart of Islamic territory, when you know you are going to be taken as prisoners as soon as you land, certainly these two have reasons to be afraid.

173

Mustafa has been in prison before. He has been tortured. And now he has Christ! He has nothing to fear. His two new friends do not have the same footing that he has. He faced death fearlessly without Christ. Now he faces death with Christ. Now he is truly fearless. He prays for clarity, he prays for his companions, he prays for their mission and the people they will meet. He knows his calling is to reach the unreachable; teach the unteachable. He was part of ISIS, he was one of the unteachable. But he was only unteachable because the true Word of God was not allowed to be proclaimed.

He'll break that barrier. He'll reach the unreachable.

As the plane begins its final approach into the Bekka valley, he ends his personal prayers and prays with his friends. Then he gives them a few words of advice. "Keep quiet as much as possible. I will do the talking. Do not let anything scare you. God says many times to not be afraid, He is with you. We're walking into the valley of our enemies. If we do it with the confidence that God is with us, then no one can stand against us."

The tires of the small plane touch down on the baked tarmac of the remote airfield. The passengers look out at the parched fields with scrub grass clinging to life here and there. It is a barren area. Mustafa knows it is the perfect place to start a revival. He walks to the plane's door. As he turns to speak to his fellow passengers, the earth rumbles. Not a minor earthquake. A serious earthquake. The ramshackle buildings that make up the airport's tower and maintenance facilities begin to crumble due to the heaving of the earth's core. The tarmac and air strip begin to rip apart as the ground moves in violent undulations.

174

Chapter 28, Fires, or food?

It is late afternoon, and the church grounds are swarming with people. Over two hundred volunteers are on site, more are streaming in. The video of Shawn parting the waters has gone viral. It has created a media buzz that no one expected. Fox News ran a story on it and has even sent a local news crew to cover the evening's event. The sensationalism of the act has even made MSNBC and CNN comment on it. They continue to report it as a hoax, even though the eyewitnesses they interview confirm the authenticity of the event.

As evening approaches, news vans start to converge on the church campus, as well as people seeking answers. Julian takes a moment from his cooking duties and looks at the gathering crowd. It is before five o'clock and his suppliers will still be open. He hands a list to his chief food manager. "Amy, see if you can order more. We need double what we already ordered. We're going to need to feed three thousand, not one thousand." He whistles as he looks at the growing crowd. "We may need to feed five thousand." Amy gets on her phone and starts ordering the required food while sending vans out to pick up what is available from her suppliers.

***

In the church office discussions take place. How will the evening's gathering progress? Who will open? How much music will they play? Do they have the right videos? Pastor Michael asks one of the church secretaries for an update. She peers out the window. "We have at least three news crews and about a thousand people on the grounds right now. I think we're doing pretty good," she smiles as she looks at the pastor.

Pastor Michael wants to smile. He wants to be joyful for the large crowd that is descending on his church. But he is apprehensive. He has doubts. Is this really happening? News crews? A prophet? Thousands of people? If it is true, could this be the fulfillment of prophesy?

Pastor Michael stands. "We need to pray," he states. The people in the room stand and clasp hands. They all feel that something big is about to happen. Seeking God's guidance must be the first step. The pastor proceeds to pray for them all and for what is to come. After his prayer, they all feel relieved and encouraged.

Shawn looks out the window as more people arrive. Over two-thousand people swarm the campus. Cars are lined up to enter the few remaining parking spots. One of the church secretaries is already on the phone with the local police department to arrange for extra traffic control. The local fire department is contacted as well.

Georgeanne chimes in. "This is not going to stop. Expect thousands more to come. This is trending off the scales on my site. And now we have national news media covering us. This is going to blow up!"

Through the open windows, they hear the lead singer of their praise band open up. It is not yet time for them to start, but she instinctively knows to start. The band begins with a few southern rock songs. Songs that bring people together, songs most of them know. Before six o'clock arrives, close to five thousand people have come on to the church's grounds. "Let's get this thing rolling," Pastor Michael states. He walks out of the office and enters the throng of people that have encamped on his church's complex. He takes his time making his way to the stage. Shawn and Clarissa follow along with other prominent members of the church.

The band finishes playing "Lean on Me." Pastor Michael walks onto the stage and grasps the mike. "I'm humbled that so many of you have come here seeking answers. God answers prayers, so let's start this assembly of God's people with a prayer." He waits for the crowd to hush and then bows his head. "Our Father, Creator of heaven and earth, we love You and appeal to Your love. Allow Your love to spill out on those who have come here seeking answers. Allow Your Holy Spirit to enter them that they may spread Your love to all the people in their lives."

The band starts to play quietly, bringing some drama to the pastor's words. "Dear Lord, Your words are not to be preached just here on this campus, at this church. The Bible proclaims that your Word is to be proclaimed to the nations. We know Your true Word is the love of Jesus Christ and the salvation from our sins that He offers." The band grows louder with the beginning chorus of 'Holy Spirit.' "Abba, our Father, Your Holy Spirit is truly welcome here!" Pastor Michael proclaims loudly, just as the band begins singing.

The band sings three songs, entertaining the crowd and setting a mood of praise and worship. One of the church elders takes the stage as the music dies down.

She smiles as she looks out over the large crowd. She guesses that over five thousand people are spread out across their large campus. She glances to the road and sees stalled traffic as more people are trying to get to the event. She is almost overwhelmed; she has never talked to a crowd of this size. She raises her hand and bows her head. The crowd quiets as she prays silently for His grace. As she opens her eyes, she feels strength and clarity.

"Welcome to Shiloh Baptist Church," she states with enthusiasm. "We thank you for coming out for this night of praise and worship. We have a young man who will be speaking to you soon. He has a powerful testimony. For those of you who are hungry, we have food available at our pavilion. There are comfort facilities available if needed. This is a much larger crowd than we anticipated, so please be patient and considerate. Our musicians will entertain you for about an hour while you eat and mingle. Then we will introduce our main speaker. Let me say a blessing over our food." The elder blesses the food and all who partake of it. A migration of people towards the food pavilion ensues.

***

Julian is about to freak out. "We have food for a thousand people. I have more food coming, I have more food cooking. But there

177

are over five thousand people here! How do I feed five thousand with five hundred chickens?"

"Tell the servers to portion the meals and keep on serving," Pastor Michael states. "We will feed those that need fed. These people did not come here for a free meal. They came here to hear the Word of God. That is the nourishment they need."

For an hour, more food is cooked, more food is served, and the line never diminishes. The lead chef of a five-star restaurant scrambles, grumbles, and implores his people to keep pace. He is amazed as the line grows but the food never seems to diminish. As the serving platters dwindle, more food is brought out. As more people step into line, more food is brought forth. Meanwhile the band plays praise music and the crowd gets geared up for the main speaker. They all saw the young man part the waters. They all saw the video. They want to hear from this modern-day prophet. As the sun sets, the band finishes up with a rousing modern version of 'How Great Thy Art!"

The twenty-five-acre complex is overflowing with people. Cars on the street are still trying to find a place to park. People continue to file into the few remaining empty spaces on the sprawling complex. The traffic control officers have to wave people away from the area as the nearby streets are unpassable.

The crowd is overwhelming and exuberant. All the lights on the stage are shut down and a single spotlight shines stage right. The church's technical people know how to stage a show. Shawn walks on to the stage, into the spotlight.

***

Halfway around the world, Xi smiles as he walks onto the rickety stage. He knows that his country will swiftly and violently suppress any uprising. But how can they suppress this uprising? He clearly hears a voice: *'If I am with you, who can stand against you'*. By mid-morning over two thousand people have come to hear what he has to say, despite the imminent arrival of the government train and its mighty forces that will coldly suppress any rebellion.

"Thank you all for coming," Xi starts. "I love that you all came here to hear God's Word. My message will be brief, then you all must return home, as if nothing has happened." Xi pauses, "I have a new message for you. You are all created by God, in His image. You did not evolve from some swamp creature. God loves you and wants to see you in heaven. He came to the earth in the form of Jesus Christ. He died on the cross as the final sacrifice for our sins. We do not owe the state anything. All we have has been given to us by God. We're not here to serve the state. We're here to serve God, our Father and creator. The state offers only enslavement and death. God offers freedom and eternal life. Remember this and seal it in your heart. You are not a servant of the state that only sees you as a tool to further their power. You are a servant of the Lord, who created you and wants to see you flourish here on earth and be with Him in heaven. Tell your family, neighbors, and friends that they don't have to be slaves to the state. I implore you to come forward and be baptized in the Holy Spirit so you may leave this village and go forward to tell everyone you know about God and His love."

The crowd is hushed. Some are crying; they have never heard this type of message delivered with such confidence and power. Others are hushed and bewildered. Who is this man to defy the state so blatantly? But what he says rings true. The state did not create them. Does God really exist?

Baptismal lines form. Two of the village elders, just baptized the day before, help with the baptisms, as do other new converts. Xi's wife shows up with a new box full of Bibles they had hidden in their shed. As they did the day before, the Bibles are partitioned and sent off with the new believers.

The day before, the new believers were treated to a feast and rejoicing. Today the new believers are encouraged to disperse as quickly as possible. They all know why. The government train will be arriving soon. Any who openly proclaim Christ will be arrested.

Two-thousand new believers flee into the remote countryside of northern Manchuria. They barely know the scriptures, but they know God in their hearts. They know they heard a new message, one of love and forgiveness. They carry with them portions of the Bible. They carry with them a message of hope.

"Xi, you must flee with your people," one of the village elders implores. "We're already lost. Our village is in rebellion. We will be jailed and humiliated to make sure other villages do not rebel."

Xi has no intentions of running to the hills. He feels words of wisdom come upon him. "Jesus treated the Roman centurions the same way he treated the prostitute at the well. Paul treated his jailers the same way he treated his best and truest friends. God's love is for everyone. It is easy to preach God's love to the oppressed. Now I must bring God's love to the oppressors. I'm glad you are willing to stand with me. I will stand with you. We will both stand for God."

The elder bows down before Xi. "Truly you are a man of God. I believe in the loving God you proclaim."

Xi reaches down and pulls the man to his feet. "Do not bow to me. Bow only to God. Let us pray." Xi praises God for the many new believers that were baptized this day. Then he prays for their safety and their mission to spread God's Word. He also prays for fortitude to face the challenges to come and for strength to meet those challenges.

Xi looks around. There are only a few dozen stout hearted people around him, all of them are new believers other than his wife and children. The stout guard and two of his friends are nearby. Xi walks over to his wife and two children. "Wu, you must leave. Take the children and go. I will be okay."

"How can you say that?" Wu responds. "You know full well that you are going to be arrested. I'm just supposed to slink into the mountains, knowing you have been arrested and probably killed?"

"I will not be killed. I'm sealed." Xi responds. "Trust me, my love, you must flee. Spread the Word. I will send two of these guards with you to keep you from harm."

"But what about you? Who is going to keep you from harm?" Wu implores.

"God will protect me. I have to do this." Xi looks at the two imposing guards. "Protect them, keep them safe. I'm in God's hands. He'll prevail."

They hear two long and blaring blasts from a locomotive's horn. The government train is coming into the village.

***

"This situation needs to be flipped on its head," Abaddon says over a securely encrypted phone to one of his top lieutenants. "I funded you to establish the radical movements in the United States. Why are your people not disrupting this clearly racist religious movement? Where are your people on the ground? These people moved fast. You need to move faster. Get it done or I will find other ways to get it done."

The woman on the other end of the encrypted call trembles. She has worked for senators and presidents. None of them carried the power of the man she is talking to now. The voice on the other end of the call is the source of all her power. The voice put her into the position of power she now holds. If the voice decides to replace her, then she becomes a liability. That is not something she wants to contemplate.

She composes herself before she responds. "There will be disturbances before the night is done. You will see violence in the cities of America. We will not sit by and allow all we have worked for be torn down." In response she hears a click as the line goes dead.

A similar call is made to a high-ranking officer in the politburo of the Chinese government. The official assures the voice on the other end of the line that drastic measures will be taken to quash the rebellion in Manchuria.

Abaddon leans back in his chair. He knows something is coming that will test all that has been put in place. Everything that has been done over several centuries to devalue life, corrupt people's morals, cause civil unrest and cause doubt in every institution, is coming to a climax. People are starting to fight back against the immorality that he has been spreading. He knows the source of the power that the people are using to fight back. He dreads that power.

Chapter 29, Tremors

The remote airstrip in the Bekka Valley has not seen this much attention since Saddam Hussein supposedly sent his chemical weapons there to hide them from the Americans. Al Qaeda and Syrian troops have secured the perimeter. Representatives from three of the most powerful Imams of Islam are present. Sleek black SUV's line the runway while heavily armed technical trucks prowl the perimeter of the air strip.

Mustafa jumps from the small plane and crumbles to the pavement as the earth heaves around him. Earthquakes are rare in the Middle East. The trembling earth shakes everyone at the remote airstrip to their core. Even the most hardened soldiers are shaken by the violent upheavals of the earth. Some of the technicals topple in the violence. Two of the shiny black SUV's sink into the chasms created by the shifting earth.

As the tremors subside, Mustafa stands on shaky feet to surveil the situation. His friends are dispersed in the SUVs and technicals lined up to greet him. He had told his allies to expect the unexpected. Although Mustafa knew God would be with him, he did not expect and earthquake to be part of his return to Syria. He gains his footing and helps his Orthodox priest friends off the now disabled plane.

Mustafa turns and looks around at the destruction caused to the small airstrip. He sees some of his allies start to emerge from the wreckage. He signals for them to gather and unite. Before any of the other forces can recover, Mustafa is surrounded by his loyal followers. The Syrians, ISIS, and Iranians stumble to their feet as their leaders try to assess the situation. As the dust settles, Mustafa and his crew clearly are in control of the situation.

Mustafa smiles. He knows God made this happen. "Lay down your arms," he commands. "God does not want us to fight. There has been too much fighting. Lay down your arms!" he says in a commanding voice.

Mustafa's men have the rest of the militias in a bad place. For ISIS or the Syrians to fight back would be suicide. They are caught off guard and have no other recourse. If they were to try and fight, they would be decimated. Mustafa is known as a brilliant leader and valiant fighter. The men around him are clearly ready to fight for him. Slowly, the fighters who were set up to ambush Mustafa begin to drop their weapons.

A captain of an elite Iranian unit looks to an Imam standing next to him. "Who is this man who arrives during an earthquake and is able to win the battle without a shot being fired?"

"He is the devil. He must be killed," the Imam responds, as he raises his hands, pretending to surrender.

Mustafa sees the imam rise from behind an overturned SUV. He runs towards the Imam. He once knew him as a teacher at a madrasa he attended as a young child. He breaks out from his circle of protection to embrace the radical Islamist. The Imam's security people are quick to react and take Mustafa into custody. The people Mustafa rallied to protect him are dumbfounded. The man they just risked their lives to help has run into the hands of the enemy.

The imam has no choice but to embrace Mustafa as he runs into his arms. "You have strayed far my son. You have become an apostate. You have been condemned to be crucified."

Mustafa steps back and looks right into the eyes of the Imam. "No, my brother, it is you who have strayed. I'm here to bring you into the fold."

The imam is stunned. He should have been referred to with reverence, not as a brother.

Mustafa's crew is ready to fight, their weapons are held steady as they watch this odd reunion. They have no idea of what is happening. Their crew emerged from the earthquake with the upper hand. And now their leader has run into the embrace of the enemy.

"I have been set free by Christ," Mustafa states, beaming love at his former teacher. "I'm here to share that love with you. You are still under the yoke of the devil. Your duty is to arrest me. Go ahead, arrest me. You will take me to my destiny. But I must have one final word to my friends who helped me get here."

The imam's hands, arms and chest feel like they are burning. He lets go of Mustafa in bewilderment, his eyes grow pale. "You are the one!" the imam exclaims. "What they say is true!"

"No, my brother, I'm not the one. I'm one of one-hundred-and-forty-four-thousand."

The imam spits. "That is blasphemy. No wonder they want you."

Mustafa grasps the imam again. Not forcefully, but gently, turning the imam to face him.

"My brother, you await the arrival of the twelfth imam. He is to crawl out of a well. You taught that tale to me many times, drilled it into my head. But it is foolishness." Mustafa leans back and laughs. "Why would the savior of the world come crawling out of a well? No, the Savior of the world will descend from heaven. He'll not crawl out from the depths of the earth, dirty and soiled. He'll come from heaven, clean and unblemished."

The imam shakes away from Mustafa's gentle hold. He glares with indignation. "You will not call me brother. You will call me teacher! I will not stand for this insolence and blasphemy."

"That is fine by me my friend, let us sit and discuss our differences."

As this discourse has taken place, Mustafa's allies have moved to take control of the airstrip. The ISIS, Iranian and Syrian forces are being disarmed, separated, and secured. The two Orthodox priests have moved close enough to hear this debate. They listen intently but do not go near the two as the debate continues.

Mustafa turns and looks at the younger priest. "Bring us some tea please, and figs. Tell Mahmoud he has done good work in securing the area. Let him know he must be ready to move within an hour."

Mustafa turns back to the imam. "Please, sit with me and let's discuss our faiths. This is important to you and me, but it is even more important to the millions of people who follow your edicts."

"I will not stand for this!" the Imam snarls. "You may have won this battlefield, but you will be crushed. A Syrian battalion of armored vehicles will sweep into this valley soon and sweep you and your infidels from this place."

"Don't be so shallow," Mustafa replies calmly, as he takes a seat on one of the rocks so recently upheaved from the ground. "The battle that is about to be fought has nothing to do with this air strip or this desolate valley. It has nothing to do with tanks and battalions. It will be a battle for the souls of men and women. Do you want to be on the winning side of that battle?"

"I am on the winning side of that battle," the imam declares defiantly. "I will die fighting apostates like you! When the battle turns, I will be the one who cuts off your head and burns your body at the stake. Allah will reward me for killing you."

"No. That is not going to happen," Mustafa replies. The young priest returns with tea and figs retrieved from the disabled plane. The discussion he hears intrigues him and he sits down to listen.

Mustafa turns and smiles at the young man. Then he turns his gaze back to the imam. "Here is a man of true faith. He has come here to spread the Word of God's love. He has already won the battle. You

186

speak of arms and armies. He brings us figs and tea. My brother, why does your heart turn to stone when you can see right before your eyes acts of love? Do you really believe your savior will crawl from the bowels of the earth?"

The imam, still standing, turns and glares. "Your words are wind in the air, meaningless and unheard."

Mustafa looks at the well-known Islamic leader as questions arise in his mind. Wind is not meaningless and makes a loud noise. The imam's words sound wise but make no sense.

Mustafa turns to the imam. He takes a deep breath and exhales in the direction of the imam. A great gushing of wind swirls around the imam and throws him back ten feet. The Islamic leader crashes into a new outcropping of stone. His eyes glaze over for a moment, then he regains his composure.

"I love you, my brother," Mustafa states as he looks at the disheveled imam. "You are right. My words are like the wind in the air. But you deemed the wind to be of no power. Winds are very powerful, and so are the words of truth. I tried to talk with you. I was hoping you would take me to your leaders, into the fire. But you have been stubborn. I shake the dust off my sandals. I will not waste any more time with you."

Mustafa gives the rally signal, and his protectors gather. Fifteen minutes later a rag tag group of fighters and evangelists head south, towards the Sea of Galilee.

Mahmoud turns to his driver as they head towards Israel. "Do you know what's going on? Whose side are we on? What does Mustafa have up his sleeve?"

"Boss, I'm totally confused," the driver responds. "Did you see him blow the Imam into the rocks? He has the power of God behind him."

"We took that airfield without firing a shot. I knew Allah was with us then. But the confrontation with the imam? That was crazy. And we have two Orthodox priests with us? He seems to like to hang with them. This is weird. Now we're heading towards Israel. None of this makes sense."

"Tell me what makes sense these days," the driver replies.

Chapter 30, The Revival

Shawn walks onto the stage, the bright lights shine on him and into his eyes. He has never been on a stage like this. Other than the pool party, he has never been in front of any large crowds. There are cheers and applause as he makes his way to the center of the stage. The lighting crew does some weird things that makes the lights flash and swirl. Many of the church volunteers are professionals that work in Hollywood. They know how to dramatize a stage. This fires up the crowd. They cheer and applaud even more. Shawn sits on a tall stool in the middle of the stage, dumbfounded. All these people are cheering him on. He has always been a confident young man. You can't be a street runner, facing down impossible obstacles without having some self-confidence.

But this is overwhelming. Even though the lights limit his view, he knows there are thousands of people out there waiting for him to speak, and news crews will be recording his every word. Pastor Mike and Clarissa had told him over and over to just tell his story, that God would give him words. He also remembers that they told him to pray. Right now, he wants to hear the voice in his head. *"I am with you, I will never leave you,"* resounds in his head as the spotlights focus on him.

Shawn looks up and smiles. "I want you all to know that I'm scared out of my mind. I'm not someone who comes onto stages like this. But just now, God told me He is with me." He looks up, "Thank you, God," he says sincerely.

He turns and looks out into the bright lights. "Wow. I'm new to knowing God. But when God tells you He is with you, that's a wake-up call! How many of you know God? How many of you know that the power of God is with you?"

There are cheers in the audience. Shawn waits a few moments for the cheers to die off.

"I hear you cheering," he begins, "but how many of you really tap into the miracles that God performs every day? How many of you see the miracles that are happening all around you? When you look into the eyes of a loved one, do you see the miracle of sight? When you look at the stars in the sky, do you see the miracle of creation? When you feel peace in your heart, do you savor the miracle of salvation through Christ's crucifixion and resurrection? Our God is an awesome God! Can I hear an Amen!" The crowd cheers and amens are said loudly and repeatedly.

"Amen brothers and sisters, Amen," Shawn echoes the crowd as they quiet down to hear his words. "Now, we know through scripture that God warned us of false prophets. My friends, the false prophets have been around since the time of Christ, but today, they are squarely rooted in our society. They are the enlightened ones. They tell us to believe in the big bang theory. They tell us there was nothing and then all of a sudden, the universe was created from this 'big bang.' "

"They mock us for believing that God said, 'let there be light'." Shawn pauses. "The smart people say there was nothing and then in some 'big bang' there was everything. Are they telling us the universe happened by accident?" He queries. "In our version, there was nothing and then there was everything, and it happened because God ordered it to happen." Shawn pauses again, then continues. "Yet we're the crazy ones? It doesn't make sense to me that they are following the science and we're religious zealots."

Shawn stands and looks into the lights. "My question to you is which do you believe? Big Bang or Creation? Both say there was nothing and then there was everything. Did it happen by accident? Or did God make it happen? Creation lays out a plan on how it happened, over seven days. Big Bang says it just happened for no reason at all. They say our ancestors crawled out of some primordial soup. We say God created us, that God knows us. He knows every hair on your body. We say we are created in His image and He loves us."

190

Shawn turns and walks back to his stool. He sits down and hangs his head for a moment. The crowd is hushed as they listen to his commonsense argument.

"Were we created by God, or are we the descendants of a lizard?" Shawn asks quietly, his head still looking down at the floor of the stage. He stands from his stool and looks out around the vast audience. The lights still blind him, but he knows the audience is out there. He raises his hands to the sky. "God, I choose you!" He looks out to the audience. "I am not the descendant of a lizard. I am a child of God! Loved, adored, and forgiven! Each and every one of us is a child of God, loved, adored and forgiven!" He sweeps his hands around pointing at the vast unseen crowd as he makes this proclamation. The crowd erupts in applause, cheers go on for several minutes.

"Shawn, step aside for a minute," he hears in his ear. He looks around, dumbfounded, is God talking to him again? "Shawn, the band is going to play 'Child of God', then you can continue, you're doing great," the stage manager tells him through his earpiece.

The band comes on stage and plays 'Child of God' and 'So Will I'. The audience becomes even more enthused.

Clarissa and Pastor Mike talk briefly with Shawn while the band plays. They give him encouragement and pray with him. "You are speaking God's Word," the Pastor states. "Say what is in your heart."

As the band winds down, Shawn walks back on stage. He motions to the band to bring it down but to continue playing. He looks over the vast crowd intently, causing some to feel angst. "We need to pray." He pauses. He bows his head. "Please pray with me. Dear God, You are my Lord and Savior. I'm a sinner but through Jesus Christ, Your Son, I'm forgiven. You are my Father and Creator, and I believe in you." Shawn looks up and smiles. He knows that people prayed that prayer and souls were saved.

The band stops playing as he sits back down on his lone stool in the middle of the stage. He wipes some sweat from his brow. "You all probably think I'm a preacher, that I could go on citing scripture and telling you about the Bible and what it says. In reality, I'm just a punk, a street runner, a college kid with no background in theology. But God spoke to me a few days ago. He told me to proclaim the Gospel. I wanted to run and hide. But God did not let me do that. I came to the realization that God is real, that He loves me and that He has a plan for me."

"Some of you probably saw the miracle of me parting the waters. But I didn't part the waters, God did. He did it to bring us back to him. I'm just the messenger." Shawn pauses as he shrugs his shoulders and looks around. "Why am I to be the messenger?" he asks the crowd with humble honesty. "I'm nobody."

He walks to the front of the stage. "God called me to be the messenger. I'm to let you all know that you are to be messengers too!" he states passionately. "No one knows the time of His return, but it is coming! No single person can spread the Word. We all must spread the Word. And the Word can only be spread through love. Christ gave us two commandments. Love God and Love your neighbor. I implore you to do both. Don't just say it, live it."

"As I said, I'm not a preacher so I'm going to wrap this up right now, no long sermon. If you have come to Christ this evening and want to be baptized, please come forward to be cleansed of your sins. If you are already a Christian but want to be anointed to renew your commitment, please come forward. And to all of you, know that you are a child of God." The band starts playing softly again. "Please join me in a final prayer. Dear God, we invite Your Holy Spirit into our lives. We ask that You guide us and inspire us. We ask that we always feel Your presence in all we do. May we bring others to come to know You through our love and our actions. In Christ's name we do pray, Amen."

The band breaks out in full song, starting with 'Holy Spirit'. Hundreds of people line up to be baptized or anointed. Shawn's short talk inspires the crowd. The Holy Spirit moves them. The actions of those present will move people around the world.

***

The news media wraps up their coverage. No waters parted, No fire and brimstone. No miracles from their point of view, just another evangelist speaking nonsensical religious diatribe.

"This is Jane Roberts reporting for KLAW at Shiloh Baptist Church. To wrap things up, there was no explanation of the parting of the waters, just your standard come to Jesus sermon. To sum it up, the pool party was a prank, a stunt to get us here. Back to you in the newsroom. Reporting for KLAW this is Jane Roberts signing off." The young woman signs off figuring her feature won't even make the eleven o'clock news. Nothing happened.

She turns to her cameraman and small production crew. "Well, we can wrap this up. Did I hear something about the fires nearby? Maybe we can get something newsworthy there."

The camera man licks his fingers. "Did you get any of this chicken? It's amazing. The coleslaw and potato salad are the best I ever had. Hey, Rich did you get an extra plate for Jane?"

The crew leader replies, "before you pack us up for another assignment, put some food in your belly, Jane." He hands her a brimming plate of food. "I think we should do a story on the food. This is amazing. More people would go to church if they knew they served food like this."

She intends to turn up her nose at this offering but the aromas from the plate are too enticing. She takes a bite out of a chicken leg. It melts in her mouth in a burst of subtle flavors. She takes another bite and relishes the taste of the meat. She lives on take-out dinners and prepackaged microwaved foods. This chicken is as good as any five-star restaurant she has ever been to. She tries the side dishes; they melt in her mouth.

"How does a podunk church put out a meal like this?" the reporter asks.

"Maybe that's the story," the producer suggests. "They fed thousands of people a gourmet meal. Maybe we could do a goodwill story on that? The editors always like a goodwill story. I know you wanted miracles, but this might be something we can roll with."

***

Minutes later the news crew sets up near the church's bar-b-que pits. After a few inquiries, they manage to get chef Julian for an interview.

"Chef, I'm extremely impressed with the food you have provided today. How were you able to provide a quality meal to thousands of people?"

Chef Julian is disheveled. His apron is dirty, his chef's hat is askew, his face is smudged with grease and flour. He looks at Jane sternly. "You have no idea! I cook the best for everyone, beggars or paying customers. But this, this is crazy! This is a miracle!" He gestures all around as a wide smile crosses his face.

He grabs Jane's hand firmly. "Let me show you." He takes Jane and her crew into the firepit area where the last few chickens are being split, rubbed with spices, and put on the grill. Around them people scurry to fill the final orders for the assembled crowd while other volunteers start to clean up.

"We're used to cooking for large crowds," Julian states. "We ordered food for a thousand, which we got delivered in one day! That alone is a miracle. At four o'clock we saw the size of the crowds and knew we needed more, so we ordered more. But the crowd grew! We have cooked nonstop for six hours. And I tell you this, everyone gets my best. I don't cut corners."

Julian pulls Jane in closer and talks in almost a whisper. "How did this happen? I still have food. We have fed over five thousand people! We did not have enough food to feed even two thousand people. Come and help yourselves to more. We have plenty."

Jane pauses. There has to be an explanation. "Well sir, not everyone here may have come to get something to eat."

"No, we count everyone who comes through the line," Julian responds. "We have people designated for that purpose. Five-thousand-four-hundred-and-sixty-four people have been fed. And we have food left over. Would you like to take some home?" Julian asks sincerely.

Jane does not know what to think. How does she make a report out of this that the editors will post? The headline would be 'Miracles happens at church event, Thousands fed'. That's not going to get her on the nightly news. That's not what the editors are interested in broadcasting.

"Where's the street runner? The one who parted the waters?" Jane asks, hoping to get some kind of story that will make the news.

Julian looks toward the stage and clearly sees the young man that has rattled him yet inspired him. "He is at the stage. I'm sure he'll welcome your questions." He points the way for the news crew. Jane and her crew make their way to the stage where many people are still lined up to be baptized or anointed.

As the news crew approaches the altar, they are stopped by a friendly but vigilant crowd. "We just want to film what is going on, so we can report on what is happening here," the producer states honestly.

"Would you film and publish the birth of a child?" a woman asks.

The producer is taken aback. "No, not without permission."

The woman responds, "asking Jesus Christ into your life is being reborn. It is not something to be filmed like a documentary. It is a holy thing. Please respect that." The woman looks at the producer with eyes that are alive and glowing. "Do you know Jesus as your Savior?"

"I know who Jesus was, a first century philosopher who preached love and respect. He was executed by the Romans for telling his followers he was the Son of God," the producer responds.

"Then you do not truly know Jesus, young man," she responds. "Why do you think they call it the first century?"

"Oh, come on, we all know that is based on the birth of Christ, but that is a western culture thing. Many countries go by different dates. Surely you have a better reply than that."

The woman looks at the young man with curiosity. "Do you know where Jesus is buried?" she asks kindly.

"Um, well, ah, at the temple mount, right?" the producer responds.

"Are you sure of that?" the woman asks. She pauses a minute before continuing. "The temple mount is where the original temple to God was built by King Solomon. It is where Jesus was tried and sentenced to be crucified. Seek out any historical records you want. Jesus was entombed and his tomb was guarded by Roman soldiers. After three days the stone was rolled away; Jesus rose from the dead. His death and resurrection atoned for all of mankind's sins. Go ahead and check your history mister reporter man. There is no historical record that denies any of Christ's miracles and his resurrection. Your job is to investigate things. Why don't you investigate that?" she asks sincerely.

The producer is caught off guard by the simple yet logical statements of the Christian woman. He stands flatfooted. He assumed most Christians went to church because that's what their parents did.

He thought it was more of a ritual than a belief. He thought the true believers were just hoodwinked rubes. Jane Roberts has listened to this exchange and is intrigued. These people truly believe in the fairy tales told in the Bible. She decides she has to interview the 'prophet'. There has to be a story there, a way to expose the charade. She pulls out her press pass and asks a person who seems to be helping usher the crowds if she can have an interview with Shawn. The elderly man looks at the press pass and then back at Jane. He ponders for a moment before responding. "I'll see what I can do, Miss Roberts."

A few minutes later, the elderly man returns and beckons Jane and her crew to follow him. He leads them to a small pavilion in the middle of the large amphitheater, it is obviously their production facility. The light and sound crews are still breaking down and packing up their equipment. "Make yourself at home. Shawn will be here shortly. Is there anything I can get you? Water or sodas, maybe something to eat?" They all say they're okay and the elderly man heads back to his duties.

The producer looks around at the engineers who are breaking down the equipment. The production equipment is of high quality. A bit dated, but almost as good as what they have at their own studios. He is impressed at the efficiency and care taken by the volunteer staff. The church volunteers make small talk with the production crew and answer all their questions. The production crew comes to realize that the volunteer church staff is just as knowledgeable and capable as they are. For the most part, the church volunteers all work for some of the area's production companies, they are all skilled technicians and engineers.

Soon they are left alone to wait for their interview. As they are waiting, they hear a disturbance in the distance, people shouting and yelling. They see people moving towards the disturbance and the news crew is about to move to see what is going on. But the disturbance quiets, then they hear singing and rejoicing. A few moments later a large crowd passes by, heading towards the cooking pits where Julian's people begin feeding the new crowd of people

Shortly after that, Jane sees a tall and charismatic young man approach their pavilion with two young people; one is a striking young black woman, the other is a woman of Asian descent. The three stride with confidence towards them, laughing and smiling. As a news reporter, she is used to people being serene and austere, intimidated by her presence. The jovial, almost joyous mood of the three people approaching her throws her off balance.

The Asian woman approaches Jane first and extends her hand with a smile. "Hi, I'm Georgeanne Haquani, I'm Shawn's media consultant. We're completely open to an interview with you, but we will be having our people record the interview too, okay?"

Jane stops for second, the name rings around her head. Then she recalls hearing about her as a social media darling among religious and conservative circles. And she wants to record the interview herself? She could get blown up for asking misleading questions or performing biased edits. Damn this new media. Ms. Haquani probably has more followers than she has as nightly viewers! She is going to have to play this straight and tight.

"That's okay with me, Georgeanne," Jane replies with a tight smile. "I think the more open we can be with each other, the better informed the public will be." Jane watches as some of the same people from the church that her crew were just complimenting as being professionals, set up to film the interview.

Shortly, Shawn and Jane settle into two chairs to start the interview. The lighting is all set, the microphones are in place and the sound checks have been completed. The interview begins.

"Let me introduce you to Shawn Masters. You all saw him perform the parting of the water's mirage Yesterday at the public swimming pool. I have an exclusive interview with him now. Let's see if we can find out how he performed this trick of the eye."

Shawn smiles. "Jane, you and all your media friends keep calling it a hoax, a prank, or as you just said, a mirage. God works miracles. He worked a miracle yesterday to help wake people up. I'm here to help people wake up from their sleep. Our society crumbles as we walk farther and farther away from God."

"But no one can part the waters. Do you really expect us to believe God did that?" Jane asks.

"Well, Jane. You can only believe in miracles if you believe in God," Shawn replies. "Do you believe in God?"

Jane stutters for a moment. She knows she'll lose half her audience if she says yes. She is the one who is supposed to ask the questions. Her crew will not be able to edit what the social media queen releases. "What I believe is not the question. What do you believe?" Jane asks.

"Actually Jane, you are right. It does not matter what you believe," Shawn states, turning to look into the camera. "What matters is what the people watching right now believe." Shawn turns to Jane. "I love you, Jane. I want to see you in heaven. I want you to believe in Christ as your Savior. But my mission is not to proclaim salvation to just you. My mission is to proclaim salvation to the thousands if not millions of people watching."

Shawn reaches across and lays his hand on Jane's knee. She feels an energy like she has never felt before. She jumps back in both surprise and fear. "Jane, do not be afraid. You have a mission too. You need to speak the truth. Quit hiding from it. Make a choice; truth and freedom or deceit and lies. The choice is yours. God has always given us that freedom. We can believe in Him or we can deny Him. What happened when God parted the waters yesterday, it was a miracle, it was a wakeup call for all of us. God's redemption is coming. It is coming soon."

Jane feels a power around her. A power she cannot deny, but she fights it. She has been told all her life that the Bible is a fairy tale. The big bang theory and the theory of evolution are known science. Or are they? It is all theory. None of it is fact. Her mind swirls as all she believes comes into question. Is she the result of an amoeba crawling out of the primordial soup? Or is she created by God? How can she abandon all the science that has been drilled into her head for her entire life?

She pauses to regain her focus. Her production crew can see she is rattled. She looks down for a few moments, then looks back up, her eyes clearer. She looks at her producer. "Three, two, one," she states to let the producer know she is ready to continue. Her pause will be edited out of the news cast.

"So, you think you are here to proclaim the return of Jesus Christ? Every generation has a crackpot that says, 'repent now, the end is near'. You don't seem like one of those crackpots. You seem like an intelligent young man."

Shawn relaxes in his chair. "I don't think it, Jane. I know it. I'm here to proclaim Christ. I don't know if Christ is coming today, or tomorrow or in five hundred years. But I do know I have been given a mission to proclaim God's Son as our Savior."

Shawn leans forward and points to his forehead. "Do you see this scar? It is a seal. Jane, there are 144,000 people spread around the world right now who have this seal. They are the 12,000 descendants from each of the twelve tribes of Israel as foretold in the book of Revelation. I'm a descendant of Abraham. I can recite to you my heritage back to the original tribes of Israel. If you want a real news story, go out and find the others who are proclaiming Christ."

Jane smiles, she knows she has a crackpot story that the editors will eat up. "If you know you were sent by God to perform miracles and proclaim Jesus as our Savior, why don't you perform a miracle right now. Prove it to us."

Shawn smiles again, which confuses the reporter. She knows she is just one step away from tripping up the religious zealot. But he seems unfazed by her snappy reporting.

The comely young black woman walks over with a stool and sets it down next to Shawn. She smiles at Jane and the camera crew. "Jane, the miracle is happening right now," Clarissa states. "Thousands of people are hearing and seeing a report on the return of Jesus Christ. Thousands of people are being awakened. Jane, you yourself are doing God's work. You are helping to spread the good news. I pray that you are strong enough to do the job God has given you."

Jane's jaw literally falls open. She wants to use this interview to expose the religious zealots. They think this interview will spread the Word. She thinks back. What have they said that is so alarming? That people were created by God and did not evolve from a Lizard? Quite frankly the idea that she evolved from a lizard is a bit revolting.

Clarissa looks directly at Jane. She pulls back her frizzly hair and puts it into a bun, clearly exposing a mark above her temple.

Jane's eyes open wide. "Is that a mark? Are you sealed like Shawn said?"

Clarissa smiles. The joy and love that beams from her smile almost melts Jane's heart. "I saw Shawn in heaven singing Christ's praises. I'm a descendant of Abraham too, as are you. You have a job to do, Jane. You are a reporter who is supposed to report the truth. I pray you report the truth. That decision is up to you and your team."

"Three two one, that's a wrap," Jane's producer states. He is conflicted by what he has heard and seen. His mind races as he directs his crew to break down their equipment. He thought as Jane did, that they would expose some Christian zealots as crackpots. Their editors would eat it up. But he does not think that story will fly. No matter how much they edit the tapes, the story these people told was genuine. Not to mention what will get released by Georgeanne, the media consultant. 'Report the truth' rings around in his head as he walks up to Shawn to thank him for his time.

"You speak powerfully for such a young man," the producer says as he shakes Shawn's hand. "Jane normally rattles the people she interviews. You managed to rattle her. You spoke truth to some of the things I have been questioning. I'll try to make sure you get a fair hearing in the final edit."

Shawn clasps the man's hand firmly. "God loves the truth." He looks the producer in the eye with love and compassion. "Don't question any longer, embrace God. He knows you are in a tough position. You need your job to take care of your family. If you push too far, you may lose your job. You need to know that God will provide. If you follow God's calling, He'll take care of you. Scripture says that God takes care of even the smallest sparrow, so surely He'll take care of you."

"I believe in what you are saying," the producer responds. "But it's hard to embrace. If I were to edit this news cast the way I feel I should, I would lose my job. I have kids to feed, a mortgage." The man turns and starts to walk away.

Shawn clasps his hand and pulls him back. "The truth will set you free," he states with conviction. "I have a news tip for you. Earthquakes are occurring all around the world. The USGS has shut down its own site or altered the data to keep it quiet. Investigate it. I'll give you my data to confirm what I know."

The producer looks at Shawn bewildered. "How do you know this? Why didn't you mention this to Jane?"

"I'm a geology major at USC in my senior year. I have access to a lot of data including the USGS website. Jane would have just used it for more evidence in writing her 'crackpot' report. Investigate it. It may be nothing. Or it might be something really big."

Then, as if God is speaking the truth, the earth trembles under their feet. A few light stands fall over and the tables full of expensive equipment rattle and shake. The producer ducks for cover. Shawn stands firmly, his arms crossed in resolution as he looks around. It was a minor quake for Southern California, something all long-term residents have experienced. But the significance of its timing is not lost on either man.

The producer regains his feet and turns to Shawn, there is both fear and respect in his eyes. He looks around to make sure none of his people have been hurt. Assured that all is okay, he returns his gaze to Shawn. "I will do my best to make sure your story gets told truthfully." He gives Shawn his card. "Email what you know about these earthquakes. I've seen other reports from around the world. The Chinese are worried the Three Gorges Dam may be compromised if there are more quakes in that area."

Shawn takes the man's card and hugs him. "Know that God is with you. He knows every hair on your head. Do not be afraid, for if God is with you, who can stand against you?"

Chapter 31, Assessments

General Shapiro looks around at the few select staff members that surround him. "Reports of weird and strange things continue to pour in from around the world. The president is not pleased with what I have been able to tell him. The earthquakes continue to happen across the globe as do other disturbing events, like the antipolice riots that broke out in several cities last night. On the other side, there are reports of religious zealots popping up all over the place. These are not your wackos with a sign board saying the end is near. These are everyday people who are preaching Christianity boldly and loudly, and they are gaining traction.

"Let me go through the list: A woman in Argentina, the president of a worldwide cosmetics conglomerate, was interviewed on their most popular morning TV show and had an alter call with over five thousand people in attendance. In Nigeria, a crowd of twenty thousand people attended a sermon given by a schoolteacher. In France ten thousand Catholics attended mass outside the remains of Notre Dame. In Los Angeles the street runner college student that supposedly parted the waters at a public swim party drew over ten thousand people to an event last night. He made an even bigger splash by having a report on the event this morning on a national news program. The reporter actually gave the young man some credence!"

He looks around the room at his trusted advisors who are supposed to have a handle on everything that is happening around the world. "What the hell is going on! Can someone give me a logical explanation for all of this?"

"You missed a few things, General," Henry, his intelligence officer states. "There is a Christian uprising going on in Manchuria. The Chinese government is aware of it and apparently has not been able to stop it. The movement now encompasses a large part of the rural farmlands and is starting to spread to the larger towns and cities.

The Gideons have taken notice and have launched a program to move thousands of Bibles into the area."

"We can't leave out what happened in the Bekka Valley," Frank states, he is the general in charge of operations. "Our foot-washing ISIS fighter left Albania with two Orthodox priests and flew into a remote airstrip in Syria. He apparently allied with ground forces ready for his return. Here's the weird thing. The moment the ISIS traitor stepped foot on the ground, there was a massive earthquake. 7.2 on the Richter scale. The men loyal to the traitor apparently were warned this would happen, because they were unfazed by the quake and immediately took control of the airstrip. Two dozen men loyal to the ISIS traitor took down a hundred Syrian, Iranian and Hezbollah fighters in a matter of minutes."

"A reliable source tells us that the ISIS traitor talked with one of Iran's lead imams who was there to capture the apostate. The discussion did not go well, and the ISIS traitor literally blew the imam to the ground. Listen to this, our source says the traitor blew the Imam to the ground like we would blow out a candle!"

General Shapiro rolls his eyes. "Tell me, where is our ISIS rebel going now?" Then he raises his voice. "And why the hell haven't you brought this guy in! Why do we have a five-billion-dollar operational budget and yet one rag tag ISIS rebel can elude us? What does this guy know and why does half the Islamic world want him dead?"

Henry speaks up. "We know where he's going. He's leading a small convoy of loyalists towards the Golan Heights and the Sea of Galilee. He has a half dozen technicals and a couple of armored trucks. The Israelis know he is coming. We have given them updates, but they seem to know everything that is going on. They have their own drones and satellites monitoring the situation as well as Mossad units on the ground. They apparently have direct contact with the ISIS traitor."

"So, you're telling me we know what is going on. But does anybody have any idea why this is all happening? And I don't want to hear about Biblical prophecy. Every generation since Christ's death has thought that Christ was coming soon. I want geopolitical recommendations on how America can maintain its influence around the globe. How can we use these developments to our advantage? That is what the president is going to want to know. We'll meet again in eight hours. I want concrete answers."

Frank, the G3, assesses everything he has heard. He makes his own report and forwards it to his contact. He questions if he is doing the right thing, but it is too late to turn back. He made a decision years ago. America's never-ending wars have to stop. He will do whatever he can to stop the bloodshed of Americans.

Chapter 32, Rebellion

The landslide on the tracks has been cleared, the government train finally makes it into the village. This is not the normal train with a few dozen cars to haul the produce and livestock back to the major cities. This train has three extra cars; two are full of well-trained soldiers, and one car carries an elite group with an officer that is well known at stopping local rebellions. The elite soldiers move swiftly and efficiently. This rebellion will be stopped. The senior officer has direct orders to quash this religious movement with all haste and by any means necessary.

Xi is taken into custody by two heavy handed guards. A short, strong-willed man dressed in the full regalia of the Communist Party complete with chest ribbons to pronounce his loyalty and service, looks at Xi. He smacks Xi across the face. "You are a disgrace to the country! You were given land and the freedom to work that land. And how do you repay the country that let you live in freedom? You rebel against it with these wives' tales of a God! You are a disgrace! This entire state is now in rebellion. Thousands will die because of your misguided adventure."

Xi is humble and allows the rough handed soldiers to bind him. He does not fight back or attempt to retaliate after the smug officer slaps him. He prays for wisdom and patience as he endures the humiliation thrown at him. He thinks of all that the apostles went through; he is willing to endure anything the communist state can throw at him. He knows his final destination. And he embraces it.

The officer becomes agitated at Xi's silence. "Where is your fight? Do you not have any self-respect? You are a little man. Tonight, I will show your wife what a big man can do. Your seed will be eliminated. Your wife will bear my child!"

"The seed I have planted cannot be eliminated," Xi responds quietly. "I have planted the seed of hope, of salvation. It is like a mustard seed. It is tiny, but it will grow strong, and it will multiply by the thousands, by the millions. You can take my life. You can take the life of my wife and my children. But you cannot stop the Word of God. It has been firmly planted in fertile soil. It will grow and spread beyond your comprehension."

The communist officer pulls his gun and points it at Xi's forehead. "I will kill the head of the snake right now. The snake will die." The officer begins to pull the trigger, bringing back the hammer that will drive the firing pin into the rim of the bullet that will end Xi's life.

"Don't kill him," a junior officer states. "We need to interrogate him. We need to find out who he talked to. How can we stop this infection if we don't know who he's infected?"

The officer moves his pistol a few inches and fires. Xi's left ear rings at the report fired only a few inches from his head. He honestly thought he was going to die, but he knows he has been sealed. He'll be in heaven singing to God when he dies. Does that mean he can't be killed? He does not know. But he does know he is going to heaven. That is all the assurance he needs.

"You are right," the officer states. He spits in Xi's face. "Interrogate him. Round up the village council for interrogation as well." He turns to another officer, "shut down all travel into and out of this precinct. We must treat this like a virus, like what happened in Wuhan. Set up plans to lock down the entire province if we find the infection has spread. These simple-minded people, why can't they just obey the state? Why must they seek a higher calling? Isn't serving the state enough to fulfill their ambitions?" The officer shakes his head, truly pondering these questions. He is fully loyal to the state. He never questions its authority, and never questions the authority he has over the people. It is the way it is. If people begin to believe in God, it will turn everything upside down. This movement must be stopped.

***

Twenty miles away, in a barn full of people, a young woman reads from the Book of Matthew. She stops and looks up. Her eyes are full of light and hope. "How often have we been told to spy on our neighbors? We have been told to rely on the state. We have all known in our heart that spying on our neighbors is wrong. Here is the truth! We should love our neighbors. We should not be jealous of our neighbors; we should embrace them and lift them up. We all know this. But the state has us hating each other. That is not good. Let me read more and then we will pray. My friends, there is a God, and he loves us. We don't have to live under the yoke of the state any longer."

In another village across the Songhua River, a middled aged woman reads from the Book of Psalms. She is a teacher by profession, and she reads with passion and enthusiasm to those who have gathered. She pauses for a moment to look at the people around her. "Can you imagine the love and respect the writer of this poem had for his God? His God is benevolent and loving, so powerful that even the mountains sing His praises. Look at this," the teacher states as she holds up the half inch thick Book of Psalms. "These are all poems written by people praising this God. A God of love and redemption. We're supposed to love our state? A state that kills our babies and treats us as slaves. These poems are written about a God of love. We all know the state does not love us. We're the state's slaves. I would rather trust in this God of love."

The teacher is a woman of passion. Her words reach into the hearts of those who are listening. The holy spirit moves among the crowd, humbling them, quieting them. A group of dissenters gathers. They are a few hardliners loyal to the state. One of the loyalists throws a rock at the teacher. It glances off her forehead, causing a bleeding wound. The teacher's eyes are opened at that moment. She is a child of God. She sees heaven. What Christ sacrificed is fully revealed to her. At that moment she knows. She has a calling, she has a mission to the people of China. A mission of salvation and freedom. She stops reading from Psalms and begins to tell of salvation through Jesus Christ.

"What the heck happened there," one of the dissenters ask? "You hit her in the head with a rock and she digs in deeper?"

At the center of the action, the teacher proclaims salvation through Christ. Eternal life in heaven. She asks for all that are willing to come forward and be baptized. She is fully moved by the Holy Spirit in both her words and actions. As she talks, her mind is filled with the words of God. Her words truly become God's words. And people come forward to be baptized in Christ. Word spreads of a miracle happening. The Chinese do not even know what a miracle is. So, they come to see. And they hear the Word. And they become part of the miracle.

***

Xi is abused by the state's soldiers. He is whipped and beaten. The village council is brought in to watch as he is interrogated and abused. The communist officer paces in front of the council. He has to report back to a senior politburo member about what he has found. He must be thorough and relentless. "We know some of you helped this happen," he says to the council members. "We have statements from your fellow councilmen. We know who you are. You not only let this man spread his fairy tales of a God, which is against state regulations, but some of you have embrace this God."

The state officer cracks a whip on Xi's back. "There will be no dissension in this village. There will be no dissension in my precinct. The spreading of some fairy tale religion will stop right now. We know that science has proven there is no God."

Xi, strapped to the whipping post, prays to the Lord for strength. He prays for strength for his new believers, that they may fight back. "I will suffer so that others may live, Lord. I pray that you give others the strength to stand up and proclaim you," he prays out loud.

One of the council members speaks up. "I'm one of the people who has embraced Christ, I helped start this uprising. Put me on the

210

whipping post next to my brother." The councilman steps forward and kneels next to Xi, fully willing to bear the consequences of his actions. He knows he may die. He knows his family will be exiled, possibly killed for his actions. He prays for their souls, that they have heard the Word and accepted it. The whip cracks on his back, ripping through the fabric of his threadbare smock and drawing blood.

"Round up his family," the precinct officer sneers. "I will rape his wife in front of him. I will rip out the hearts of his grandchildren as he watches. I will castrate his children in front of the entire village. Unearth his parent's bodies and feed the rotten bones to the pigs. We will make an example of this ungrateful heathen."

***

Halfway around the world, Abaddon watches the scene play out live on a high-definition computer screen. He hears and sees every word and action through the Wi-Fi camera on the officer's helmet. His lips grow wet. His heart palpitates. This is what he lives for. This is what his god Baal, wants to see. He feels his own power grow as the apostates are belittled, brutalized.

***

The elder prays once again, as the whip cracks on his back and blood stains his garments. "Dear God, protect my family. Cloak them from this evil. Allow your Holy Spirit to infect them with the will to proclaim your love and salvation. Allow them to know that the state is not triumphant, that You are triumphant."

The officer hears these words and is enraged. He turns to one of the burly guards. "Beat him. The state cannot stand for such insolence. Beat him to an inch of his life."

The guard hesitates. "He is praying to his God. How can I beat him while he is praying?" the guard asks, not fully grasping the situation. He knows he should obey the command of the officer. But his heart tells him not to. "Let him finish his prayer, sir," the guard states humbly.

The officer looks at the guard with cold eyes. He raises his pistol and shoots the guard between the eyes. "The infection has spread to our own ranks," he states as he looks at his second in command.

Unnoticed, a young man slips away from the crowd surrounding the public beatings. He finds his friend, a grandson of the village elder. Word of the beatings, threats, and execution spread quickly. Some choose to stay and be reckoned with. Others choose to flee. Those who have accepted Christ pray together for strength and wisdom. They all feel an enlightenment. Those who will be staying will see God soon. Those who are fleeing, will be spreading the Word. They are scared and shaken. But they feel an inner peace. They have been afraid of the state for their entire lives. Now they have something to look forward to. Now they have a purpose.

The older man from Xi's church who had time to study the Bible gives them all a scripture to guide them. "Remember these words of God; 'If God is with you, who can stand against you.' Now go and proclaim Christ. Dust off your sandals and move on when you need to, but stand firm when the time is right."

"Father, aren't you coming with us?" a young boy asks. "Who will be our leader?"

The older man smiles at the young boy. "You have a better leader than me. You have found the Holy Spirit. Even in your darkest hours, He'll be there to comfort you. Follow His path."

Hundreds of people flee the village, commissioned to spread the Word of hope and salvation. A few committed souls stand to face the wrath of the state. The older Christian has seen miracles happen that he never thought could happen. He is going into town to see if there are more miracles in store. He is going to free his pastor from the whipping blocks. He knows his pastor's work is not yet done. He has no plan other than to expect miracles.

Chapter 33, New Mission

"What are we doing? Where are we going?" the driver of the technical asks his navigator.

"Mustafa has everything under control," the navigator states calmly. "He told us to be ready when he landed, to expect the earth to move. I thought he was just being dramatic, but he was right! The earth freaking moved! My friend, Allah is on our side."

"But why did we truss up and bind our allies?" the driver asks. "Whose side are we on? We have always fought alongside ISIS and the Iranians. Yet we just trussed them up and fled the scene. It would have been better if we had killed them. Now they know who we are. They will come for retribution."

"There will be no retribution, my friend," the navigator states. "Mustafa blew the Imam down. He put him in his place. Mustafa is the one who has Allah on his side. We need to stick with him. He has been called."

The driver follows their small convoy through the desert landscape of southern Syria. They are heading towards the volatile area of the Golan Heights, an area controlled by the Israelis but under constant attack by the militant Hezbollah militia, allies of the Iranians. They will soon be coming into the Hezbollah controlled area of southern Syria.

The driver is not a geopolitical philosopher. But he is smart enough to know things are out of whack. "What happens when we hit the Hezbollah checkpoints? They have to know we're coming. What happened back there at the airport, surely Hezbollah knows about it. We have two Orthodox priests with us. We'll be killed as apostates. They won't wait to hear our side of the story."

"That's not our problem, my friend. I'm sure Mustafa has that all figured out," the navigator responds. The navigator is the commander of their technical which holds four men, the driver, the navigator, a gunner who mans their machine gun, and a fighter whose duty is to keep the machine gun loaded and to provide security as needed. They are all hardened fighters for the Islamic cause. Despite their young age, they all bear the scars of men who have seen combat.

The lead vehicle of their convoy pulls off the desert road. It is a fully up armored Hummer with a fifty-caliber machine gun mounted on the turret. The Hummer is one of many resources the militant Islamist acquired from the United States Army after it left the area. The other ten vehicles pull off as well, forming a defensive perimeter, prepared for any attack. They see Mustafa call for the leaders of his convoy to join him. Soon ten men stand and listen to Mustafa's plan.

Mustafa embraces all the loyal fighters that helped him take control of the Bekka Valley airstrip. He thanks them for now following him on their current mission. His embrace is strong and loving as he reunites with many fellow battle-hardened fighters who he has shed blood with. Over the years they have fought together, they have lost friends and family members. They have bound each other's wounds on the battlefield. These fighters have placed their trust in Mustafa. Mustafa has placed his trust in them.

As the camaraderie starts to wan, the navigator asks a question all his comrades want to ask. "Where are we going, leader? We're headed towards the Golan Heights and Israel. What is our mission?"

Mustafa stands tall and looks around the people surrounding him. There are ten commanders and about fifty fighters in his small army, nothing more than a heavy platoon. "We're going to Megiddo," he pronounces with a smile. "We're going to be at the site of the last battle."

The people around him are hushed. Megiddo? The site of the last battle? Armageddon?

215

Mustafa speaks up over his people's murmuring and confusion. "We're going to fight the last battle. I have seen it. I'm to be there. You all will be there too. Do not doubt me." The two priests are stunned by this statement. More so than Mustafa's allies.

"Megiddo is in Israeli held lands," one of the combatants points out. "We have to cross Hezbollah lands and then the Israeli's checkpoints. I can see us getting through the Hezbollah lands, but how do we take an armed convoy into Israel?"

"God is working miracles," Mustafa states. "We all should have been killed at the airport in the Bekka Valley. But God was with us. Now we're going to move through the lines of the Hezbollah militia. You saw how the power of God blew down the imam? The Imam was preaching hate. Our God is a God of love, not hate. That is what we have been told, right?"

The men around him mumble and grumble. They are men of war, they are fighters. It has been drilled into their heads from a young age that to die in battle for Allah is the way to heaven. They also have been told that Allah is the God of love. So how do they turn away from Mustafa's preaching? Megiddo is the site of the final battle. They all want to be at the site of the final battle. That would be the highest honor. It would secure their place in heaven.

Mustafa continues as his men ponder his words. "God has shown me the gates. The gates will be open for us. The final glorious battle is coming soon. Follow me to glory and freedom."

These words rally his men. They are fighters. They know all about the last battle at Megiddo. If Mustafa will lead them there, they will follow. They know it will take miracles, but they have already seen miracles. They have no idea of the miracles yet to come.

As the navigator gets back in his vehicle, a question lingers in his mind. "Mustafa kept referring to God, not Allah," he says out loud. "That is a Gentile word."

"What, boss?" the driver asks as he looks at his commander. "Is there a problem?"

The navigator is confused but he follows orders. "No, no problems, follow the convoy. We're going to the place of the final battle. Mustafa is on a mission and God will work miracles to make it happen."

***

General Shapiro has been on the phone, using up favors and offering favors. His people have finally located Mustafa and they can see he is heading towards the Golan Heights. They have no idea why he is heading that way. There is some concern that he is looking to link up with the Hezbollah fighters. "General, that can't be his aim. There were Hezbollah fighters at the airfield. He had his people hogtie them. He wants to get to Israel," Henry, his G2 states.

"Why would Israel accept him?" General Shapiro asks. "He's a bull in a China shop. He's wrecking everything he comes across."

"General," Henry responds, "he declared himself a Christian and defied all of Islam. He's an apostate worthy of being stoned to death. He wants to get to Israel where he'll be safe. We need to do everything we can to help him. Once he is in Israel, we can have the Mossad pick him up."

"I don't know," the general responds. "He is causing mayhem with the radical Islamists. Maybe we just let him roam around Syria and Iraq and continue to cause mayhem."

"That's a bad idea and you know it. If this guy wants to get to Israel, then we have to help him. If he manages to get through the Hezbollah checkpoints, then we need to make sure he gets through the Israeli checkpoints too. You have the contacts to make that happen."

"Okay, okay," General Shapiro responds. "If this guy wants into the Holy Land, I'll make sure it happens." He makes a few phone calls and is stunned by what he hears. He shouldn't be. He always underestimated the Israeli intelligence resources. The Israelis know all about Mustafa's small army and where they are heading and why. One of Mustafa's commanders is a Mossad resource.

After hanging up the phone, the general turns and looks at his two senior advisors. "The Israelis are going to assist his arrival. They want to talk with him as much as we do."

The general leans back in his chair and looks at the ceiling. "Earthquakes are happening to an extent that the USGS has shut down so the public can't see its data. Fires are burning around the world, more so than any global warming activist could ever explain. And Christian zealots are popping up all over the globe."

"Earthquakes happen, we know that," the general begins a rambling stream of thought, talking to himself as much as he is talking to his advisors. "So do fires. We know there have been more fires because we have neglected our forestry management. But all these disasters happening at the same time. Is it coincidence? Or does it mean something? Add to that, a bunch of people show up and proclaim God's retribution is coming soon."

The general looks up and addresses his staff. "The same questions persist. How does this effect our diplomacy and how we position our armed assets? A few nut jobs around the globe and some natural disasters should not affect our military or economic influence, right?"

Henry, the intelligence officer, speaks up. "Quite frankly, a few agitators in the right place with the right message can totally disrupt the world as we know it. We have game planned this many times. But we have always game planned it with people promoting a communist or socialist message."

Frank, the operations officer, adds his opinion. "Socialism and communism never work out, so our scenarios always showed us winning. But the message being delivered is different. Our computers and our programs are not built to figure in a religious movement like this."

"So, it comes back to this zealot trying to get to Israel," General Shapiro states.

"No, it is more than that. Our reports of a religious revival are worldwide," Henry replies. "We must look at this as a vigorous religious revival and we cannot discount all the other events that are happening around the world. Too many coincidences."

The general rolls his eyes. "So, this is some kind of God inspired event? The final battle is coming as the earth is destroyed by massive earthquakes and raging fires? Don't come at me with that crap right now. I have too much on my plate as it is. Let's deal with what we can control, with what we can understand. I have to report to the president and joint chiefs with something solid. We'll start by focusing on the Middle East. Then we'll plug in additional information and possible actions we can take. I need to offer a commonsense report by tomorrow morning."

Chapter 34, The Big One

"This is Ken Mathews reporting from KLTV. As has been predicted for many years, a massive earthquake has hit the Los Angeles area. As you can see behind me, there are fires burning everywhere and the loss of life is expected to be very high. Off in the distance, you can see downtown Los Angeles. You can see that the skyline has been decimated. I'm reporting to you remotely because our studios are not operational." The reporter looks down. "Oh my God," he states. He looks back at the camera, tears pouring from his eyes. "I'm sorry people, I want to be professional, but I know thousands of people have died. Our studios have been crushed, people I know and respect are dead. I have to sign off."

A national news anchor starts to speak. "This is a rapidly developing situation. A massive earthquake has hit the Los Angeles area. That was the latest report available by satellite that we have from our local affiliate in Los Angeles. The city has been rocked by this massive earthquake. We don't have much to go on as most cable and internet connections are down. The United States Geological Survey says it was an eight-point five earthquake on the Richter scale. As you could see in his video feed, fires are burning everywhere. But more significantly, the towering skyscrapers of downtown Los Angeles have been leveled. It is early morning on the West Coast. Normally tens of thousands of people would have been in those buildings. If fifty story buildings were toppled, how many residential buildings have crumbled?" The newswoman fights to maintain her composure. Tears start to pour from her eyes as she thinks of the devastation. "We must pray for those people," she says as tears flow down her cheeks.

The news cast switches to another anchor. "Breaking news. Just minutes ago, a massive earthquake devastated the downtown Los Angeles area. We have reports of large-scale destruction. We're trying to get live feeds from the area, but internet and cell service have been completely disrupted. Initial reports show that the skyline has been toppled. From what we have been able to learn, the buildings were built with buffers to withstand an eight-point-two earthquake. The earthquake was an eight-point-five according to government sources."

The news anchor looks up at the camera. "People, this is serious. I'm the third person that this story has been handed to, because everyone else has broken down. People, I have family that lives in the Los Angeles area. This is not a normal earthquake. From what I'm seeing there is widespread destruction. Pray. Please pray. I'm not a religious person. But I ask you to pray. At some point in everyone's life you come to realize that there are things that are out of your control. At that point, you realize there is a God. At that point you pray. This is Ron Samuels signing off."

"Don Jenkins here to continue our reporting of the massive earthquake that has hit Southern California. We have reestablished our live video feed with Ken Matthews from KTLV. Ken, we turn it over to you."

"I'm here Don, I'm okay. I have a job to do, and I'll do it as best I can. What I can show you, Don, is not easy to see. If you look in the distance, that is what used to be downtown Los Angeles. All the major buildings are toppled. The tops of some buildings are resting on other buildings. A tremor could bring more buildings down. Let me have my camera man adjust the view to show you what else is happening." The screen pans and yaws as a new view is brought into place. The screen is full of fire and destruction. The blaring lights of fire trucks can barely be seen in the chaos. "As you can see, the fire departments and EMS teams are doing what they can, but the situation is way beyond their control. Don, this city has been hit harder than anyone ever anticipated. I'll keep reporting as long as I can. We know the world needs to see this. Our vantage point seems safe for now." As he says this, a massive explosion is heard and the picture from the camera rolls and tumbles as the cameraman is tossed to the ground from the shockwave of the blast.

The picture quickly returns to the news anchor in New York who is obviously shaken. "Ladies and gentlemen, the situation in Los

Angeles is very precarious. It seems that a massive explosion occurred close to our reporting team. As soon as we know what has happened, we will let you know. We now bring on Professor Michael Johns, who has a doctorate in plate tectonics to find out what he has to say."

"Professor, this is a massive quake that has caused great destruction. What can you tell us?"

The professor, a wiry man in his middle age looks at the camera with a grim face. "This earthquake is unprecedented in modern times. Los Angeles is on the San Andres fault. Everyone predicted a large earthquake would happen. No one predicted a quake of this magnitude. An eight-point-five magnitude earthquake is beyond belief. The building codes in Southern California were revised for buildings and infrastructure to handle an earthquake of eight point two, which is higher than any earthquake any geologist predicted for the area. The devastation and destruction from this quake will be massive. We're going to see total failure of most of the infrastructure and most major buildings." His face is sour as he reports this news.

"What about other faults?" a cohost of the news show asks. Should people be worried about other fault lines?"

"I don't want to be an alarmist, but my gut reaction is to say yes. This past week has been marked with a significant increase in tectonic movement. The USGS public site has been taken down because of the sharp uptick in activity."

The news anchor interrupts him at that point. "We have our news crew back online from Los Angeles. Give us an update Ken. Are you and your crew okay?"

Ken Matthews comes on the screen. His face is dirty. Blood trickles from a cut on his chin. His shirt is torn at his shoulder. His hair is disheveled. "Ken Matthews reporting from Los Angeles where a massive gas explosion has erupted only a half mile away from us. Our entire crew was blown off our feet and our production truck has been literally blown on its side. Don, it is total mayhem here and we're going to try to get out of the area, to a safer place." In the background the news truck is seen laying on its side. A makeshift crew of people can be seen trying to rig hoists and chains to put the vehicle upright.

"Don, we're going to pan to the left so you can see the fire from the ruptured gas line. Let me warn you, this is a cataclysmic site." The picture pans left to show a huge flame billowing into the sky. "That was a major natural gas transmission line that is on fire, spewing flames a quarter mile into the air. Everything within a quarter mile of the explosion has been leveled and is on fire. We're worried about more explosions like that. There are refineries, pipelines, and storage facilities throughout the entire area. Fires are burning everywhere. Don, I have never reported from a war zone, but this has to be worse. We have a crew working to get our truck up righted. Then we will try to move to a safer place and continue reporting."

The news feed goes back to the seasoned New York network anchor. He does not know he is live and is caught with his eyes wide open and his jaw hanging in shock. As he realizes he is live, he turns to the camera with a grim look. "Our nation has been rocked by a devastating earthquake. You have seen the destruction. It is beyond anything anyone could ever have imagined. People, these are not clips from a Hollywood movie. This is real. "

The co-anchor speaks up. "Don, this just in. We have reports of a tsunami warning for the entire west coast from the Baja peninsula to Alaska and the Hawaiian Islands. There are international tsunami warnings for the entire Pacific ocean all the way to Australia, Japan and China."

"This is an event of biblical proportions, Jane. We now go to our White House correspondent."

"Don, the president will be addressing the nation shortly," a young blond haired reporter states. "Just a few moments ago we were issued a short statement from FEMA. A state of emergency has been declared for the entire nation. Apparently, there is concern that the quake in California may be a prelude to additional tectonic movements around the globe. FEMA has requested that all nonessential workers around the country return home. They have also requested that all schools and businesses close and all travel be limited to essential services for at least the next few days. Don, I have never seen a response to an earthquake like this."

The news reports continue throughout the morning. The death toll is expected to be in the thousands, maybe even the tens of thousands. Video begins to pour in of the toppled skyscrapers and crumbled bridges. An aftershock causes more buildings to fall to the ground. The site is more horrifying than when the Twin Towers fell. A city of twelve million people is decimated. Panic and mayhem are everywhere as people try to flee the fires and destruction. But the highways are decimated too. Every overpass and bridge has fallen or is structurally impaired. The people are trapped in the city that is burning to the ground and crumbling around them.

***

Abaddon licks his dry and cracked lips as he watches the scenes of devastation unfold across the screen of his computer. His heart races as he knows thousands are dead, probably tens of thousands. How many thousand more will die? Maybe it will be millions! He becomes flushed. He turns off his computer and orders a sumptuous breakfast from one of his maid servants. He is not worried that she may report about what she has seen. She is a slave. She has never left his complex from the day she was brought there at the age of fourteen. The food and pleasure she will provide will keep him energized for what is coming.

***

Clarissa looks around at the jumbled mess of their shaken apartment with cracked walls and broken windows. She hears sirens blare all around them; car alarms, security systems and the wail of emergency vehicles heading in all directions. "We knew this was coming," Clarissa states with agony in her voice. "We should have

224

done more to warn the people." She buries her face in the couch and sobs.

The stress is evident on Shawn's face. Did he cause this? Is he somehow responsible for this horrific event? He feels an inner resolve, an inner strength. "Yes, we knew this would happen. But we didn't know when. It was predicted thousands of years ago. How were we to know it would happen today? Clarissa, this is just the beginning. We know. We have to let people know. We have already started that mission. Now is not the time to second guess our mission. Now is the time to step forward boldly. What we have done so far was just preparing us for what we're going to do."

Clarissa raises her head from the couch. Her hair is tossed and knotted. Her eyes are red from crying. Her lips are tight and dry. "I know," she says. "That's what scares me the most. I can't just crawl into bed and let it all pass. I have to do what needs to be done." She falls to her knees and prays. "Dear Lord, give me the strength to follow Your will. Give me the will to follow Your path. Allow me to follow Your path with wisdom and righteousness. Allow me to be Your humble servant."

Shawn raises his bowed head and says "Amen." He then turns and looks at Clarissa. "We should get to your church. They have the resources to start helping people. They also have people who can help to guide us."

* * *

By video conference, General Shapiro meets with the president, the Joint Chiefs of Staff and the president's national security staff. The president's first question is very blunt. "Could any of our adversaries have caused this? Could this have been caused by some weapon we don't know about?"

His chief of staff speaks first. "That question has been discussed. There is no evidence of any subterfuge. This was strictly a natural disaster. It was an earthquake no one could have predicted."

225

The scowl on the president's face is less pronounced at this news. "If some bastards made this happen, that would have been an act of war," he states as he looks into the conference call camera and addresses his joint chiefs of staff and his national security team, the most powerful people in the world. "So, what can we do to help out the people in Los Angeles?"

"We're trying to determine the extent of the damage and what facilities are still operational," the head of the air force states. "We think John Wayne International Airport in Orange County can be made operational by the end of the day. Then we can start to airlift people and supplies."

The head of FEMA speaks up. "We're gearing up a massive rail and truck effort to bring supplies and people to the area. The city is essentially destroyed. We need to treat this like a rebuilding effort in a war-torn country. They will need mobile hospitals, pharmacies, and food distribution centers. But first we need to get the civilian population stabilized. They need EMTs and fire fighters right now, followed by debris removal crews and skilled construction crews to get essential services back up and running."

"An evacuation option needs to be looked at," the vice president says grimly. "There will be millions who will just want to leave. And that might be a good thing. If we can help people relocate, it will make clean up and rebuilding easier."

"You're all looking at tomorrow, even next week," the president interjects. "What can we do today? I want concrete action. I want mobile medical hospitals activated, I want search and rescue teams with search dogs on planes within the next hour. I want firefighting crews dispatched already. I want the west coast fleet fully activated. I don't want to talk about it, I want it being done. We can't let a major American city burn to the ground."

The president turns and looks around the room. Half the people he looks at are physically in the room. The rest are present through video conference. "What happened in Los Angeles is the most important event of the day, but are there any other issues that need to be addressed, especially anything that might be connected to this earthquake?"

The Special Forces general tries to bite his tongue. He tries not to speak, but he can't hold back. "The earthquake in Los Angeles is not the only tectonic anomaly that has happened recently. Over the past week there has been a major increase in tectonic activity around the world. Mr. President, did you know the public side of the USGS website has been shut down because it didn't want the public to see all the seismic activity?" The room goes quiet as the general speaks.

The Special Forces general continues. "I have told you about the ISIS traitor. The moment he landed in Syria, an earthquake hit the Bekka Valley, allowing him and his allies to take control of the area."

The general decides to go all in. "I have not reported to you what we have determined to be his final destination. He and his small army are headed to Megiddo, the valley of Armageddon, the site of the last battle."

Many in the room gasp or sigh. The head of FEMA is the first to speak up. "End of times? Is that what you are saying? C'mon man. That's right out of the conspiracy playbook."

The Special Forces general will not be silenced. "There are earthquakes happening all around the world. The Chinese are worried the Three Gorges Dam may fail. There are fires burning out of control on four continents. Add to that the religious revival movements that are spreading like wildfire; so, yes, I think an end times situation may be a logical assumption." The three-star general knows he just ended his career. But he had to say it, he had to put it on the table.

Half the people on the teleconference meeting begin talking at once. "That's crazy talk!" "What ISIS fighter are you talking about?" "Where is Megiddo and what is that?" "USGS shut down its site?" "What do we know about the stability of the Three Gorges Dam," "Don't listen to that nonsense!"

The chief of staff speaks up forcefully as the teleconference begins to break down into chaos. "Quiet now, everyone, quiet. This is a discussion, we need to find solutions, not argue with each other. You all heard the president's orders. First priority is to get first responders to the area as quickly as possible, followed by field hospitals and supplies. Evacuations need to begin as soon as possible. FEMA will take the lead in the operation and all military branches will provide all assistance available." Mr. President, do you have anything to add?

"Thank you, George," the president responds. "People, we need to move now and move fast. I don't care if it gets chaotic, because what is happening on the ground in Los Angeles is beyond chaotic. I want planes full of first responders landing as close to the area as they can as soon as they can. I want battalions of rangers airdropping as soon as possible. I want our navy to lift anchor within the hour. Let's get moving now, even if we have to figure out the exact mission later."

"I expect an update from everyone in six hours. That meeting will convene at four o'clock this afternoon. May God bless you all. You are dismissed."

***

"George, what the hell was General Shapiro talking about and why am I in the dark?" The president barks after the secure room has been cleared and all the video connections have been closed.

George takes a deep breath and sits down. "He knows more than we do right now. The rogue ISIS fighter was in one of his briefings a day or two ago when he explained that big dust up in Syria. There have been mentions of the other things the general brought up, but no one has put them all together."

"Why hasn't Colleen put this all together?" the president asks. "That's her job."

228

Colleen Davoe is the Director of National Intelligence, DNI. She is a long-time member of the Washington establishment and has worked her way up through the ranks, starting as an aide to a senator on the intelligence committee then working through the system to her current high-ranking position. "Get her here now." The president demands

Ten minutes later Colleen is sitting in the situation room with the president, the vice president, and the chief of staff. "I got here as quickly as possible sir. I know things are chaotic right now. How can I help?" she asks politely.

"There are things happening that I didn't know about. I'm hoping you can enlighten me," the president responds. The chief of staff plays the short tape of General Shapiro talking about the weird things happening around the world. Colleen sits back and absorbs what is being said on the video, carefully watching the faces of the speakers. Colleen works for someone way more powerful than the president. She has to be very careful in what she says.

"I don't know what your concerns are, Mr. President," she responds calmly. "Most of what the general said I'm aware of and most of it has been reported to you in the daily briefs."

"There is nothing about the USGS shutting down its public site in any of your reports," George states. "And there is nothing about a religious revival. Yet accounts of a religious revival can be found on many local news feeds. Like the guy who parted the waters in Los Angeles and the businesswoman converting thousands in Argentina."

"I can't include accounts of fables and myths in my daily briefings, sir," the DNI says to the president. "The USGS site needed to work out some glitches. It was reporting some hyper-activity that would have alarmed the public."

The president stands in anger. "The USGS site was reporting some hyper-activity a few days ago, so they shut down their public site! Was that a good idea considering what just happened! Tens of thousands of people have probably died, and millions will be affected!"

Colleen shirks at his outburst. "Sir, I didn't order the USGS to shut down its site."

"No, you didn't," he says harshly, glaring at her. "But did you or anyone else tell me? Don't you think the seismographs going off the charts might be something of interest? And what about this guy who parted the waters in California? You don't think significant religious activity is worth talking about?"

The seasoned Washington insider is trying to hold her own, but the president's wrath is directed straight at her. "Sir, getting worked up at a moment like this is not necessary. The country needs you to be cool and calm right now. Many Christian zealots pop up now and again. We have to use discretion in what we report."

"Colleen, I was raised in the church. I went through catechism and all that. I have gone to church fairly regularly over my sixty years here on earth. I'm not an evangelical person. But I know the Bible. Do you know the Bible?"

"I don't know what the significance of the Bible has to do with this situation," she responds.

"Two billion people believe the Bible is the Word of God. Do you think that is significant? The Bible predicts earthquakes, fires, and a great revival before the return of Christ. I think Christ said it himself."

Colleen stands and looks at the president indignantly. "Are you telling me you believe in the myths told in the Bible? All these years I thought you were enlightened. I thought you were one of us!"

The president stares directly at his defiant DNI. "If you don't consider all options, you are negligent in your job. If you dismiss certain possibilities because of your religious biases, then you are not ignorant, you are obstinate." The president sits down and clasps his hands. "I like you, Colleen, you are smart. But you shouldn't dismiss the improbable or even the impossible."

Colleen is a bit shaken, but she sits down. She thought she was on the verge of being fired. She was already anticipating writing a bombshell tell all book.

"I need you to consider biblical prophecy in this matter," the president states. "Something is going on. It may just be the earth's movements. It may be something more than that. You're smart enough to think bigger. You're smart enough to think both Biblically and earthly. I want a report in four hours that includes the biblical implications of what is going on. You have a good staff, get on it."

Colleen stands and shakes the president's hand. "I'll have my staff get on it immediately, sir." As she is walking out the door, she ponders what to do. Her president thinks biblical prophecy may be coming true. She knew he went to church, but is he one of those religious zealots? His request is not normal. But two billion people do believe in the Bible. Is it wrong to include biblical prophecy in her reports? If that is what the president wants, that is what she'll give him. It will include her own bias. She knows what is expected from her. Overall, she is sure it will come to nothing. Now, who on her staff has any biblical knowledge? She can't think of anyone.

Chapter 35, The Battle Starts

The old man hobbles down the lane that will lead him to the village square where Xi and the village elder are being whipped. Even from a half mile away he can hear their cries at the crack of the whip. He winces and stumbles as he hears the suffering cries of the two men. He feels demons trying to attack his weary bones. He carries a Bible in one hand and a walking stick in the other and prays as he walks, commanding the demons to leave him be. He moves as fast as his old bones will allow him. He continues to pray with each step he takes. His strength in the Lord grows as he nears the center of town.

As he approaches the main square, he takes notice of his surroundings. He grew up in this village, he has never left it, he has never been more than a day's journey away from it. The village was never a happy place. Communism and its harsh realities never generate happy memories, but it is his home. It has always been a busy place, a place of hustle and bustle as people bartered and traded, working hard to make a living, and trying to please the state.

Today there is no hustle and bustle. The normally active village streets are almost vacant. He has seen a few people fleeing through the alleys, burdened with loaded packs, toting scared children. The air of defeat hangs heavy as the village is basically deserted. Armed soldiers from the state have taken over.

The old man turns the corner taking him into the main square, where the beatings are taking place. A few dozen townspeople watch and cheer. They are the few who benefit from the state through bribes and favors. He hobbles closer to the scene, unnoticed. To these people he is nothing. They could look directly at him and not even notice he exists. He is a plebe, a serf, a slave to the state. They do not even acknowledge his existence. He continues to approach the town center, ignored by all. He prays to the Lord. "I have been nothing to these people my whole life. They have never acknowledged that I even exist. Dear Lord, may I continue to be nothing in their eyes. I will do Your will, because I know You see me, You love me. I pray that You keep their eyes blind to me. May Your will be done."

The old man continues forward into the square full of soldiers and state loyalists. The few people who do know him do not even acknowledge him as he continues his steady plod towards the two men being whipped. He walks right into the middle of the town square and stands next to Xi. He looks around at the enraged crowd.

"Why do you whip my brothers?" he asks the assembled crowd. "What have they done to harm you?"

The crowd hushes and the whippings stops. "Who said that?" one of the officers asks. "Who questions our authority?"

The old man is startled at their response. "I question your authority," he states boldly. "We have been loyal to the state. We have met your quota, yet you beat this man. Why? He is my friend. The other one is a leader of this village. Why do you beat men who are leaders and who help the state to survive? That does not make sense."

Everyone in the square steps back and looks around, they are blind to the old man speaking to them. "Who are you? How do you know who we are?" a village elder asks as he looks around in astonishment. "This is none of your business. Show yourself so we can talk."

The old man is confused. He is standing right there. The elder who questions him is a long-time friend. "I'm right here you fools! What is wrong with you? Are you blind?"

The elder and the officer turn this way and that, trying to see who is talking. The small crowd begins to disband, feeling something is wrong. Xi and the village elder remain tied to the whipping posts.

The old man can see the people are scared, including the state's soldiers. "Leave now!" he commands. "I will tend to my brothers." He casts his hands out as if to send demons away. The townspeople and soldiers flee, with terror on their faces.

The old man looks around, bewildered. He looks up to heaven. "Thank you, Jesus, thank you God." He knows a miracle just happened. He is not sure how, but he knows God's hand prevailed.

He kneels down and begins to release the binds of the two men. Xi is barely conscious, the village elder is close to death. How is he going to get these two men out of the village? They need medical attention. Where can he go to get these two men the attention they need? Five soldiers seem to appear from nowhere. They have two stretchers. One is a medic with all the supplies an EMT would normally carry. The EMT turns vaguely towards the old man, "Follow us. We believe." The five soldiers trot off with the two stretchers, going in the opposite direction of the railhead and the soldier's encampment.

The old man looks around. The village square is empty. His two friends are being carried away to safety. The state's soldiers are in disarray. He looks up to the sky as he falls on his knees. "Oh Lord! Never let me doubt You. This is a miracle!" The man prays while on his knees and begins to weep as he praises the Lord for what has happened.

A few moments later he feels a jostle to his shoulder, he comes to full alert. "We can't wait any longer, we have to go." It is the EMT that took his friends away just a few moments ago. "Follow me. I'm your sister; you are my brother. You will be safe."

The old man feels a calm as he turns to look at the EMT. He can see in her eyes that she is true, she is a believer. She puts her arm around the old man as they walk away from the village square and the whipping post. "How did you do that? That was a miracle." She begins to question the old man as they walk towards safety.

The old man starts to talk as they leave the village square. "I had to rescue my pastor. He would have done the same for me." As the old man says this, the earth begins to shake. It is not a tremor like they have been feeling for the past few days. This is a violent shaking that causes houses and walls to tumble to the ground. The EMT tries to hurry the old man away from the village, but a piece of wall tumbles down on them. A five-hundred-pound stone lands on the old man, crushing him. The EMT is horrified. The old man just rescued two believers, only to be crushed by a falling rock. The EMT checks for vital signs, as she is trained to do. But she knows he is dead, crushed by the heavy stone. She screams at the Lord. "Why take this good man? I Just rescued him!" As her words echo through what is left of the village, the earth shakes again. She sees the walls falling around her and she flees the scene. There are still two survivors she needs to tend to.

The village elder who lived in the fifth-floor penthouse apartment is with the three senior communist officers when the quake hits. The poorly built building crumbles to the ground, taking the lives of the four highest ranking communist officials in the area. The soldiers assigned to qualm the unrest are left without leadership in the midst of a major natural disaster.

***

Abaddon turns from the computer screens and spits. A victory has been snatched from his hands. He tosses the delicacies that the maid servant had brought. The servant trembles at what might come next. She breathes a sigh when she sees her master begin to brood, ignoring her.

***

The four stretcher bearers stumble as the earth shakes beneath their feet. They struggle to get their patients to open ground, away from the falling rocks of the surrounding hillsides. Their leader, the medical specialist, arrives shortly, making her way through the newly fallen rockslides. She is sobbing as she makes her way towards their hasty encampment. The stretcher bearers have started fluids and administered what limited first aid they know to their two patients.

As the trained medic stumbles into their brief bivouac, she tries to regain her composure. But her strength is drained when one of her crew asks the obvious question. "Where is the old man? You went back to get him. What happened?"

Her mind vividly recalls the rock smashing the old man to death, and she shakes. The Holy Spirit works on her mind as she responds. "He did not make it. He was crushed in the earthquake. But the Lord did not crush us. He has spared us. The old man, a true believer, completed his mission. We need to complete our mission. We have saved the prophet and his helper. We need to complete that mission, just as the village elder, a devout Christian completed his mission."

"What is that mission, sister?" one of the men asks.

The EMT looks up from attending to the deep wounds on Xi's back. She looks at the smile on the face of the village elder who is receiving care from one of her crewmates. How can a man smile after being so brutally beaten? She turns and looks at her crewmate. "We will move on. We will tend to their wounds and then we will move on. These men stepped out in boldness. We will help them. They have a mission."

The EMT turns Xi over, having cleaned up and bandaged all the wounds on his back.

Xi's eyes open and he looks at the EMT. He grimaces. "Thank you, sister," he says feebly. "I have a mission and we must move on. We cannot stay here. The state will be after me. But more importantly, I must proclaim the Lord's Word of salvation."

"We'll move soon, preacher," the EMT replies with a smile. "Before we go trekking across the hinterlands, we need to get you and your friend stable. Despite our crude accommodations, we have saline solutions and other medications to help replenish your fluids and revive your energy." As she attends to Xi's wounds, she brushes the

236

hair back from his forehead. The fresh scar is revealed. For a second the EMT ignores it. But then she starts to think.

"You have a mark on your forehead, a recent scar. How did that happen?" the EMT asks in a hushed voice.

Xi smiles and looks at the young woman attending to his wounds. "God gave me that scar. God marked me. I'm sealed. I'm to proclaim His Word to the nations. Sister, you are supposed to help me do that. God put you here for a reason."

The EMT diligently continues to clean Xi's wounds. Many thoughts race through her head. Finally, she speaks up. "The last person God sent to save you got crushed by a five-hundred-pound rock. So, what happens to me? Am I going to die in a hail of bullets?"

"Does it matter how you die?" Xi asks gently. "We all want to die in our old age, surrounded by our children and grandchildren. But if we die proclaiming Christ's love, is that a bad thing? Are we supposed to die fighting on a battlefield, as the believers of Islam think? With swords in our hands to kill the infidels? No, my sister. Our sword is the truth. Our sword is love, unconditional and everlasting love."

"God does not want you to die fighting for Christ," Xi continues. "When you die, God wants only one thing. He wants you to die loving Christ. Nothing else matters."

Chapter 36, Broadcasting

"End Times. No one wants to hear about it, but we all think about it." The camera zooms in on the well-know news anchor. "Massive earthquakes, raging fires, civil wars. We have all seen disasters in our lifetime, but have we ever seen so many disasters at one time? Our next guest puts this all in perspective. Please welcome Dr. Jerome Yantzy, a professor of tectonic and geologic history at Yale University. Professor, what do you think of what is happening?"

Dr. Yantzy comes on screen, a well-dressed man in his mid-fifties with a trim beard and rimless glasses. "Well Jim, we have to look at this in the totality of the timeline of history. Every generation since Christ's death has thought that Christ's return was imminent. Every generation thinks that the end of the world is coming. Rubbish. First of all, if God created the world, why would He want to end it? I have never received a reasoned answer to that question. But let's move on to the events of today."

"Yes, doctor. Can you put the recent events into perspective?" the news anchor asks.

"Certainly, my friend. The earthquakes are not because God is angry. The earth is angry. It always has been and always will be. Over the past five billion years there have always been violent movements of the earth. Five billion years ago there was just one continent, Pangea. Now there are six. That was caused by the movements of the tectonic plates. The continents move. Sometimes a little every year. Sometimes they move a lot. Yesterday, they moved a lot."

The news anchor looks at his guest intently. "So, you are saying there is nothing to worry about. That this was just some extreme earth movements."

"You are half correct," Professor Yantzy responds. "Yesterday's events were caused by extreme tectonic activity. But to say there is nothing to worry about, that is not correct. I think we will see more extreme tectonic movements. I think there will be a lot more major quakes as the earth settles into a new alignment. The tectonic plates will need to adjust to the major shifts that happened yesterday."

The news anchor's face goes pale, he tries to maintain his composure. "So, you think we can expect more violent earthquakes, Doctor? Can you tell our viewing audience where you think they may occur?"

The professor looks down, thinking through his answer. He is an academic, he wants to answer responsibly, truthfully. After he thinks things through, he looks at the news anchor. "This shift in the tectonic plates was very violent. No one predicted it. Any fault line could be suspect right now. Yellowstone could blow its top, or any one of the volcanoes on the Pacific Rim could erupt. The New Madrid fault line could heave like it did two hundred years ago. We have never seen this much tectonic activity. We know this has happened in the past. But it has never happened in the past few hundred years."

The camera zooms back to the news anchor. "That was Dr. Jerome Yantzy, one of the world's leading experts on tectonic activity. What we have experienced may just be the beginning as he tells us the earth's crust needs to adjust to yesterday's seismic movements. With that, we shift to our crew in Los Angeles where fires still burn from yesterday's massive earthquake. Joan, what can you tell us."

"The scene here is horrific, Mike. First responders and search crews are all over the city, but they have not even come close to the downtown area where there are major buildings that have crumbled to the ground. I'm here at the Rose Bowl in Pasadena that has been designated a first aid and refugee site. It has already been overrun by those who have been left homeless from the horrific earthquake. I have reports that John Wayne Airport is overrun too. FEMA is trying to bring in needed supplies and search crews. Mike, it will be days until the people here can stop the fires, let alone finish up with search and rescue missions."

"What about evacuation missions?" Mike asks.

239

"In a way, that is a bit of good news. Bus loads leave every few minutes. It is heartbreaking to see them leave. These are people who have lived in Southern California all their lives. But, they know their homes and neighborhoods have been leveled. They get on a bus not knowing where it is going. It could be Denver. It could be Wichita Falls. They just want to get away from here, even if it is with only the clothes on their backs. Mike, these people are scared."

***

Twenty miles to the northeast of the Rose Bowl a church is the center of activity for their local recovery effort. The damage in their area is not nearly as extreme as in downtown Los Angeles. The night before, many people came to know Christ and many more were anointed as His apostles. These commitments are not ignored. Just after the crisis occurred, people started arriving at the church, some needing help. Most wanting to help. By ten in the morning a thousand people have gathered at the church.

"What do we do?" an associate pastor asks. "These people are here to help. We're not set up to provide disaster relief. We send money and mission crews around the world to help disaster relief efforts. But we have never done this so close to home."

"We figure it out," the lead pastor responds resolutely. "Do you think the people in Puerto Rico knew a hurricane was coming? Do you think the people in the Sudan prepared for a civil war? Yet we sent them money and people to recover. They figured it out and moved forward. So will we."

"We need to start moving these people into work crews," Julian states. "I know the cook team and can get started with at least a soup line. I have people who can scrounge for food. We should also set up a first aid team and a prayer team. Those should be easy to get going."

"Great idea, Julian," one of the church elders exclaims. He is a generous donor to the church, an executive of a large construction company. He is used to making decisions under pressure. "We have many doctors and nurses in our congregation. We'll set up the gymnasium and fellowship hall as our triage and treatment area. Julian, you can set up the firepit area as an outdoor kitchen with the church kitchen as your prep area. Are you with me?" the church elder asks. The lead pastor nods as others express their enthusiasm for his ideas. The middle-aged man is dynamic, he has seized the moment. He is using the skills God blessed him with to rally his congregation.

He continues with his plan, thinking out loud. "We need a team of people willing to swing a hammer or use a chainsaw, skilled laborers. They will start going out to clear the streets and rescue people who may be trapped. They will need some EMTs with them. Let's have those people meet at the main pavilion. I'll take charge of that crew." The man looks around at the church staff and other leaders who have gathered. He is a man of action, and he has laid out a plan of action. But there is not a lot of compassion in his plan.

A church secretary speaks up timidly. "I think what you said is good, but where is God in your plans? I think we need a prayer team. Some people won't be able to help cook or clear trees. We should have a prayer team."

"Yes," the executive replies. "We can use the sanctuary as a place of prayer. You and the pastor can lead that team. So, let's get announcements on the loudspeaker system. We need to let these people know we're going to start doing God's work. We're going to start to help out our neighbors, we will be God's hands and feet right here and right now."

***

Georgeanne, Shawn and Clarissa sit in a corner of the large room and listen to the plans being made. They are glad to see the church using its assets to help the community, but they all know something is missing.

"None of them fully grasps what's happening," Georgeanne states. "They think it's just a disaster that has happened close to home. Jeremiah and Isaiah could both appear on Santa Monica Boulevard, and they would feed them soup, thinking they were common beggars."

"That is brilliant!" Shawn exclaims. "This church is doing what it is supposed to do, helping those in this area. But we need to do what we're supposed to do. We're to proclaim the Word to the nations. From the time of Abraham through the New Testament, God says his Word will bless all nations. Georgeanne, your channel can reach millions, right?"

Georgeanne looks at Shawn. He is animated and excited. She just met this young man and believes he has a good story. The tape of the 'pool party miracle' doubled her following to almost four million people. But is she willing to give that kind of power to someone she barely knows? A voice speaks to her. *'Why are you here? Are you here to spread the Word? Why do you hesitate? You have been blessed.'*

Georgeanne looks up, startled. The Holy Spirit has settled her questions. "I'm in! Let's put together a message and get it broadcast."

Clarissa looks at the slight woman with a smile. "I think the Holy Spirit just spoke to you. Game on. Let's get Shawn dressed up in sack cloth to make it more dramatic as he lets God's children know what's coming."

"Yes, with ashes in his hair," Georgeanne responds.

"Whoa, ladies!" Shawn responds. "You're getting a little carried away."

"Are we? You want to tell everyone that the end of the world as we know it is coming soon. And I'm the one getting carried away? I think sack cloths and ashes are the least you can do."

Shawn is caught flat footed. The women's argument makes sense. And it will grab people's attention. "Okay, you and Clarissa win. Get something that looks like sack cloths and gather some ashes from the firepit. I'll let the pastor know what we're doing. We could use the prayer team covering us with their blessings."

Shawn walks away from the group, heading out into the church's campus, looking for the lead pastor. As he walks, he prays. He prays for strength, wisdom, compassion and humility. "Dear Lord, you have chosen me for this mission. You moved the waters as Moses did. Help me to alert the people as Isaiah did. In Christ's holy name I do pray."

As he finishes his prayer, he catches site of Dan, the youth pastor. He catches up with him and explains what they plan to do.

"Shawn, what you did last night was great. You got the message out to thousands of people through Georgeanne's media and the TV coverage we received. I have never seen so many people respond to an altar call. You are doing God's work; I'm sure of that. But we're in the middle of a disaster. We need to respond to the needs of our friends and neighbors. I don't think this is the right time for another one of your stunts."

Shawn stops for a moment, downfallen at the response he has received. He wants to respond in anger. 'A stunt', he thinks. 'God's work is not a stunt!' But a calming voice speaks to him. *'Be the calm in the storm.'*

Shawn tugs at Dan's shoulder and stops the young clergyman. "The people need more than a blanket and a cup of soup. The people need the truth. Christ is coming. Is He coming tomorrow or in a hundred years? I don't know. But they need to know the truth. One of my professors taught me that you should never let a crisis go to waste. He meant it in political terms, but it is something that is Biblical. The prophets always used the crisis that the Israelis faced to proclaim God's Word that His people needed to return to Him. Now is our time to be the prophets of old. We have strayed far from God. His wrath is coming upon us. We need to return to God. If we, as Christians don't proclaim this now, when will we proclaim it?"

Dan stops. He wants to carry on with helping the first aid station get set up to bandage the wounded. But what the young man has said rings true. When are Christians going to stand up for what they believe in? Boys aren't girls. Babies in the womb are people. Big bang and evolution are both theories, not fact. Creation is sneered at. The Bible is thought of as a bunch of fables. When are Christians going to stand up to the false teachers that surround them and corrupt their children? Why not now? Why let a crisis go to waste? Dan stands tall as he turns to face Shawn. "You're right. We need to proclaim God's love now more than ever. How can I help you?"

Shawn is dumbstruck. After receiving such a strong rebuff, he did not see Dan offering his help. His prayers have been answered. He stammers a bit before replying. "I, uh, we, uh well, we just wanted to let you know. We, uh well, we'll be broadcasting from your church. Um, we thought you all should know. Uh, I guess that is the main thing."

Dan grabs Shawn up in a big hug. As he releases his embrace he steps back and smiles. "I have never seen you tongue tied, my friend."

"I told Clarissa that I wasn't good at public speaking." Shawn replies. "That is when she told me about Moses and Aaron. We know what that led too. But I know God is with me, He talks to me. I'm supposed to be here, He'll give me the words." Shawn states with complete sincerity.

The two men turn and start walking back towards the main church. Dan is intrigued. He has always assumed that God would give him the words he needs at any given time. He has four years of theology behind him. He knows his scriptures. Yet here is a young man with very little Bible training proclaiming a simple and basic faith in God's Word deeper than he has ever known. Part of him wants to be jealous, but the better part of him is in awe, and praises the Lord.

244

***

Twenty minutes later they are in the church sanctuary. In the flood of volunteers, Mike found two of their technicians to help with sound and lighting. True to her word, Georgeanne, along with Clarissa's help, has found sack cloths and brought ashes from the roasting pits. Shawn is now being dressed as one would expect Jeremiah or Isaiah to be dressed during the fall of Jerusalem.

Georgeanne and Clarissa are trying to put ashes on Shawn's face, but the effect is not right. "Stop! We don't need makeup and theatrics. This is not right." He sheds the sack cloths and dons his own street clothes. "I'll be back," Shawn states. He heads out of the church, looking for a work crew. It does not take him long. Twenty minutes later he returns with real sweat, ripped pants, dirty t-shirt and grime on his hands, arms, and face. Rubble has been removed from the doorway of an apartment building; several people have been rescued. "Okay, this is real. I feel better. Let's do this."

Georgeanne nods her approval. "We go live in two minutes."

Chapter 37, New Visions

Mustafa's ragtag but heavily armed convoy heads into the lands held by the Islamic Hezbollah freedom fighters. The Hezbollah commanders have been told by higher authority to let the convoy pass. They are confused about this decision but follow their orders. Some of them think Mustafa may be the twelfth imam and he'll lead them all to the final battle, to the final destruction of Israel. Others scoff at his meager convoy and note that there are priests in the convoy. "He's a fool on a fool's errand," one Hezbollah fighter says to his compatriot. "Does that make us fools?" he asks out loud.

"I have heard so many stories, I don't know what to believe," his fellow soldier responds. "I hear he knocked a senior Imam to the ground just by shouting at him. Now he is supposed to be heading to Megiddo. It's too much for me to think about. I'm good so long as today's mutton is edible."

"You are right my friend. What happens tomorrow is not in our hands." The guard spits the dust stirred up from Mustafa's convoy from his mouth. "Allahu Akbar!" he yells at the convoy as it dips over the horizon.

***

"That's the front lines of the zionist state," the driver says, as his crew commander looks around in wonder. They are in no-man's land, between the erratic Hezbollah front lines and the well-defined territory controlled by the Israelis. The convoy has pulled up and formed a defensive perimeter in the disputed land. The firepower of two warring factions have them in their crosshairs.

Mustafa steps out of his vehicle with confidence and pride. He beckons for his commanders to come to him. "Do not be afraid!" he hollers. "God is in control, my friends. He has brought us this far. He will not fail us now. Come, let us make our final plans before we enter the Holy Land. Before Joshua crossed the Jordan into the promised land, he consulted the Lord and his people. You need to know the plan before we enter into the promised land."

The twelve commanders of the twelve vehicles gather around, fully aware that their every move is being watched from both sides of the border.

Mustafa looks at them all and smiles. "Twelve loyal commanders, just like the twelve tribes of Israel. God works so many miracles." Mustafa turns to the west, looking over the fertile lands of Israel. He looks to the sky with his arms held high, then spreads his arms wide towards the promised land. "Sometimes it is too much to fathom. Our tradition tells us that we're all the sons of Abraham and that God promised us this land. He promised Abraham that his offspring would be more numerous than the sands on the beaches and the stars in the sky. He told Abraham that his legacy would be a blessing to all nations."

Mustafa turns back to his commanders. His eyes are bright. His movements are swift and agile. His words are strong and powerful. He points to one of the commanders. "Gad," he hollers and points to the next man and shouts, "Levi". These two commanders fall to their knees and begin to weep. Mustafa continues pointing and naming the tribes of Israel. "Reuben! Judah! Asher! Ephraim!" More of the Islamic commanders fall to their knees and begin to weep as their eyes are opened. If they are sons of Abraham, then they too are sons of Israel. How had they been blind to this significant fact. The remaining six commanders are dumbstruck as their fellow Islamic fighters seem to be overcome. Mustafa continues to call them out by name. "Manasseh! Naphtali! Benjamin! Zebulun! Issachar!" Despite their will to fight, they all fall to their knees as their eyes are opened. They believed they were the sons of Ishmael. But the blood of Isaac has been spread to all. They are kin to the people they have been told to despise. But most importantly, they realize that they are all the children of God.

Mustafa stands tall, surrounded by his commanders, his army. He raises his arms to the sky and prays in a loud voice. "Our Lord, Father, Yahweh, Allah, God Almighty! We have strayed so far. We have followed false prophets, and continue to follow false prophets. Allow us to see Your majesty. Allow us to unite and proclaim Your love. Let us mere mortals lay down our sinful ways and embrace each other in love as You have embraced us in love. In Your holy name I do pray!"

***

Twenty meters away, a driver knocks on the knee of a gunner who is watching the perimeter. "Abram, look at what is going on. Mustafa is bringing all our commanders to their knees. Look at that! Maybe he is the twelfth imam!"

The gunner takes a brief glance towards the gathering of the commanders, then looks back out over the no man's land they are stuck in. "Not the right time for them to decide to talk with Allah. We got guns pointed at us from both directions. Mustafa needs to get this show on the road. If he has a path into Israel, then let's follow it."

The driver is pale as he responds to the gunner, having heard and seen all that happened. "I think Mustafa just opened that road."

***

Halfway around the world, the entire scene has been broadcast onto the screens in the Special Forces command center by a drone circling five miles overhead. "What just happened!" General Shapiro asks with passion, looking at the live shot from the drone. "He just put his commanders to their knees by pointing at them. What the heck was that? Damn, I wish we had audio."

"He has faith, he has the power of faith," the young sergeant responds. "If you don't know Jesus, then I can't explain it."

"Don't be smart with me son," the general responds. "Are you telling me he has some supernatural powers?"

The sergeant takes a deep breath. He says a silent prayer. He is strong in his faith. He turns from the high-tech screens and looks at the general with respect. "General, that is not an easy question to answer. I have to ask you a question to answer your question. Do you believe in God?"

"That's a ridiculous question. I have been to church. I know there is a God!" General Shapiro states with a bit of indignation.

"Okay, sir," the sergeant replies. "Follow me here. I'm trying to explain what you have just seen from my prospective. You brought me and the chaplain here to help you evaluate this situation because of our faith. If you don't understand our faith, you won't understand our explanation." The sergeant looks up to the senior chaplain who nods his approval.

"I don't mean to be out of line, sir," the sergeant states, "but do you believe that God created the universe?"

The general is a bit flummoxed and impatient. "Of course, God created the universe. How else did all of us get here?"

The chaplain's eyes widen, and he responds. "Then you know that the big bang theory is rubbish. The universe did not just happen, it was created."

"Well, the big bang happened because God wanted it to," the general responds.

"The universe was created because God willed it to be created," the sergeant responds. "But it occurred over four days. The Bible tells us that very plainly. There was no big bang."

General Shapiro looks at the sergeant as if he just spoke in tongues. He looks to the chaplain, a Captain, the highest-ranking clergy in the navy. "You bring this illiterate young man in to help me understand what's going on? Where was he schooled that he questions the Big Bang Theory?"

"General, you just stated that the big bang is just a theory," the navy captain responds. "It is not proven, it's just speculation, a theory. You have always had an open mind. Listen to what the young man has to say."

The general harumphs and sits down with his arms crossed. "I don't see where this is going but I'll sit through this charade for a bit longer."

The captain nods to the sergeant to continue. "One more question, General. Did you evolve from some primordial lizard that crawled out of a swamp four million years ago?" The sergeant asks this question without blinking an eye. "Or did God create Adam who is your genetic ancestor?"

The general stands up and explodes. "What kind of question is that? Who do you think you are? I'm not some descendant of a primordial lizard! How can you come in here and throw these insulting questions around? Both of you leave! That is an order. You have wasted enough of my time. I thought you had some insight on this situation."

The chaplain and the sergeant stand to leave. They salute the general as they gather their papers and personal effects.

The other person in the room speaks up. It is General Shapiro's longtime friend, Henry, the general in charge of intelligence, the G2. "General, you are being too hasty. These two men are trying to point out that God is real. If God is real, then miracles can happen. You began by asking about supernatural powers. The nature of your question would cause a person of religion to explain God. How else would someone have supernatural powers?"

The chaplain stops at this comment. "Let me correct what you have said, General. A person does not have supernatural powers. The power is all in God's hands. But a person of faith can use God's power to do supernatural things. It happened time and again throughout the Old Testament. It is documented to have happened in the early church. The apostles repeatedly performed miracles. There have been documented miracles throughout recorded history. Miracles happen. But you will only recognize them if you believe in God."

The commanding general is still worked up as he stands behind his desk and stares down his guests.

The young sergeant speaks up. "General, may I speak?"

The general's faith and patience are being put to the test. He relinquishes. "Go ahead young man."

"Weird things are happening around the world. Massive earthquakes, raging wildfires, and seemingly miraculous events. I know that I did not evolve from a lizard. God created me to be here at this time. General, did God create you to be here at this time?" The sergeant nods to the chaplain then salutes as he leaves the room.

The general's face goes red. But the man he wants to yell at is already gone. He looks around the room and calms down. His eyes settle on the chaplain who remains firm in his position, despite being told to leave. "You believe in all this bull crap, don't you, captain?" he asks.

"If I didn't believe," the captain responds, "I would be running with my tail between my legs. God is allowing the destruction to occur, and He is helping the miracles to happen. I firmly believe that. That is my report."

"And how does your report help me make decisions?" General Shapiro asks. "How am I to use that information when I report to the president? I can't tell him this is all happening because of God's wrath. Despite all you have told me, I still don't believe that. We often have earthquakes. Fires sometimes rage out of control. When times get bad, religious people attract large crowds. I can blame most of this on global warming, or climate change, whichever my public relations aides think will be better received."

The general stands there, trying to work out in his mind how to tell the president that everything is going to be okay. Surely, he can explain away the recent events as only a few blips occurring at the same time. Things will be back to normal soon and they should concentrate on rebuilding Los Angeles. That will be the basis of his report.

The naval chaplain interrupts the general's thoughts. "I have been dismissed, but feel free to call me at any time, General. We will be praying for you; we always do." The chaplain leaves, gently closing the door behind him.

The three-star general in charge of special operations is left alone with his two-star general in charge of intelligence. The two men have known each other for years. There is friendship and trust that binds the two men.

General Shapiro sits down and looks at his longtime friend. "Henry, don't let those kooks in here again. That was crazy talk."

Henry ponders his response. "Jerry, you asked about the supernatural. Did you expect them to tell you something different? The only real explanation for the supernatural is God. Unless you think the Avengers are behind all this." Henry looks at the general intently. "Do you have a better explanation? You know that even if climate change was a true crisis, it would not cause massive earthquakes. Henry pauses for a minute, then continues. "How do you explain the religious revival? How do you explain the ISIS fighter?"

General Shapiro looks at his long-time friend. "Deep down, I think you're right. But I ain't gonna be the crazy guy at the strategic meeting. I'll be heaped with scorn. Maybe even fired."

"The young sergeant said you are here at this time for a reason. Maybe this is your purpose and your time."

***

"We're going to Israel my friends. We're going into the promised land," Mustafa says to his followers. "We have a lot of work to do. Our enemies are now our friends. What a joyous day!" he exclaims. "Today we will all be baptized in the Jordan River. We're all one people. We have always been one people, but the enemy has divided us. The enemy will be defeated."

One of his commanders looks at Mustafa with open eyes. "Why have we been fighting for so long, teacher. Our own scriptures tell us we're the brothers of the Israelis. Why have we been taught to hate them?"

"That is a deep question my friend. War is used to keep people united against a perceived foe. It is good for building a kingdom. But war is based on hate. Hate is the currency of the devil. He wants us divided. If we're divided, we fight each other. There is no room for God when we hate each other. We will be the start of unity. The enemy hates unity."

"How do we tell our fighters that we're going into Israel to be baptized?" another commander asks.

"You tell them the truth. You tell them that they need to be clean to enter the Holy Land," Mustafa replies with a smile. "The time has come, we must move. Hezbollah will get twitchy fingers if we tarry here too long. And the Israelis never like an armed force to linger on their borders. The Israelis expect us. Mount up. We will stop at the Jordan river to be cleansed."

Chapter 38, Failures

"Where do you want us to go, teacher?" the leader of the group who rescued Xi asks. "We're with you. How can we help you?"

"We must go to the valley of the Yangtze River," Xi states forlornly. "The Three Gorges Dam is unstable. Millions could die. We will try to save their lives while we try to save their souls."

"That's three hundred miles away!" one of the drivers exclaims. "How are we supposed to travel three hundred miles while the state is looking for us?"

Xi walks over and gives the young man a hug. "My brother, it will all work out. The Word of Christ is spreading as we speak. As the Word spreads, the state's stronghold diminishes. China has a long history of freedom and free-thinking people. The strong grasp of communism is against our culture. We have let loose the idea of freedom and redemption. It will move across this land like a wildfire. We will help that movement by warning the people in the Yangtze valley that the Three Gorges Dam is unstable. The people have always been worried about the stability of the dam. They never trusted the government nor its engineers. The recent earthquakes will have all the people alarmed. And rightfully so, because the dam is going to fail."

The young man steps back, alarmed. "I believe you teacher, but you want us to go into what could be certain death? What if the dam fails while we're alerting the people? We'll get swept away in the flood!"

"No one wants to die tomorrow," Xi states with compassion. "Yet, no one knows when they are going to die. We have the ability to save millions of people. We could do nothing and save ourselves. That is the wrong decision. I'm willing to take the risk to sound the alarm that will save millions from the flood. At the same time, we can spread the Word that will save millions from the fire. Have faith, young man, have faith."

The young man is troubled, but the words sink in. He is going to die sometime. He might die tomorrow at the hands of the state. Or he could die sounding the alarm that will save millions. "Okay, teacher, but I'm sticking close to you. I have a feeling you're going to escape the flood."

The decision is made, the mish mash convoy sets off to the southwest. Three hundred miles through the heartland of China is nothing like three hundred miles through the heartland of America. The winding mountainous journey could take a day or more. It could take even longer if they encounter government soldiers willing to use force to stop them.

***

"Look, there it goes again," a senior geologist at the USGS says, as they watch a screen that shows worldwide seismological activity. "Los Angeles was not an isolated event, and you all know it. More major quakes are coming. We're looking at worldwide tectonic movements like we have never seen before."

"I see that too," the director of the USGS says. "But what the data shows, it's not enough to raise an alarm. We can't have worldwide panic. That would be catastrophic."

"You already shut down the open side of our site," the senior scientist sneers. "The public doesn't know what is happening. We know a real catastrophe could be at hand, and still you don't want us to tell the public what's really happening? This could lead to a super volcano. Yellowstone could blow up. Yet you want us to keep everyone in the dark? That's not right!"

"It's a complicated situation. It's something that the White House is aware of," the lead scientist explains. "We need to follow their guidance."

"Well, that's freaking backwards. I thought they were supposed to act on our guidance. Do they know the freaking earth is going through massive movements, that we're seeing activity that is literally off the scales!"

"I have submitted reports through the appropriate channels. You know how these things work. We don't want to raise an alarm without having gone through the proper protocols."

"Protocols be damned! sir. The New Madrid fault could buckle next, making what happened in Los Angeles look like child's play. Chicago, Cincinnati, Memphis, Nashville, and St. Louis could all see major earthquakes. And those cities don't have building codes that even come close to the west coast high standards. You have to act sir."

"Please calm down," the lead scientist states calmly. "As you said, this is a worldwide event. Other countries need to be notified before we sound the alarm here. It needs to be coordinated. That is why the decision needs to be left to the White House. If we sound the alarm here, it could cause worldwide panic."

Frustrated, the senior geologist throws his papers to the floor. "I don't give a damn about what the Chinese or the Russians do. If we tell our people now, they'll have some time to react." The frustrated scientist storms off.

A few states away, engineers methodically check the Hoover Dam for any signs of damage or weakness. Across America inspections are being done on many major infrastructure projects. In Yellowstone National Park an evacuation has been ordered, scientists hastily gather and analyze new information. The evacuation is truly pointless. If the major cauldron below Yellowstone erupts, the devastation will be felt for hundreds of miles. The effects will be felt around the world.

***

Halfway around the globe, at the Three Gorges Dam, Chinese engineers look for any indications that the dam may be compromised. They all know the engineering was not ideal. The dam itself is solid and will withstand almost any upheaval the earth may conjure up. The weak points are where the dam is secured to the sides of the valley. If the mountainsides that the dam is anchored to begin to fail, then the dam will fail.

The dam's spillways have already been opened in an effort to lower the lake level and relieve pressure on the dam. It is a futile effort. The massive lake behind the dam took years to fill. A few days of the spillways running at maximum will lower the level of the lake by a few feet at most, barely effecting the pressure on the dam.

Downstream from the dam, alarms are sounding, letting the locals know that the river level may rise dramatically in a short period of time. The alarms are meant to keep fishermen and boaters from getting caught in a dangerous situation. The locals hear the alarms and get off the river or head to higher ground. For several hundred miles downstream from the dam, people heed these warnings. They happen often, especially in the spring. It is no big deal, just a new part of their lives.

Chapter 39, The Sermon

Drums begin sounding with a rhythmic beat, followed by a base guitar with soul reaching chords. A piano begins playing a dramatic tune. Shawn walks through some piped in fog and onto the small stage. He looks directly at the camera which closes in on his handsome yet sincere face.

"This is what the Word of God says." Shawn holds up a Bible and reads from it. "The book of Mark, chapter 13, verse eight. *Nation will rise against nation, and kingdom against kingdom. There will be earthquakes in various places, and famines. These are the beginnings of birth pains.*"

"These are the beginnings of birth pains." Shawn repeats as he looks down and pauses. Then he looks directly at the camera. "Birth pains, the Bible says. From what I have heard it is an excruciating pain. That is what God has in store for us. My friends around the world, God is angry. Our world has strayed far away from him. We follow false prophets. We worship false Gods. What is wrong is accepted as right. Our world has been perverted. And God is angry."

"This massive earthquake didn't just happen; God is sending a message." Shawn pauses. "They say to follow the science, which tells us there are two genders. Then we're told there is no gender." Shawn raises his hands in frustration. "We're told to believe in evolution. They tell us an amoeba came to life from some primordial soup hundreds of millions of years ago. That blob of life evolved into some kind of lizard that crawled out of the ocean. Over a few million years that lizard evolved into the dinosaurs, which became birds. And somehow the birds turned into apes and the apes became man." Again, he raises his hands in frustration.

The music plays dramatically in the background as the camera closes in on Shawn's face. "I look at my face in the mirror every morning. I can tell you this with confidence, my ancestors were not lizards! Follow the science, they say. Yet their science makes no sense!" The camera zooms out to show several people of multiple nationalities on the small stage. "We're the children of God, created in His image! We're beautifully made, and He loves us! That is something I can believe in. Is it wrong to think we were created by God? I think it is more crazy to think I'm the descendant of an ape."

The camera zooms in again. "I have an urgent message to bring to you. Walk away from the mayhem. Walk away from the darkness. Walk away from all the doubts placed in your head. Walk away from the divisions that our society is placing between us, walk away from the darkness that seems to be surrounding us. Walk towards the light. The devil resides in the darkness. Jesus is the light. The light will always overcome the darkness."

"All you who are watching this, pray with me in this time of darkness so that we can be the light." The camera zooms in on Shawn's face again. "Dear Lord, we know You are the Father and the Creator. We know Jesus is Your Son who died for our sins and then defeated death, laying the path for our eternal life with You. Give us the strength during this time of darkness to reject the false teachings that surround us. Give us the strength to be Your true prophets, to proclaim Your Word of love in all we do. In Christ's most holy name we do pray, Amen."

The camera zooms way out. In the foreground are people hugging and crying around the small stage. In the background is the devastating aftermath of the earthquakes. Scenes of devastation start rolling across the screen as a calming voice begins a narrative. "Children of God, reach out to your neighbors in love. Now is the time to act boldly. You have a place in heaven that Christ has prepared for you. Step out, as the apostles did, and proclaim God's Word. Step out as the apostles did and help your neighbors. There is no room for hate. There is no room for fear. Be fearless warriors for Christ here on earth. Do the work that needs to be done. And do it for the glory of God. Birth pains lead to new life. Understand that we're going through birth pains that will lead us to a beautiful new life."

As the message comes to an end the screen shows a video of Shawn and a group of volunteers clearing the rubble from an apartment doorway. As the doorway is cleared, a young woman emerges with an infant child, they are dirty, bruised, and bloodied, but they are alive and well.

***

Under Georgeanne's skilled guidance, the video is shot and edited in less than an hour. There are things she would have liked to clean up, but under the circumstances, she knows it is the best they can do. She feels like she is in a video herself, as the reality of everything happening around her sinks in. As she presses the 'post' button she can't help but to break down and weep.

The video is posted. Its effects are almost immediate. Many of her followers in southern California have no cell service or internet connection, but she has a few million followers across the country and around the world. They know she is in the heart of the disaster area. They quickly check on her post. The heartfelt message is reposted and soon goes viral. People begin to search their souls.

Christians become emboldened in their faith, not as street corner preachers, but as caring neighbors. Random acts of kindness happen. People start talking to their neighbors and friends, food is shared with the elderly and the infirm, small chores are done for those in need. In many instances, faith is shared, and prayers are given up to the Lord. People sense that the world is not right. The outreach of love is calming to all.

***

The video, along with a report, is forwarded to the Special Forces general a few moments before his video meeting with the president and his staff. A second video is forwarded as well. It is of a senior scientist from the USGS telling anyone who will listen that the earthquakes are widespread and that the USGS is hiding critical information. The senior scientist states that major earthquakes could begin occurring around the world. The video has not gone viral. But its message is very true and could have chaotic repercussions in the very near future.

**

Back at the church campus, relief efforts ramp up as the volunteers spread out into the community to offer help, clear rubble, and help rescue those who are trapped. Other churches around the country begin to ramp up their community outreach programs. There is a vitality in the air, a sense of urgency. People seem to be aware of an impending disaster. Shawn's words ring true in many hearts; God is angry, the world has walked away from His teachings. They know it, they have known it for years, and they have done nothing to stop it.

Soon, the presidential symbol fills the screens of television sets around the nation. A few minutes later the president addresses the nation. "My fellow countrymen, a natural disaster of epic proportions has struck this country. A massive earthquake occurred in the Los Angeles basin at approximately 6:15 Pacific time this morning. The United States Geological Services recorded the earthquake at 8.5 on the Richter scale. As you have all seen, downtown Los Angeles has been devastated. The loss of life will probably mount into the tens of thousands and the property loss will be in the billions. I ask you all to keep these people in your thoughts today. I dare say, I ask you to pray for them if that is your nature."

The president changes his posture as he continues. "FEMA is already responding to this event. All resources available are being sent to the area. Search and rescue teams from around the country are being flown in to help our fellow Americans. Heavy lift crews and equipment are being mobilized as we speak to be deployed in the rescue and cleanup operations. America will unite around our brothers and sisters in southern California."

"Many of you may have questions about this event," the president continues. "Could there be more serious earthquakes around the country, or around the world? I have consulted with our most senior scientists. While there have been other small earthquakes around the world, our best and brightest minds assure me that the event in southern California is an isolated event. There will be more aftershocks, but I assure you that the rest of the country can concentrate on helping with the relief effort without fear of more earthquakes. I thank you for your time, and may God bless America."

A news anchor comes on the screen. "As you can see, the president is very concerned about what has happened in Los Angeles and we can be comforted in knowing that FEMA is fully in control of the situation. We can also be assured that the president has consulted our most senior scientists. As you heard, there is no threat to the rest of the country of additional earthquakes."

"Mikki, I know you want to reassure the country, but to say that FEMA is fully in control of the situation is a bit of a stretch," the cohost responds. "It is comforting to know that FEMA is responding, and I'm sure they will be fully operational soon. But I have a question. Why did the USGS site shut down? Is it just an anomaly? A coincidence? That doesn't work in my world view."

"I have asked about that too, Jim," Mikki responds. "The USGS has major offices in southern California, their offices have been severely damaged. They say the system will be back up soon."

"Okay Mikki, except the site went dark two days ago. I'm not sure how that all works out. There have been local reports that the USGS has been hiding its data. Now, onto other news. A rebellion in China continues as tens of thousands of people are revolting against the government in a northern Chinese province. Landslides have slowed down the response of the army to put down this rebellion in the remote farmlands of Manchuria."

"This is the second day in a row we have heard about this story," Mikki responds. "Could the Chinese be starting to lose control? Normally, any rebellion is quashed before we even know about it."

"Yes, Mikki," Jim responds. "This is an unusual situation. The state has not been able to stop this rebellion. The fact that we have even heard about it is amazing. They must have some significant forces guiding this revolt. I hope that the authorities can bring this under control. To have China in turmoil would be adding fuel to the fire in this chaotic world. China has always been a bright spot for us in their ability to keep everyone under control."

"You're right Jim," Mikki responds. "We have seen firsthand what can happen if people have too much freedom."

"I know, I know," Jim says as the camera turns back to him once again. "Now, on to the weirder side of the news. A new cult has formed in Australia as a woman in tattered clothing and ashes in her hair has gained tens of thousands of followers as she proclaims the end of the world is near."

"With all that is going on Jim, I'm not sure that even ranks as weird," Mikki responds. "What else have you got? "

"How about this, Mikki? A remote church in Nigeria says they have the Ark of the Covenant. The wacko priest in charge says now is the time to reveal its presence, so it can help prepare the way for the new kingdom."

"This I like, Jim, only because I picture a young Harrison Ford. That will bring me new life!"

Laughing, Jim responds. "I'm good with the Ark being found. Just close your eyes when all those serpent ghosts start swirling around." Both anchors laugh out loud.

Jim looks back at the camera. "That wraps it up here. This is Jim Nayborough signing off for the NNH network. Thanks for watching 'All the News that Matters'. We'll see you again tomorrow morning for another edition of America's most trusted morning news show."

Chapter 40, The Discussion

"The destruction and mayhem happening around the world should be playing into our hands," Abaddon states to a few of his elite followers on the secure video call. "Yet there is a Christian revival happening. This is not good." Abaddon shakes his head. "Around the world we have been able to promote the sacrifice of children through abortion, we have perverted the idea of sexuality, we have destroyed the idea of the traditional family. We are on the verge of pushing all morality into the abyss. As we push the world into chaos, our time to rise up and take control of the world will come."

One of the richest men in the world speaks up. He is the developer of software used on virtually every computer. "Sir, our efforts to implement population control have been quite effective, yet there is a consistent value for life that we have not yet been able to stifle. The generation now coming to age has learned that the life of a human has devasting effects on the life of the planet. It is a long-term project, but we are having an impact."

"You have done well in helping to abort the human parasite from the face of the planet," Abaddon responds. "But we face an urgent situation. We don't have time for long term solutions. The enemy needs to be quashed now. You have the ability to quash the voices that go against our agenda, I expect you to use your resources to silence the voices that oppose us."

The billionaire trembles. "How can I do that? We have laws. The people of my country have rights."

Abaddon sneers. "That has not stopped you before. You are known to suppress news that is not in line with your political ideologies. How is my request any different? You have the ability to do what I ask. You only need to continue to do what you are already doing."

Abaddon turns to his communist ally. "Why is the apostle in Manchuria still alive? He should have been killed yesterday."

The communist leader is bold and strong. He has always been stubborn. His allegiance to Abaddon is only for his own motives, but he tolerates the strong-willed man. He has no idea of how far Abaddon's influence extends. "We have our best men tracking down the heretic. His voice will be silenced soon. You can trust that we will do everything we can to continue on our path to total state control."

"You claim to be in control, but you are not." Abaddon looks into his camera intently, staring at the communist leader with a calm yet chilling iciness. "The viral infection of the Word spreads. It spreads faster than the virus you let loose on the world from the labs in Wuhan. It is way more dangerous, yet the infection spreads. What have you done to stop the spread of this virus?"

The communist leader is stunned to be challenged. He thinks of Abaddon as a tool for him to use to implement his agenda. He has no idea that he is the tool being used by Abaddon. The communist responds with indignation. "It is none of your business how we deal with this little insurrection. The man will be caught. He and his people will be dealt with. How we do that is none of your business."

A man steps into the picture behind the communist leader. In a flash, a garrot is put around the small man's throat. In an instant, the man is dead. The other people on the video call see the execution happen. A few have seen it before. To them it is a normal high-powered act of influence. To others it is a gruesome act. It is a startling signal that they could be next.

Abaddon casually leans back in his chair. He looks like a normal grandfather, wizened and kind. But he has a sinister look to his eyes. He gazes casually into the camera that is broadcasting his image to the rest of his compatriots. "The general failed in his mission. I'm sorry you had to see that. You all know what needs to be done. Please don't fail me."

Chapter 41, The Crossing

The hodgepodge convoy passes through the village of Kidmat Tsvi heading towards the town of Gadot smack in the middle of the DMZ on the east side of the Jordan river. They come up to a small bridge that crosses the Jordan River north of the Sea of Galilee. The land around them is full of productive farms and remote compounds. They are in an area that was settled thousands of years ago by Noah's children and grandchildren. The convoy pulls off the road at an access site to the river. The trained militia fighters immediately set up a defensive posture. Many look around with wide eyes. They are at the doorstep to the promised land, the holy land.

Mustafa dismounts from his vehicle and confidently walks over to the outlook site. The Jordan river flows before him, less than a hundred feet away. It is more like a stream than a river at this point, only a few feet deep and less than fifty feet wide. He smiles as he reaches his hands to the sky. "Yahweh, Almighty God. I thank You for Your forgiveness and the blessing of being part of Your holy army. As we enter the promised land, I pray that You bless us and protect us. May Your will be done."

Mustafa then turns and addresses his ragtag group. "Come, all of you come. We're safe here. No one would dare attack us here. You all must come and allow this glorious moment to sink in. We are about to cross into the promised land."

His soldiers are hesitant. Their commanders beckon them to come and gather. What they are doing is against all their training, against everything they have learned on the brutal battlefield. They are all going to congregate together, undefended, with no guards. The entire situation is surreal. They fight their instincts and gather together at the outlook, with the Jordan river flowing before them.

"Do not be afraid, my brothers," Mustafa begins. "We're in God's hands. This is an historical site, a site of great reverence. The Israelites, under the leadership of Joshua, conquered these lands thousands of years ago, when they first entered the promised land after their exile in Egypt. These are the ancestral lands of the tribe of Manasseh. Across the river are the ancestral lands of the tribe of Naphtali. These lands have been fought over for thousands of years. King David and his armies marched through these lands. The Assyrians and the Babylonians marched down this valley. The Romans fought battles here. The Persians amassed armies here."

Mustafa turns to look at the men who have followed him this far. "I cannot tell you of all the conflict and strife that has happened here. The conflict and strife must stop. Love will win the battle. You all have lost brothers, sisters, parents, and friends in the wars of the past few decades. It makes you angry. It makes you hate. Anger and hate are the work of the devil! It only leads to more death and destruction."

"Today is a new day. Today we embrace love and forgiveness. Today we start a new life, a new path. No more hate, no more fighting, no more killing. Today we embrace peace and love. That is God's true message. The Koran says it, the Talmud says it, the Bible proclaims it. From this time forward, we're a brotherhood of peace, as the Lord almighty wants us to be."

The men around him are stunned. The commanders have already had their eyes opened and they talk with their men. "The time for fighting is over," "God wants this to happen," "It is time to lay down our arms," are things heard throughout the assembled fighters.

Mustafa feels emboldened at the words he is hearing. He knows God is with him. "We're going to enter the holy land in triumph! We will enter the holy land cleansed of our sins and empowered with the Word of God. Come now, we will be baptized in the Jordan river. Then we will go throughout the land in peace, proclaiming God's love."

The sun breaks through the scattered clouds and a slight breeze wafts through the valley. A flock of white doves descends into a small cluster of olive trees. An older man and his two daughters trundle down the road with three donkeys toting fully laden carts. The man stops at the spectacle. He looks over the large group of hardened and scarred fighters standing at the edge of the Jordan river. "Welcome, my friends. I can see you are hard men. You carry regret and sin. Wash in the river, be cleansed, and walk in God's path." He nods towards the stream and smiles as he and his daughters continue on across the bridge.

"The signs of peace are all around us," Mustafa exclaims with authority. "We must embrace this moment. We will start a movement!" The group is stunned, but they move with Mustafa as they lay down their arms and follow him towards the river. The surrounding lands are going to be conquered once again. But this time, no blood will be shed. The fighters leave their arms on the west side of the river. They are baptized and move on to the east side of the river. As they emerge, they have no possessions except the shirts on their backs. But they have an awakening and a purpose. Some break down in tears, others gather in wonderment. They all see the world in an entirely different way. The Holy Spirit moves in them all. They leave everything behind and start to walk the path they know they are supposed to walk.

***

"Someone please explain what just happened!" Frank, the special forces general in charge of operations demands.

Mustafa's crew has been followed by mile high drones for several hours. The Americans expected Mustafa to enter Israel and start a running gun battle that would trigger an Arab uprising that could have led to another full-blown war.

Henry, the intelligence officer smiles at his compatriot. "You just saw another miracle. Those men were baptized. They laid down their arms. They are walking into the unknown with no possessions, no weapons, no provisions. They are acting on faith. I saw this coming, and still I'm amazed."

"Is this more of your end times talk?" Frank asks. "General Shapiro doesn't want to hear it. The president won't hear it."

Henry sits up and looks at his friend. "I'm to give you reasoned explanations of the events of the world, based on known intelligence. Earthquakes are happening around the world at such an alarming rate that the USGS shut down their site so the public wouldn't be alarmed. Then a massive quake hits LA. It has not been well reported, but massive fires are burning around the world, from the Russian steppes to the Brazilian rainforests. The west coast and many of the rocky mountain states are experiencing massive wildfires. Add to that the religious revivals happening around the world and the miracles we have watched happen. We just saw a miracle in real time. General, in my opinion, the events occurring around the world are Biblical. The hand of God is at work. I have no other reasonable explanation."

Angry, Frank replies. "Put that in writing. Damn it, what am I supposed to tell General Shapiro?"

"The truth," Henry replies as he rises to leave the large and ornate office. "If I had a better answer, I'd have told you. I'm not being an evangelist; I'm giving you my best evaluation of what I've seen. That's my job."

The G3 looks at his friend. "Don't leave yet, Henry. Let's see what becomes of Mustafa and his gang of ruffians."

The G2 sits down next to his friend. "They are no longer ruffians, you know," Henry states.

"Once a warrior, always a warrior," Frank replies. A specialist with a very high security clearance adjusts the screen to track Mustafa and his crew of warriors. As he leaves the room, he deftly picks up a thumb drive. Within minutes the entirety of the previous conversation and all the highly sensitive data he acquired has been sent to an unknown recipient. Frank's security specialist will be well paid for his act.

***

The farmer with the three cartloads of ripe olives enters the village of Gadot. He greets a long-time friend, a high-ranking officer in the Mossad. Gadot is smack in the middle of the DMZ and no official Israeli forces are allowed without the proper credentials and permission from the Palestinians. But the Israeli intelligence corps, the Mossad, is well established in the area. The farmer did not just happen upon Mustafa's crew at the border. He was on a mission. He reports to his friend.

"When does something like this happen?" he asks before getting into his report. The Mossad officer knows that all truthful sources are chatty. Information that is too precise, too accurate, is often information that has been planted by the enemy. "About forty men were there, all hardened fighters. You could see their scars, even in just passing. But the leader, he was something! He was telling them about Joshua and the twelve tribes. As we passed through, I felt the presence of God. I invited them to wash away their sins in the river. After we crossed the bridge, I turned back to see them in the river and crossing to the eastern bank. They left everything behind! Their weapons, their vehicles, their equipment, everything! They'll be here in a few minutes, you will see."

"Thank you, my friend," the Israeli officer responds. "Your information and service is invaluable. May God bless you and your family." The officer presses a large gold coin into the man's hand.

The man pushes the gold coin back, "This is God's work. I don't need to be paid for doing God's work. Miracles are happening, you will see." The old man turns and heads toward the olive press that has been in operation for hundreds of years.

Ten minutes later, the forty men come up the road. They are singing and shouting as they come. The joy on their faces is radiant. The undercover Mossad agent gets on his secure communications to his headquarters. "I have an alarming situation here. Code red."

"We know of your situation," is the response he receives. "Welcome your new friends. This has gone to the top. The pilgrims have left their arms behind so welcome them as friends."

***

Mustafa leads his men into the village as they dance, sing and shout in joy. Many of the villagers seek shelter. Being on the front lines between the Hezbollah warriors and the Israeli army, they have seen too much violence. This strange procession is new, but the villagers know to keep their heads down and be ready to find cover.

"Do not be afraid!" Mustafa proclaims as he sees the villagers scurry for cover. "We come in peace. We come proclaiming peace. We're your brothers. Look at us. We carry nothing on our backs. We have laid down our weapons. We carry something more powerful than weapons; we carry the truth."

The Mossad agent steps into the village square to greet Mustafa. He looks at the large man sternly, as a village elder would. "You are warriors. You have the scars of hardened men. But you sing and dance as you enter our village. We're a peaceful people, just trying to earn a living in this no man's land. What do you want? We don't need any more war, any more strife. Why are you here?"

Before the well-trained Mossad agent can react, Mustafa wraps him up in a bear hug and kisses him firmly on the cheek. As the bear of a man sets the Mossad agent back on the ground he smiles. "We're here to celebrate the Messiah," Mustafa pronounces with joy. "I can tell that you are a respected man in this village. Bring out the fathers of the village. I have a message for them, a message for all men of goodwill."

"I can relate that message, my friend," the Mossad agent states firmly. "This village has seen too much trouble to trust a man like you."

"You judge me without knowing me," Mustafa replies. The large man steps back, his face scrunches up as he thinks through the situation. Suddenly his eyes grow bright. "Bring me water and a bowl. Bring me a quart of your best oil. Do it now, don't hesitate." The Mossad officer is stunned at the request but orders a few hidden villagers to heed the large man's orders.

"Take off your boots," Mustafa says kindly. "Have your people take off their shoes and sandals." Mustafa kneels down and begins to wash the Mossad officer's feet. Mustafa turns to some of his most trusted followers. "We must let these people know we're here to serve them. Come and join me as we wash their feet." All of his people come forward to help wash the villager's feet. More villagers come into the square to watch the spectacle and to get their feet washed.

Mustafa pours a small dab of olive oil on the Israeli officer's feet. "My friend, I can see you are a soldier, probably a member of the Mossad," Mustafa says as he massages the oil into his feet. "We're being watched from both sides. My men and I are going into Israel with the same message we bring to you. Do you have a mind and a heart that is open to hearing God's Word?"

"How can you insult me like that?" the Mossad agent asks as he hastily puts his boots back on.

"Please, listen to me," Mustafa replies, calmly. "I'm no different than you. I did not understand. We're all brothers. We both agree that there is only one God, the Creator and the Father. But what both you and I missed, my friend, is the Son. Jesus is what separates us. And he is what will unite us." Mustafa takes a palm full of oil and pours it on the Mossad agent's head. "Awaken my friend and see the truth."

The Mossad agent grabs Mustafa's hand and pushes it away. But the blessed oil has already been applied. The Mossad agent falls to his knees as his eyes open and he believes. For two thousand years his people have denied the obvious. The Israelis have always rebelled against God. It is man's nature to be sinful, rebellious.

The full truth comes down on the Israeli soldier as he looks into Mustafa's eyes. "Christ is the Savior! We rejected him, denied him. We're such a hardheaded people. And the whole time, God never abandoned us. He saw us through the worst of times, even the holocaust. We're his people and he loves us, and Jesus is his Son. That is why you are here. You are a prophet. But you are not going to tell us of what is to come. You are going to tell of what has already happened."

"Rise up my brother," Mustafa says gently. "I'm not a prophet; I'm just a humble believer. As a believer I have to be an ambassador. You too will be an ambassador. Once you know the path to true peace, to eternal life, how can you not resist the urge to tell everyone! You now know the truth. Join me, let us walk into Israel and tell the truth to God's chosen people."

The Mossad officer stands and embraces Mustafa. He knows full well the mission God has laid before him. It is totally contradictory to what he has done his entire life. For his entire life he has protected the state of Israel, its faith and traditions. Now he will be telling his countrymen that they missed the boat. Their messiah came two thousand years ago! But he will be carrying the good news that the Messiah is eternal, everlasting.

The villagers have been watching what has happened and they begin to come out to greet the travelers. They bring food, wine, and clothing for the strangers. Mustafa's men, his new converts, begin mingling with the villagers. They express great joy and humility among those they meet. No words of conversion are exchanged. Only love and compassion.

Curiosity arises among a few of the Jewish people. "Why are you here? You are men of war, but you bring peace? What is your mission?"

"We're here to bring peace," one of Mustafa's men states. "The Messiah would want us to love even our enemies. But you are not our enemies, you are our brothers. We're here to embrace you as our brothers, even if we had once been enemies."

One of the Israeli merchants looks at the fighter with a grimace. "The Messiah, you say? What do you mean by that?"

The former Islamic fighter is bewildered. "Jesus Christ, the son of God! He is the one who was sent to save the world. He is the blessing for all nations that Abraham was promised by God. He is the Messiah. You know of him, but you obviously don't know Him." The former warrior begins to site prophetic scripture from the Talmud, the Koran, and the Bible. Many villagers gather around as he speaks. He wraps up his short sermon. "Only yesterday I was blind to what is so obvious. Today my eyes are open. God is the creator, and He loves us, but we're sinners. Jesus was sent to atone for our sins, the final sacrifice. There is no need to perform sacrifices and rituals to atone for sin. If you accept Jesus as Lord and Savior, then you know the final sacrifice has been completed. Believe in Christ as the final sacrifice. Know that he rose from the dead as God's Son, and all your sins are forgiven. If he could defeat death, then he can defeat all the sins of this world."

The villagers look at the former soldier, stunned. No more sacrifices to atone for their sins? The ISIS fighter looks at their blank stares and has an idea. "Bring me your sacrifices that the Bible appoints to atone for the sins you have committed," he says in a bold voice. Quickly doves, grain, a few goats and even a large ram are brought to him. He is an experienced fighter who has lived off the land, he quickly dispatches and skins all the birds and animals brought to him.

The soldier looks over the carcasses and then looks over the people around him. "If I were to offer this meat on the altar, you believe God would be appeased. But God's Son died on the cross. Do you think this rotting pile of meat means anything to God compared to his Son? You can take your pile of meat and walk away as the Israelis have done for thousands of years! Or you can embrace God and his Son, Jesus Christ."

The soldier turns and walks away from the hushed crowd. They are stunned, shocked at the blunt message. Some are outraged. Others are humbled. What if Jesus Christ was the Son of God and was the final sacrifice? What if they missed the message? It was promised that the Messiah would be king over all nations. All nations would bow down to Him. Christianity has spread around the world. Yet the Israelis remain confined to their small country. And now an avowed enemy is standing in their village espousing love in the name of Jesus Christ.

Once again, the earth shakes as it has so often in the past week. The villagers of Gadot tremble, some fall to the ground. The man of peace continues to walk away from them, seemingly unaffected by the trembling earth.

Mustafa greets his friend with joy as they prepare to head towards the Israeli front lines. "I'm not a good convert," his companion states. "I think I insulted them. I told them their sacrifices were like a rotting pile of meat compared to what Jesus did for them."

The large man laughs out loud. "I need to remember that line my friend. Turn and look, you have done well." The former ISIS fighter turns around to see several dozen people following him.

"Teacher, tell us more. You have knowledge and power." Many people from the village converge on the former ISIS fighters, not in anger, but with joy, and questions.

"Now is not the time for questions," Mustafa proclaims in a loud voice. "Now is the time for action. The earth trembles because God is going to bring judgement. Our mission is to bring the Word to God's chosen people. It is written in the scriptures that God will save not only his people, but all the nations of the earth. Join me to spread the Word to the chosen people."

Mustafa turns to the Mossad officer. "It is only a few miles to the border checkpoint; we can walk there. They know we're coming; you need to tell them we come in peace."

***

"So, what's going to happen when this mob reaches the Israeli border?" Frank asks Henry, the Intelligence officer. "They can't just let a couple of hundred people come strolling into their country."

"Most of them are Israeli citizens," Henry replies. "They have no reason to stop them. They may try to stop Mustafa and his crew, but they are unarmed. Arabs pass across the border every day. The Israelis don't want an incident, so I think they all will pass through the border unmolested."

The security specialist enters the room and discreetly slips Frank a typed paper message as he once again adjusts the screen, and fine tunes the high-tech equipment. Frank read the message. "The apostate must be terminated. All with the mark must be terminated immediately." Frank reads the message and tries to digest its significance as he continues to talk with his friend.

"This is unfathomable. How do I explain this to General Shapiro?" Frank asks, as many thoughts churn through his head.

"Don't explain it. Just show what is happening," the G2 replies. "I'll have my people put together a comprehensive video. Short but concise. Make sure General Shapiro lets the president see it. His advisors and the chiefs of staff can figure it out."

As Frank ponders this for a moment, alert notifications come flashing across their screen. An aide bursts into their office. "Sir, Japan has just been rocked by a massive earthquake. Osaka has been hard hit, worse than Los Angeles. Tsunami warnings have been issued. Osaka is in a large, confined bay, we could have tsunamis happening within the next few minutes."

The high-ranking technical NCO scans through his feeds and soon has live video from Osaka. One shot shows the city's skyscrapers thrown down as if Godzilla had rampaged through the city. Another video shows the beach as the water drains away. The shoreline goes haywire as the water rapidly recedes from the beachfront. People are scrambling everywhere, running from the crumbling buildings, running from the beach, knowing what is happening. Another live feed shows a wide-angle view. The low rolling wave can be seen moving back into the bay. The two generals along with the two senior NCOs watch in horror as the tsunami washes ashore. The wave is powerful, a long and hard flood of water. It is not a towering wave that comes crashing into the city. It is just a massive push of water that is unstoppable, unrelenting. It sweeps up everything in its path.: cars, cabanas, food booths, trees … people. They watch the sickening violence as the water pushes inland for over a mile, inundating everything in its path, grinding through the valleys and over the rubble dams created by the buildings that are still crumbling due to the earthquake. They see the people caught in this nightmare of violence. All of the soldiers watching the video have seen combat. None of them have seen such violent destruction and horrific loss of life.

Chapter 42, The Innocent

A young woman stands on a street corner In Rio de Janeiro, not fully understanding the mayhem occurring around her. The news of the massive earthquake that hit Osaka has the city in a panic. Those who can, the elites, are fleeing the large city. But millions of people are stuck in the slums and barrios built into the steep hillsides and narrow valleys of the coastal city. They have nowhere to go. Many flee their shanty shack homes and head to the small coastal plain, hoping it will be a safe area. A large earthquake would cause massive landslides to come crashing down the unstable hillsides, burying their homes. In the chaos, looting starts as the impoverished locals invade the high-end beach districts.

"Dddd,on't run. Ddddon't move ssso fast. It ssscares me. Wwwwhy are yyyou all ssso scared?" the young woman stutters, pleading to the people swarming around her. "Sssstop and llllisten. God isss good. He issss here. Dddon't be afffraid. God ssssayss that in ttthhhhe Bible allllot."

Several dozen people scurry past the busy corner. But some pause. Some pause to take in the spectacle, others pause out of compassion. Some pause to listen to what the young woman has to say.

"Rrrrrruning away is not gggggood. Face whhhhat is happening. I knnnow Jesus. I'mmm not afffraid. Whhhy are yyyyyou afraid?" Some of the people who have paused move on. Others linger as the young autistic woman has struck a chord with them. Why are they running? Many of them are good Catholics. They have been taught that God is in control.

The young woman turns this way and that as the crowd grows around her. People are listening to her! In her twenty-five years of life, very few people have ever listened to her. "God llloves you all," She proclaims with joy. "Ttttttturn to God. Go tttttto your chhhhurch. Love your nnnnneighbors. Rrrrrunning is not gggggood."

278

An older woman who has stopped to listen turns to her husband. "The young girl is right. Why are we running? We should be going to the church. We should be looking for a way to help. Running is not the right thing to do."

"The mountain could come sliding down at any minute, burying us all. Are you going to listen to this simpleton woman?" the husband responds angrily.

"This simpleton girl is proclaiming love and faith. That is a better message than I have heard from the simpleton I have been married to for forty years," the woman responds. "We're not going to run. We're going to help. Come with me or run like a coward." The woman looks at her husband with defiant eyes. He succumbs to her will and they turn back into the barrio where they start to help the elderly and disabled.

***

Two thousand miles to the north, in central California, one of Georgeanne Haquani's aides stumbles across a video of the autistic woman calling for calm in Rio De Janeiro. She brings it to the attention of the team. Georgeanne looks at the video and is immediately convicted. "Use it, you know what I want, get it produced. I want to see the final product but move fast." Using the laptops they have available, running on the church's backup generator, her production people put together a short video featuring the autistic woman espousing God's Word. They show it to Georgeanne, who suggests a few tweeks. A few moments later Georgeanne shares the video with Shawn, Clarissa and the church staff.

"I'm ready to hit the publish button," Georgeanne says softly. "But we have developed a community here. I want your approval before I act. This is so moving. I'm sure many people will connect with her simple message."

The lead pastor speaks up. "Social media has been used far too often to spread evil ideas. Here is an opportunity to spread a pure and simple message of love and reliance on God. That message needs to be shared." All the people in the impromptu meeting agree. Georgeanne hits the publish button. It takes twenty-four hours for the message to start to go viral. By that time more chaos has begun to happen around the world. The simple and honest message resounds with the people. 'Turn to God, go to church, help your neighbors, don't be afraid.'

The message being proclaimed by someone who is autistic, makes the message stick. 'This autistic girl can figure it out. She can find peace. Why can't I?' many people think. They start to think through what they believe and why they believe it. 'What if there is a God? If there is a God, and I believe in him, then I don't need to be afraid.' The young autistic woman and her simple message begins to resound around the world.

***

"End times!" the president states angrily. "That's your assessment! What am I supposed to do with that!" The president sits down as he looks at a screen providing real time news footage. The Chinese are evacuating the valleys below the Three Gorges Dam. The scene switches to the mayhem that is going on around Osaka. A brief report is given about all the minor earthquakes happening around the world and the fact that the USGS site is still not functioning. The focus of the news switches to Los Angeles and the still burning city.

General Shapiro responds. "Sir, I'm telling you the truth. I'm telling you what we have observed and what we know. It is up to you and your advisors to decide why it has happened and what to do. The scriptures say events like this will happen. That is not my opinion, that is the truth. The scientists have not given any comprehensive answer to why there are massive earthquakes happening around the globe. They only offer theory, but no truth. None of their scientific models predicted what is occurring."

The president's trusted cabinet members and chief advisors all start talking at once. 'preposterous!', 'right wing religious zealot',

280

'follow the science'. Some curse, others get louder with their opinions as the room disintegrates into confusion and dissent.

The president's chief of staff sees the meeting start to melt down. She wishes she had a gavel. She finds a large book and slams it on the table several times. The third time that she slams the book on the table, it lands fair and square, sending a resounding smack that catches everyone's attention.

The room goes silent as she begins to speak. "This is the president's office, the highest office in the land; it will not become the site of a shouting match. You asked for the man's opinion. He gave it to you as honestly as he could. I don't care if you don't like what he said, it does not give you the right to shout him down. Let's bring this discussion to order. I will not tolerate more outbursts like that." The woman looks around the quieted room sternly. "The nation's business will be discussed calmly and with respect."

"How am I to respect the notions of a religious zealot?" the secretary of health and human services asks loudly and with defiance.

"You respect them with dignity," the president responds in a soft and gentle voice. "I'm a man of faith. Does that make me a religious zealot too? I appointed a cabinet with diverse views not to argue, but to have constructive discussions from various views. C'mon man, let's hear each other out without shouting at each other."

"That would have worked," the secretary of state responds, "if you hadn't let a right-wing general into the discussion. How are we supposed to get anything done when we let extremists dictate the agenda?"

The secretary of state's insulting remarks to the four-star general in charge of special operations makes the room go quiet. General Shapiro is more in touch with what is really going on around the world than anyone else on the planet. His people are on the ground, in the hot spots. He knows facts where most of the people in this room rely on speculation.

The general says a prayer. It is not something he usually does. He normally reacts on his own accord. He asks God to give him humility and patience, two things he knows he lacks. The general feels a sense of freedom descend on him. The tenseness in his shoulders goes away. The stiffness in his neck abates. He feels a strength in his soul. 'tell the truth' resounds in his mind.

General Shapiro looks at the secretary of state. "Madam, you only want to hear what you have already determined is the truth. I'm here to tell you the real truth. I'm not a religious zealot. I'm a soldier doing my duty. I apologize if that offends you. I have offended a lot of people throughout my career. There are many people in war zones around the world who are now dead because I followed your orders, because they offended you. You, Madam are the zealot. You are a zealot to your political ideology." The general turns to the president. "Sir, I cannot serve your administration and the views that it espouses." He takes the four stars off both his shoulders and places them on the president's desk. "I was raised in the church, but I never considered myself a religious man. I think now may be a good time to become one." He gives a final salute, then turns and walks out of the ornate Oval Office, leaving behind a stunned crowd of Washington insiders.

The secretary of state looks at the president, "Did he just resign?" she asks.

The president picks up the twin ribbons of stars laying on the corner of the Resolute Desk, "I would say so."

The secretary of state smiles. "Now we can put one of our people into that position. We can't have dissent among the leaders of our armed forces." Around the room people nod. They have all come to know that discussion is not really allowed. They are puppets picked to approve what the true power players have already decided.

The president is humbled. A man with enough conviction to resign is a man he wants on his staff. A senior aide is sent after the general to inform him that his resignation has been denied by the president. The president wants to hear the opposing views.

The words of his friend echo through the general's mind. 'God put you here at this time and in this place for a reason'. The general thought he had done his duty. Apparently, his mission is not yet completed.

***

While this act of valor is taking place, General Shapiro's operations officer, Frank, has issued discreet orders; Mustafa and anyone with the mark of Christ is to be eliminated. In black op rooms, targets are established, and missions are set in place. Those with a mark must be killed. The people assigned with the mission do not question why. They are in place to follow orders, not question them.

Chapter 43, God Is In Control

"The power of the Lord is greater than the power of the state," Xi proclaims from the tailgate of a pickup truck. "The power of the Lord has been awakened. His wrath is coming, and it is coming soon! How many babies has the state ripped from the wombs of our women? How many people have been killed for their religious beliefs? The elites have pillaged us, enslaved us, mocked and ridiculed us. They have turned neighbor against neighbor, brother against brother. This is not the way of our forefathers!"

"We're an ancient and proud people!" Xi implores, sparking a fire in many who know the long and proud history of the Manchurian people. "We have always enjoyed freedom and the fruits of our labors. Our ancient society grew because of our industriousness and our intellect. The state wants to strip our dignity, our heritage away from us. They have turned us into mere slaves, beholden to the state. Now they want to strip away any form of religion. They know that belief in God will undermine their authority. Therefore, God himself must be destroyed."

Xi looks down and shakes his head. He rises up and lifts his arms as he looks out across the large crowd that has gathered. "God cannot be destroyed! The creator of heaven and earth, the father of man, cannot be destroyed by what he created! Only God himself can destroy what he created. And it is foretold in the scriptures that God will once again bring ruin to the earth. But God is merciful. He sent His Son, Jesus, to save us from His wrath. He tells us that if we believe in Jesus as our Savior, then we can be saved."

"The state says you are their slave, their property. Did they create you? How can you belong to them if they did not create you? God created you. You belong to God! Please, turn away from the state. Turn to God, your creator, the one who loves you and has a place for you in heaven. Take these words into your heart."

Xi turns and points his finger upstream at the massive dam only a few miles away. "God did not create that. God can bring it down with the touch of his finger. God's hand has been decimating the works of man around the world. Two great cities have fallen, and the earth continues to tremble. Take to heart the words I have given you and flee this valley. Flee from all that man has created and turn to God, your eternal father."

The driver of the pickup that Xi has been using as a stage honks his horn as he sees government troops trying to make their way through the massive crowd. Xi plops down into the bed of the truck as the small convoy begins to roll. The crowd converges around the government troops as Xi and his convoy head out of town, traversing the steep roads that lead to the next town below the dam. As they bump along, Xi prays that his message has reached its target. He spoke from his heart; he spoke what God laid on him. An hour later he is in Yichang, a much larger city. He gives the same message.

***

Xi has no idea that his message is being heard around the world. Cell phone video clips of his short sermons and confrontations are making their way through the social media platforms, reaching millions of people. An enterprising and media savvy young priest in Australia creates a YouTube channel of Xi's exploits. In just a few days it has gained several million followers. The young priest downloads Xi's speech from in front of the massive dam. 'A modern-day Jeramiah', he thinks. 'This message has to be told.' Thirty minutes later, the message is posted accompanied by supporting scripture. The young priest adds a final comment. "This man tells those who are around him to flee from the dam, a man-made structure. There is a perfect metaphor here. We, as Christians need to flee from all the man-made constructs that have been erected. I plea for you to turn to the truth that can only be found in the Bible and by knowing God."

***

Halfway around the world, one of Georgeanne's people comes across the priest's YouTube channel. Soon the group in Southern California meets to discuss what is happening. The city around them continues to burn and crumble into chaos. Their people are in the streets doing their best to help out; to spread the message through their acts of kindness and in their message of love. But they all know more needs to be done.

Twelve devout Christians sit around the large conference table. They are tired, they are dirty, they are out of their element. A change of clothes would be a welcomed renewal. With water in short supply, no one has even had a sponge bath. Twelve people who are used to all the luxuries ever available to mankind sit in their own filth and stink to discuss their options. The mood is not good.

Clarissa sees the despair and knows that the group needs to be uplifted. She begins to slowly tap her feet and hum a familiar tune. Shawn picks up the soft rhythmic beat and starts to tap on the conference table. The others around the table look at Clarissa and Shawn. They are at their wits end. They want this true nightmare to be over. And here are these two young people smiling and humming the beat of a familiar song.

Before anyone says anything, Clarissa softly begins to sing. Her melodic voice stuns the group. The first words out of her mouth brings tears to the eyes of those at the table. "Amazing grace, how sweet the sound, that saved a wretch like me..." She sings on and the others join in. Clarissa knows all seven verses by heart. The rest follow along as best they can. When the verse about praising the Lord for ten thousand years is sung, they all stand and sing to the Lord with all their hearts.

When they finish singing, they all turn to each other, hugging and sharing. The air of despair has left. A renewed effort sweeps into the room. Despite their despair, they must continue with their mission.

The lead pastor of the large church, Michael, speaks up. "What do we do? We know Christ is going to come back, but we do not know when. How can we proclaim the events of the day as a sign that Christ is coming?"

"Christ is coming soon," Shawn states. "He told us that two thousand years ago. We must always be aware that he is coming soon. We must always be prepared. But we cannot proceed using the news of today to proclaim Jesus as Savior. Today's events may be the wrath of God for turning away from him, but we will not win souls through fear. We will win souls through truth, and that truth is found in love."

"The only way to reach the people in an effective way is through mass media," Georgeanne states. "Everyone is tuned in now, looking to see the next great event. My people are taking the latest videos from around the world and are putting together a new message. Well, it is not a new message. It is a message that is two-thousand-years old. Christ could proclaim it to a few thousand at a time. We're going to proclaim it to millions, even billions!"

"Yes, we need to do that," Pastor Michael states. "But what can the rest of us do?"

Shawn responds. "What we are already doing. Love on our neighbors in any way we can, and pray. We need to be doing what we're asking others to do. Let's take a short break. We'll regroup in thirty minutes. We've been through a lot. Let's take some time to think things through."

Michael pulls Shawn aside as he is rising to join Georgeanne and Clarissa. "You seem to be a gifted man Shawn, but how do we know we can trust you? You say you are chosen. What does that mean? Clarissa says she has seen you in heaven. The Bible warns us to be wary of false prophets. The Bible tells us no one knows the time or the day of his return. What if the earthquakes are just the rumblings of the earth? Why so much urgency now?"

For a moment Shawn is rattled. A senior pastor, with many years of service to the Lord is questioning him. He is new to his calling. Is he stepping on the pastor's toes? Is he making the pastor feel small? Is it like a Pharisee questioning Jesus? He quiets his heart and looks at the seasoned religious leader. "I'm chosen in the same way you are chosen. God laid on your heart to preach His Word. You studied His Word, you prayed for His guidance, and He blessed you. You have built a strong faith community and have spread salvation through both words and deeds. But not all paths are the same. I assure you I'm following the path that God has laid before me."

"You parted the waters," Michael responds. "You performed a miracle, or the devil is in you."

Shawn smiles and chuckles a bit. "My friend, the devil can tempt people, but the devil cannot perform miracles, only God can. Yes, the waters parted, but only because I truly believed that God could do it. You have done it too Michael, in your ministry. You have parted the waters and moved mountains through your faith. Don't doubt that faith because it is needed now more than ever."

The pastor ponders that response and acknowledges to himself that throughout his life miracles have happened, sometimes they were small, sometimes they were big,

"But you say Christ is coming soon," Michael states, with concern. "Christ himself said no one knows the time or day. Yet you seem to project that you know when he is coming and that our days here on earth are numbered."

Shawn looks at Michael with some frustration. How did what he so plainly state get twisted into this false premise? He sighs in frustration. The devil is twisting his words. "All that has happened is overwhelming for us all, pastor. I did say that Christ's return is coming soon. I said it in reference to what Christ said two thousand years ago. We should lead our lives everyday as if Christ will return tomorrow. None of us know when that will happen, including me. I'm not proclaiming Christ's imminent return. I'm only proclaiming that he will return."

The pastor ponders what Shawn is saying and begins to nod in agreement. Everything the young man is saying is true to the scriptures. In a matter of days, the young man has transformed his church from a local establishment into a hub with worldwide reach. He needs to be reassured that they are truly doing God's work, spreading God's message.

"You have a large fresh scar on your forehead. Clarissa has a prominent birthmark on her cheek. She says she saw you in heaven. How do you explain that?" the pastor asks.

"I'm a descendant of the tribe of Gad, Clarissa is a descendant of the tribe of Rueben. In the book of Revelation, John says that one hundred and forty-four thousand descendants of Israel will be sealed. Their place in heaven is secure. In the book of Mark, Jesus states that His Word must be proclaimed to the nations before He returns. I believe in my heart that we're those messengers. I believe in my heart that the people we have seen around the world bravely proclaiming the message are part of that group."

The pastor stands silently for a few moments as he processes what he has just been told and what he has seen over the past few days. It makes sense, but it seems too farfetched. Is God testing him? Is the devil tempting him?

"If you are part of the twelve thousand from each of the twelve tribes of Israel, that would indicate that Christ is returning soon. Doesn't that contradict what you just said?"

"It is a circular argument, pastor. Christ said he was returning soon. I say Christ is returning soon. Was Christ right but I'm wrong?" Shawn asks calmly.

"Pray with me," the pastor says as he reaches his hand out to Shawn. "God, show me the truth. If this man is part of Your kingdom, show me a sign. If it is Your will, grant me the wisdom to help him. I pray this in Christ's name. May Your will be done."

Shawn looks up to heaven and says, "Amen." He turns to the pastor with a knowing smile. "God will answer your prayer, in the meantime let's go and see what Georgeanne has put together."

A few minutes later they are in the church's recording studio where Georgeanne and her people have compiled a five-minute video showing the events of the last few days. It shows dramatic scenes from the earthquakes in both Los Angeles and Osaka. It shows clips of other scenes from around the world that people have posted to you tube and other video sharing channels. They all watch intently. The message is powerful. "Turn away from the corrupt world that man has created, turn to what God desires, a world of love, forgiveness, and redemption."

One of the church elders is in tears. "That is a powerful testimony. The ending with the young autistic woman telling people they need to go to church; I still have tears in my eyes." The ending of the clip remains on the screen showing a still shot of the face of the autistic girl as she exclaims God's love.

Pastor Michael looks at the screen with some puzzlement. "Can you zoom in on the woman's face?" he asks. A technician zooms in so the screen only shows the young woman's face. It is striking to all of them. There is fear in her eyes, yet there is determination. There is spittle on her dry and cracked lips. They can even see a bit of a run on her nose. But Pastor Michael sees something else that only Shawn and Clarissa see too. Square in the middle of the young woman's forehead is a birthmark, an odd-shaped birthmark, roughly resembling the continent of South America.

The senior pastor turns to Shawn and Clarissa. He reaches out and touches Shawn's scarred forehead. He then turns and caresses Clarissa's birthmark. A tear forms on his cheek. "I don't' need to be struck by lightning to see God's truth." He looks at Shawn. "I'm sorry I

290

doubted you, my friend. Both of you are truly blessed. We will do everything we can to help you."

Minutes later, Georgeanne's video is posted. They wait in anticipation to see if the message is seen and shared. Georgeanne looks at the gathered group as the view count hits 84. "Give it time. Let's get something to eat." She shoos the bystanders out of the small studio, and they all move to the food line where they are served a thin soup. It is the best the church can do with food supplies starting to run low.

Chapter 44, Movements

"Forty-one targets in site. No visible arms. No visible explosives," the young corporal reports from her front-line position. Her job is to report what she sees as accurately as she can. No commentary, just the facts. She is serving her two years of mandatory service in the Israeli military. Her sharp eyes and keen mind have put her on an outpost near the Sea of Galilee. It is an area that is normally very quiet, where Arabs and Israelis trade across the disputed border and usually live in peace, except when the Arab militias decide to fire some rockets and stir things up.

She continues with her report. "There are at least two hundred civilians with them. Some are dancing and singing. Others look troubled. I have never seen anything like this. It looks like a combination of a wedding festival and a funeral procession. They are definitely heading towards our border checkpoint. They will pass beyond my viewpoint in a few minutes."

"Message received," she hears in her ear bud. "Stay put, keep alert. Situation is still amber."

The corporal taps the young man dozing next to her, her outpost partner. "I reported everything. We're to stay put. We're still in amber status, nothing to be alarmed about."

The young man turns and smiles at his foxhole partner. He runs his finger up her slender thigh. "Well, we can tell them what we did a few hours ago. That would give them something to be alarmed about."

She slaps his hand away. "Don't get any new ideas. I was bored then. And I'm stilled bored."

Chagrinned, the young man looks out over the broad valley and the large group of people heading west, towards the border checkpoint. "So, what's up Sheila? What does our vaunted commander think of this rather large caravan of refugees?"

"They're not refugees, they're immigrants, I think. I'm not sure how they will be classified. Some of them are ISIS fighters. Most of them are Israeli settlers. Apparently, they are expected." She hands the high-powered binoculars to her teammate. "None of them are armed. Go ahead and check them out, see if I missed something."

The young man takes the binoculars and looks at his trim mate. "I can assure you that you didn't miss a thing," he replies with a smirk on his face. Sheila slaps him once again. "That will never happen again. Now do your job!"

***

Mustafa and his small group leave Gadot and head towards the new Jewish settlement of Mishmar HaYarden that straddles the disputed border. The surrounding countryside is abundant. It is full of thriving vineyards, fields of lush vegetables and groves of heavily laden olive trees. Ancient homesteads are scattered across the landscape; some are well maintained and still in use. Others have fallen into disrepair, having been vacant for decades, even centuries.

As the group comes over a small rise, the Israeli settlement comes into view. Over a hundred trim and neat homes can be seen, laid out on straight and well paved roads. There is a village square that is the marketplace for the settlers, as well as a small modern strip mall with a few stores, a gas station, and a hardware store. There is also a military garrison at the border crossing checkpoint.

Mustafa crests the hill with many of his followers surrounding him. He has marveled at the abundant fields and vineyards, even stopping to enjoy some of the freshly ripe grapes of a roadside vineyard. At the crest of the hill, he can fully take in the surrounding land. "This is a blessed land!" he exclaims. "It is no wonder that this is the land God led Abram to." He spreads his arms out wide. "Look at this land, my friends! Have you ever seen anything like this in Syria or Iraq? Even their most fertile valleys don't compare to this. This is truly land blessed by God."

The forty former ISIS fighters look around, most with wide eyes. All the way to the horizon they see lush vineyards, sturdy olive groves and well-kept homesteads. "We have been taught that the Israelis have been cursed by God and are evil," one of Mustafa's commanders exclaims out loud, bewildered. "Surely we have been lied to. We live in poverty while right next door the Israelis live in abundance!"

The entire group has now stopped at the crest of the hill as they take in the beauty of the land before them. Mustafa gathers the crowd around him, both his former ISIS fighters and the Jewish converts, Messianic Jews, that have followed him. "This land has been fought over for thousands of years. Our small army is going to bring a new invasion to this land. We're going to bring the truth of Jesus Christ. The Jewish people are proud; they are stubborn. They are going to reject our message. They rejected it two thousand years ago. Most will reject it again. But God loves His chosen people. It is our mission to proclaim His love so they might be saved."

The people around him gawk in amazement. A young Israeli girl uses her GoPro camera to catch the events for her YouTube postings. "Israel is about to be invaded by a new kind of army, an army of Christian warriors, an army of former enemies who have changed their ways. I have witnessed the power of their words; I have witnessed their conviction. They are not like the curious Christian tourists. These men come with a conviction to convert the Jewish nation to Christianity. I have heard their leader speak. He speaks with knowledge and passion. He lays out how Christ truly fulfilled the prophesies. He is correct in saying we're a stubborn people. We were stubborn in the days of Isaiah and we're still stubborn to this day. He convinced me that Jesus Christ is truly the Savior. I pray that my people listen. Please stay tuned as I document this earth changing event."

As she closes her video feed, the earth trembles, rocks shake. Old buildings in the area tumble down, sending clouds of dust into the crisp clean air.

***

A thousand miles to the south, in the Great Rift Valley of Africa, a massive earthquake creates new chasms and causes massive landslides as the remote location experiences a huge tectonic shift. Gorges two hundred feet deep are ripped into the valley floor as the earth violently heaves. Ridges a hundred feet high and miles long suddenly project from the earth. In a matter of a few minutes the tectonic plates realign. New mountains arise, some mountains crumble. Ancient lakes drain as new lakes are formed. Rivers are diverted as the continent of Africa begins to take a new form.

Technicians watch their scientific gauges and start to sound the alarm. Geologists around the world scramble to understand what is happening. None of their models work. Their science fails them, and they begin to panic.

The scientists at the USGS headquarters in Reston, Virginia record and report their findings methodically. Earthquakes registering over 6.0 on the Richter scale are usually rare events. For the past few days, they have been regular occurrences. The scientists and geologists have been scurrying and brainstorming to develop a sound reason for what is happening. They have looked at everything from the alignment of the planets to the strength of the polar magnetic fields. Nothing explains what is happening. They have tried to keep the earth's trembling's hidden from the public to keep people from panicking, but when cities begin to crumble, they can no longer hide what they know.

"We have another major shift," a technician hollers. "Great Rift Valley in Ethiopia. 9.4 on the Richter scale." Several senior scientists rush to the woman's cubicle. She pulls up a real time satellite shot on one screen while two other screens show a plethora of real time technical data. "This is serious, people," she states, trying to be calm. "The Nile river looks like it may shift its path and flow through Nigeria and to the Red Sea instead of flowing through Sudan and Egypt. Land mass shifts are greater than anything we have ever seen."

A senior scientist watches the satellite feed and data screens as the earth begins to take on a new shape. The largest river in the world may change its path. The largest lake in the world may drain out, forever changing the African landscape. "I want two more stations to monitor this. George and Diane, you need to work up a world call now. If the Nile shifts its path, Egypt needs to know now, not tomorrow."

"Earth dam, we have an earth dam being created in the Nile valley," another technician hollers out. He has just shifted his screens to the new hot spot. "The valley walls have crumbled into the Nile river just south of the Sudan border."

The senior scientist rushes over to see the satellite feed. "That's going to create a new lake," one geologist states.

"And the Nile will shift to the Great Rift Valley," another geologist exclaims in wonder. "What else is coming?" she whispers, scared to her core by what she is seeing.

The senior scientist sees panic starting to spread across the floor. She needs her crew to remain calm. She steps up on a nearby desk and addresses the vast room of people monitoring the data screens from around the world. "My friends and colleagues, please remain calm. We all know that we're seeing unusual earth movements. But are they that unusual? We have only been monitoring tectonic plates for a few decades. What we're experiencing has happened in the past. It will happen again. We just happen to be the first people to record it. The great New Madrid earthquake caused the Mississippi river to flow upstream for several days. The earth is changing as it always has. It is just changing a little faster than normal these past few days. Keep calm. Everything is going to be okay."

Just then a loud beeping echoes around the room. It sounds every time an earthquake over 7.0 is recorded. A few days ago, that was a significant event. This is the fourth alert today. A technician quickly hits the reset button silencing the shrill alarm. "Manchuria, 7.2," a technician yells over the hubbub. A gasp of silence follows his pronouncement. A moment later he gives a short report. "It looks like the Three Gorges Dam remains stable."

The Three Gorges Dam is the largest man-made dam in the world. Some geologists wondered if the weight of the water behind the dam would cause the earth's rotation to be altered. It was built to withstand a 7.8 earthquake, according to the Chinese engineers. But what shortcuts did they take? Did the contractors truly build it the way the engineers designed it? If the dam fails, a wall of water would sweep downstream for hundreds of miles, killing millions of people.

Chapter 45, Broadcasting

Yichang is a city of a half million people on the Yangtze river only a few dozen miles south of the Three Gorges Dam. By Chinese standards, it is a village, a rural outpost of no consequence. But the five hundred thousand inhabitants of Yichang value their lives. They have feared the construction of the dam since its inception. Despite the government's ability to quash the news, the residents of Yichang have heard of the massive earthquakes happening around the world. They know that a massive earthquake would send a wave of water hundreds of feet high down the Yangtze River, inundating their town.

Xi has arrived as panic begins to spread. His message to fear the government and trust the Lord hits home. As he is speaking, the earth trembles violently. It drives home his message. Thousands are baptized in the river before they flee to the surrounding mountains. As they flee, they carry a message, the message of redemption, the message of forgiveness.

Two hours later, Xi is on the road once again. He is heading for the city of Wuhan. A city of over twelve million people. If the dam breaks, this major city straddling the Yangtze River will be the worst hit. The flood from the dam breaking will no longer be a massive wave. As the flood waters spread out into the many valleys upstream, the flood will turn from a wave into a massive surge. The surge of water will inundate the vast city in a matter of minutes. Even with hours of notice, there would be no way to evacuate twelve million people. The highways would be jammed as the massive surge of water pushed down the river valley. The death toll would not be in the tens of thousands. The death toll would reach into the millions.

And no alarm has been sounded. The massive earthquakes that have happened around the world don't make the news. There is no report of the earthquake that may have weakened the dam a hundred miles upstream. The twelve million people in the city of Wuhan go about their business, oblivious to the possible destruction they face.

Five hundred miles away, in Beijing, the Chinese Politburo makes two decisions. The news blackout will continue. And three divisions of troops will be sent to Manchuria to eliminate the religious revolt that is unfolding. A special search will be made for anyone with a mark. They are to be shot on sight.

As Xi and his small caravan approach Wuhan, they see many cars, trucks and buses leaving, heading into the surrounding countryside and higher ground. Some are civilian buses and private cars. Many more are military caravans and government transport vehicles. Someone has ordered an evacuation. The military and high-ranking government officials are getting out of the city's flood plain. How long will it take for the civilian populace to get wind of what is happening? Xi knows the rumor mill will crank up quickly. The Chinese people instinctively mistrust the government. Once word of the massive earthquakes happening around the world begins to circulate, these roads will be jammed with people trying to flee the city.

"Six hours. That is all the time we have here to spread the message. How do we spread the message to Twelve million people in six hours?" Xi asks the large jail guard who has remained at his side this entire time. "I can't reach twelve million people from the back of a pickup truck."

The guard sees a situation up ahead and asks the driver of their SUV to pull over. All four of their vehicles pull over too, the occupants wondering what is happening. The guard gathers their makeshift security detail together and they hastily make a plan. He tells Xi they will be back in a few minutes. He asks the entire group to pray for them. Without explanation two women and six men set off on a daring and bold mission.

On the other side of the highway from Xi's convoy is a military truck that has broken down. A command vehicle has pulled aside as well, to assist. Xi's security people are walking toward the two military vehicles on the opposite side of the road. Xi's first thought is that he is being betrayed. He sees himself being placed under arrest and he plots out in his mind what he would do. He closes his eyes and begins to pray for strength and guidance. He knows from the scriptures that many of the apostles were jailed, but God intervened. He prays for that same kind of divine intervention.

As he is saying amen, an older man in the back seat grabs Xi's shoulder. "Look teacher!" he exclaims. Xi opens his eyes and looks towards the vehicles on the other side of the road. A scuffle is taking place. His people surprise the soldiers and quickly overwhelm them. Faster than Xi can react, Xi's guards have the Chinese soldiers subdued. Moments later the soldiers are secured in the back of the military truck and Xi's guards return with smiles on their faces. They each carry bundles of clothing.

The jail guard jumps in the SUV. "Let's roll! We need to get out of here." Their convoy quickly pulls back onto the road, and they speed down the highway towards Wuhan, leaving the scene of the crime as quickly as possible.

"What did you do?" Xi asks, exasperated.

"We acquired a few military uniforms and a bit of military equipment," the guard responds as he holds up a radio. He turns it on and makes a few adjustments. Soon they are listening to the military's command channel. "Don't worry teacher. We didn't kill anyone. A few people may have been bruised, but no one will die. And we're only borrowing the uniforms. We'll give them back when we're done." The large man smiles and chuckles at his own joke.

Xi is still stunned by what just took place. "Why do we need the uniforms?" he asks angrily. "Dressing up as the people's army will not win us friends among the people."

"You are right, prophet. The people do not like the army. But they respect the army. So when we march into the local radio and television station, we will be respected and obeyed." The guard smiles at Xi with pride.

"What are you talking about? What radio station?" Xi says, anger still in his voice. Then he sits back as what his guard has said sinks in. A smile begins to form on his face. "How do we reach twelve million people? You found the answer." He turns and looks at the burly man. "I underestimated you, my friend. This is a stroke of genius."

"That is one of the reasons I hate the state," the guard replies. "My test scores should have put me in the engineering curriculum. But they judged me by my size and strength. So, I was put in law enforcement and ended up as a jail guard."

"God blessed you with talents," Xi responds. "I guess He is using those talents now."

***

Thirty minutes later the convoy passes in front of a concrete and glass building with several satellite dishes on the roof as well as a few large antennae poking into the sky. A block away they pull into the parking lot of a large warehouse.

One of the guard's people speaks up first. "There was only one security guard at the gate. I didn't see any military vehicles in the parking lot."

"Good eye, Zhou," another guard responds. "I think their security detail has beat feet. Maybe they are the ones we rolled on the highway!" This draws a few smatterings of laughs from the serious looking group. They are changing into the military uniforms. They hastily make a plan. There will be no violence. They will walk in as if they own the place; order people around as if the chairman himself sent them on this mission. If they act with authority, the people will comply. The people are used to complying to authority.

Xi is amazed at the boldness of the plan. He is amazed at the boldness of the people who only just a few days ago came to know Christ. It confirms his thought that the newest believers have the most passion. These people are willing to walk into a very uncertain situation so that he can preach the Word. The thought humbles him. He prays for strength. He once again sees a vision of heaven. In this vision, he sees a multitude of people, the people surrounding him now, and tens of thousands more people. He falls to his knees. Is this the fruit he is to gather? He is humbled, but he also feels a great burden fall on his shoulders.

In his prayers, he hears a voice. A voice he has not heard for several days. *'I will not give you a task that you are not prepared to handle. If I am with you, who can stand against you?'*

Xi feels the burden fall from his shoulders as the Holy Spirit fills him. He knows he is following God's path. He is embarrassed that he doubted. He turns to his compatriots with newfound faith. He prays a blessing over them all. They are about to do God's work. They will preach the Word of hope to the twelve million people of Wuhan.

***

Twenty-four people march into the broadcast studios barking commands and demanding action. The presence of eight soldiers, including a colonel, impresses upon the technicians and producers that they need to follow orders. The facility broadcasts on three television channels, two AM frequencies and four FM frequencies. There are larger broadcast facilities in the area, but this will do.

The eight 'soldiers' bark orders, and the facility's technicians start to assist Xi and his people in their mission. They develop their message and get ready to go live. They will begin the broadcast with a short message of love. "We're messengers from God. He loves you and will never leave you. Turn to him now and ask for forgiveness. The state has been lying to you. The world is in trouble." This is followed by short videos of the earthquakes happening around the world including scenes of the Three Gorges Dam. A crew member provides narration that will help make the radio broadcasts make sense.

At this point, Xi begins a short sermon. "My name is Xi and God has sent me to proclaim this message to the people of this once great nation. We have become a pagan nation. We kill our babies in the womb. We succumb our children to slavery. We have forsaken any notion of God. We all know this is wrong. Our ancestors celebrated life. Our ancestors enjoyed freedom. But now we're slaves to the state. Rise up against the state. Take back your freedom. Take back your wholesome spirit that you were born with."

"People, there is a God. He created you and He loves you. The state is tyranny. God is freedom. Turn to God.

"You have just seen the videos of what is happening around the world. You have seen those videos because we have taken over this state-run broadcast facility. The state does not want you to see what we have shown you. The earth is trembling. As God predicted, the earth will be remade. Turn to God, and flee this valley filled with evil spirits and evil deeds. Flee from the state that has turned our people away from God."

"Do these things now to purify your soul. Love God who is here to save you. Love your neighbors as you love yourself. These are the values of our forefathers. These are the values of a good and just people. These are the values that will bring you peace in your heart and eternal salvation."

"My name is Xi, and I bring these words to you from your loving father, God almighty."

Xi sits back and exhales. Sweat is pouring from his brow, his shirt is soaked in sweat. He looks through the heavy glass that separates the recording studio from the engineer's room. He sees many of his followers in tears. Some of the technicians are in tears too and his people embrace them. They begin praying with them. Other technicians are red faced, angry. Their studio was just used by rebels. They will be branded as rebels as well, just for allowing the short broadcast to happen. A scuffle breaks out, but Xi's guards quickly take control of the situation.

Xi's new friend and right-hand man steps into the studio. "We have to go teacher. Our radios tell us that troops are heading this way. The message has been put on a loop and will continue to be broadcast until someone stops it." The large man wraps Xi up in a warm hug. "You did it, We did it. We proclaimed God's Word to twelve million people. And we did it in three hours. Now let's get out of here. I don't think God is done with us."

Xi stands up and follows his friend. He's in a bit of a daze. He passes a television screen in the lobby as they head out the door. He sees himself proclaiming the Word. He sees his own resolve and compassion expressed to the people through the broadcast. It strengthens him. Their group heads into the parking lot and the small caravan gets ready to roll. He looks in the side mirror of the passenger seat and sees two of the station's trucks join their caravan, a satellite truck, and a production truck. The guard smiles. "We have gained a few new allies, or I guess I should say converts."

They merge into the growing stream of traffic. Xi pushes the search button on the radio and he is soon hearing their short broadcast. He smiles as he closes his eyes and says a silent prayer.

***

In a highly secured mansion on the shores of the Black Sea, an old and decrepit man is notified of the events happening in the city of Wuhan.

"Take me up to my villa," the old man states. "I need to go to my place of worship."

His aides escort him from the beach where he was enjoying some time in the sun, watching the waves roll in, and the boats duck and dive as the fishermen haul in their nets.

Soon he is alone in his inner sanctum where he bows down before his image of Baal.

"Why do you allow the enemy to boldly proclaim their faith? Why must I always worship in the dark?" Abaddon pleads. "We are winning, my lord. Child sacrifice has become accepted around the world. Science has become the new god. Worship of earth has supplanted worship of the creator of the earth. Humanity is truly on the verge of choosing self-service over self-sacrifice. Yet I worship you in the dark."

Abaddon does not get an answer from the carved block of stone. He did not expect one. He moves to his situation room and issues more orders. He has let down his god. He will correct that. He will have his people proclaim his god. He knows that the next news cycle will feature people proclaiming the science of climate change and that mother earth must be respected. In his cold and calculating ways he will use influential people to turn the masses away from the creator of the earth and have them begin to worship the earth itself. His allies are true believers. They do his bidding willingly, seeing the control they can exert over the masses and the power they can gain by making the earth an object of worship.

Chapter 46, Tsunami

"A third major quake happened, and more rumblings are occurring around the world. What more evidence do we need to claim that Christ's return is imminent?" a church elder asks.

"The wildfires are spreading," another woman, their head of Christian education states. "Three interstate highways within ten miles of us are closed due to the wildfires. Add to that the rumors of a major civil uprising in China. These are scriptural events, prophesy fulfilled. That video from Argentina shows a husband turning against his wife, brother against brother."

The senior pastor sits calmly as his own people seem to crumble around him. They are not in panic, but they are close to it. They want him and Shawn to do a joint message proclaiming that Christ is coming now. They want a powerful message to be delivered and broadcast by all means available.

The pastor understands their passion. All signs point to the fulfillment of Christ's message. The rapture could occur at any moment. Those who know Christ will be taken to heaven. Those who do not know Christ will be left behind as God's wrath sweeps across the earth. All Christians want to spread the message. All Christians want everyone to know salvation.

But one message from Christ is very clear. No one knows the day or the hour of His return. To proclaim His imminent return would be false prophesy. How does one proclaim the urgency of the moment without becoming a false prophet? Other preachers have already begun to claim the end is near. Some sound foolish and bombastic. Others give reasoned explanations, sounding deep and thoughtful, but not relatable to the common man. He tries to explain this to the strong believers around him. This only brings about more arguments. Brother is truly fighting brother.

Shawn and Clarissa listen and watch. But they don't have the answer. They don't know the time nor the day. They only know they have a mission. But all Christians have the same mission. Shawn and Clarissa have just been more adamant. They have been sealed, but all Christians are sealed. What makes them special? They had a dream they were in heaven. Who hasn't had that dream? Are they really chosen?

Both of them hear a still and quiet voice. *'How will they hear without one who proclaims Him.'*

They turn to each other at the exact same moment. Their eyes meet and there is a moment of clarity. They have a mission to fulfill. Just then, Georgeanne bursts into the room. She is excited, more worked up than normal. "You all have to see this! This is from some city in China. It's going viral, over a million views in just twelve hours." The tech savvy woman jabs at her tablet and a few moments later the screen on the office television shows Xi proclaiming the Word to the citizens of Wuhan. They are all moved by his words, related by a translator. The senior pastor, Shawn and Clarissa all note the fresh scar on the man's forehead.

Once the video has played through, Michael stands and addresses the room. "We have to act now. It is our time to be bold. We must act on faith. This man, Xi, our fellow Christian who is under great duress, is mounting a revolution in his country. A revolution of faith. We will mount our own revolution, a return to Christ and the moral principles our country was founded on. Georgeanne, put together the dramatic videos that you are so good at finding. Clarissa and Shawn, are you with me on this?" They both nod, smiling to see some action starting to take place. The pastor continues. "Good, we'll meet in the studios and hash out a short but precise message. I'm a pastor who can get long winded. You two are used to short and concise messages. I think we can put something together that relates the urgency of the moment but is true to the scriptures."

The room quiets down. The elders are pleased as decisive actions have been put in place.

***

Michael, the senior pastor, looks at the people around him in their small studio. "As I see it, our message needs to have three points. One, our country has moved away from our moral principles. Two, the country needs to embrace Christ and his love, God's forgiveness. Three, this has to happen now. I could make this an eighteen-week sermon series. This message needs to be given in less than ten minutes."

Georgeanne interrupts the pastor. "It needs to be less than three minutes. People will not click on a ten-minute video unless they are already committed to your message. The curious, the newcomer won't click on anything longer than three minutes. And if you don't grab their attention in the first fifteen seconds, they'll click off."

"Maybe we can make it three messages," the church's Christian education leader suggests.

"That would work if the first message is compelling enough for them to listen to a second message," Georgeanne responds. "The second message can be longer, maybe five minutes, because the viewer is already interested. But the first message has to be really strong."

"We should do both," Clarissa states with confidence. "We produce a three-minute comprehensive message as well as a three-part more in-depth message. We link them all together. It's not like we're buying ad time, we can post what we want, right Georgeanne?"

"Basically, your right," Georgeanne responds. "Unless big tech throttles us, or the government shuts us down, we can post as much as we want. Our last video post has over three million views. It has gained sponsors at this point."

"Sponsors?" One of the elders asks sternly. "God doesn't need sponsors to proclaim his message. Does the cross need a corporate logo? I've never trusted this whole internet thing. God's Word should not be exploited by capitalism."

The room goes quiet. The woman's words ring true. There is tenseness in the air.

Michael shifts in his seat, thinking this through. "How many times have any one of us watched a sermon on television? Do you think that was free? No, the sponsoring churches paid to have their message aired. Why do you think Christian radio stations have fund raising drives? Airtime is not free. If Georgeanne's web channels have corporate sponsors, then so be it. They are paying for the Lord's Word to be proclaimed. They should be upheld, not defamed. They should be thanked, not cursed." Michael looks around the room as many heads nod.

The dissenting woman nods to Michael. "What you say makes sense, Pastor. We pay to have your sermons broadcast on a local cable station. It just seems dirty to have a sponsor to proclaim God's Word."

Clarissa speaks up once again. "In the book of Romans, Paul tells us that we all should give according to our talents, the talents that God has blessed us with. He alludes that good businessmen should be generous. I don't think it is sinful to be economically successful if one gives back to the church. That is what these sponsors are doing. They agree with the message that Georgeanne is proclaiming and are willing to support that effort."

Shawn is chomping at the bit. Ideas are rolling through his head. He knows the questions that have been raised needed to be hashed out. Now they need to act. He stands as he speaks. "We need to get people moving," he states. "Are we in agreement that we push forward as quickly as we can?" He pauses for a moment and no one dissents. "Michael, would you pray for us and this mission?" he asks as he turns toward the church's lead pastor.

Michael looks around the room, he feels good that they are acting as one body with one mission. He says a short prayer for them all, and their compatriots around the world.

***

The screen shows real video of the mayhem that is occurring around the world. Superimposed across the screen is a simple question. "Why is this happening?" The scenes are disturbing to watch, but real. Then the scene switches.

The screen shows a man and a woman walking together in the woods. They are naked and beautiful. A voice comes on calmly. "God created them, man and woman, this is what the Bible says." The screen switches to two strands of DNA swirling together, the calm voice continues. "Science says that the X and Y chromosomes determine our sex. We're told to follow the science, yet we say God is wrong. I don't understand this. We're genetically born as a man or a woman. How can science be right, but God is wrong when they both say the same thing?"

The screen switches to a small spec blasting outwardly. Bright points of light are scattered across the screen, depicting the creation of the universe, resulting in the brilliant stars throughout space. The calm voice resumes its narration. "In the book of Genesis, we're told that God created everything from nothing. The scientists say this is foolish nonsense. They want us to believe that everything was created from nothing for no particular reason at all. It just happened in one big bang."

The screen switches to Shawn who looks intently at the camera. "Let me get this straight. If everything came from nothing, then I'm a scientist. But if everything came from nothing because God did it, then I'm a religious zealot."

Shawn turns to a new camera. The background is a void of blackness. "If I believe in nothing, I'm a scientist." As Shawn continues to speak, the background bursts into explosions of color that meld

310

together to form a field of wildflowers. "If I believe in God, then I'm like most of you. Join with me in revolting against the science of nothing. Like most of you, I believe in God. It is not too late to stand up and believe in the truth. It is never too late."

The screen switches back to the man and the woman in the woods. "God created the earth," Shawn states. As he continues to speak, the scene decays into the chaos of the day. "He can destroy the earth as well. We have turned our backs on the one who created us. We have decided we came from nothing. We have placed our faith in nothing." The screen dissolves in an explosion and then goes black.

A woman's voice is then heard, distant but joyful. "God our creator loves us and wants us to be with Him." As she begins to speak a vague image starts to appear on the screen. "God knew we would turn from Him and become sinful." The image on the screen emerges into a cross. "He sent His Son to die for our sins." The image transforms to an open grave with a ray of light shining down from heaven. "He defeated death and rose to heaven where He has made a place for all who believe in Him."

The scene suddenly switches back to Shawn. In the background are scenes of mayhem. Shawn looks intently into the camera as he gestures at the mayhem behind him. "Jesus warned us of this. He told us in the Book of Mark, *'When you hear of wars and rumors of wars, do not be alarmed. Such things must happen, but the end is still to come. Nation will rise against nation, and kingdom against kingdom. There will be earthquakes in various places, and famines. These are the beginnings of birth pains.'"*

"I urge you to turn away from believing in nothing, I urge you to believe in God. What we're seeing now are just the birth pains." The screen fades from the mayhem, and transforms into a screen of beautiful wildflowers, with majestic mountains in the background. Shawn's calm voice is heard once again. "Share this video with all your friends and join us for more videos as we explain God's promise of redemption." The video fades to bright white with the appropriate links displayed in gold lettering.

**

"How did that work out?" Pastor Michael asks Georgeanne. "It seemed a bit long, but I could have gone for another hour if I was giving the message." He turns to Shawn, "Believe in nothing or believe in God, that was great. You boiled down the truth in a few lines. Have you ever thought about going to seminary school? You would make a great pastor."

Shawn smiles as he embraces the pastor. "God has given us the gifts, we need to follow His path, to do His will. My path is different than your path"

"Two minutes and forty-eight seconds," Georgeanne shouts out, answering the pastor's question.

"Perfect," Clarissa states. "Your visuals and audio background make it really poignant. You truly have a talent."

"You and Shawn's words make the video. I just dressed it up," Georgeanne responds. "You laid the groundwork to bring people in for more. What will be the essence of your next message? I'll start compiling videos for visual effects."

Shawn looks at Georgeanne, startled. "My next message? I'm worn out from that message. Maybe I do need to go to seminary."

Their conversation is interrupted by a loud rap at the door. They have been in the small studio for several hours. The loud rapping draws all their attention. One of the sound engineers opens the door. A young woman enters the room, breathless and shaken. "Another one has happened," she blurts out. "Mount Etna has exploded."

Michael comes to the young woman's side and gives her a comforting embrace. "You mean Mount Etna has erupted again?" he asks. Mount Etna is an active volcano in Italy.

312

"No, Mount Etna has exploded. The island of Sicily has been transformed. There are tsunami warnings over the entire Mediterranean sea." The young woman gulps for air. "They think underwater landslides have occurred. The resulting tsunamis could wipe out entire coastal towns and villages."

The people in the studio look around at each other. Mount Etna is one of the world's most active volcanoes. Georgeanne quickly brings up Fox News. In the background they can see what resembles a mushroom cloud. A young reporter tries to calmly explain the situation. "As you can see behind me, there is a giant mushroom cloud. I'm in Naples. It is over a hundred miles from Mount Etna. The cloud from the explosion is clearly visible. Some wonder if a nuclear bomb was dropped, but I can definitively state it was not a nuclear bomb. Mount Etna exploded. All across the Mediterranean there are tsunami warnings."

Michael closes his eyes and begins to pray. He has been to the Mediterranean on a trip to the Holy Land. He knows the geography. He knows a tsunami running unchecked in that confined sea could bring massive destruction to the seaside communities.

They watch as the reporter gives her eyewitness report. "Claxons are sounding. and people are starting to respond, but it seems like a lot of people don't know what to do. Some people are running to high ground. I guess they are locals who know what to do. If you look at the picture closely you can see what looks to be bellhops and barmaids urging the seaside guests to flee from their oceanside cabanas and divans. I repeat to you, this is Shana Divan reporting from Naples, Italy. Thirty minutes ago we heard distant rumbling explosions. My sources tell me that it was a massive eruption of Mount Etna. We have a tsunami warning due to the explosion of Mount Etna only a hundred miles away. I'm reporting from the third story of a beachfront hotel. In front of me, tourists are being urged to leave the beach. I can see others fleeing inland as the claxons sound all around me."

Halfway around the globe, in California, which has already been devasted by massive earthquakes, a half dozen people pray for the coastal cities of the Mediterranean sea. They watch as the reporter continues to give them a live feed.

The reporter continues. "This is surreal. Many people are fleeing inland but others seem to not care. We all heard the massive rumbling explosion. We all can see the mushroom cloud on the horizon as it continues to bellow higher into the sky. Yet many tourists seem unwilling to leave their prime beachfront locations." The camera shakes a bit as the scene changes. "Here you can see locals and others fleeing. I hope this is not another disaster like we saw in Malaysia."

She turns her camera back to the sea. "Oh crap," she exclaims. The camera shows people running inland as the sea draws away from the shoreline. "I pray for those people," she states. She drops the camera and is heard hollering. "Come up here! Come up here! Run up the steps! Run up the steps! You'll be safe. Move people, move!" The people watching the live feed can hear the desperation in the reporter's voice as she urges people away from the looming danger.

Someone picks up the camera and points it towards the beach. The American news anchor comes on. "You are watching live footage from Naples Italy where one of our reporters is covering the situation live. She is trying to spread the alarm to those on the beach of what could be imminent doom. In her panic she apparently dropped the camera. Someone else has picked up the camera and we can clearly see that the water has receded from the beach. We're told that this is what happens before a tsunami wave rolls ashore." The news anchor pauses for a moment as the video shows the water still receding from the beach. The newsman continues. "You may want to take your children away from the screen as we have been told from reliable sources that a tsunami wave is imminent. We intend to continue with our live coverage of this cataclysmic event."

The camera wiggles again and the on-scene reporter comes on camera. She is breathless and shaken. Her hair is disheveled and there

314

are smudges of dirt on her face. "I apologize to the viewers," she says emotionally. "Tragedy is happening right before me. I had to try and help. There is nothing more I can do. A tsunami is about to hit this town. Anyone who has not reached safety is in extreme peril. Many have fled inland. Did they flee far enough? Others have fled into the high-rise buildings like the one I'm in. Are these building strong enough to withstand the coming surge?"

The camera view changes to the oceanfront, which shows a beach devoid of people, but with no water. The camera zooms in to the waterline. The reporter adds her voice to what the people are seeing. "The water has receded at least a half mile from the coast. This is not good. All that water is going to come rushing back in. And when it does, it will push inland, wreaking devastation in its path."

The news anchor comes back on. "We're watching live coverage from Naples Italy. Mount Etna has exploded, not just erupted, our sources say it has exploded. You can see the mushroom cloud in the background of our reporter's video." The screen clearly shows the still growing mushroom cloud from Mount Etna. "We have a reporter on site in Naples Italy where a tsunami is imminent. We return to her live coverage of the impending disaster."

The screen switches back to the reporter on the third story of a beachfront hotel. The screen focuses on the distant beach. "I can see the water is starting to roll back in. If you look, you can see a mounting wave heading this way. From what we know of previous tsunamis, it is usually more of a strong and persistent surge, not a large wave." The reporter grows quiet as the video of the incoming wave continues. On the screen a large wave can be seen building as it closes in on the beach. After a few moments, the reporter starts speaking again. "As you can see a large wave is heading towards the beach. The wave is at least twenty feet high and gaining by the moment. Anyone still on the streets will be swept aside as this wave crashes ashore." The camera pans the streets below, which are mostly vacant, just a few people running into buildings or fleeing inland. "The claxons are still ringing but it looks as if most of the people have found some type of shelter," the reporter states.

The camera turns to show the incoming wave. It is clearly visible, and it is massive, well over thirty feet tall. The massive wave is only a few hundred yards from the beachfront. The camera stays focused on the wave for a few seconds as it rolls towards the coastal city. As the wave nears the coast, showing no signs of abating, the reporter is heard saying "Oh my God." The camera is dropped to the ground. The camera continues to broadcast as the wave rolls in. A few seconds later the camera goes dark as the forty-foot-high wave blows through the third story balcony of the ocean front hotel.

The news station switches to their news anchor. He is caught off guard, in shock by what he just watched. He sees the red light that lets him know he is live. He tries to compose himself. Choked up, he manages a few sentences. "That was traumatic live footage of a tsunami. We'll be back after a short break." The screen switches to a commercial for 'Botox'.

***

Pastor Michael and his entire crew are in shock by what they just witnessed. They sit in stunned silence.

One of the engineers finally speaks up. "That was a tsunami." He wipes the sweat from his brow and continues in a soft and mournful voice. "That reporter probably died. That wave was massive. No one has seen anything like that, ever."

Michael speaks up. His throat is dry. His voice is weak. "Tens of thousands are dying as we speak. That wave is still rolling into the countryside. We need to pray for them and their families." Michael's voice trembles as he says this. He knows he has prayed too many times and has not acted enough.

Shawn is stunned, horrified at what he just saw. The scar on his forehead begins to throb. He puts his hand to his head and feels a

316

dribble of blood. He looks over to Clarissa. Her birthmark seems to be glowing. What is God trying to tell them? Are they not doing enough? Do they need to be bolder? What more can they do?

The news station comes back from a prolonged commercial break. "This is exclusive breaking news. The president will be addressing the nation at eight AM today to reassure the nation amid these troubling times. We'll pick up coverage of the tsunami in Italy as soon as we can establish contact with our on-scene reporter."

The church secretary pokes her head into the office again. "Sorry to interrupt, but there is someone on the phone who wants to talk to Shawn. He says he is from the military. Someone from the Special Forces command center. What should I tell them?"

Michael instinctively says, "Take a message. Find out what they want." He is not thinking, just reacting.

Shawn fully comprehends the importance of the call. "Tell them I will be right there." He jumps up and heads toward the door. "Clarissa, come with me," he states as he heads out of the studio.

A few minutes later he is on the phone with an army colonel. "Are you the one who is on the video that proclaims the end is coming?"

"There's a lot of videos like that circulating the internet," Shawn replies. "If you are referring to the video from Shiloh Baptist Church in southern California, well, that's not actually what I said. I said to be prepared for the end to come. No one knows when Christ will return. There are lots of videos out there right now proclaiming a lot of things."

"Your videos are different. Your videos are getting millions of views. You're the guy who parted the waters," the colonel responds calmly. "Your videos have caught our attention. We want to talk with you."

Shawn pulls the phone away from his ear and hits the mute button. He looks at Clarissa. His normal naive exuberance vanishes. The government, the army, has sought him out. "What do I say?" he asks his soulmate.

Clarissa has a look of both concern and determination on her face. "God is working here. We don't know his ways. Talk with the man. Find out what he wants. I'll go get Pastor Michael and Georgeanne to help guide us."

Shawn quickly unmutes the phone and puts the audio on speaker. "Are you still there Colonel Harris? I'm gathering some of my associates around me. I'm putting you on speaker phone so we can all talk together."

"I'm still here young man. I fully understand the precautions you are taking. I have a few questions. First, how did you part the waters at the pool party? Before you answer, I want you to know our experts have studied all the tapes and interviewed many of the people who were there."

Shawn looks around the room before answering. His friends know his answer and they nod for him to tell the truth. "I must be truthful with you, Colonel Harris. I did not part the waters. God did." He briefly retells the events of what happened that day. As he winds up, he repeats his conviction. "God wanted to get the people's attention. He performed a miracle. The fact that I'm talking to you proves that God does work in strange ways."

The line is silent for a few moments before the colonel responds. "I was told to look for that response," the colonel responds. There is a different tone to his voice. Less authoritative, more respectful. "I have another question. What do you know about what is happening in China?"

Clarissa looks at Shawn and their eyes light up. Shawn answers truthfully. "I have only seen what has come across the internet; our news media has stifled this story. There is a man who is proclaiming

Christ as the Savior, just like I am here. He has gained many converts to Christ."

There is another pause from the army colonel. "There is something distinguishing about this man. Do you know what it is?"

Shawn looks at Clarissa who points to her birthmark. "I know what you're talking about," Shawn replies. "He has a fresh scar on his forehead, just like me."

"Do you know this man? Are you coordinating with him?" the colonel asks, his tone is frustrated, almost angry.

Shawn replies truthfully. "Yes, I know him because he is my brother in Christ. But I have never spoken to him. He is following the path he was asked to follow. I'm following my path."

"What do you know about the border breach in the Golan Heights?" the colonel asks.

"The Golan Heights?" Shawn questions. "What is happening there? We just watched the tsunami in Italy, but I don't know anything about the Golan Heights."

"You don't know a man named Mustafa?" the colonel asks.

"I have a few Arab friends here in southern California. But I don't know anyone by the name of Mustafa."

"We'd like to talk with you. Would you be willing to sit down with some of our people?"

Georgeanne mimics a slash across her neck and shakes her head. Then she speaks up. "We're talking with you now Colonel. We have answered all your questions without hesitation. What more do you want?"

"I assume this is Georgeanne Haquani talking," the Colonel responds. "You are the media guru for your group. You have done well. You have risen to one of the top one hundred media influencers on the web. We could have you shut down if we wanted to, but that would not be helpful to the situation."

"You are right, Colonel," Georgeanne responds. "The Word of Christ cannot be shut down. Even the totalitarian Chinese overlords have found this out. So, get to the point. Why is a low-grade army officer calling us?"

The line goes quiet for a few moments. The Colonel is not used to people talking back. "You are speaking to a Colonel because my bosses think you know something that they need to know. If we thought you were not important you would be talking to a sergeant, not a senior officer. There are thousands of calls like this happening right now. Your group is at the top of the list."

"Okay, then let's talk," Michael states. "We'll help in any way we can."

Georgeanne speaks up before the colonel can respond. "We're speaking the truth to the people, something our government hasn't done for years. Call back when you get serious about telling the truth." Georgeanne reaches out and disconnects the call. Some in the room, including Shawn, look dismayed.

"You just hung up on the man!" Shawn states, dumbfounded. "That was rude first of all, second, why?"

Georgeanne stands and stretches. Then she turns to her companions. "They need us more than we need them. We're proclaiming God's Word, and people are listening. The people are tired of the lies told by our media and our government. We have put their monopoly of power in jeopardy. They want everybody to live in fear. We're saying there is nothing to fear. We're offering a better outcome. This makes us a threat to the state."

"But what if people in the state are beginning to see the light?" Clarissa asks. "What if that guy was an ally?"

320

"He'll get back to us," Shawn replies as he ponders the situation. "If he truly sees what's happening and thinks we can help him, he'll get back to us. In the meantime, we need to find out what is happening in the holy land. Who is this Mustafa guy? And what is he doing?"

***

Abaddon is probably the only person on earth that celebrates the explosion of Mount Etna. He watched the death and destruction with a stoic face, but his soul found glee at the mayhem. He knows the destruction is being brought on by his god. He believes that things are turning in his favor. The news reports are all about an angry and abused earth revolting against mining, fracking, farming, and logging. He laughs at the stupidity of his followers.

He takes a sip of his wine as he replays the coverage of the tsunami hitting Naples. A smile crosses his face as he envisions the massive wave rolling inland, inundating thousands of helpless people. His revelry is interrupted by a flash message on his secure phone. "The California prophet refused to cooperate." Is the short message he receives.

Abaddon replies brusquely. "Eliminate the messenger."

Chapter 47, Invasion

The video of the crowd is calm and steady. A teenage woman, a newly converted Messianic Jew, films the arrival of Mustafa and his entourage at the official border of Israel with its military outpost and formal checkpoint. Mustafa and his twelve former ISIS commanders now lead a thousand people. Most are newly converted Christians, compelled by the power of Mustafa's message and his knowledge of the scriptures. Some are simply curious followers. The border guards have never seen anything like it. They have been in communication with their area supervisor for several hours as they watched the situation develop.

Now the crowd is at their checkpoint. They go about asking their normal questions. They do not want to rile the mob or cause an international incident. They want peace. Arabs and Israelis cross the border every day for trade, work and even just family visits. Many Israeli residents are Arabs that enjoy full citizenship. Border crossings are a normal part of their daily routine. The border guards have been advised to treat this abnormally large crowd as they would any other group of people trying to cross the border.

After each pilgrim is asked for their passport, the normal questions are asked, 'What is your country of origin?' 'What is the reason for your travel?' 'Have you ever been convicted of a violent crime?' 'How long will you be in Israel?'

The crowd begins to get loud and impatient as the border guards go through their rituals. Mustafa encourages his people to be patient and to pray. The Word is spread throughout the crowd. The often-belligerent Israelis quiet down and begin to pray. Mustafa is praying for a miracle. Few of his people have passports, and all of them are surely to come up as known ISIS fighters.

Since most of the people in the crowd are Israeli citizens, the border guards try to hasten the process. They shorten their questions and get lax on their passport inspections. Mustafa and his men are scattered throughout the crowd, but they are getting close to the checkpoint. Without a clean passport, they will be denied entry into Israel. Most of them will be arrested.

Mustafa is only a half dozen people away from the border guard. He knows he'll get into Israel. But he does not know how. He says a silent prayer. He wishes to follow God's will. As he says 'Amen', a young man bumps into him.

"Oh, I'm sorry teacher," the young man says. "My apologies." The young man bends down briefly and picks something up off of the ground. "I believe you dropped this," the young man states as he hands Mustafa a passport. Mustafa knows it is a forgery, but his keen eye sees that it is a good one. "Again, I'm so sorry. Is there anything I can do for you?" the young man asks sincerely.

Mustafa looks at the young man and smiles. "You have been very helpful my friend. Thank you for noticing my fumbling fingers. We all should be so blessed to have such a friend as you."

"Teacher, you and all your friends have been a blessing. Your faith alone is a blessing." The boy replies. He smiles and dodges back into the crowd.

A few moments later a border guard asks Mustafa a few questions and briefly looks at his passport. The border guard hands the passport back and tells him to move along. Two steps later, Mustafa is in Israel. He wants to cry. He wants to drop to his knees and pray. But he keeps moving. There will be plenty of time for crying and praying. He looks around him as he walks forward. He is in the promised land. He is walking on the same soil Jesus walked on. A calmness and peace comes over him. He feels great joy and great sadness all at once.

The large crowd continues to pour through the border crossing. It takes two hours for them all to pass through. By this time more people have gathered, wondering what the pilgrimage is all about. The group has moved into the countryside west of Mishmar

Hayarden along Route 91. They gather around Mustafa. They are now in the Holy Land. They came because he inspired them to turn to Jesus as their Savior. They are all full of the Spirit and the peace that He brings. They are ready to proclaim the Word, and eager to learn more.

Mustafa stands on a large stone so that those around him can see and hear him. The crowds quiet to hear him speak. "God gave his chosen people ten commandments. They are rules needed for any civilized society to survive. But he gave two higher commandments. The highest commandment is to love God. The second is to love your neighbor. The ten commandments guide us to lead righteous lives. The two higher commandments challenge us to live holy lives, lives of service. To be a follower of God is not to just follow his laws, it is to lead a life of service. This is not a New Testament commandment. It is stated in the Old Testament too."

Mustafa pauses for a moment and looks over the growing crowd. He notices a few military people on the fringes of the crowd, keeping an eye on things. His keen eye also spots several people who look like Mossad operatives. This does not surprise him. Israel is a tightly secured country. A mob of this size would not enter the country without ringing alarm bells in their vast security operations. But he and his people have been peaceful. They have not given the authorities any reason to stop them.

He continues his short sermon. "Why is the earth trembling? Are the scriptures of old starting to be fulfilled? Is Israel going to be reborn?" Mustafa pauses again and gazes across the still growing crowd. "Here are the answers to those questions that God has laid on my heart. The earth is trembling because God's people have rejected him. Science and politics are the new religion. This violates the first commandment."

"The scriptures of old came true two thousand years ago, when Christ was sacrificed for our sins. Many Jews, including the apostles, saw this. The promise to Abraham was fulfilled."

"The final question is about to be answered. Abraham was promised that his offspring would be a blessing to all nations. Christ came and died for the sins of everyone. That means Jew and Gentile. I pray that you all come together, Jew and Gentile, as God's kingdom is reborn. The New Jerusalem will be rebuilt as the apostle John told us it would. It will be the rebirth of Israel, with all nations and all peoples, just as God promised Abraham."

Mustafa's voice rises and carries over the countryside. "The God of Israel is the God of all the earth and of all the peoples. Jesus Christ was His son and was the final sacrifice for all our sins. Believe this and your place in heaven is secure. Let the Holy Spirit into your heart knowing you are redeemed. Let God's love into your heart. And then spread that love. Spread the message of forgiveness through Christ, our redeemer, our Savior.

Many in the crowd are overwhelmed by the power and conviction of the speaker. They bow down and confess their sins. They turn to Christ as their Savior. Others walk away. They dismiss the man as another zealot. They think the true messiah of Israel has not yet come.

***

Georgeanne and her people pick up the video that the young Israeli woman posts to her twitter account. Before they even talk with the others, they repost the video to all of Georgeanne's followers. The video soon goes viral. The massive earthquakes around the world have driven a surge in demand for religious content videos. In small bedrooms and in large halls, people see the message of redemption being brought to them. Some turn it off, switching to mindless dribble about their favorite celebrity. But others reach out. They call upon Christ to forgive them. And as most new believers do, they share the message!

***

Abaddon watches the video and searches the peripheries for an assassin. He expects to see one of the Mossad agents or an ISIS infiltrator shoot the prophet dead. He spots several people in the crowd that he believes will kill the evangelist. He waits patiently, but it does not happen. A frown of disappointment forms on his face. First, he will go to his place of worship. Then he will reach out to a few very powerful people. He will make things happen.

***

Back in Israel, the crowd grows as Mustafa and his followers head south towards the town of Capernaum on the shores of the Sea of Galilee. Some come to see the commotion. Some come to hear what is being preached, others come to jeer and mock. As the crowd makes their way south, several men come up to Mustafa. They are some of the men that Mustafa recognized as Mossad operatives.

Mustafa's people try to stop these men from getting close to the prophet. Mustafa scolds them. "Let the man come and speak with me. If his aim is to do me harm, he'll answer to God. Otherwise, his intent must be to help God proclaim his Word." The crowd parts. The man and his guards are allowed to meet with Mustafa.

The prophet looks over the man with a keen eye. He is slender, with a wiry muscular frame. A man stronger than he appears. His eyes are open and wary, taking in the surroundings without even looking. Behind his gray eyes is a mind that is working, thinking. This is a man of great intellect, a blessed man.

The man steps forward with an outstretched hand. Mustafa steps in past the man's hand and embraces him. "Welcome my fellow soldier, we have much to talk about." The Mossad officer returns Mustafa's embrace but is unfazed by the welcome. He has seen it all, he has been in situations far more dangerous. As they step apart, they eye each other up; like two heavy weight fighters sizing up their opponent, trying to figure out the next move, trying to stay a step ahead.

326

Mustafa begins to weep as he sees the situation through new eyes. "I'm sorry to weep in your presence, my new friend," he states. "For a moment we both looked at each other as enemies. I'm not your enemy. You are my brother. We're all children of God."

The Mossad agent looks at Mustafa with his steely gray eyes. Not even Mustafa, with his years of experience at reading hard men can tell what the man is thinking.

"You do not believe me. You think I'm an intruder, an invader." Mustafa pauses for a moment before continuing. "In a sense you are right. I come to bring the message of Christ as the salvation for all of mankind. He is the salvation for the Jewish people too. That is why I'm here."

The quiet man stares at Mustafa, his steely gaze seems to penetrate into Mustafa's soul. In a calm voice the man asks him a direct question. "Do you truly believe Jesus is the Son of God?"

Mustafa pauses. Could he be taken to jail as a heretic? Could he be tried as an insurrectionist? He knows Peter denied Christ three times. But that was before Christ's resurrection. Mustafa knows of the resurrection and the salvation. He knows it deep in his heart. He found it during the midst of a raging battle. It is not something he can deny.

"For God so loved the world that He sent His only Son," Mustafa replies softly. His voice rises a bit as he finishes the well-known verse. "All who believe in Him shall not perish but have eternal life."

The Mossad agent reaches out and firmly grasps Mustafa's forearm. The wiry man's grasp is firm, like a vice. Mustafa looks at the man, confused. Then he sees a smile grow across the man's face. The wind gusts and blows the man's hair aside for a brief moment. A birthmark is revealed close to his hair line. Most would not notice it. To Mustafa it is quite apparent.

The vise like grip of the Mossad agent pulls Mustafa into a bear hug. "We're brothers. It is my turn to weep. I'm a Levite. We have much work to do. For now, you are my captive. The Mossad knows you are ISIS. Trust me."

"I will trust God. Take me where you think we can best be used," Mustafa says. He steps back and holds out his hands to be arrested.

***

"As you can see, the leader of this movement has just been arrested," the young Israeli woman reports. "I fear things could get violent. They just arrested this man, and he has thousands of people following him." The camera shifts focus to a scuffle breaking out. Out of nowhere Israeli defense forces in full riot gear appear, pushing back Mustafa's people. "This is not good, this could escalate into a riot," the newly minted on scene reporter states. The view from the camera is jumbled for a bit then points out over the crowd. The woman's voice is heard, strong but almost hysterical. "This is wrong! Do not fight! We have a mission. Stop the fighting! They have taken the teacher, but they have not taken us."

In the sideways view of the camera, the crowd is seen to be stopping its forward push against the riot police. The young woman continues to implore the crowd to shy away from violence. "If we're peaceful, the police cannot stop us. The teacher taught that Jesus would want us to love each other. Violence is not love. Step forward in love. Follow the path of love. The police are our friends, our brothers and sisters. Embrace them with love. It is an unstoppable force. It is the force of our God through Jesus His Son."

The camera view tumbles around a bit again and then focuses on Mustafa being taken away. All around him, the crowd slowly pushes in. But not in anger. They push in, embracing the riot police, literally kissing their shields, and then hugging the soldiers. The woman with the camera scans the crowd as they push in with love. Finally, she speaks up, breathless. "I, I wanted to be a reporter, Um, I, well, I became part of the story. Sorry about that. But I had to do something. And look! A truly peaceful protest! These people could hug and kiss these soldiers all the way to Jerusalem! This is truly miraculous!"

*   *   *

Georgeanne has been monitoring the twitter feed and rushes into Pastor Michael's office with the last post. "These people are connected to Shawn and Clarissa and all the others we have seen around the world. Pastor, they all have a birthmark or a recent scar on their forehead. They all are claiming Christ as the Savior, and they are doing it with a power never seen before. Billy Graham did not speak as powerfully as these people. These are common folks, farmers, college kids, a reformed terrorist and even an autistic woman. You have to watch this video from Israel. It is amazing."

Pastor Michael and a few of the church elders watch as Mustafa is arrested. They see the near riot turned into a scene of love that causes the Israeli defense forces to crumble. "God is working miracles," Pastor Michael states quietly.

One of the church elders speaks up. "Rewind it to when the terrorist is arrested, what did you say his name was? Mislaffa?"

Georgeanne starts the recording just before the arrest. "His name is Mustafa," she replies politely. "What are we looking for?"

"Right there!" the elder exclaims. "Go back to where the wind blows the wiry man's hair. The wiry man has a mark too!" They find the spot on the video and zoom in. Sure enough, they see the birth mark. "He didn't arrest him; he's taking him to where he needs to be!" the older man exclaims. "Good Lord Almighty! May your kingdom come. If I ever doubted, now I truly believe!" The man turns and rushes out of the room. They can hear him as he shouts with joy. "It is true, It is true. Christ is the Savior, and he is coming soon. Oh, glorious day. Oh, glorious day!"

The remaining people in the room look around, at first perturbed. But as it sinks in, they start to smile, then they start to laugh with glee. Pastor Michael speaks up. "We all have our doubts now and then. To have those doubts erased! That is a glorious day! We need to join him; we need to celebrate this day. All doubts need to be washed away."

"Make a joyful noise unto the Lord," a woman states, one who is active in the churches worship ministry. "We should have a parade."

"A parade? In the midst of our city falling to the ground, with fires burning out of control?" Michael asks with dismay.

Shawn and Clarissa enter the room at that moment. "Ya'll serving cocktails in here?" Clarissa asks. "I just saw a punch-drunk crazy man racing across the grounds telling everyone that it is true, to have no fears."

"We only serve the wine of Jesus's love," the female elder replies, "and our cups runneth over. I'm so overwhelmed with joy that I want to have a parade."

"A parade?" Shawn asks, a smile coming across his face. "Everyone loves a parade. I'm all in."

Pastor Michael replies grimly. "Downtown Los Angeles is in ruins. The freeways are shut down. The store shelves are empty. People are going to get real hungry real soon. And you want to have a parade?"

"People are hungrier for the truth, for the Word, than they are for food," Shawn replies. "They need both, so let's combine them. We're a food distribution point where people come to get food. We'll take the food to them. And we'll do it with praise and worship."

Georgeanne, the most creative one in the crowd lights up. "A food caravan accompanied by people singing praises to the Lord, with music and dancing! This is gold. This will go viral. A man on a street

330

corner with a clapboard is boring and trite. A parade of joyous music handing out food to the needy! That is Christ's love in action. We won't be waiting for people to come to us, we will be going to them. Pastor, you have to see the message this would deliver."

"You frame this in a new way," the Pastor responds. "It will be a relief parade. I can buy into that. Let's hash this out. It has potential."

Chapter 48, Theories

General Shapiro mulls over the situation. "The California kid rebuffed us. Mustafa is in Israel, arrested by the Mossad. The Chinese farmer has gone underground. Meanwhile we're truly having biblical earthquakes. The Nile river has switched courses. The Egyptians will run out of water in a matter of days. Eighty million people denied their primary source of water. Los Angeles' destruction will pale in comparison to what is going to happen in the Nile delta."

"You barely touched the surface of the situation, General," Henry, his intelligence officer responds. "In the past week the earth has been in upheaval. We have seen a major surge in religious activity. It's not just the Christians that are compelling people to turn to God. Well known Islamic leaders are proclaiming that the return of the twelfth imam is imminent. Buddhists are proclaiming the time of deliverance. The Gia crowd is telling its followers that mother earth is angry, that she'll not tolerate any more destruction caused by man."

"Or is the earth just going through some serious growing pains?" Frank, the operations officer asks. "This all could be a natural cycle that we have never experienced."

"If the earth is five billion years old, how come this is the first time we're seeing this type of seismic activity?" Henry asks. "Surely the scientists would have records of a similar event from all their core samples and computerized models."

"The records are not that old and not that accurate," a senior staff member replies.

"The Bible says it happened about five thousand years ago," Henry replies flatly.

The room goes quiet for a few moments. One of Frank's staff members speaks up again. "Are you implying the great flood actually happened?"

"Every ancient culture on earth has a reference to a great flood," Henry replies. "You are supposed to be 'woke'. Are you denying the cultural past of billions of people?"

"Are you basing your thoughts on ancient stories?" the senior staffer asks, mystified.

"What are you basing your recommendations on?" the intelligence officer responds.

"Science, you old fool. The science we all know to be true."

"I assume you are talking about the Big Bang theory and the theory of evolution?"

"Exactly. That is known science," the senior advisor states, flabbergasted that this conversation is even taking place. "We have all grown up being taught the science of evolution. Why bring up the myths of the Bible once again?"

Henry swivels in his seat to look at the man ten years younger than him. "I can see that you are a well-educated man. So surely you can tell me the difference between a fact and a theory."

"Of course," the officer responds. "A fact is something that is provable. Why do you ask such a benign question?"

"A scientific fact is something that can be observed and repeated," Henry replies calmly. "No one has ever observed the evolution of a species into another species. Changes within a species happen all the time. My beloved dog is a cocker doodle. But that is a blending of two dogs. Can you show me where a species evolved into a new species?"

"Of course, General! That is how all living things came to be. Your question is inane."

Henry stays calm despite the insult to his intelligence. The colonel he is talking to does not realize the flaw in his argument. "I'll ask you again, my friend, can you name one time that a new species has evolved from an existing species? Has it ever been observed and has anyone been able to repeat it?"

The colonel is mystified that a senior officer is questioning what he has been taught all his life. "Evolution takes thousands of years, sir. No one has actually seen it happen. The earth is billions of years old. Man has not been around long enough to actually see evolution occur. We all know this, so what is the point of your argument?"

"You have made my point, Colonel. Evolution is a theory, not a fact. Has our society turned science into a false god? Do you believe in evolution, Colonel? "

"It is a theory based in fact, General," the colonel replies firmly.

"But Colonel, you just admitted there are no facts, there are no scientific studies that confirm evolution. How is that different than someone who believes in creation? You cannot prove evolution happened. I cannot prove God exists. You say to believe in God is a religious myth. How can you believe in evolution when there is no factual evidence? Neither can be proven, yet one is a myth, and the other is a science. How does a critically thinking man justify that?"

The colonel turns red in the face. He turns to the commander of the Special Forces. "Do you take the advice of a man who denies science?"

"Colonel, I think Henry made it pretty clear that there is science and there is theory," General Shapiro responds. "Evolution is a theory, not science. The big bang is a theory, not science. So maybe there is a God. If so, don't you think we should take that into consideration as we decide what to do?"

The colonel is humiliated. Is he surrounded by people who believe in myths? Are decisions that will affect not only the nation, but the world, to be made by heathens that believe in some unseen god? He stands and looks around the room. "I'm a man of principle. I cannot be part of this discussion. If you all believe in myths over science, then you can go your own way. I will go my way." He turns to the commanding general. "It has been an honor to serve you sir, but I must request that you give me a new assignment."

The commanding general looks directly at the disgruntled colonel. "Sit down colonel," he commands. "Everyone may not agree with you, but that does not mean your input won't be heeded. I'm not looking for consensus, I'm looking for advice. You have a sharp mind. You wouldn't be at this table if I didn't appreciate your input."

The colonel remains standing. "These people believe in God, sir. These people believe in a myth. I' don't see how I can be of help to you."

"You believe in a myth too," the general responds. "Or are you willing to make the jump from theory to fact with no scientific proof?"

The senior advisor hesitates for a moment, then sits back down at the large conference table. In his mind he begins to think; everything he has been taught is only a theory. But he knows God is a myth. He has seen too much of man's cruelty to believe there truly is a God. "I'll stick around, General. But don't kick me out if I disagree with you."

"My friend, we just asked you to stay, because you disagree."

***

The city of Wuhan is in upheaval. The words broadcast by Xi were recorded and rebroadcast. The rumors of earthquakes happening around the world cannot be suppressed. Even the state-run Chinese news starts to broadcast some of the current events, including mention of the massive earthquakes that have happened. But these items are downplayed, buried. The state-run news talks more about the great things the state has done. The Three Gorges

Dam is featured; it is proclaimed how strong it is, how the great Chinese engineers designed it to handle any and all earthquakes.

The people of Wuhan know they have been lied to over the past fifty years. They wanted to believe the crop production estimates, but knew the numbers were inflated as they lived on meager diets. They wanted to believe the economic forecasts, knowing they were lies. Many want to believe the Three Gorges Dam is safe. But they all know better. Many fought against the dam being built, knowing a catastrophic failure would wipe out their city. Now the earth is trembling. It is trembling at a level that could cause the dam to burst. If the dam is compromised, they would be given notice. But it would only take two hours for the massive wave to hit Wuhan, a city of twelve million people.

The people see the government officials leaving the city. They see panic as critical laboratories are being shut down. The military along with its supplies and equipment are heading towards the surrounding hills and mountains. Some people are too scared to move, generations of oppression keeping them in their place. But other people begin to move. They know their proud history and have always hated the oppressive government.

Those who have heard Xi's message of hope break free from their fear of the government. They embrace the idea that there is a God who created them and loves them. They find each other in small groups that soon join into larger groups. A few missionaries and underground church members emerge from their silent walk with Christ to embrace these new believers. As the streets of Wuhan are vacated by the state officials, the new believers become emboldened to proclaim their faith publicly. In the confusion and fear that envelops the city, these groups of new believers are points of light.

The Chinese have always been a society that embraces hard work and moral standards. The idea of respect for family and love of one's neighbors is not new to them. For centuries, the Chinese flourished because they had a moral society and free trade. The

Christian message they are hearing rings true to many. It is the reason that China was seeing a rapid expansion of Christianity prior to the current expungement of any religious expression. In the current chaos, Christ becomes a beacon of hope. Tens of thousands are converted and their numbers grow as they organize their own exodus from the threatened city.

A missionary, who was born in Wuhan, studied biology at UCLA. While in America he found Christ. When he returned to Wuhan, he managed to start a small Bible study that expanded over the years. Another disciple of Christ met a Mennonite while studying agriculture in Kansas. He too started a Bible study upon his return to Wuhan. It is these people and many others like them who now carry the Word openly to their friends, family, and neighbors. They lift their hands in praise as they see their lost countrymen become found. These are the Christians who fuel a conversion of great magnitude. They lead as many as they can away from the city.

Through back channels, reports and videos of what is happening make it out of the country. Christians around the world find these videos and rebroadcast them. The cataclysmic events that have been happening has the entire world on edge, seeking answers. Some use the upheaval as a reason to promote acts of evil. Many people turn to their most base instincts, gluttony, deceit, lust, robbery, rape and murder. Others see what is happening and seek out the Lord.

Chapter 49, Conversions

Mustafa sits calmly in the back seat of the Israeli police cruiser. He is handcuffed and has shackles on his feet. The Mossad agent who arrested him sits in the seat beside him. A young and fit woman drives the car. A well-armed guard sits next to her in the passenger seat. As they turn a bend in the road, Mustafa sees Jerusalem in the distance. Clearly visible is the bright gold dome of the Al Aqsa Mosque. Mustafa lets out a sigh. "It is such a shame that a mosque sits where a temple to the Lord should stand." He turns to the Mossad agent next to him. "If you give me a chance, I'll place the foundation stone for the new temple myself." He laughs heartily. "I will carry that two-ton stone myself and lay it in its place."

The Mossad agent looks at him and smiles. "I do not doubt your will to do that."

"You will help me!" Mustafa replies with a smile and a hearty laugh. "You are stronger than you look. I know this. You and I will place the foundation stone for the new temple. A Jew and an Arab, both sons of God, both descendants of Abraham. I like that my friend. Do you like that?"

The Mossad agent frowns, but he knows it will happen. He has seen it.

"Don't frown my friend," the ISIS fighter says. "We do not seek to do the improbable. We seek to do the impossible. Christ said he would rebuild the temple in three days, and he did, when he died and was resurrected! He passed that power to us. It is in the scriptures. We're His ambassadors. An ambassador's word carries the power of the nation he represents. We represent the kingdom of God. Our words carry great power." Mustafa leans close to the Mossad agent. "Are you willing to use the power that God has given us? Are you willing to step out and be bold?"

The Mossad agent is silent and frowns again.

Mustafa leans back in his seat and laughs heartily. "I now know why God chose us! I'm bold and reckless. You are cold and calculating. You are planning what is to be done. I can see in your eyes that you are both scared and determined. I'm scared too my friend, but I face fear much differently than you."

"You fear losing. You fear humility," the Mossad agent replies quietly. "I fear failure. My people are stubborn. They are not going to listen. They rejected the Messiah two thousand years ago. What is going to change their minds now?"

"What changed your mind?" Mustafa asks as they come into the city and the driver begins to negotiate the heavy traffic and narrow streets.

"Six days ago, on a mission in the Gaza Strip, I was in a gun fight. I was injured with a grazing wound to my head. It knocked me out. I woke up in heaven. You were there. So were many others. Tens of thousands of us were there. We were praising God. And God commissioned us to proclaim his name to the nations." The Mossad agent turns to Mustafa, a small teardrop forms in the corner of his eye that he quickly wipes away. "The Savior was there with God. The nail holes were obvious in his hands and feet. His side was pierced. But he was alive and sitting on the right side of God. He smiled and blessed me." The Mossad agent begins to weep. "I have never felt so loved in my entire life."

Mustafa thinks of his calling in the middle of a chaotic battlefield, he can relate to the stunning revelation. He tells the Mossad agent his story. A common bond is formed. A mission is established. Together they will lay the foundation stone of the new temple. Prophesy state that the laying of the foundation stone will herald the coming of the new Jerusalem and the return of Christ. It will take the strength of God to complete this task.

***

A hundred miles to the north, Israel is being invaded. The Messianic Christian followers of Mustafa have not given up on their mission. They travel by foot into the northern kingdom proclaiming Christ as King and Savior. Most Israelis shut their doors and windows, not wanting to hear the message. But others are willing to listen. The powerful conviction of the new believers gains many new converts. By nightfall, a large gathering of people has come to hear what the new converts have to say.

None of the newly anointed missionaries have any idea of what to say to the gathering crowd. Their leader has been arrested, yet they are supposed to continue his mission. None of them have any experience in talking to a crowd. One of Mustafa's commanders offers to start things off. "We all have a story to tell. Let's just get out there and tell our stories. Christ has changed all our lives in just the past few days. I now have a peace I never knew before. I used to dream of seventy-two virgins. That dream was not always pleasant! Now I dream of an eternity in the presence of God. That dream is beautiful."

One of the Israeli converts speaks up. "Benjamin, that was beautiful. You are right. We just need to speak openly and plainly of how we feel and what we know. Let's get started. If you go first, I'll go second." The middle-aged woman looks around at the other new believers. "Who else is willing to tell their story? Who wants to share their joy?" A half dozen hands are raised. Some immediately, some hesitantly. The group begins to get organized. A makeshift stage is put together, someone comes forward with a karaoke machine that will work as a loudspeaker system.

Benjamin steps up onto the small platform and gazes out over the people who have gathered around. He is not schooled in the Bible. His knowledge of Christ's life is limited. He now knows that Christ is the Messiah that God sent to save the world. He is willing to share that good news. He does not know that the location of their gathering is only a few miles away from where Christ gave the 'Sermon on the Mount'. Their gathering will be almost as important as that famous sermon.

The newly convicted Arab begins to tell his story. He tells of his background and being recruited as a young man by ISIS. He tells of his association with Mustafa including some of the cruel and violent acts they committed together. He describes all the events that happened in Syria and his sudden revelation and conversion. He breaks down in tears and kneels as he prays for forgiveness once again. He prays for all those around him to find the salvation that he now knows.

Many people in the crowd fall to their knees and pray too. His testimony of transition from a life of brutality to a life of joy is powerful. He does not speak like a rabbi or a missionary. He speaks from his heart. He speaks with the power of Christ, with conviction. Some of his fellow converts move out into the crowd to embrace those who have been touched. Their loving embrace brings these people their own realization. The Holy Spirit is alive and moving through the crowd.

The middled-aged Israeli woman speaks next. She tells of things in her own life that even her husband did not know. She lays bare her soul, knowing all she has done has been forgiven. Again, her plain talk resonates in the crowd. They are not hearing a sermon from the pious. They are hearing true life and true love. Some turn and walk away, not wanting to hear, not wanting to confess their own sins. But even more show up as the word spreads. Something new is happening. Something of great joy. Something historical. Something prophetic.

The revival lasts for several hours. A group forms to lead the crowd in songs of praise. Food is brought in by some local catering businesses. Small groups form and make plans to evangelize. The cataclysmic events of the day are not talked about, but the awareness of them spurs the group on. Surely the day of redemption is near. Those who have found forgiveness and redemption are enthusiastic to share the good news. The peaceful invasion of Israel will continue with renewed zeal.

***

"So, the ISIS fighter is now in Jerusalem?" General Shapiro asks Henry, his longtime friend and chief of intelligence.

"As best we know, General," Henry responds. "As usual, the Mossad is vague about what they know. Our sources say there may be an upheaval within the Mossad. To add to the fire, there is a Messianic Jewish uprising on the shores of Galilee."

"You're gloating," General Shapiro responds. "You proclaim to be a Christian. You should not gloat," he chides his friend. "Tell me about the Messianic Jews."

Henry continues to smile as he eyes up his friend and boss. "I hope I'm not gloating. I hope I'm seeing a man come to know the truth that I know. That is why I smile. As for your inquiry, Messianic Jews are Jewish people who accept Christ as their Savior. Our reports indicate that the people Mustafa left behind by the Sea of Galilee have organized their own movement. There are hundreds of social media videos circulating the internet right now. Some are going viral."

"Back up a bit. What do you mean by the people that Mustafa left behind? The Israelis didn't arrest the whole crew of misfits?" General Shapiro asks.

"They would have had a revolt on their hands," Henry responds. "The Israelis would have had to arrest hundreds of their own people."

"And now your reports say the movement has grown into thousands of people spreading across northern Israel." General Shapiro responds. "I have seen some of the videos you sent me. These speakers are good. I almost broke down and cried."

"And they intend to carry their message throughout the country," Henry replies.

The commanding officer of the Special Forces rubs his chin thoughtfully. "Okay, back to business. What happens if this Christian conversion continues? How does that change our operations?"

"First of all, you must understand that a great conversion of the Israeli population is prophetic. It is another sign of Christ's return," Henry states. "If you take that into consideration, then you must take into consideration that the final battle is at hand."

"This all is above my understanding," General Shapiro responds as he buries his head in his hands. "This is information the president and the joint chiefs of staff need to be considering."

The G2 sits back in his chair. "You're right, General. But is anyone else giving this kind of input? The president only has a handful of people around him that will even consider providing him a Biblical world view of the current events. Most of his staff and the four-star generals are mired in DC politics. They only see the world from a geopolitical and geo economical point of view. You are the only one who has brought the Christian world view to the table."

"And I'm going to be dismissed from the table after our next meeting if I tell them we need to prepare for the final battle."

"You control a lot of valuable assets, General. It is the reason you are the only three-star general with access to the inner workings. Let's bring in the G3 and put in place a plan for our assets," Henry replies. "We will know we did our best in this battle to come. We will have stood firm with God's chosen people."

An alarm sounds and disrupts their strategic planning. Their eyes begin to scan the computer screens that surround the office. They soon focus in on a screen that shows the Tibetan Plateau. The Chinese army has initiated a large armed incursion into the Indian held territories of Uttarakhand and Himachal Pradesh. The Indian army is fighting back and has scrambled their air force.

"Wars, and rumors of wars." The Special Forces Commander shakes his head. "I hate to admit this, my friend. You have been right and continue to be right. Gather the staff and we will develop and implement plans for the 'final battle.' After we have our plans established, then I will talk with the president."

Chapter 50, The Parade

The site is almost comical. Over a thousand people have come to be part of the 'parade'. Dozens of food trucks are fully stocked and equipped, ready to serve. Three high school marching bands are present. They are not at full capacity, but they are warming up with drum rolls and bleating horns. Several food pantries have showed up with truckloads of food to be handed out to those in need. Four church choirs are there, ready to sing to their neighbors.

But of great importance are the work crews that will lead the parade. Several tree service companies are on hand, their skilled men ready to clear the way. Excavation companies with back hoes and front-end loaders line up as well, willing to help in any way they can. To help those in dire need, a medical team is in place consisting of several doctors, dozens of nurses and eight ambulances.

In support of this missionary force are several hundred men and women willing to help. Some will get their hands dirty helping with debris removal. Some will keep their hands clean as they serve food and administer first aid. Others are just there to provide moral support, willing to listen, willing to care. Their mission may be the most important of all. It is easy to take action. To truly love, to truly care, that takes compassion.

"Do you see this?" Georgeanne gushes. "Look at this gathering! They are all here willing to help at a moment's notice. I bet you half of them have never been to church. But they are willing to help out. God is alive and working miracles!"

Pastor Michael smiles at the woman's exuberance. "This is an amazing site. So many people coming together in less than a day. Look at the work crews ready to lead the way. Who would have thought we could pull this off?"

A church elder looks at the pastor with a smile. "God did this. As you have always preached to us, we're His hands and feet in this world, His ambassadors. You're preaching and His will is coming true."

One of the choirs begins rehearsing 'How Great Thou Art'. The woman wipes a tear from her eye. Meanwhile Georgeanne's crew is taking videos of everything. They will post a short video later in the day.

And then the 'parade' begins. The Christian army begins moving towards downtown Los Angeles, fifteen miles away. They have no idea how far they will get, two miles? Five miles? It does not matter. They will bring relief to those they encounter and wrap them up in love.

Shawn and Clarissa are at the leading edge of the mission, urging on the crews as they cut through downed trees and clear rubble from the streets. They soon see the complete devastation. Trees down, buildings devastated, homes crumbled. The people are happy to see the trees being cleared and the rubble removed from the roads. But the true shouts of joy come when the food trucks show up, followed by the semi-trailers full of food. The marching bands let everyone in the neighborhood know something is happening. Crowds start to form. Some wait for food, others see what is happening and start to help with the physical labor of clearing the streets. As the food relief supplies dwindle, more is brought in. All the while, the church choirs sing and the high school marching bands play.

Shawn and Clarissa circulate among the crowds as do many other compassionate believers. They hear two questions. "Who are these people?" and "Why hasn't the government done this?"

By midafternoon, the 'parade' has moved almost four miles and enters an area hit hard by the earthquakes. The streets are strewn with debris and people are still searching for survivors in the rubble of crushed buildings. Search and rescue teams are brought forward and the medical crew springs into action. Up until now, they had been treating minor injuries. Now they are seeing major injuries that have not been treated for days. It is quite apparent that no relief has been able to enter this area. The doctors and nurses are horrified at what they see, treating days old injuries. The work crews truly start to dig in as they know there are still survivors buried in the rubble.

346

The marching bands continue to play as the food trucks and pantry trucks roll in.

As the newly arrived relief crews start to clean up the largely Hispanic neighborhood, the starved local populace swarm the food trucks. It has been days since they have had fresh food. Even the strongest men are on the verge of collapse from lack of a good meal. While all this goes on, the marching bands and the church choirs continue their music and praise.

An older Hispanic man wipes the sweat and grime from his face. "That is good music your people are singing. You are people of faith. We should all return to our faith. That is how we were brought up. But my children, my grandchildren, they do not know faith. I think I failed them. I did not bring them up in the church the way I was."

"It is never too late to turn to Christ," one of the compassionate crew members states. "The prodigal son was greeted with a feast. Bring your family around. We may not be able to provide a feast, but we can provide a good meal. Tell them of how you were brought up. Maybe it will ignite a spark. Maybe you can still be the light they need to see."

Scenes like this play out as the mission parade continues to help those in need. Many come to know salvation. Many just take advantage of a free lunch. As night begins to fall, some lights come on, powered by a few mobile generators. The cleanup operations slow down and small groups gather. Discussions of what has happened get intense. 'Is this the end times?', 'Earthquakes, fires, wars, famine.'

Clarissa takes part in one of these discussions. "'No one knows the day or the hour,'" she relates. "But the day and the hour may be soon. Are you ready? Do you believe in God? Do you know Jesus as your Savior?" Many ponder that question, but others reject her thoughts vociferously.

"Don't listen to that jive! She's just a white woman in black skin," a heavily tattooed young man hollers. "She just wants you to follow the white man's preaching."

Clarissa stands and looks at the street punk, a very hardened man who has obviously seen time in jail. "Jesus does not see color. God created just one race. Why do you want to sow division by the color of our skin? Look at the children here. They are all playing together. Do they notice the color of their skin? Now tell me and everyone here, what do you have to offer? Why should these people continue to listen to you?"

"You is stupid," the man responds. "I control this neighborhood. These young ones are my dealers. These people rely on me for food, for protection. So get your sorry butt out of here, we don't need you." The thug pulls a gun and points it at Clarissa. "Now get, leave all your goodies and get out of my neighborhood. We don't need you around here."

"So, you take care of these people?" she asks. Clarissa looks around at the chaos around her, ignoring the gun pointed at her. "Why did it take our caravan to bring food to your people? You're a helpless fool." She begins to walk towards the crack dealer. "Give it up Jarod. Your time is done. These people are now free from your depraved edicts."

Jarod begins to back up as Clarissa approaches. "How do you know my name? Are you some kind of witch? Stay away from me you evil woman." Clarissa continues to close the gap, walking deliberately towards the frightened yet belligerent man. "Why are you coming for me? Back away, Back away!" the man hollers. Clarissa closes the gap to just a pace away. Jarod tries to pull the trigger on his pistol, but Clarissa reaches out and grabs it. She expertly pulls it from his grasp. The crowd cheers as Jarod looks on in horror, disarmed by this fearless woman.

Clarissa reaches out and touches the man. "Lord have mercy on this man. He has never heard of your mercy. May You have mercy on him. May You open his eyes to Your love." Clarissa puts her hand on his forehead. "You have been forgiven. In the name of Jesus, I cast out the demons that have infected your soul."

Jarod falls to the ground and writhes in pain. A dark cloud swirls around him and then blows away into scattered bits, dwindling to nothing.

"Stand and be the man God intended you to be." Clarissa states forcefully.

Jarod stands, his head is downcast. "I'm a sinner." He lifts his face and looks around the crowd. He sees his mother standing next to his young sister and he feels remorse. He moves his glance and sees one of his girl friends who is holding one of his children. Something inside him clicks. He sees all the bad decisions he has made in his life, but he also sees all that can go right.

He glances around the crowd and sees his fellow gang bangers. He knows he has a choice to make. If he embraces what is in his heart, his gang bangers will come against him. But what is in his heart is strong; stronger than any bond his gang offered. What is in his heart is true peace. His mind races as he knows all eyes are on him.

"Yo! Y'all need to stand down," Jarod exclaims to the crowd, his directive is meant to reach his gang members. "This is our sister, and she is here to help. All these people are here to help. Things are bad. We're in no shape to turn down help from anyone. What good is it to defend our turf if our turf is in ruins? Let it be known that these people are our friends."

***

Abaddon watches this scene play out in real time from an on-scene reporter using a gopro camera. He slams his fist down on the large ornate oaken desk in his elaborately decorated office with marble floors and oak paneled walls. He watches in dismay as the young woman casts the demon from the gang banger. Even he winced as the woman proclaimed Jesus's name. He looks up to the carved image of Baal that dominates his private office. He bows before the image and prays for the power he needs to win the battle that is being waged. The carved image does not respond. But Abaddon's mind swirls with ideas. He knows that man has embraced science over God. He needs to use the tools of the intellectuals. Science will defeat the myths of God. The tools of science are already on the march, making headway against the voices proclaiming God.

He turns to his trusted aide. "Tune in one of our trusted news channels. Our people will be making a mockery of these evangelicals. We will win the war by using science to defeat the notions of these evangelical rubes."

"Yes, my lord," his servant replies as a worldwide news channel is displayed on the screen.

The servant tarries and Abaddon becomes disturbed. "Why do you linger? I no longer need your assistance."

"The ISIS fighter in Israel. He has joined forces with the Mossad," the servant replies.

"The Mossad arrested him. Our people will soon have him in custody," Abaddon states. "That factor has been taken care of. Do not be alarmed on that front, now go, leave me be."

"The Mossad do not have the ISIS fighter," the servant responds humbly, knowing he could be killed just for reporting this disturbing news.

"I watched him be arrested!" Abaddon shouts. "How do our people not have control of him! Trusted people oversaw the operation! He should be in an interrogation room right now."

"The agent who arrested him has gone rogue," the servant responds. "The entire Mossad is in disarray. The Messianic movement has infected their ranks to the highest levels."

Abaddon's eyes light up fiercely. "The Mossad knows all about the Foundation Stone and the movement behind that conspiracy theory!"

"Yes, my lord," the servant replies humbly.

"Leave me now!" Abaddon shouts. "I must think this through."

The servant slips out. Glad to still be alive.

Abaddon contemplates what might happen if the foundation stone is placed at the original temple mount. He determines that this action cannot be allowed to happen. But his best allies in the area, the crazed Islamists, want the foundation stone to be place at the temple mount too. Religious zealots do not make good allies. He will use his next best option, bribery. Money trumps religion … usually.

Chapter 51, Connections

"Why do our people hate each other?" Mustafa asks as he slices a piece of mutton and follows it up with a handful of moist and well-seasoned rice. "Abraham is our father. God created us all. Some of us have the blood of Ishmael. Some of us have the blood of Isaac. But we all have the opportunity to embrace the blood of Christ that flowed to forgive us all. My brothers are bent on evil, they are corrupt. I know it, I have seen it. How do I bring the word of truth to them?" He swabs some bread through the thick gravy and slurps down more of the delicious food.

Some in the clandestine gathering sneer as the large man gobbles down the feast. Other see an opportunity that God has brought to them. Mustafa is in the middle of a very mixed group. Some are Orthodox Jews, some are traditional Jews, some are Messianic Jews. They have one thing in common. They all believe that the rebuilding of the temple will begin the rebuilding of a new nation.

Rebuilding the temple has very significant meaning. The Orthodox Jews believe that rebuilding the temple will bring about a great earthly kingdom. The Messianic Jews believe it will bring about a great new heavenly kingdom. Mustafa knows it will be the start of the new Jerusalem. He has seen it. He was there. Yet he knows God's plan must play out here on earth. God's last call for salvation must ring out to all nations. God's people must have their last chance to spread his Word.

Mustafa begins to devour a large slice of pecan pie that has been served as the dessert. "What news do we have about what has been happening around the world?" he asks.

"Earthquakes, fires, tsunamis, wars," one of the rabbis replies with a bit of scorn. "You know the world is in chaos. You are in Jerusalem; you will be protected from these catastrophes."

"You speak of the earthly Jerusalem. You need to know the heavenly Jerusalem to be protected," Mustafa tells the Orthodox rabbi. "That is a big difference."

The Orthodox rabbi looks sternly at Mustafa, "Who are you to tell me what the scriptures say?"

Mustafa looks up at the man in his flowing robes and meticulous head dress. The Spirit enters him as he stands to address the rabbi. "The promise was given to Abraham that his seed would bless all nations. It was also foretold by Isaiah. It was fulfilled through the life of Jesus. His crucifixion and resurrection were the fulfillment of all the prophesies. You deny the obvious. That is what the scriptures say. For two thousand years you have denied the scriptures. I'm here to give all of you one last chance to embrace the truth. Who are you to deny the truth of the scriptures?"

The Orthodox rabbi sits down. Sweat forms on his brow. He has never been so forcefully confronted. Could this unOrthodox man be speaking the truth? What if Jesus was the Messiah? His mind races. But his heart hardens. They are God's chosen people. He is one of God's chosen priests. Surely, he would know. Surely God would let him know. His hard heart does not see that God is trying once more to reach him and his people.

"Do you have internet service?" Mustafa asks, turning to one of the technical people who replies in the affirmative. "Search for any videos of Christian outreach. I won't help you lay the temple's foundation stone until I know that God's Word is being proclaimed to the nations."

The Orthodox rabbi looks up for a moment. "That is what the scriptures say will happen. God, forgive me for not seeing the truth."

One of the rabbi's followers looks at his mentor. "Rabbi, What are you saying? We're the chosen people. We have suffered for thousands of years. God is about to finally redeem us. We're on the verge of rebuilding the temple."

"The temple was rebuilt two thousand years ago, when Jesus was resurrected," one of the Messianic Jews states. "The rabbi is finally coming to that truth. It was prophesied that the temple was to be rebuilt in three days. Jesus rose from death in three days. Your rabbi just came to the truth."

The rabbi looks up. "We have been so wrong. How did we miss it? God has protected us even though we rejected the Savior. God has protected us for thousands of years. But now I see. God has given us grace. God has fulfilled his promise. God, forgive me for being blind to your grace. May your grace sweep through this room and sweep across this nation."

A breeze blows through the open windows of the home. With it, the Holy Spirit infects all those in the house. Some jump for joy, others break down and cry. Mustafa and his messianic friends begin to sing, praising the Lord. They all sing the same song in different languages. Mustafa sings It in the ancient Aramaic language. The harmony echoes throughout the neighborhood. People passing by on the road below stop and listen to the beautiful song.

The woman with social media savvy returns to the upper room. As she climbs the steps, she is overwhelmed by the Spirit too. She looks around and sees the people in the room glowing, radiating a warmth and love that encompasses her entire body and soul. She stops as she feels an absolute joy surround her. For a moment she kneels as she lets the love flow into her being. Her life changes in an instant.

But her lifestyle does not change. Now she sees the importance of the reports she has gathered. She has true news reports ranging from South America to South Africa, from the west coast of America to central China. The gospel is being proclaimed to the nations. This is what the prophet wants to know.

A dark cloud crosses her mind. 'Do not tell the prophet,' she hears in her mind. 'Humanity will see a great suffering. Keep quiet. Be like Eve, your mother. Blame me and move on. It will not be your fault."

She turns and sees a snake at her feet, talking to her. She hesitates.

Mustafa sees the woman coming up the steps and smiles. But then he sees the smile on her face turn to fear. Seeing the snake at her feet, he quickly reaches for a hidden knife that even the Mossad agent didn't find. The keenly sharpened deadly weapon finds its mark, severing the head of the snake from its coiled body. The woman rushes up the stairs.

"Evil has not yet been defeated," Mustafa states. "It will be nipping at our heels until the final battle. As we sit here, the devil is still working in this world, bringing doubt and division. False prophets will be proclaiming science over miracles. Others will proclaim mother earth over God's will. We must stay united."

The young woman rushes up the steps and grasps Mustafa in a bear hug. "The snake spoke to me. It gave me doubts. I felt like Eve in the garden. You truly are a man of God. You killed the snake. I have no doubts any longer."

"Welcome home my sister. Now let us see what you have found."

"You will find this interesting, priest," the woman responds as she sets up a video display for them to see. She plugs in her laptop and pounds on a few keys. The flat screen TV in the room starts to play the videos she has downloaded. The first five minutes are news reports of evangelical ministries from around the world. The last three minutes show clips of what is happening in Israel, including news reports referring to the 'prophet'. Mustafa sees videos of himself leading his small following into the Jordan river to be baptized. It is followed by a video of the crowds around him as he proclaims the Word as they entered the promised land.

The screen changes to a newscaster;s feed. "There you have it, Melissa. Some kind of miracle worker has entered Israel. His disciples are spreading the Word as we speak, but he is nowhere to be found. Reports from the locals are that he was arrested by the Mossad. We'll have more on this developing story later tonight."

Chapter 52, Martial Law?

"Do you see the activity we're getting?" Georgeanne ask one of her tech people, astounded. "We have over two million views in less than twenty-four hours. Only mega stars get that kind of reaction."

"People are searching for answers. Our posts are providing answers," Clarissa responds as she enters the room. "What other news is there about a Christian revival?"

"Mainly the news is about the mayhem happening around the world," the tech responds. "The corporate media is still saying that global warming is causing it all to happen. There has been no word from the elites of a Christian revival. But the social media sites are on fire. Many are Gia sites, telling people that mother earth is angry because we have decimated her resources. These sites are dominating the web traffic. But other sites are showing our world view, the biblical world view."

"Only the faithful will be saved. It is our mission to reach those who do not know the truth," Georgeanne responds. "We must access all channels to get the truth out. Share everything you have coming in. The autistic girl we saw in Argentina, repost her video. She makes a powerful statement."

Georgeanne's crew works tirelessly to broadcast God's message on every platform available. In some instances, they get videos aired on some local television networks and a few radio outlets broadcast snippets of their audio. But the angry mother earth narrative is the predominate explanation on the worldwide media.

***

"The global activists were right, Mr. President. We acted too slowly and now the earth is going through the convulsions that they predicted," the Secretary of state says. "It may not be too late for us to turn away from our pillaging of the earth. We could issue an executive order stopping all mining and shutting down all fossil fuel power plants. Maybe that would stop the earth from rebelling."

"We have emergency plans in place to stop all travel," the Department of Homeland Security offers. "We can lock down the country at your order. We used the Covid emergency protocols to do this. We could use this as our reason to lock everyone down again. All you need to do is issue a decree of martial law. We have plans in place to implement your orders. Having people travel during these turbulent times is not wise. We should lock the country down until we know what's going on."

"Most of the country has not been affected by the natural disasters that have happened'," the President responds. "Our people have reacted with great resolve to help those in need. If we shut the country down, we'll shut down those relief efforts."

"FEMA and the Department of Homeland Security are in a much better position to help those in need," the DHS secretary states with authority. "You can clear the way for us to do our job if you declare martial law. This is a much bigger catastrophe than anything we have ever faced. The local help will be overwhelmed without federal help."

"Since when has federal help been better than local help?" the vice president says. "Yes, we should empower all available federal assets. But shutting down the country to do that; that is asinine. We need people helping people on a local basis."

The DHS secretary speaks up. "We should take advantage of this crisis. We can use this crisis to implement martial law. We can't let the local populace think they can respond on their own. They need to know the federal government is in charge. This is our opportunity to let the governed know who is in control. This is our opportunity. We must seize it."

General Shapiro has been quiet. Now he speaks up. "If you implement martial law and Jesus comes tomorrow, how will you be judged?"

All eyes turn. The DHS speaks up. "What do you mean? How is that relevant?"

"Do I need to repeat all that has happened? Do we not realize Biblical changes are occurring? Where does Mother Gia appear in the constitution? Don't be stupid. We're to shut down the country because you think we have made 'Mother Nature' mad. Yet you dismiss the idea that God, our creator is mad. You want to shut down local relief efforts to wait for federal relief? Why can't we let the locals continue on their relief efforts while the federal agencies support them?" the general asks. "Why do you think we need to implement martial law?"

"You are so far out of the loop," the DHS secretary responds. "We need to take control of the people. Covid allowed us to start to manipulate the people. With everything that is going on now, this is the perfect reason to fortify that position. We can't let the people think they can continue to live in freedom. They need to be controlled. The science tells us that this free-market experiment is wrecking the earth. And now the science is proving to be true. The earth is imploding because we have exploited its valuable resources."

The secretary of the interior speaks up, "Mr. President, that's a bunch of malarkey. There are no scientific studies that predicted what is happening now. I've been talking with our geologists and climatologists. They have no idea why this is happening. The earthquakes are random and widely spread. They are trying to find some linkage, but it's just not there. The climatologists flat out state that climate change would not cause the tectonic movements like we're seeing. A more likely scenario is that the tectonic shifts and resulting volcanic eruptions will cause climate change."

"Which is why we need to declare a state of emergency," the Secretary of State implores. "We don't know what's happening and we have to lock the people down until we figure it out. It's for their own good."

"Wait a second," the president interjects. "DHS says the science is settled, but you two say the opposite, that the scientists are still trying to figure it out. And what about the general's argument. I grew up believing in God as a loving creator of earth, now you want me to believe in an angry earth god?" Several people start to speak at once.

The chief of staff bangs her gavel several times. All eyes turn to her as she begins to speak. "Mr. President, let me sum up what I think the majority of those present believe. First, no one knows why the current events are happening, which is why you are getting contradictory information from a scientific standpoint. Second, the majority of your cabinet wants you to declare a state of emergency, martial law, so that the federal government can control the people and stop any chaos that might arise. Third, this is an opportunity to move towards a world governance that many in this room believe will bring about worldwide equity and peace."

Many heads in the room nod in agreement. No one else was willing to put it so bluntly.

One man shakes his head. He feels like Isaiah preaching to the corrupt leaders of Israel. He stands up, gaining everyone's attention. "You say no one has offered an explanation. You are wrong. I have offered a perfectly sound explanation. Believe in the one true God, the God of creation. If you don't, you have two options. Believe in science, that has no answers, or believe in Gia, who thinks mankind is a parasite that needs to be destroyed."

The prestigious Oval Office erupts in chaos. There are shouts, booing and hissing as the few who agree with the general are shouted down and chastised. The president watches in dismay. But the chaos erupting in his own office convinces him that he cannot let this same chaos envelop the entire country. He'll implement a national state of emergency. The problem is too big. It will take all the federal government's resources to solve. His mind starts to race as he sees himself in charge of such a great nation. He'll implement plans to rebuild the nation, plans to reform the nation, plans that may take years, even decades to fully implement. And he'll be the all-wise ruler that will save the nation, see the nation through this crisis, no matter how long it takes …

Chapter 53, The Foundation Stone

The foundation stone is not impressive in any way. It does not look like any of the other large building stones found throughout Jerusalem. It is not expertly cut. It is not square and smooth like the thousands of stones around it. It is odd shaped, in its natural state, as God created it, untouched by human tools. It is the foundation stone of the original temple. Legend says it is the stone that Abraham used when God asked him to sacrifice Isaac. God spared Isaac and Isaac became the father of the nation of Israel. King David had all the rest of the stones of the temple cut over three-thousand years ago. King Solomon oversaw the foundation stone being laid into place and then constructed the first temple around it, erecting for God a monument that would be respected by all nations.

The temple was looted and destroyed by the Babylonians in the sixth century BC. Numerous prophets told the Israelites to repent from their evil ways or their kingdom would be destroyed. But just as a drug addict must hit rock bottom before they need help, the Israelites needed to hit rock bottom too, and the original temple was destroyed, and the walls of Jerusalem laid low. The temple was rebuilt less than a hundred years later and stood for another six hundred years. The second temple is prominent in the life of Jesus. But it was destroyed by the Romans in the second century AD.

The true rebuilding of the temple occurred when Christ was resurrected from the grave. God stated that He would tear down and rebuild the temple in three days. Christ was resurrected three days after his death. That is when the new covenant was established. Those who believe in Christ will have their sins cleansed and know eternal life with God in heaven.

Now a diverse group of people are going to place the foundation stone where King Solomon placed it at the height of the Jewish kingdom of the Old Testament. The placement of the foundation stone has many implications to many divergent peoples. The Orthodox Jews believe it will bring about an earthly kingdom and an earthly ruler that will lead Israel to greatness and punish all the people who have oppressed God's chosen people over the past centuries. They have all the building blocks laid out and ready to go. They will rebuild the temple in three days, bringing glory to the homeland.

The Christians have a different view of the foundation stone. They know the temple was rebuilt in three days when Christ was crucified and rose from the dead. To them the placing of the foundation stone is the start of the coming of the New Jerusalem, as prophesied by the Apostle John in the Book of Revelation. No one knows what will really happen. There are many divergent views. Some think It will be the start of the great tribulation. The rapture will occur, bringing all the faithful to heaven. Those left behind will see the rise of the antichrist and all of the prophesies of destruction and plagues fulfilled. They think that during this time, there will be a second revival as people come to realize that Christ was the true son of God.

Another viewpoint is that the tribulation will be experienced by all Christians. There is no rapture. The persecution of Christians will test their faith so God will know who is truly righteous. All humanity will feel God's wrath as the antichrist rises to power. But God's love will prevail. His followers, those who remain faithful, will proclaim him, bringing about another great revival.

Finally, there are the Muslims who believe that rebuilding the temple will bring about the final prophesies of Muhamad. The twelfth imam will arise. This will also bring about a great battle, Armageddon, with the faithful to Islam winning the day.

It is a divergent group of people who are willing to work together to lay the foundation stone of the ancient temple. Mustafa pulls aside the Mossad agent and a few trusted friends. "We must pray about what we're planning to do. Placing the foundation stone may bring about the fulfillment of prophecies that are thousands of years old. Are we all sure this is the right time? Are we the right people to do this?"

The Orthodox Christian priest speaks up as he looks around at his new friends. "Look at this group. The nature of the group fulfils prophesy. I'm an Orthodox Christian whose roots go all the way back to Paul's ministries. You, Mustafa are a converted ISIS fighter who like Saul, persecuted the Christians and Jews until just a few days ago, and now you are a fearless advocate for Christ. Benjamin is a Messianic Jew who is still an agent of Israel. Most of the others here are Christians from around the world, with a single mission: to proclaim Christ as Lord and fulfill the prophesies for his return."

"The most important prophecy is that Abram's offspring would be a blessing to all nations," a woman responds. "Jesus commanded us to preach the gospel to all nations. As we have seen, that is happening. China is in revolt because Christ's Word is spreading. South America is returning to its Christian roots because of the simple words and kindness of an autistic woman."

Another man speaks up. "We see Christian revival messages going viral on the internet. In Africa, even as fire ravages the continent and wars are breaking out, we hear reports of the Word of God reaching the people. Even in Egypt, as the Nile river begins to run dry, our Christian brethren are spreading the Word of God. People see that what they knew and trusted is coming to an end. They know it was an act of God. People everywhere are looking for answers. Christians everywhere are rising up and showing people the truth. The truth does not lie in science. Salvation does not come from the government. God is the answer. He is the way, the truth and the life."

"So, the time is right?" Mustafa asks. "This is the will of God?"

Those around him nod solemnly.

"Then let us pray." All bow their heads. "Dear God, creator of heaven and earth, may Your perfect will be done. We're flawed, sinful, but we have turned to You for forgiveness. Your people have proclaimed Your greatness and love. The Holy Spirit has filled Your people and we are proclaiming Your message to the nations. Your faithful servants are preaching to the world the final sacrifice of Christ and pleading to the sinful to return to righteousness.

'Dear Lord, we know that Christ will return in triumphant victory. We go to lay the foundation stone of Your temple in a show of faith to You and our belief that Christ is the true foundation of our faith. We know Your true temple was rebuilt through Christ. So, your faithful servants will make this gesture of love and faith. We pray that You will bless not only us, but all who know You. We pray that Your hand of protection will be upon all who know You and proclaim You. In Christ's name we do pray. May Your will be done."

***

The small group emerges from the upper room of the large warehouse. The Mossad agent gives a slight nod to a trusted foreman. The trusted foreman gives the signal for the operation to begin. There are no cheers. There are no shouts of joy. Moving the first stone, the foundation stone of the Lord's Temple, will require more than just stealth and intrigue. It will take a true miracle. It will only be done if God wants it done.

The temple mount is occupied by the Palestinians. The group of believers will have to pass through the Palestinian checkpoints not only with the eight-thousand-pound stone, but with the equipment and manpower to put it in place. The plan to do this has been in the works for years. The route has been carefully plotted. The manpower and equipment precisely planned. Everyone knows what they are to do. The groups at the wailing wall are infiltrated with activists who will spring into action at precisely the right time. Other diversionary tactics have been carefully prepared. Precise execution is needed for the plan to work. Even the Israeli military will come against them once the mission begins to unfold. Years of studying the people and security in the area have gone into the planning of this mission.

***

Shawn sits on a large piece of rubble and begins to pray. He had been helping to clear debris from a partially collapsed apartment building. The workforce of their relief parade is now at the front lines of the devastation. They are miles away from the downtown area and the need is beyond his comprehension. They have a steady caravan working to take people out of the devasted areas to where they can receive more aid and transportation to the interior of the country or find temporary quarters. FEMA has finally showed up to provide relief, but only for those who can get to their aid stations. Shawn's people are the ones on the front lines actually getting the work done and directing people to the aid stations.

A middle-aged man approaches Shawn. He is a local volunteer who recruited his own team after Shawn's crew arrived in the neighborhood. "Pardon me my friend. I'm Jose Olivia. You and your team helped rescue my sister and her two children. I want to thank you for what you have done here. Your drive and your help inspired us to begin to take things into our own hands." He pauses for a moment. "We were waiting for the government to help us. That's what we seem to always do. Thank you for being here, to remind us that we can take care of ourselves. They tell me you are a prophet, a man of God."

Shawn smiles, despite the stress he feels. The man's genuine appreciation calms him. "If believing that God exists makes me a man of God, then that is a true description. I don't claim to be a prophet, I only claim that eternal salvation is found through believing in Jesus Christ. What can I do for you, my friend?"

Jose reaches out and shakes Shawn's hand. As he does so, he pulls him into a bear hug. "Thank you, thank you," he says sincerely. Then he steps back and looks around at the crews working to clear the rubble, searching for survivors. "I hear rumor that we're to cease our relief and recovery efforts. We're supposed to wait for the government agencies to show up. They're worried we may get hurt or cause harm to those in need. They say we're supposed to wait for FEMA and their professional people to get here."

Shawn's eyes open wide. This is the devil at work. The Christian relief crews are helping the people and spreading God's love as they do it. Apparently, the government cannot allow this to happen, the government must be the savior. Shawn looks around before responding to Jose. There is destruction and chaos as far as the eye can see. "FEMA will never be able to respond to all the needs. We don't need the government to tell us what to do. Loving and moral people know what to do. Tell your people to keep working. Neighbor helping neighbor is how we will solve this problem. For far too long we have relied on the government to solve all our problems. It is time to rely on God and his love for us. He commands us to love our neighbors. That is what we're going to do. That is how we're going to clean up this mess."

"Amen, prophet," Jose responds. "I have been to church, my brother, but I want to know God like you know God."

Shawn stops. Now is the time, for just one soul. "Then pray with me." He reaches out and takes Jose's hand. They pray together, and a soul is saved.

***

After fleeing the nearly deserted city of Wuhan, Xi's small caravan approaches a mountain top village. There is a totem pole in the middle of the village with the faces of many false gods carved into it. Over a thousand people are in the village square, bowing down to the false gods, wailing and weeping, crying for the gods to forgive them.

Xi steps out of his vehicle and immediately feels the evil in the air. He looks up to the Lord and asks for faith to move mountains. He is overwhelmed by the Holy Spirit and wades straight through the crowd of pagan worshippers. He walks right up to the small rise where several pagan priests are offering sacrifices to the totem gods.

A few men rise to stop him, but he raises his hand against them, and they wilt back into the crowd like cowering dogs.

He approaches the pagan symbol with his arms raised. The pagan priests finally notice him but cringe in fear. The power emanating from Xi causes them to fall to their knees. "There is no god but the one true God!" Xi proclaims loudly. His voice echoes around the amphitheater in which the villagers have gathered. He grasps the totem pole with both hands, and it bursts into flames.

The pagan priests are horrified and try to put out the fire, but their long flowing robes catch on fire. In a gruesome sight, the pagan priests are burned alive as the totem pole crumbles down in burnt ashes.

From the top of the hill, Xi's followers watch, mesmerized. Truly he is a man of God. Some of them begin to move, knowing they are going to be needed.

Xi turns to the crowd. "God the creator does not tolerate false gods. Know that the false gods have been cast away. God the creator loves you. Cast aside your demons. Allow God's love to forgive your sins. Come forward and be baptized. You have been forgiven by the blood of Jesus."

Xi's followers come walking through the crowd. They sing loudly as they proceed, making a joyful noise to the Lord. The crowd looks on, astonished. Many feel the love and joy emanating from the Christians. They felt a great weight fall from their shoulders when the totem pole was incinerated, and the false prophets cast down. Evil spirits have been cast aside. The Holy Spirit moves in. A baptism pool is set up and the villagers begin to come forward, drawn by the love they feel in their hearts as they cast aside the demons that have been tormenting them.

***

Around the world, the 144,000 step forward in similar ways. They draw upon the power of Christ to cast out demons. They speak powerfully and confidently. They act with boldness, fearlessly proclaiming Christ as the Savior and redeemer of the world. When they are mocked and chastised, they boldly condemn the doubters, sending them cowering into the shadows. Never before have so many spoken so boldly about Christ. Never before have so many been convicted by God's love. All the while, false prophets arise, trying to lead people astray. The governments of the world actively try to suppress the Christian revival. The powers of the world continue to push the immorality that they have been spreading for years.

***

Abaddon and a few of his closest allies watch a monitor that shows the totem pole being incinerated. They cringe in fear as their pagan priests burn alive, left in agony as no one comes to their aid. Abaddon's lead counselor bends down at his feet and offers prayers for the frail man.

"Be gone from me you sniveling fool," Abaddon responds as he slaps the man across the face. "I have worked for decades to appease you, to appease our god. I have done everything the great one has asked. In return he has given me a life of power. But it is all crumbling down before me. Everything I have worked for is crashing to the ground. My life of service to Baal has been useless. Is our god powerless against the God of the Jews? Have you led me astray for all these years?"

A dedicated female servant dares to approach Abaddon in his rage. "My master, look at what is going on in Jerusalem, on screen 4. It looks like the conspirators are moving the foundation stone. Informants from the area confirm this unusual activity."

A caravan of trucks and heavy equipment is seen leaving a warehouse close to the temple mount and entering the crowded streets of Jerusalem. Several live scenes from the ancient and holy city scroll across the monitor. All the scenes show a clearly agitated state. The recent cataclysmic events and religious uprisings have all sides agitated. Muslim, Jew, Christian, agnostic: all religious sects seem to be in the streets.

Abaddon turns to the sniveling priest cowering on the floor. "You said this would never happen. You said this could never happen. You said that it was all a myth. Yet here it is. The detested Jews, the irredeemable Muslims, and the self-righteous Christians are going to do what you said would never happen!" Abaddon glares intensely at the pagan priest. "What happens if this fabled stone is laid at the temple mount?"

The priest looks up timidly. "No one truly knows, my lord. The New Jerusalem as described by the apostle John could be established. Christ could come and gather his believers to heaven as God's wrath envelops the earth. Or nothing could happen at all." The pagan priest slowly rises to his feet. "The power of their so-called god is just a myth." The pagan priest stands tall before Abaddon. "I assure you, there is nothing to be worried about. The vast majority of mankind will follow their base instincts. They will turn from this idea of a virtuous God and follow the true god that we know."

Chapter 54, What Happened?

Mustafa is in the truck that carries the ancient and holy foundation stone. They enter the labyrinth of streets that make up the ancient city of Jerusalem. The city is in chaos as the news of civil unrest around the world spreads. The streets are full of people. Some are Messianic Jews proclaiming Christ. They are surrounded by large crowds. Muslims and Orthodox Jews find themselves united in protesting against the Christian revivalists. Other Muslims begin to riot, burning stores, synagogues, and churches. Israeli state officers try to quell the mayhem, but the crowds are too large for even the vaunted Israeli armed forces to handle.

"Your well-planned mission is not going to work," Mustafa says to his Mossad friend who is driving the vehicle. "There is no way we can make it through these streets as in intact convoy. We need to adapt. We just need to make it to the temple mount with the foundation stone."

The grim face of the Mossad agent speaks volumes. "I'm listening ISIS fighter. What do you suggest?"

"We must do the unexpected!" Mustafa says with a chuckle. "Rather than sneaking in, we will proclaim our intentions and boldly go to the temple mount and place the foundation stone."

"My people won't let that happen," the Israeli officer states.

"My friend, look around," Mustafa replies. "It is chaos. Your people won't be able to stop us. The Muslims want the stone to be placed because they think it will start the final battle that they are sure they will win. The Christians want the cornerstone placed because it will bring about the New Jerusalem as foretold by the apostle John."

"Okay, you're the battlefield technician. What do you propose we do?" the Mossad agent asks.

"They expect us to sneak in through the back door. I say we walk in triumphantly through the front door."

"You are a wanted man by Hezbollah, ISIS and the Iranians. Don't you think that might cause a problem?"

"Not if we come with the foundation stone. The very stone that will cause the return of the lost Imam. I will be greeted as a hero," Mustafa replies. "My friend, this is the greatest plan of all. The Muslim's will help us. Yet we know how the battle will end; Christ will be victorious! Turn left here, that will bring us around to the front gate of the mosque. I will tell them what we have. They will help us."

The Mossad agent turns the wheel, taking them off the designated path. Horns blare and the radio begins to squawk. The Messianic Jew says a prayer as he heads into the Palestinian quarter of the city. He jukes and jives around the heavy traffic and swarms of civilians. He looks in his rear-view mirror and sees that none of the convoy is behind him.

"Turn left here, on to Bab Hutta and just keep going," Mustafa commands. "There will be an armed gate. Don't stop, just keep going, barrel right through it."

"This is nuts! You said they would let us in!" the Mossad agent exclaims as he makes a hard left and hits the gas. Crowds of people scramble as the triaxle truck barrels down the narrow street, its shrill air horn blaring.

The Palestinians who guard the Al-Aqsa mosque are taken by surprise. Usually, the disturbances occur by the wailing wall on the Jewish side. To see a large triaxle truck barreling towards the mosque from the Palestinian side is not something expected by anyone. The large crowds that have gathered are already more than the beefed-up security detail can handle. Now a maniac in a massive triaxle truck is barreling towards the gate. The guards freeze, not knowing what to do.

The imposing truck smashes through the gate, sending metal and concrete shards flying in all directions. The truck bounces and jumps as it smashes through walls and careens into the olive grove that adorns the northern side of the mosque. The truck comes to a stop a hundred yards past the security perimeter. More chaos erupts as people pour through the gaping hole created by the marauding truck. Mobs pour into the Al-Aqsa mosque grounds. The security detail is stymied. Who busted through the perimeter? And now the grounds are full of Palestinians. They can't take the chance of killing their own people if they fire on the occupants of the truck.

Mustafa and the Mossad agent look out around them. They are the most holy place in the world. It is revered by Muslims, Jews, and Christians. It is where God spared Isaac's life as Abraham showed his ultimate faith in God. It is the place where Jesus walked and preached. It is where Muhammad supposedly was taken to heaven. They are keenly aware of the aura of the Holy Spirit. Their vision seems sharper, the colors are crisper, their sense of being is heightened.

"We're here, my brother," Mustafa exclaims. "Can you feel it? God is here with us! My brother, we're about to do God's will. The original temple was built three thousand years ago out of reverence for God. It was built again and then destroyed by the Romans. For the past two thousand years it has been corrupted. Today we will lay the foundation stone that will bring about the new Jerusalem! Oh, what a glorious, glorious day!"

Mustafa turns to the Mossad agent. "We are brothers. We have seen heaven. We have seen the New Jerusalem. These people have no idea of what is in store for them. It is majestic, joyful! Words cannot describe heaven. To be in God's presence, to see Him, to talk with Him. I'm fulfilled just knowing what is to come."

The Mossad agent smiles. "I know it, I can feel it, my friend. But first we need to deal with the current situation. We have not yet placed the foundation stone and we'll soon be surrounded by some very angry people."

Mustafa looks in the rearview mirror and sees the guards rushing towards them. "I will deal with them. They will be our allies, our helpers."

***

"We found the ISIS fighter," a high-level officer tells Henry, the G2. "He's in Jerusalem. More exactly, he's at the Al-Aqsa Mosque."

"That's not surprising. I suppose he is preaching God's Word to those who will listen at the wailing wall," Henry responds.

"No sir," the security specialist responds. "He is in the olive grove to the north of the mosque. He has gathered a large crowd around him. He crashed the gates in a large truck carrying a large stone."

Henry's face goes pale. "Bring up a live feed and get the Mossad commander on the line ASAP."

The security specialist enters a few commands on his computer. "I have two live feeds on your monitor now. One is from an Israeli drone and the other is from one of our satellites. We're connecting with the head of the Mossad right now, stand by to be connected with General Getty."

"Reuben, this is Henry. Give me your assessment of the situation," the G2 asks the head of the Mossad.

"Are you speaking of the crazies who just crashed into the temple mount? Or are you asking about the wave of Messianic Jews sweeping down from the north?" Rueben asks.

"Give me a world view assessment," Henry responds.

"Where is your heart? Are you righteous?" Rueben asks. "Because I think the judgment day is upon us. Are you right with the Lord?"

"I'm a sinner, but I'm right with the Lord. Tell me your true assessment."

"Spoken like a true believer. I'm starting to believe myself," the head of Israel's security states with a slight tremble in his voice. "What we're seeing is scriptural. It is foretold in the Talmud and by Christ himself in the Christian Bible. The earthquakes, the raging fires, wars breaking out around the globe, brother turning against brother. It's all been predicted."

"And it has all happened before, Rueben. Every generation has thought the same thing. Heck, World War II was horrific. Why do you think this is different?"

"The Christian revival, Henry," Rueben replies, his voice still a little shaky. "Christians are boldly stepping forward. They are performing miracles. What the kid in California did was just a start. What is happening around the world is disturbing. The movement in China is unheard of. Around the world there are reports that are astounding. In Zimbabwe, a man stared down a warlord and his men. He clapped his hands, and the armed thugs dropped their weapons and fled screaming like deranged animals."

"I hadn't heard about that, but similar reports are coming in too fast to comprehend," Henry replies.

The head of the Mossad continues. "Some of the revivalists are openly claiming that they are God's chosen people, part of the 144,000 as described by the apostle John in Revelation. They are to proclaim the Gospel to the world. That is a prophesy that goes all the way back to Abraham, the father of the Jews."

"And the father of the Arabs too," Henry replies, "through Ishmael. I agree with everything you are saying. Now tell me what is happening at the temple mount and its implications."

Rueben takes a deep breath. "Mustafa bin Salman, the ISIS fighter, is there with one of our agents. We think our agent is now a believer and is doing what he thinks will bring about the final battle and Christ's return. They have driven into the temple mount area with a triaxle truck that we believe carries the original foundation stone of the temple built by King Solomon over three thousand years ago."

"Why is that significant? Why would the ISIS fighter do that?" Henry asks.

"The temple has been built twice and torn down twice. Rebuilding the temple for the third time is prophetic. It will mark the return of Christ and the beginning of the final battle of good against evil."

"Maybe it's time for me to ask you if you are right with the Lord. Rueben, you know the prophesies. Are you right with the Lord?"

"That's something I have to think about," Rueben replies, his voice still shaky. The line goes dead. The G2 says a prayer for his Jewish friend.

***

Mustafa jumps out and clambers onto the hood of the large truck. A crowd is beginning to surround them. Some are fascinated by the large man and his audacity. Others are angry at his defilement of a holy place. The Palestinian guards are about ready to shoot him dead but are not sure what to do.

Mustafa's mind flashes back to when he was standing atop the tank, surrounded by people at war with each other. He quickly takes off his turban and waves it in the air. This turban is checkered blue and white, the colors of the Palestinians. Once again, he hollers as loud as he can. "Pax, pax, pax."

The surging crowd stops, not knowing what to do.

"Listen to me people, listen to me now. The final battle is about to begin," he bellows. "Whose side are you on? Now is the time to decide. We have the foundation stone with us. The very stone that Abraham placed Isaac on to be sacrificed in the ultimate demonstration of obedience to God. The very stone that was the center of the Holy of Holies in the First Temple. The very stone from which Muhammad ascended to heaven to meet allah. Jew, Muslim and Christian revere this foundation stone. We have it with us. It is time to place the foundation stone and bring about the final battle!" Mustafa pulls aside the tarps covering the holy stone and the crowd gasps.

***

The video feed from a drone shows what is happening at the Temple Mount to all those assembled at the Special Forces command center six thousand miles away.

"That's the real foundation stone," a technician states solemnly. "He ain't messing around. Our records indicate that he's got the real deal, general. What should we do?"

"It is completely out of our hands young man. I suggest that you pray."

***

Three thousand miles further to the west, Shawn gathers all the people in the area around him. He does not know why he has the compelling urge to pray. But he feels in his bones that the time has come.

"Now is the time of judgement. People, pray for forgiveness. Pray for our brothers and sisters who do not know the Lord. The time of judgement is here.

***

Around the world the chosen, a hundred and forty-four thousand strong, give a last passionate plea to the nations. Repent your sins and acknowledge Christ as God's Son and Savior.

Some come to know Christ. Many more walk away.

***

Abaddon falls to the ground as he sees all he has worked for has been nothing but false promises. He clasps his hand to his chest as his blood pressure rises. He feels a dull ache in his left shoulder as a clot stops the flow of blood to his heart. His last sight is of the holy stone in a holy place. He realizes how wrong he has been. His mind grows dark before he can atone for his sins

***

The crowd at the temple mount grows to a feverish pitch. The Muslims think placing the foundation stone will bring about the return of the last Imam and the conquest of Islam over the entire world. The final battle will be fought. The crowds make a path for Mustafa and his truck to the place where the sacred stone is to be set. The clouds overhead begin to gather in a foreboding manner. The earth begins to tremble. The triaxle truck backs up to the exact location of where the foundation stone was placed by God over four thousand years ago.

Mustafa begins to raise the bed of the truck that will cause the stone to slide off the triaxle truck and nestle into its destined position. Muslims, Jews, and Christians all wait, holding their breath. What will happen?

The stone slowly begins to slide down the bed of the large truck. A corner of the stone hits the ground, and a large clap of thunder is heard. The clap of thunder is heard around the world, from Miami to Mozambique.

The truck rolls forward, allowing the foundation stone to settle into place.

Nothing happens. Then everything happens. Are you ready for His return?

THE END

Author's thoughts

I state again, I am not a theologian. I do not know all the prophesies and all the workings of Christ's return. Truthfully, no one does. I wrote this book to make you think about your faith.

No one knows when Christ will return. Are you ready?

No one knows who the chosen are. Are you one of them?

We're all called to proclaim Christ to the nations.

Speak up. Live your life with faith.

Proclaim Jesus to the nations in everything you do, because if you know Christ, you have been called. By the way, do you have a mark?

Other books by Timothy A Van Sickel

<u>Righteous Gathering, Righteous Survival EMP Saga, Book 1</u>

<u>Righteous Bloodshed, Righteous Survival EMP Saga, Book 2</u>

<u>Righteous Sacrifice, Righteous Survival EMP Saga, Book 3</u>

<u>Righteous Soldiers, Righteous Survival EMP Saga, Book 4</u>

<u>Righteous Survival, Righteous Survival EMP Saga, Book 5</u>

<u>Righteous Revival, Righteous Survival EMP Saga, Book 6</u>

All books available on Amazon in both print and eBook

You can contact me at <u>vansickelauthor@gmail.com</u>

I am on facebook, but I am not very active, well, because it's facebook.

I am not on twitter or any of the other sites. I rely on word of mouth to sell my books. If you like what you have read, post a review on Amazon or Goodreads or anywhere else that you feel will get the message of this book out. Tell your friends and family.

Made in the USA
Las Vegas, NV
16 September 2021

30450711R00213